PRAISE FOR CATH

'Confirms Catherine Kirwan as a major new talent in Irish crime fiction. Her deviously plotted mystery, filled with vivid characters, distinctive dialogue and a detailed and loving portrait of the "real capital of Ireland" is captivating'
Irish Independent

'Has a vividly drawn sense of place, an amused eye for character, class and all manner of Corkishness and, above all, in Finn a winning, vital lead character; her vibrant energy and good humour animates and drives the action at break-neck pace. Hugely enjoyable'
Irish Times

'Pacy, twisty and ingeniously plotted ... a real page-turner'
T.M. Logan

'Pacy, gripping and atmospheric ... a cracking read!'
Andrea Carter

'Dark and twisted ... powerful'
Woman

'A clever twisty tale that feels completely authentic'
Jane Casey

'Chock full of secrets and with a compelling plot ... will keep you glued to the pages!'
Lesley Kara

'Another clever plot from Kirwan ... full of smoke and mirrors and musty old college secrets'
Meath Chronicle

Catherine Kirwan grew up on a farm in the parish of Fews, County Waterford. She studied law at University College Cork and lives in Cork City where she works as a solicitor.

A LESSON IN MALICE

Catherine Kirwan

HACHETTE
BOOKS
IRELAND

First published in Ireland in 2023 by HACHETTE BOOKS IRELAND
First published in paperback in 2024

1

Cataloguing in Publication Data is available from the British Library

ISBN 9781529381443

Typeset in Bembo Book Std by Bookends Publishing Services, Dublin
Printed and bound in Great Britain by Clays Ltd, Elcograf S.p.A.

Hachette Books Ireland policy is to use papers that are natural,
renewable and recyclable products and made from wood grown in sustainable
forests. The logging and manufacturing processes are expected to conform
to the environmental regulations of the country of origin.

Hachette Books Ireland
8 Castlecourt Centre
Castleknock
Dublin 15, Ireland

A division of Hachette UK Ltd
Carmelite House, 50 Victoria Embankment, London EC4Y 0DZ

www.hachettebooksireland.ie

For Michael, Molly and Elizabeth

Author's Note

This book is inspired by a great many walks through the beautiful grounds of University College Cork, although eagle-eyed locals will spot that I've taken such major and minor liberties with the procedures, administration and geography of the university as the plot requires.

For example, there is a very fine law school at UCC. You will find it at Áras na Laoi, off Gaol Walk, a little to the west of the main campus. UCC School of Law is a place of learning and research, rated first in Ireland and eleventh in the EU in the QS World Rankings. UCC School of Law is not the nest of vipers depicted in this book, which is entirely made up by me for my and, I hope, your enjoyment. Consequently, any resemblance here to anyone, living or dead, is coincidental and unintentional.

My fictional law school is to be found in the Horgan Building, a make-believe structure adjacent to the (real) Iris Ashley Cummins Building (previously known as the Civil Engineering Building), and the (really wonderful) Crawford Observatory. Finally, other than in these pages, a woman has never been president of UCC.

CONFERENCE DINNER SEATING PLAN

Location: UCC President's Private Dining Room, East Wing
Time: Wednesday, 7pm

Professor Martin Casey
(UCC Law)

Me

Dr Padraic O'Flaherty
(University of Galway — ex
PhD student of Kirsty MacM)

Nathaniel 'Nate' Simpson
(Lexbonay Investments —
event sponsor)

Professor Kirsty MacMillan
(Queen's, Belfast)

Sophie Dignam
(PhD student, UCC Law)

Professor Lia de Barra
(UCC Law)

Dr Cormac Ryan
(UCL, London —
but ex-UCC student)

Dr Agnes Heaney
(UCC Law —
conference organiser)

Dr Béatrice Mbemba
(Paris)

Professor William Atkins
(Melbourne)

Professor Nell Deady
(UCC President)

Others present in the East Wing during dinner
Magda Kozlowska (catering manager)
Ian McAnespie (conference technician, law student)
Ciara Boyle (tour guide, waitress, law student)
Rory Donnelly (College security guard)
Davide Rossi (chef)

SATURDAY

Annabelle Leahy had just turned seventeen and for a long time she had been top of her class. The arrival of new girl Zoe Harris had changed everything. Zoe Harris and her willowy blondeness and her perfectly accented French and her genius-level maths and her A pluses in English. Barely six months into the school year and the top student award that Annabelle had won easily for the last four years straight was slipping further and further out of reach, even though she worked as hard as ever. Late at night, every night, in the privacy of her bedroom, Annabelle cried. And she was tired of crying.

So, she showered early and blow-dried her hair. Pulled on her favourite black leggings, the ones that made her belly disappear, and wore lenses instead of glasses even though the contacts made her eyes sting. After a light breakfast — sourdough toast with a scrape of hummus, which Annabelle considered a more planet-friendly spread than butter — she cancelled her Saturday-morning chemistry Zoom study group and left the house in the small 1970s estate where she lived with her parents and two younger brothers. She told her mother only that she was going for a ramble, a breath of fresh air. She said she didn't know where she might go. But she did.

Striding quickly downhill from Shanakiel and on through Sunday's Well, she entered the narrow gap between two high walls. Descending the steps to the river, she crossed the north channel of the Lee via the pedestrian suspension bridge universally known as the Shakey. She did not pause to sample the characteristic wobble as Cork people invariably do, or to admire the gracious period homes and the long lush gardens overlooking the water.

Barely glancing right and left, she crossed Western Road and the small slatted footbridge over the south channel of the river. After a restorative uphill pull through the Brookfield medical faculty complex, she turned onto College Road. It was student party central all around this area for most of the year, apart from the little convent of the Poor Clares – where the nuns depended on donations and never left their compound and were so old-fashioned they probably didn't even have wi-fi – and, further along, the Bon Secours, a large private hospital founded by a different order of nuns who, Annabelle guessed, weren't remotely poor.

She made her way to the main campus and kept going until she came to the quad, four perfect squares of lawn divided by neat gravel paths, surrounded on three sides by buildings, open to the south. A polished brass plate inscribed 'PRESIDENT'S OFFICE' gleamed on one of the three doors to the East Wing, which was closed, as it always was at the weekend, but the other two wings were open.

Walking amid the carefully tended shrubs and herbs and climbers, and the old stone that was the same colour as the sky, Annabelle felt calmer than she had in weeks. She checked the time. Three minutes to ten. As a weak sun struggled through the clouds, she sat on a bench and shut her eyes. She told herself that none of Zoe Harris's achievements, however stellar they might be, had anything to do with her. Annabelle would still get the grades she needed. She'd still be able to study medicine, and specialise in paediatrics. Probably. Or become a GP. Maybe. Whatever. The details didn't matter. The point was that, in less than two years, she'd be here in UCC every day. And the misery that Zoe Harris had caused would be ancient history.

Time passed, and Annabelle started to feel cold. She rose from her seat and went inside, to the Aula Maxima. Pausing, she inhaled the silence. Before now, she'd been here only when the hall had been full, with other students from her school on the College open day. They hadn't been allowed up to the gallery, though they'd been shown the narrow door off the corridor, and the steep steps immediately behind it. They'd been told that, for health and safety reasons, it was closed to tour groups. That they were lucky to see the stairs. Luck wasn't something Annabelle believed in, either the good or the bad kind. She believed in science and in hard work. But Zoe Harris moving from Dublin and rolling into Annabelle's class at Mount Mercy? That was just random, which, when you thought about it, was another word for luck.

Annabelle walked towards the back of the room, running her fingertips along the grating that protected the shelves of musty leather-bound books. It was darker underneath the gallery and the air was denser there, thicker. When she reached the internal door to the East Wing, she pressed her palm against it. It opened. She went through it and walked quickly to the far end of the corridor, trying most of the doors with her left hand as she passed. They were locked. Returning more slowly the way she'd come, she noticed an odd unnameable odour. And she remembered the little door to the gallery. She hadn't tried that one. She went to it. Stood for a moment. The smell seemed stronger here. She pressed her nose to the wood. Definitely stronger. She turned the knob. The door creaked as it fell open. She took a single step but went no further.

Because blocking the cramped staircase was a man. Wedged against the steps. Hunched in a position incompatible with life. Bloated. Starting to leak.

It took several seconds for her brain to analyse what she was seeing. Then a scream began in Annabelle's throat that she forced herself to swallow. Wrapping her scarf tightly over her mouth and nose, she turned her back on the open bloodshot eyes. On the gathering stench.

She called 999. Got the words out somehow. No, she was sure that an ambulance wouldn't be needed. Just the gardaí. She ended the call and *waited. Preserved the scene. Kept vigil with the corpse. Tried to say a prayer. Couldn't.*

And she couldn't help thinking that, whoever he was, no one had come looking for him. That he had been left to die. To decay like a rotting magpie she'd seen once on the riverbank at the far end of the Lee Fields where the footpath runs out and, in summer, the vegetation grows wild, and high enough to make it scary, if you're a girl on your own. Annabelle had almost forgotten that magpie. But she would never forget the dead man's red staring eyes.

THREE DAYS
PREVIOUSLY

1

THAT DAMP WEDNESDAY IN APRIL, I WALKED FROM
Western Road, through the ornamental ironwork gates that
marked the main entrance to the campus. Before leaving my
house less than half an hour earlier, I'd scraped my long, thick
black hair into a tight high ponytail. It swished back and forth as
I moved, reminding me that I should've washed it.

Fifteen minutes to nine and the avenue was busy with staff
and students, all on foot, all trudging forward without visible
enthusiasm. Some branched off, via the stone staircase, towards
the south. I kept on, up the curving slope, edged with mature
greenery and trees that met in the middle. Ahead of me, where
the ground flattened, lay my destination.

But I was early and so, to kill time, swerved right in the
direction of a small paved viewing promontory by a wall topped
with railings. Gripping the narrow vertical bars, I peered over
the cliff edge into the watery meadows below and the wrinkled
Lee rushing eastwards. I wished for a little wooden boat, a blue
one. I saw myself floating with the current under bridge after
bridge, past the tip of the island and the mouth of the harbour as
far as the open sea. Except I had this thing to do, a thing I should
never have said yes to in the first place.

Turning, I passed over grass and tarmac and up the seven steps and through the carved limestone Gothic doorway that was the rear entrance to the Aula Maxima, one of the university's original buildings.

Unbuttoning my charcoal raincoat, I emerged from the short vestibule into the hall – large, vaulted, book-lined. Parallel to the back wall, a table with a floor-length white cloth was set out with stacks of cups and saucers and a Burco boiler. Along the side wall, above the bookshelves, huge pointed north-facing windows lit the space, empty but for the wall of past presidents' portraits – all male – staring darkly down from their gilt frames. Moving up the aisle briskly, between the banks of seating to the front, I sent a text message: *In the Aula. Am I in the right place?*

Seconds later, the reply came: *Through the left-hand door at the back of the dais. Coffee and other fortifications await.*

A sudden loud noise, as if a book had fallen off a shelf, startled me. I jerked, swung a half-circle on my heel. But the room was as empty as it had been and I found no likely source for the disturbance, although, it has to be said, I didn't look very hard. I went on about my business and thought little of what had happened, putting it down to a cross-draught, a creak of the old wood.

With the benefit of hindsight I see how wrong I was that morning. About how the day would go. About what I would do that evening. About nearly everything.

2

THE 'OTHER FORTIFICATIONS' TURNED OUT TO BE the conference attendee's friend, an artery-clogging array of mini-pastries — croissants, *pains au chocolat* and the like. I stress-ate a couple in quick succession and washed them down with an unwise quantity of black coffee. We were in an over-furnished peach-coloured room, the chief organiser of the event Agnes Heaney, a former classmate who'd roped me in close to the last minute when one of her other speakers had had to cancel, various other people who seemed to belong, and me.

'I've never been in here before,' the thin man standing beside me said. I'd noticed him a few minutes earlier, chatting with Agnes. He'd worked the room briefly, nodding and smiling, before coming to a halt by the buffet table. He was my height, five foot eight, and looked about thirty. He wore a slim-fitting navy suit, white shirt, red tie and pointy tan leather shoes. I had on a navy suit and white shirt too, though my suit was pinstriped and the skirt was too tight, thanks to the ten pounds I'd gained in the past few months, and I was wearing flat black shoes. I can't be doing with heels lately. Or earrings. 'Have you?'

'No,' I said.

I bent my head to read his nametag. 'Sean?'

Too quickly.

'Senan,' he said. 'Dr Senan Dunford. I know who *you* are. Finn Fitzpatrick, I ...' He spoke with a flat Limerick accent. He had a nice face and the kind of charm people called boyish. Though it might have been the Communion suit. All he was lacking was a white rosette. He went on, 'I'm, em, I'm down from Limerick for the day. But I did my undergrad degree here. I went sideways at it. Did commerce at the start. Hated it except for the law bits. Got a transfer from comm to the School of Law in the end. Took a while. Certain people didn't lay out the welcome mat.'

He made a face, tipped his head in the direction of Professor Martin Casey, the dean of the faculty, who had taught me property law, just then harvesting another pastry from the buffet. I remembered him as a great lecturer of an unpopular and difficult but necessary subject. Strict, though. Demanding. I could see how he might rub a person up the wrong way.

'What do you do in Limerick?' I asked.

'I, well, I'm attached to the law school at UL. Came down this morning. The traffic! They really need to do something about that road.'

'Right.' There was no way I was getting dragged into a discussion on the controversial stalled Cork–Limerick motorway project. 'I'm sorry, Senan, I have to, um, check the timetable with Agnes.'

'I have a spare,' he said, and swiftly handed me a typed lilac A4 sheet. 'You're in the first panel. Speaking second. After me, in fact.'

That soon?

I grabbed my bag from the side table where I'd left it. 'Too much coffee, I need to ... See you inside. Looking forward to your paper.' I gave what I hoped was a regretful smile and slipped out the side door into the Stone Corridor, an enclosed cloister containing the high point of the UCC walking tour – twenty-seven ancient Ogham-inscribed pillars, as straight and silent as a platoon of soldiers on inspection. Dim daylight filtered through the diamond-leaded glass windows.

After washing my hands, I stood by the sink and checked my script again. Cobbled together from my notes on a recent high-profile murder case I'd been involved with, 'New perspectives: the view from a very peculiar practice' was no more impressive than it had been the last time I'd read it. I drew a diagonal line through an especially weak paragraph and folded over the pages. I dug an old lipstick out of the bottom of my bag – Russian Red. It went on smoothly and took some of the grim from my face but I was about to wipe it off again when the door behind me opened.

'There you are,' Agnes Heaney said.

She dashed into a stall and locked it. Smaller than me and heavier than the last time I'd seen her, she had a faded flyaway mousy bob that could have done with a trim or a run of the straightener. She wore a baggy pilled black knitted dress that made my dull suit look designer.

Through the door Agnes said, 'You're hanging around for dinner, aren't you?'

I said, 'I'll stay for as much of the conference as I can. I'm sure it'll be … So, I was thinking I'll head away, not immediately, of course, but maybe later on this morning.'

There was no maybe about it, as far as I was concerned. I had a pile of work waiting for me back at the office and, that night, a hot date with a takeaway and my Netflix account.

But when Agnes came out of the cubicle, she'd gone pale. She grabbed my upper arm, her fingers pressed into the bone. 'Whether either of us likes it or not, you're here now,' she said. 'You *have* to stay. All day. And the evening.' Quickly, she ran cold water over her hands. She didn't stop to dry them. 'Come on,' she said.

In the long months since the events of that day, I've become convinced that, if only I'd asked her at that point, she might have told me; that if I'd known sooner, it might have changed what happened later. Instead, to avoid the temporary discomfort of an argument, I said nothing.

On such seemingly insignificant decisions, the world turns.

3

WHEN WE RETURNED, THE FRONT HALF OF THE HALL
had filled with a smattering of students and eager post-grads,
various lecturers from the law school and visiting conference
participants from other Irish universities and overseas. Mercifully,
there were no local solicitors or barristers present to watch me
making a holy show of myself, though some might sign in later
to collect a few Continuing Professional Development hours,
before being 'unavoidably' called back to the office. CPD points
excepted, the conference – 'Lies and Consequences: whither
the rule of law in a post-truth world?' – was too highfalutin to
attract the interest of most lawyers in practice. And too vague.
Or maybe that was the point? Make the topic flexible enough
for speakers from differing specialisations to get away with
rabbiting on about it for twenty minutes? It was going to be a
long morning.

Agnes went to the lectern and tapped at the microphone. A
very young curly-haired man in a headset, wearing an open red
checked shirt and a grubby Thin Lizzy T-shirt, and carrying
a small handheld video camera, stepped forward to assist her.
They seemed to know one another well. I glanced around and
spotted a second, more professional-looking camera on a tripod

being operated by a man in a suit. At some point in the future my speech, or extracts from it, would probably surface on YouTube. I winced. I *definitely* should have washed my hair.

Throughout all of this, Professor Martin Casey was sitting in the front row, tutting loudly and shaking his jowly head, like a disappointed clergyman. I took a seat with the rest of the speaker panel at the far side of the platform between Senan Dunford and a woman I hadn't yet been introduced to. Beside her was a man I hadn't met before either. They each shook my hand in turn and murmured their names.

Surreptitiously, I glanced at the programme: Dr Béatrice Mbemba lectured at Panthéon-Assas University in Paris; Dr Padraic O'Flaherty at the University of Galway. Any other day, I wouldn't be breathing the same legal air as these people. I didn't have a master's degree, let alone a doctorate. A jack-of-all-trades, I worked out of a tiny attic room at MLC, a corporate law office in the centre of town. Barely tolerated by the partners because the fees I generated were considered too pathetically low to justify my employment, I was retained for the simple reason that I was useful – useful for cleaning up the multifarious messes that tended to arise every now and again for the staff and clients of a big firm like ours and that none of the other solicitors would deign to touch. Also, over the last while, I'd developed a sideline in investigative work. It was one of those cases that Agnes had asked me to talk about.

She'd called me on my work number on Friday of the previous week. My surprise at hearing from her had intensified as she delivered her request. We'd been in the same year at UCC, neither friends nor enemies, mixing in different circles, apart from a few shared tutorial groups. She was intelligent and focused, quietly on her way to first-class honours from day one, but always helpful to everyone else, sharing her spectacularly comprehensive notes willingly if anyone happened to miss a session. That kindness was surely at the root of my inability to say no to her. That and the thought that, if Agnes was asking me of all people, she and the law school, to which I owed some fealty, had to be badly stuck. Plus, she'd been forceful on the phone. I hadn't felt like I had a choice. I'd been left with the very definite impression that another speaker had cancelled late and that she needed me to fill in.

I wondered about that now. Had she mentioned a name? Going over the conversation in my mind, I became sure that she hadn't. And that she'd never actually used the word 'cancelled'. Taking out the timetable Senan had given me, I ran my finger down the schedule. All of the other events had three contributors. Ours, the opening session, was the only one with four. Even more oddly, I was listed as a 'special guest'. Yet the way she'd spoken in the bathroom had me thinking she hadn't wanted me here at all. That she'd been stuck with me?

I looked up from the page. At Agnes. Saw her properly for the first time. Too shabby for her big day. Too pasty-faced to be healthy. My pulse quickened. Something strange was going on.

4

I WAS INTRIGUED. IF AGNES HADN'T WANTED ME
to come, she had to have had another reason for the invitation.
Presumably she'd let me know what it was eventually. But, until
my speech was done, I had to concentrate on that.

Agnes made the usual contradictory opening remarks:
welcoming everyone with one hand and, with the other,
imparting dire warnings on escape routes in the event of fire or
other cataclysmic events. She spoke succinctly, assuredly. She'd
been doing this kind of thing a while. She'd published several
books. Whatever was wrong, her work couldn't be the problem.
After less than five minutes, she gave way to Professor Casey.

'Settle in,' Senan Dunford, beside me, muttered. 'He may be
some time.'

He was. Effusive gratitude to all distinguished guests.
Special mention for the event sponsor Lexbonay Investments
(an 'ethical fund', according to the conference programme, that
had 'a well-established and mutually beneficial relationship'
with the law school) and a particular welcome, with a round
of applause, for their CEO Nathaniel Simpson (in the front
row, directly in front of the lectern, a sleek, bald man with
a tan, wearing an expensive open-neck white shirt with the

sleeves rolled up and a chunky watch with a steel bracelet). Long pauses for brow-wiping and water-sipping. All followed by an almost interminable exposition of his own thoughts on the conference topic.

'The rest of us might as well pack up and go home,' Senan said.

I disguised a laugh as a cough. Casey paused and glared at no one in particular but, as the fidgeting and throat-clearing in the audience increased, had the good sense to declare the conference 'well and truly open' and to finish.

Senan Dunford was next. Agnes retook her place at the microphone to introduce him. She spoke with real warmth, reciting his academic achievements, the scholarly articles he'd written and that he was just 'completing' a fellowship at the University of Limerick. So that's what he'd meant when he'd said he was 'attached' to the department up there. It looked like the poor guy would be out of a job soon. In the circumstances, it had been decent of Agnes to give him the opening slot.

But he was good. Nervous at the start, he grew more confident as he went on. His presentation was lucid, expertly put together. He spoke well, and with a conviction that was refreshing, as if he was sure that what he had to say was worth hearing. If he managed to get a post somewhere, I reckoned he'd grow into the kind of 'expert on everything' academic who'd turn up on radio panel shows and talking-head documentaries. For all kinds of reasons, in Ireland, such academics were rarely female.

At the end of Senan's presentation, Agnes spoke again and invited another round of applause, saying, 'You can all see why we're writing a book together. He'll keep me on my toes!'

Watching Professor Casey's response, I was mildly surprised

to note that he seemed to be clapping as enthusiastically as everyone else. It looked like the grudge went only one way.

As the room stilled, Agnes said, 'And now, our special guest, a graduate of UCC, a solicitor and, in more recent times, an amateur sleuth. Ladies and gentlemen, Finn Fitzpatrick.'

I gave silent thanks for the brevity of the introduction and made my way slowly to the podium. Although I couldn't shake the nagging sense that coming here had been a mistake, I told myself that, in fifteen minutes, my self-imposed ordeal would be over.

Adjusting the microphone, I moistened my lips and started to speak.

5

DESPITE, OR BECAUSE OF, THE FACT THAT IT BORE
more resemblance to a true crime documentary than an academic
paper, my speech appeared to go down well with most of the
audience. I retook my seat and Agnes waited by the lectern.
When the clapping ceased, she began her introduction of Béatrice
Mbemba, a lengthy note of achievements and qualifications.

Béatrice was stylish. She wore a fitted purple wrap dress. Her
black, naturally curly hair fanned out from her head like a halo,
held back at the front by a pink headband that exactly matched her
lipstick. When she spoke, her English was flawless with a barely
there French accent. In her opening remarks, she said that she
intended to talk about how moral concepts of truth and honesty
related to the legal duty to disclose relevant information. After
listening to a few crisply delivered sentences, I zoned out and
heard hardly a word she said. I had cause to regret my inattention
later but, at the time, I was mentally berating myself again.

On the Friday afternoon that the phone call had come from
Agnes, I'd called into Gabriel's office to discuss a few ongoing
cases. Gabriel was one of the founders of MLC and the firm's

managing partner. He worked on the first floor. High ceilings. Tall sash windows. Antique partner's desk. No clutter. No dust. The exact opposite of my paper-crammed garret, in fact.

He was the one who'd given me a traineeship way back when I'd passed the Law Society entrance exams. At the time, I was distributing CVs like confetti to every law firm in Cork. I had no contacts in the legal profession, and little hope of a positive response. Unexpectedly, I was called for an interview at MLC, though looking at the other candidates in the waiting room, most of whom I knew from UCC, I'd had the feeling I was a wild-card entry. Yet I clicked with Gabriel, and my meeting with him had gone as well as it could. All the same, with the possible exception of Gabriel himself, no one could have been more astonished than I was when he'd rung and offered me the job. I started a few weeks later, and I'd stayed. For sixteen years.

That Friday, we chatted amiably, concurring on strategy as, a lot of the time, we did. I liked turning things over with him, especially when he was as relaxed as this, all too infrequent an occurrence. But he'd had a couple of big successes recently and the finances of the firm were back on track after the violent death of one of the partners had led to a crisis that, for a time, had threatened to derail MLC permanently. As I'd been instrumental in helping the firm avoid disaster, my star was briefly in the ascendant. I wasn't enjoying my time in the sun much. I knew it wouldn't last. Almost as an afterthought, as I was leaving his room, I told Gabriel that Agnes had invited me to speak about the Mandy Breslin murder case at the upcoming rule-of-law conference at UCC. I told him what little she had said about the conference. I also told him that, however reluctantly, I'd agreed to attend.

I'd expected his support. Even, if I'm being honest, his praise.

He was forever telling me to get myself 'out there' more, 'out there' being a mythical place where potential legal fees grew like ripe yellow corn waiting to be cut. Instead Gabriel went quiet. He got up from his swivel chair and walked to the window, hands in his pockets. He was small and slight and was, as ever, impeccably dressed, in a beautifully tailored dark grey pinstriped suit and a crisply ironed blue shirt. After a while, he loosened his tie. Never a good sign.

Without turning around, and quietly, he said, 'I wish you'd run it by me, Finola.'

He was the only one who called me by my full name.

'Right,' I said. 'Is it that you don't want me to go or something, because—'

I was going to say that I'd be glad of the excuse to say no but he interrupted me: 'It's not that.'

'Is it the topic? That it's about the firm? I'm sorry, I hadn't thought ...'

'*Yes*, Finola. I'm surprised you hadn't considered that might be a problem. Washing dirty linen in public. Best avoided and all that.'

'I'll cancel,' I said. 'It's no problem. I'm actually delighted.' I was telling the truth.

He put his hand to his forehead and turned to face me. 'On the other hand, backing out now might only make things worse.'

He's a worrier. Then again, so am I, but I still thought he was overreacting. 'I really don't see how it could. I can tell Agnes that something's cropped up I can't get out of. She only rang a couple of hours ago. It's not too late for her to find someone else.'

'Did she say why she'd asked you?'

'I think someone cancelled.'

He nodded slightly several times. It's a tic he has. It means he's thinking. It also means he wants you to stop talking, and that if there's any more to be done, he'll be the one doing it. When he's good and ready.

After a while, he sighed and said, 'It's so hard getting trainees these days with the big Dublin firms coming down and stealing candidates who should be ours right out from under our noses. I don't want to do anything to damage our relationship with the university. So, in the circumstances, refusing isn't an option. Especially when you've already said yes ... Go. But be as discreet as you can be.'

'If you're sure?'

'I'm not.'

'But you still want me to go?'

He shrugged. 'Get in and get out,' he said. 'Don't linger afterwards.'

That was the moment when I should have insisted on cancelling my attendance at the conference. But I hadn't. And now Agnes had strong-armed me into agreeing to stay on for the conference dinner. I'd planned on being back at the office well before lunchtime. Instead, I was stuck there for the entire day. It came to me that military types called this kind of thing 'mission creep', and that terrible things usually happened as a result of it. War crimes. Massacres.

I needn't have been as passive as I was, or felt as powerless. I could have walked out of the Aula Maxima at that very second, and no one would have been able to stop me. But I didn't, and that makes me think that a part of me sensed something malevolent in the air and wanted me to stay. So I stayed.

Which was another mistake.

6

I WAS WOKEN FROM MY REVERIE BY PROFESSOR
Casey clattering noisily out of his seat. Padraic O'Flaherty was
next, a lecturer in human rights at University of Galway. He
was another good speaker, though if you paid me a million euros
I couldn't tell you what he said, apart from his opening lines,
which were in fluent Connemara Irish. As he spoke, Béatrice
leaned across to me. 'Is this Gaelic?'

'Yes,' I said.

'I like it,' she said. 'I wish I could understand.'

'He's saying it's an honour to be here and he's thanking Agnes
and the School of Law.'

'Thank *you*.'

She smiled and we both turned to look at Padraic. Mid-thirties
and red-haired, he was wearing academic smart-casual: tweed
jacket, checked shirt, corduroy trousers, brogues. He seemed
comfortable in himself and he made the audience laugh a few
times. I recall observing that, if he'd been a bit taller, he'd have
been seriously attractive.

❖

After Padraic, we had the Q and A, during which, to my extreme relief, all of the questions were directed at the other panellists. Calling them questions was stretching it. As is the way with these things, in the main people made statements exhibiting their own knowledge and seemed most interested in scoring professional points. I concentrated on looking interested but uninteresting: the last thing I wanted was to be asked a question. I was mightily pleased when Agnes wound up the proceedings and invited everyone to take a refreshment break.

And so it came to pass that, barely two hours after the welcome snacks, we were down at the back of the Aula where, under the gallery, a catering assistant was dispensing teas and coffees. Cups and saucers and far too many chocolate biscuits had been set out on the trestle table. A polite queue formed quickly. I didn't join. I was standing to one side with Padraic O'Flaherty. I spotted that he wasn't wearing a wedding ring, which, I told myself, was no indication of anything except that he wasn't wearing a wedding ring, and was, in any case, none of my business. He said a few nice things about my speech. Then he asked, 'Are you going to the conference dinner?'

'I am,' I said.

'Are you sure?'

I laughed. 'Em, reasonably?'

'Sophie's going to require more certainty than that, I'm afraid.'

'Who's Sophie? Agnes was the one who said I couldn't get out of going to the dinner.' I blushed. 'Sorry, I ...'

'*Sophie*'s the one confirming the numbers, though. Take it from me, she'll hunt you down. She takes her job *very* seriously. When not counting guests, she's Agnes's PhD student, I think.' He smiled. 'Where do you live?'

'Nearby. A short walk.'

'Convenient,' he said.

Was he flirting with me?

'Very,' I said.

Was I flirting with him too? Oh, God …

He laughed. 'I'm getting myself a beverage. Do you want one?'

'Thanks, but I can't. I'll be climbing the walls if I ingest any more caffeine.'

As I watched him walk away, half of me wishing I'd asked for something so that he'd have to come back, my eye was drawn to a group gathered around an older man I hadn't noticed until just then. He wasn't physically distinctive. Bespectacled men in their sixties aren't uncommon in universities. He looked fit enough, like he played an occasional game of golf, or went for a slow jog one Saturday morning a month. Even from a distance, I could tell he had charisma. Twinkly eyes. The lovable-rogue type. The kind who makes people feel invigorated. Makes them laugh. Which was what I'd picked up on. The too-loud laughing and, when I looked, the expressions on the faces of the people doing it. Eager to please. Senan, the guy from Limerick I'd been talking to earlier. A few others I didn't know. And Agnes, laughing so hard that I knew he was someone she needed to impress.

Him. Professor William Atkins, chair of common law jurisprudence at the University of Melbourne Law School, the conference guest of honour and keynote speaker. Universally popular, it seemed.

But I'm getting too far ahead of myself. I have to keep to what happened, and when.

7

BEFORE THE NEXT SESSION STARTED, I CAVED AND grabbed a black tea with a chocolate digestive. Then, before I retook my seat, I spotted the woman I assumed was Sophie standing near a slight, studious-looking young man in a bow-tie. I went over to her and told her I'd be at the dinner.

She said, 'So Agnes informed me.' Nevertheless, she placed a tick beside my name on a list attached to a wooden clipboard. She was wearing wire-framed glasses and a butter-cream-coloured twinset. She reminded me of a millennial Miss Marple.

'You *do* know you're signed up for the campus guided tour as well?' she asked.

What else had Agnes planned for me? I pinned on a smile. 'What time's that?'

'Five until six. Then there's a Pimm's reception in the President's Garden, weather permitting.' She glanced doubtfully in the direction of one of the high windows.

'It's supposed to clear up,' I said.

'Dinner is at seven p.m. in the President's Dining Room.'

'Which is …?'

'Through there,' she said. She gestured with her right thumb towards the door that led to the East Wing.

'Thanks for all that,' I said. 'Listen, Sophie, you don't happen to know why I'm here, do you? It's only that I wouldn't have expected to be invited and …'

She seemed surprised by the question. 'Agnes just said to add your name and I did. But as to why, you'll have to ask her yourself. I have no idea, I'm afraid. Other than the obvious one.'

'Which is what?'

'That she wanted you to come. It's the way things are going. With sponsorship and all the pressure to get traction on social media, they often include a non-academic these days.'

'A performing seal?'

'Don't put yourself down.' She paused. 'You don't recognise me, do you?'

Taken aback, I asked, 'Should I?'

'I was a summer intern at MLC. Three years ago.'

'We didn't do much work together, though? Otherwise I'd have—'

'No. I was on Mandy's team. Finance and trusts. I was so sorry when she died.'

'Me too,' I said.

'She was great. I went to the funeral. I wanted to pay my respects. I saw you there. It was good what you did. Afterwards, I mean. Finding out who committed the murder.'

'So much has happened in the last few years. I can only apologise for not knowing you now.'

'Don't worry about it,' she said. 'Three years ago, I probably looked different. I had my hair dyed black for a while. Kind of a 1920s bob.'

'*Now* I remember you. From the tearoom. A silent movie star with a fondness for sushi at lunchtime.'

She laughed. 'That *was* me. All that single-use plastic packaging. I don't know what I was thinking.'

'Great to meet you again. We must—'

I got no further because Agnes was up front at the microphone again, calling everyone back to their seats. Sophie mouthed, 'Gotta go,' and left me standing on my own. In mentioning the previous case, she had reminded me of how I used to be before. What little energy I had leaked out of me. Sneaking another biscuit from the table, I slipped into the back row, empty but for me, making myself as inconspicuous as possible.

On the dais, Agnes was going through the same sort of introductory rigmarole she had before, this time for the keynote address by Professor Atkins. At the far end of the row, a slim, dark-haired woman in her forties slid quietly into a seat at the edge just as Atkins started talking. She didn't acknowledge or even appear to see me, but I recognised her as Professor Lia de Barra from the UCC School of Law. She must have just come through the rear door of the Aula because I hadn't seen her earlier. Not even taking the time to remove her expensive soft yellow coat, she sat up straight and listened intently. She wasn't alone. The atmosphere in the room had changed. Atkins appeared to have academic star quality. It was as if Benedict Cumberbatch had taken the stage in a student production. I made an effort to listen but, as keynote speaker, his speech was at least twice as long as everyone else's.

My mind began to drift and I found myself flicking idly through the conference programme. After a while, I opened my phone and started googling. I didn't know it then but my research would come in handy later. After the murder, I mean. Because everyone at that dinner ended up becoming a suspect.

Including me.

8

BEFORE THE QUESTION-AND-ANSWER SESSION
started, I escaped out the back door of the Aula Maxima. It was
about ten minutes to one and I needed to phone my assistant,
Tina. She'd texted during Professor Atkins's paper, asking me
to call her as soon as I could. I was glad of the fresh air and the
excuse to leave early. I wasn't the only one, I noticed. Further
along the path, in the direction of the library, Béatrice Mbemba
was engaged in an animated conversation with another woman.
I didn't recognise the woman from the conference hall but that
didn't mean she hadn't been there.

Senan Dunford had left the Aula too. Leaning against the
back wall, he was smoking a cigarette and checking his phone.
He'd done that thing with his tie that some men do for reasons
I've never understood: flung it over his shoulder. It made me
smile. He smiled too and gave me a little wave. I waved back at
him, then turned away and rang Tina.

'Where are you?' she asked.

'Still up at College. I got stuck here for the day. Sorry, I
should've phoned to tell you.'

'You should've done more than that. You should be on your
way to the courthouse.'

'Oh, Jesus! One o'clock settlement discussions in Harry Bennigan's case! I'll meet you on the steps. Bring the file. Tell everyone I'm on the way. Leaving now. Running. Thanks, Tina.'

If I'd been back at work, as I'd expected to be, I'd have seen the appointment in my diary. And because I didn't have to remember, I'd forgotten it. This kind of thing wouldn't have happened to me before, but my brain had turned to mush recently.

And climbing the eleven steps at the front of the courthouse less than fifteen minutes later, a lot sweatier and more out of breath than I would have been six or eight months previously, I acknowledged that my body had turned to mush too. Admittedly, I'd had an injury. I'd been hospitalised after getting into serious trouble during the Mandy Breslin murder investigation. So I couldn't blame all of my disintegration on the breakup with Davy Keenan. Not quite all. In fairness, 99 per cent was probably a more accurate figure.

I paused beneath the Corinthian portico. During the day, the plinth operated as a sheltered outdoor smoking and consultation area. At night, surrounded as it was by busy pubs and nightclubs, the steps provided rest for weary revellers. I sent a message to Tina letting her know I'd arrived and went in by the left door.

Inside, a substantial crowd stood dispersed under the dome, which told me that Family Law District Court was going on in Court 3; that the entire morning's cases had been bogged down by something interminable; and that the judge hadn't yet risen for lunch. When she did, the place would clear out for an hour or so as people left in search of sustenance. Meanwhile, the atmosphere was tense. Solicitors whose cases had settled gathered in a scrum near the courtroom door, clutching signed agreements, hoping desperately that the judge would take rulings before she rose and that they wouldn't have to return in the afternoon. I greeted several colleagues as I passed and walked quickly in the direction of the Bar room at the far side of the hall in search of my counsel. Feeling a hand on my shoulder, I turned, expecting it to be Tina with the file.

But it wasn't Tina.

9

IT WAS DAVY, THE LYING, CHEATING GOOD-FOR-
nothing who'd broken my heart into a million tiny little pieces
and who, apart from a new but minor frown line between his
perfect brows, looked as good as ever. Possibly better. Six foot
two, strong, his beard was gone and he'd shaved his sandy hair
into a buzz-cut too short to run his fingers through but soft to
the touch. Probably. He looked like a Viking after a makeover.
His eyes seemed bluer. I looked up into them for a nano-second
and had to look away.

'Finn,' he said. 'I was wondering if I'd run into you.'

I made no response. His hand was still on my shoulder and my
breathing had stopped.

'I'm here for court. About Tom. Everything's fine, really, just
sorting a few things, you know. Better to have it down in black
and white.'

Tom was his son. The one he'd had as a result of a brief dalliance
with an ex while he was supposed to be with me. Technically,
we were on a break at the time of the actual insemination, but
that did nothing to lessen the pain of the betrayal. Plus, he'd
known about the pregnancy for months but I'd only found out
about it after the child had been born. And *he* hadn't been the

one to tell me. My best friend Sadie had seen him going into the maternity unit at Cork University Hospital carrying a small suitcase with a heavily pregnant woman by his side. Even if she hadn't been a detective garda by trade, she'd have worked out what was going on.

She'd never liked him, because of his past. I'd met him first when he'd been a client of mine. Sadie had known him because of a cocaine addiction that, to his great credit, he'd beaten. He'd gone to rehab and retrained, and I'd done the legal work on a lease for his gym, one of Cork's most successful now, with a waiting list to join. We'd become 'just good friends' for a time. It was only after a few more years that we'd got together.

But Sadie had never approved of the relationship. She'd never trusted him and she'd been proved right. A while after she gave the news to me, I'd met him once and once only to confirm the way things had to be between us. Finished. For ever.

Which didn't make it any easier. Especially as he and the ex had split up again so, from what I'd heard, he was on his own now. I hadn't yet seen him with the baby but I imagined them like one of those black-and-white Athena posters. I took in a gulp of air. And still I said nothing. I was painfully aware of how bad I must look, my face undoubtedly red and horribly shiny after the rush down Western Road from College.

'It's nice to see you,' Davy went on. 'I don't have a solicitor, actually, there was no need, hers drew up the agreement and I just signed it but—'

I found my voice. 'You're not looking for free legal advice, I hope?'

'Not at all, no. I was only explaining why I'm here is all.'

'Thanks. Because it would *really* bother me if I saw you with another solicitor.'

'Would it?'

'Obviously not. You can do whatever you want, Davy.'

At the sound of his name in my mouth, my eyes welled. I clamped them shut. Then, mercifully, I felt my phone vibrate in my hand. 'I have to take this,' I said.

Davy's hand fell from my shoulder as I walked away. I put the phone to my ear and rubbed my thumb up and down the side of my neck, the same side as his hand had been.

'I've been looking for you,' Agnes Heaney said.

There was a bubble of conversation in the background. The Q and A must have ended.

'I was called into work urgently. I meant to let you know.'

'But you'll be back? You promised.'

I supposed that I had. And I'd just spotted Tina coming around the corner from Court 1.

'Ah, yeah,' I said. 'All going well.'

I waved at Tina and ended the call before Agnes could say anything else.

10

TINA HANDED ME MY BRIEFCASE. SHE WAS NINE years younger than me and eighty times as fashion-conscious. She was, as she said herself, 'Cork's most glamorous fat person'. She had the kind of glossy red curly hair that Irish dancing wigs were invented to emulate.

'I've given you the main brief, the pleadings and two extra printouts of the financials,' she said. 'By the way, was that a certain person I saw you talking to?'

'It was. Just a few seconds. He's here for Family Law District Court. Something to do with—'

'The baby.'

'Yes.'

'Things can't be too rosy with himself and herself so,' Tina said. 'Would you ever …?'

I shook my head wearily. 'Have you seen Mary Jo around?' Mary Jo was my barrister in the Bennigan case.

'No sign of her so far,' Tina said.

'She's probably in the Bar room. And where's the client?'

'I put him sitting on a bench in the atrium,' she said. 'He doesn't know you forgot about him. I made it seem like this was the plan all along.'

I laughed. 'It was, wasn't it?' Then I said, 'Does he have someone with him?'

'No one here, no one on the way,' Tina said.

In a contentious divorce like this, having a friend or relative present for settlement discussions often helps to bring perspective. But some people value privacy over support, and I could empathise with that. One of the worst things about the whole Davy debacle was how it had made me a live gossip topic in the office and, worst of all, an object of pity. Though the talk had died down in recent weeks, this episode would serve to reignite it. All of a sudden, returning to UCC for the afternoon seemed considerably more attractive. I decided there and then that that was exactly what I would do. I could either keep wallowing, reliving my broken past with Davy, or do something else. Being at the conference, and talking to people I didn't already know, including nice-seeming guys like Senan Dunford and Padraic O'Flaherty, was an opportunity. I needed to wake up and grasp it.

'You can head away, missus. I'll find Mary Jo, and I'll take the files home with me later. I'm not going to make it back to the office today. There aren't any other bombs going off?'

'Not yet, no,' Tina said. 'You okay?'

'Why wouldn't I be?'

There it was, the sure-God-help-her-the-poor-misfortunate expression. Well meant, especially by Tina, but excruciating for me.

'I'm fine, honestly,' I said. 'Now go and have your lunch. Please.'

❖

I located Harry Bennigan and sat beside him. Tina had placed him on one of the comfortable old wooden benches, wide in the seat and well worn in, a bit like Harry himself. He was a florid man in his sixties who bore a striking resemblance to his second cousin and sailing bestie Dermot Lyons, senior partner in MLC and, as a rule, my nemesis. But, like I said before, I was useful to have around, especially for the kind of file Dermot called 'delicate'. Despite his almost permanent moaning about the inadequacy of my pecuniary contribution to the firm, he funnelled a surprising amount of work my way.

Light flooded in on us through the glass roof of the atrium. The floor was glass too, though opaque as the Circuit Court office was beneath our feet. Before the renovation, this area had been an internal void. Now it was the epicentre of the building. If you were looking for someone, chances were you'd find them here, or run across someone who'd seen them.

'How are you feeling, Harry?'

'At this stage, I want it over more than anything else,' he said.

In my experience, timing is nearly the most important thing when it comes to settling a case. If Harry's wife felt the same as he did, we might be able to do business at long last.

'Come on,' I said. 'We'll find a consultation room and have a proper chat.'

I punched in the code for the Bar room and poked my head around the door. Inside, a set of curved antique wooden tables was arranged in a ring formation, like a massive skinny doughnut with an oversized hole in the middle. The surfaces were scattered with piles of documents and other legal detritus of indeterminate age and importance. The room was cleaned, but only around the edges. The table was never touched. Mary Jo, my counsel, was sitting at the far side, a takeaway coffee cup and bunched-up empty sandwich wrapping beside her.

'Have we a client?' she asked, when she saw me.

'We're in number six,' I said.

She gathered up her papers and followed me out of the room.

We had a Consent signed and witnessed by 4 p.m. The divorce would be ruled before the judge at a later date. I exited the courthouse with Harry Bennigan and loitered with him on the corner of Washington Street for a while. It had taken two years of angry wrangling for him to get this far, and barely three hours to tie it up in a neat little bow. Often, it was hard for clients to know what to do with all that excess emotion. Harry didn't seem to want to go home, but at least he hadn't mentioned going to the pub, the main reason he'd ended up in Family Court to begin with.

'There she is coming down the steps now,' he said. 'I wonder will she say hello to me.'

'It's not the end of the world if she doesn't. Life is long. Things change over time.'

I watched as his ex-wife, an assured ash-blonde woman, walked by us without a word. The woman with her nodded a greeting as they passed. Something niggled at me. I didn't know her, yet she looked familiar. I asked Harry who she was, but he didn't know either.

'I've never seen her before but my youngest boy told me she's been getting advice from some swanky financial consultant. That must be her.'

'He didn't tell you her name, did he?'

'I did ask, but I wasn't told. I can try to find out, if you like. Now that it's all over …'

'There's no need,' I said. 'I thought I'd seen her before but I'm probably wrong.'

11

IT WAS AFTER 4.30 P.M. BY THE TIME I GOT BACK
to College. I went in through the back door of the Aula as
quietly as I could, but Senan Dunford heard me. He was sitting
near the middle door, and there was a gap between his row and
the front section of the seats, now tightly packed. Senan glanced
over his right shoulder and grinned when he saw me. He nudged
the man beside him, Padraic O'Flaherty, who made a big show
of turning around in his chair and tapping his wristwatch as if
to say, 'Where were you?' Tiptoeing up the centre aisle, I sat in
the row behind the two of them. I put my fingers to my lips in a
'sssh' sign and gazed mock-avidly in the direction of the lectern
for a few seconds. But when I checked back on the two lads, they
were both fully turned around in their seats, miming applause.
I moved into their row and sat a seat away from Senan, putting
my bag and briefcase between us. He leaned across. 'You escaped
lunch but you're coming on the tour?' he whispered.

I gave him two thumbs-ups and settled back in my chair. I tried
to engage with the lecture. The speaker was Professor Kirsty
MacMillan from Queen's University Belfast, easily identifiable
by her Scottish accent. I remembered reading in the conference
programme earlier that she'd been born in Kirkcaldy in Fife.

Hers was the final paper of the day and I have no doubt that she was well worth listening to.

Except that I couldn't. After a while, I took out my phone. No messages. I shut my eyes and attempted to concentrate but, despite my best intentions, my mind kept drifting back to the encounter with Davy in the courthouse. I hadn't seen him during the afternoon, which meant that his case had finished and been ruled. I felt mildly guilty as I thought back over our conversation. He'd said that he'd signed the agreement in relation to his son without the benefit of independent legal advice. He shouldn't have done that and, even if he was a stranger, I would've advised him to get a solicitor. But he wasn't, and I hadn't. Because his life was none of my business any more. I told myself I'd done the right thing. Even if it didn't feel like it.

12

WE GATHERED OUTSIDE THE MAIN ARCH AT 5 P.M., waiting for the campus tour to start. I was standing between Senan Dunford and Padraic O'Flaherty, who'd adopted me as a 'naughtiest girl in the school' mascot because I'd skipped a few hours of the conference. I was happy to play along with the fiction that I'd been off having fun instead of grinding out a settlement in a divorce that client confidentiality didn't allow me to tell them about anyway.

Along with us was Kirsty MacMillan, tall and spare with cropped grey hair and a voluminous multi-coloured pashmina. Senan congratulated her on her paper.

'Thanks. And it's over, which makes it even better. Now, where's the pub?'

'We're getting Pimm's after this, I think,' Senan replied.

Kirsty grimaced. 'Are you a Pimm's man?'

She was addressing Padraic O'Flaherty, who had the kind of Irish skin that only has to see the sun to turn pink. I didn't know him well enough to start recommending sunscreen, but I feared for him. The clouds had cleared and the evening was surprisingly bright and balmy. I was, I had to admit, sort of enjoying myself now, and the knot in my belly had started to unclench. It was partly the good weather, of course. What's seldom is wonderful, as the old Irish saying goes.

'I'm more of an Arthur Guinness man, Kirsty, as well you know, but I'll happily drink Pimm's, if that's what's on offer. What about yourself, Cormac?'

He was talking to Cormac Ryan – a graduate of law at UCC, though after my time as a student – who was now teaching at UCL in London and who, according to a chat I'd had with Senan as we walked along the Stone Corridor a few minutes earlier, had just turned thirty and was 'shaping up to be a *seriously* high flyer'. Ryan was a little smaller than me, with thinning dark hair, an unfortunate black and orange polka-dot bow-tie, and a worried expression. I'd seen him around in the Aula earlier in the day, but his was one of several speeches I'd missed.

'I'll skip the Pimm's,' he said. 'I might have a glass of wine with dinner but I'm on the red-eye to Heathrow in the morning so I'll be taking it very easy.'

Professor Atkins was due to be on the tour too, according to Sophie, who was standing facing away from our group, still holding her clipboard, but he hadn't appeared yet. The final two on her list, both yet to arrive at the meeting point, were Béatrice Mbemba and someone I'd seen only once during the day, at the opening session in the morning, when he'd been thanked from the podium by Professor Casey: Nathaniel Simpson, CEO of Lexbonay Investments, the conference sponsors.

We were all looking in the direction of the quad, but when the stragglers arrived, they came from behind.

'Looks like the gang's all here,' a male voice I recognised as belonging to Professor Atkins said. 'And we're the ones holding up the show.'

We turned around. Atkins it was, and Agnes, Nathaniel Simpson and a slim young woman with long brown hair.

'Not at all,' Agnes said. 'I was only delighted to help you relive past glories.'

She was slightly out of breath. She looked stressed, and her wool dress and long puffer coat were too warm for the way the day had turned out. I had my own coat over my arm and my briefcase, which had a long strap, hanging from the other shoulder. My handbag was a cross-body one, which was a help. Even so, I was laden, and I'd been sorely tempted when, first, Senan and then Padraic, had offered to assist me. But if my file went astray after they'd had a few drinks, it would be my fault, not theirs, so I kept a firm hold on all my belongings.

'When I was last here, I served and volleyed on that spot,' Atkins said. 'But I can't complain. They did a fair enough job on it.'

He was talking about the Glucksman Art Gallery, built by the river in the lower grounds of the college on the site of the former tennis courts. He spoke with a strong Australian drawl.

'Best new public building in Ireland 2005, according to RIBA,' the woman with long brown hair said. She had a high-pitched voice that served to emphasise her ultra-Cork accent. I found out when she introduced herself at the start of the tour that she was Ciara Boyle, a student in the School of Law who worked part-time as a guide for the visitors' centre.

'So you keep telling me, Ciara, though you haven't yet explained what business an organisation of Pom architects has with an art museum in Cork.'

She giggled. 'I'll email you as soon as I find out, Professor

Atkins. You're the first person ever to ask me that. But I'm sure my boss will know the answer.'

'I'll be waiting, Ciara, and didn't I tell you the name's Will? Now who else is here that I haven't met yet? It's just you, I think.'

He stepped towards me and put out his hand to shake mine. His grip was strong and his gaze was steady. I liked him straight away, as everyone else seemed to. I've thought back over that meeting many times since and I'm quite sure. I felt nothing out of the ordinary at the time.

13

AGNES TOLD US THAT SHE AND SOPHIE HAD 'A LITTLE housekeeping' to do and that they'd see us soon. Our guide Ciara waited no more than another minute and, when there was still no appearance by Béatrice Mbemba, started the tour.

Pointing to the lion and chained unicorn carvings representing the United Kingdom above the exterior of the limestone arch, Ciara explained that the lion's face had been chiselled off late one night, decades previously, by a group of nationalist engineering students who had objected to having the symbol of England in their university. As the group moved into the quad, Béatrice was walking quickly towards us across the centre.

'Uh-oh,' I said.

'Indeed,' Ciara said, with a smile. She waited until Béatrice had reached us before continuing. 'Have you finished all your exams, Béatrice?'

'*Quoi?* I mean, I don't understand.'

'Well, you see, if you haven't, you're in big trouble.'

Ciara went on to explain the superstition that walking on the quad led to 'fierce' bad luck and inevitable failure. She said that no student would dare to do what Béatrice had done, and certainly never in April when the cherry trees were in bloom and final examinations were just around the corner. It was all said in jest, and the rest of the group chuckled and jibed playfully. But poor Béatrice looked stricken for some reason, and I couldn't be sure if she'd been like that before Ciara had told the story, or if she was genuinely concerned by what she'd heard.

I wasn't the only one who noticed her distress. The event sponsor Nathaniel Simpson, whom I'd pegged as a smoothie when I'd seen him in the Aula that morning, moved beside her and put his hand solicitously on her arm, leaning in to say something to her. I couldn't hear what he said but assumed it was something like 'Are you okay?'

She shook off his hand roughly and took three or four steps away from him, giving him a filthy look, which I was sure everyone in the group found just as remarkable as I did.

Though, when I met Professor Atkins's eyes, instead of finding bemusement, I found an expression of steely calculation that morphed into a smile when he spotted me watching him.

14

AFTER A WALK-THROUGH OF THE STONE CORRIDOR
and, by special dispensation of the president, a steep scramble
up the usually closed-off narrow stairs to the Aula gallery to
see the enormous stained-glass window up close, the walking
tour wound its way slowly onwards. Up ahead, I heard Kirsty
MacMillan talking to William Atkins about his paper.

'I think you're getting more radical as you get older, Will.'

'Go big or go home, Kirsty. That's always been my view. *You*
should know that.'

The two of them moved slightly apart from the rest of the
group and continued talking but I could no longer hear what
they were saying.

A little after that, as the tour paused briefly to admire the
twin Giant Californian Redwoods, I nudged Padraic O'Flaherty.
'What was that about, the thing between Béatrice Mbemba and
the sponsor guy?'

'Genuinely no idea. They look like they might have history
together, though.'

'That's what I reckon too, and Professor Atkins seemed to—'

But I was prevented from asking any more by our arrival at
the bronze bust of George Boole. Students believe that rubbing

his nose brings good luck, and the base of the sculpture is often strewn with floral offerings and cards. Dutifully, we stepped forward to touch the nose, noticeably shiny and smooth. And that spring evening, if there was luck going around, the women must have got it.

Because one of the men would be dead by midnight.

15

THE TOUR SNAKED ON BY THE CRAWFORD
Observatory, a small but perfectly formed, and impossibly cute,
cut-stone structure.

As we went past, our guide Ciara said, 'We don't have time to
go inside but we *can* fit in a quick visit to the Horgan Building,
which is, as I'm sure you're all aware, the home of the UCC
School of Law. If you'll follow me, I believe there might be
some people here to greet us.'

A narrow path led through the grass. Like much of the green
space on campus, it was not the manicured lawn it had been
during my student days, as it was no longer cut during spring
and summer – to the unbridled delight of the thriving College
bee population. I found myself walking in front of Professor
Atkins.

'I enjoyed your presentation this morning,' he said. 'I'd love
to chat about it later.'

'Of course,' I said.

I remember turning to him and smiling, and that he smiled
too.

The front door of the Horgan Building was flanked by Professor Martin Casey on one side and, on the other, by Professor Lia de Barra. A glamorous figure on the fringes of the law school when I was a student, my earlier googling had told me that Lia was a native of County Wexford, and that she'd studied law as an undergraduate at UCD. She'd done a PhD at Durham and had come to UCC as a post-doc researcher initially, which was what she must have been doing when I'd first become aware of her. After being appointed a lecturer some time later, she'd worked her way up the promotion ladder with impressive speed.

In the middle, between Lia de Barra and Martin Casey, stood Agnes. As she had all day, she looked ill at ease. I realised she was the odd one out of the three in not being a professor and still a senior lecturer.

Agnes said, 'And I'll call on Professor Lia de Barra to say a few words of welcome.'

From behind me, I heard Padraic O'Flaherty ask, 'Are we ever going to get a drink?'

'Don't worry,' Professor de Barra said. 'I won't keep you long.'

'That'd be a first,' Professor Casey said.

'You're not exactly famous for your brevity, Martin,' Professor de Barra said.

Agnes wore a strained expression, and no wonder. If they were like this in public, departmental meetings must resemble pitched battles.

De Barra continued, 'Welcome to the Horgan Building, constructed in 1910—'

'I think you'll find it was 1911, Lia,' Casey said. 'The Civil Engineering Building next door went up in 1910.'

I looked across at Senan Dunford. He raised his eyebrows, as if to say, 'What did I tell you?' and I could see his point. Whatever had happened to Professor Casey, the years since my graduation had turned him into a bitter old grump.

'As I was saying, the Horgan Building, which commenced construction in 1910 and, as Martin so *help*fully points out, was completed in 1911 is— Oh, let's just go in and have a look. You can ask me any questions you want, but we'll aim for a quick turnaround. It's been a long day and I could kill for a canapé.'

'I think that's what's known in the trade as taking the path of least resistance,' Cormac Ryan said. He gave a little honk.

'Well, yes,' Lia de Barra said. 'You always were a good student, Cormac. I find that, in these matters, it's best to read the room, something people I *could* mention have yet to learn.'

She smiled sweetly at Professor Casey. When he stomped past her and into the entrance hall, the smile widened into a broad grin. They were each as bad as the other. I looked at Agnes. Her face wore a tense, unseeing expression and her hands were by her sides in two clenched fists, one for each of her appalling colleagues, both of whom were also, unfortunately for Agnes, her bosses. My heart went out to her.

But now wasn't the time to sympathise. Also, it had occurred to me that the exchange I'd just witnessed might have been the reason she'd asked me to come today. Perhaps she was thinking of pursuing a case for stress, or bullying and harassment, against the university. And perhaps it was the very last thing she wanted to do. I thought back on what she'd said in the bathroom that morning: 'Whether either of us likes it or not, you're here now.' It was an odd method of seeking legal advice but, if that was what it was, it was perhaps understandable. These cases are notoriously hard to win. This way, I had first-hand knowledge of the problem. Which might make it easier for her to ask for help, often the hardest thing for a plaintiff, especially ones who happen to be lawyers and who imagine, mistakenly, that their legal training equips them to deal with the heavy emotional fallout.

As I went by her, I said quietly, 'You know you can call me anytime?'

She did call me. And soon. But it wasn't about bullying and harassment.

16

THE PRESIDENT'S GARDEN IS A PLACE OF VERDANT
lawns and seasonal flowerbeds and some of the UCC
Arboretum's most precious specimen trees, but it was *not* a good
choice of location for evening drinks and nibbles after 6 p.m.
in April. Situated on the far side of the East Wing, it was at its
best in the morning and during the middle of the day when
bathed in southerly light. Now it was cloaked in shade and,
though I'd hastily put back on my light coat, it wasn't enough
to keep out the chill. To make things worse, after weeks of
rain, the grass was boggy underfoot, seriously impeding the
progress of the tray-carrying waiting staff. At least I wasn't
wearing heels.

Nevertheless, there were plenty of 'Isn't this lovely?' and 'Isn't
it great to be out?' comments, particularly from Agnes, in her
calf-length puffer, standing at the right hand of the new College
president, Professor Nell Deady, a cheery, sturdy, hockey-
playing sort in her late fifties with a fondness for fleeces, one of
which she was cannily wearing, zipped up to the neck, as well
as a quilted gilet. The reception had been the new president's
idea, and it was she, too, who'd invited the select few to dinner
in her private dining room. It was no comfort that both events

were a rare honour and that, usually, conference attendees were stuck with going to a cosy pub, probably one with a roaring fire, after the day's mental exertions, then on to a restaurant, often the award-winning Paradiso, a ten-minute stroll away on Western Road.

I was in a huddle with Padraic O'Flaherty, Senan, Kirsty MacMillan and Béatrice.

'You have to wonder what we did to deserve this,' Padraic said. 'I mean, my paper wasn't that bad, was it?'

'Well, it wasn't great,' Kirsty said.

'It was better than yours,' Padraic said.

'No one's ever complained before,' Kirsty said. 'And God knows they've heard it often enough.'

'Fair point,' Padraic said.

'How do you two know each other?' I asked.

'He was my PhD student,' Kirsty said. 'Hasn't he done well for himself? After I knocked him into shape, obviously.'

'That's true,' Padraic said. 'She did.' He beamed at her.

She patted him on the head. 'Get me another of those drinks then, and be quick about it,' she said, and he trotted off.

'Actually, I have to be away myself now,' Senan said. 'I can't stay for dinner. Which, in my current circumstances, rather suits me. I have a nine o'clock tutorial to give in the morning that I'm actually getting paid for, and that won't be happening for much longer, so I'm afraid …'

'What a pity!' I said, and meant it. I felt like I'd lost my wingman. The first person I'd spoken to that morning, he'd made me, a stranger, feel welcome in circumstances where all the other guests seemed to know each other. And I had the uncomfortable feeling that, as a last-minute addition to the conference invitees,

I might have taken his place at the dinner table. 'Give me a call next time you're in Cork. We can go for lunch.'

'Somewhere warm?'

'Definitely.' I dug in my bag and handed him my business card.

'I'm sorry you're going, Senan,' Kirsty said. 'Let me walk a wee bit along with you. I have a few ideas that might help with your job search.'

They crossed the garden, leaving me alone with Béatrice. I didn't know what to say, so I resorted to the tried and tested unpaid-tourist-board-employee hack familiar to all Irish people.

'Is it your first time in Cork?'

'Yes. I was very happy to receive the invitation from Agnes.'

'Are you here for a few days?'

'Yes.'

'I suppose you're going to Blarney Castle, to kiss the stone.'

'I have no plans to.'

'You'll probably go to Kinsale so, maybe? Or venture further west?'

'Unfortunately, I will not have time.' She drew closer to me. 'Actually, I'll be honest with you. Even if I did have time, I would not go. Is that wrong? Ireland is a very popular holiday destination in France but I like the sun. I work in Paris and it can be cold and very wet sometimes. Why go on vacation to somewhere where it rains *all* the time? I don't understand.'

'Between ourselves, I see your point, Béatrice, but it is beautiful.'

'Sure. But it's so cold.' She rubbed her hands together and we both laughed. She was easy to talk to and to like.

I said, 'I saw you having trouble with that sponsor guy

Nathaniel Simpson. I don't know him, but he strikes me as a bit of a creep.'

'Pah! That's one way of putting it. I—'

Just then, Padraic O'Flaherty and Kirsty MacMillan returned, their glasses refilled, joined by Cormac Ryan, drinking fizzy orange, and Professor Lia de Barra. Sophie came immediately after them. She whispered in my ear, 'Agnes told me to ask you to come and meet Will. Apparently he's dying to talk to you. They're over there.'

She pointed to the top of the lawn, where Agnes and the president stood with Professor Atkins. As I walked towards them, my eye was drawn to someone standing alone a short distance away, watching the party from the corner of the library: Nathaniel Simpson. His gaze appeared to be fixed on one person in particular. Who that person was, I couldn't tell.

17

'FINN, WILL WAS JUST SAYING HOW MUCH THE campus has changed since he was here,' Agnes said.

'Even since our student days, which were ... what? Seventeen, eighteen years ago?'

'Hard to believe, but yes,' Agnes said.

She had visibly relaxed, I noted, aided surely by her physical distance from Professors Casey and de Barra. And she appeared to have developed a strong rapport with Professor Deady, who was only a few months into the president role. She was English, but with Cork roots from a few generations back that she'd mentioned, without providing the specifics that might have given them a degree of currency, in every press report I'd read, as if that was somehow going to make her job any easier. As the first woman in the post, and an outsider, there were bound to be hordes of passed-over wannabes banking on her to fail. But if she was aware of any negative feelings around her appointment, she didn't show it. In fact, she looked distinctly unfazed.

'Where did *you* go to university, Professor Deady?' I asked, to make conversation, even though I knew. Along with her Irish connections, Professor Deady had frequently mentioned that she'd attended Cambridge.

'Call me Nell,' the president said. 'I went to Julian's College, Cambridge, and I worked at Cambridge until recently too. But along the way I spent a glorious sabbatical year in Melbourne, which was where I met this reprobate. When Agnes mentioned that he was coming for a visit, I decided it was an occasion worth celebrating.'

At that, Agnes moved away, leaving me with Atkins and the president.

'And now, Finn,' Atkins said, 'I'm told that we three are going to be sitting together at dinner. I hope you're going to tell us some more about those investigations. I'm curious to hear how a case starts. How you come to be involved, I mean.'

'The start is the same as any kind of legal work,' I said. 'Someone asks me to get involved. After that, there are significant differences in the—'

I didn't get any further with my explanation because of raised voices from the centre of the garden, loud enough to ensure that the reception came to a swift end. The president clapped her hands twice, and told us to move into the East Wing without further ado. Everyone complied.

Everyone, that was, except the president herself, Professor William Atkins and Agnes, all of whom moved swiftly in the direction of the two participants in the argument: Dr Béatrice Mbemba and Professor Martin Casey.

18

THE REST OF US GATHERED AND WATCHED FROM inside the door: the guests; Ciara Boyle, the law student who'd been our tour guide earlier in the evening and who also worked part-time for the caterers; Magda Kozlowska, a middle-aged blonde woman, the event manager, according to her name badge; and the curly-haired technician in the Thin Lizzy T-shirt who'd been helping with the conference.

'Are you coming to the dinner?' I asked him, and introduced myself.

'Ian McAnespie. And no. But I'm supposed to be showing ye a fifteen-minute video about the history of the university beforehand, though, fuck it, this is a much better show.' He gestured in the direction of the contretemps in the garden.

'I wonder if I should go over,' the College security guard, who'd appeared on the path outside, said. 'I mean it's not *bad*, it's not violent or anything, it's just a bit embarrassing.'

I found out afterwards that his name was Rory Donnelly, and that a passing busybody had alerted him, not realising that one of the people involved in the kerfuffle was the president. The College grounds were crowded, every bench and low wall taken up by anxious students engaged in the time-honoured time-wasting practice of library-adjacent exam-fretting. The trouble was, all of them had phones. If the president didn't manage to call a halt soon, the incident could end up on social media. Having a security guard intervene would only make things worse, given the never-ending protests by local residents about student alcohol and drug abuse, and wild parties.

'Don't,' I said. 'I'll go. Ciara, please move everyone into the dining room. Ian, I really don't think we'll be watching a video. Magda, can you talk to the chef? What's his name?'

'Davide Rossi.'

'If we can get food into them, that'll help.'

'I agree,' Magda said. 'I'll tell Davide to get dinner ready for service immediately.'

At this point, I'd gone into auto-response mode, assuming that the argument was alcohol-fuelled. It was something I had direct experience of, though not, thankfully, since my early childhood. It was the reason I never touched the stuff. But there are some things you can't forget, no matter how hard you try.

'Should I hang around?' the security guard asked. 'I'm kind of new and …'

I didn't answer him but Professor Lia de Barra did. 'Definitely,' she said.

19

IN THE END, I DIDN'T HAVE TO DO ANYTHING.
Before I reached them, they'd turned around and were walking
in silence towards the entrance. I reversed my direction of travel
and went back through the door to the East Wing. Ciara had
done a good job of clearing the hallway. It was empty, apart from
Ian McAnespie, the conference technician, and Rory Donnelly,
the novice security guard.

As Agnes passed Ian, she said, 'Video showing's off. You can
go. Don't worry, you'll still get paid in full.'

The president was next, followed by Béatrice, then Professors
Atkins and Casey. They entered the dining room in that order.
I was last.

The President's Dining Room was less plush and more
functionally corporate than I'd expected. A large mirror and a
few neutral paintings adorned the walls. The long period table
was laid with a white cloth and silver-service place settings.
The low arrangements of dried flowers dotted along the middle
looked like they'd been retrieved from a cupboard and given
a dusting. In the centre, a candelabra with nine half-burned-
down red candles evoked a Hammer horror movie. Beside the

candelabra, a few overblown lilies stood crookedly in a too-large vase. Frowning, the president spoke quietly to Agnes. Seamlessly, she moved the arrangement to a sideboard.

The room felt unused, the musty smell mostly disguised by the heavy scent of the flowers. In the old days, a president would probably have eaten three-course meals here every day, cooked and served by his personal staff. Presumably the current president was expected to grab a sandwich in the North Wing common room or a cooked lunch in the staff restaurant like everyone else.

In the original table plan, I was to sit beside the president and opposite Professor Atkins. Instead, the president swapped my place card with Béatrice's, and for good reason. But the move meant I was stuck between Professor Casey, who looked flushed and dishevelled, on one side, and Simpson, the oily sponsor, on the other. At least I was opposite Padraic O'Flaherty. I took my seat. The row in the garden had left me momentarily lost for words.

And thirsty. Pouring a glass of sparkling water for myself, I took a large gulp, then refilled my glass and those of the guests at either side of me. On my left, Professor Casey, fresh from his seemingly vicious drunken argument on the lawn with Béatrice Mbemba, seemed lost in thought. To my right, Simpson simpered.

'Call me Nate.'

'Call me Finola,' I said.

'I thought …?'

He spoke with a studied upper-crust accent that might have been English and might have been fake.

'I'm joking,' I said. 'Everyone calls me Finn. Almost everyone.'

'Oh, I *see*.'

He gave a puzzled little smile and I muffled a sigh. There were twelve guests at the table and, at the time, I was sure I had the worst seat. But at least I was still alive the next day.

20

I MANAGED TO EXTRICATE MYSELF SHORTLY AFTER
10 p.m. Leaving via the door to the President's Garden, I ambled
up the shady path by the side of the library, which was still open
and appeared busy. But as I crossed College Road, by the student
health centre, I felt a cold breeze biting. In my rush to escape,
I'd left my coat behind. I returned along the same path to the
President's Garden door. By the time I reached it, someone had
shut it.

Cursing, I doubled back and rounded the corner onto the
quad, making my way into the Aula Maxima again. The main
lights were off, but there was enough light from a side lamp on
the dais and leaking in from outside to let me see that the chairs
and trestle tables had been cleared away. Down the back, I entered
the East Wing corridor, which was well-lit but empty. I took my
coat from the stand and put it on. On my return to the Aula, I
felt the air move and saw a shadow coming in my direction. It was
Ian, the conference techie. He smelled of fresh sweat.

'I thought you'd left ages ago,' I said.

'I did, but only temporarily. I'm just packing up the
equipment. I had, em, a Film Society committee meeting that I
had to run to. That's why I left it earlier.'

'Diligent,' I said. 'Committee meetings this late in the year?'

'Ah, it's a long story. What are you doing here anyway?'

'Forgot my coat. But I have it now.'

Exiting through the main door again, I saw him from the path through the lighted windows of the East Wing. In retrospect I recalled that he was frowning and that he looked stressed, his jaw clenched, but I thought nothing of it at the time. I just wanted to get home.

I was in bed before midnight, and I was exhausted by then, but I didn't sleep well. There had been something strange about the whole day. From start to finish there had been undercurrents I hadn't understood but that had left me off-kilter and unsettled. I didn't like those feelings. I knew them too well and, because of that, I did my best to suppress them. But I shouldn't have. I should have listened to my gut. I should have opened my eyes.

THURSDAY

21

WHEN I GOT INTO MY OFFICE EARLY ON THURSDAY
morning, the tiny room felt dusty and crammed. I opened the
window to the rooftops, disturbing a pigeon. The sky was an
unreliable blue, streaked with vague, faraway clouds. Yawning, I
lingered, hoping the cool air would wake me up. After a while,
I shut the window again and sat at my desk.

I prioritised completing the follow-up tasks on the Harry
Bennigan divorce. I find that, unless I do the attendance note
nearly immediately, and file the ruling motion with the court
and deal with any loose ends, the details drift away from me,
primarily because, after a few days, I can no longer decipher my
handwritten notes.

Tina called up to me with the post around nine thirty, as usual.
She asked how the rest of the day at UCC had gone and I said it
had been a pain in the neck but at least it was over. She caught
me up on what had happened during my absence, and I gave her
a stack of reminders and queries to chase up. She asked how I
was and I told her I was 'fine'. We both knew that she wanted us
to talk about meeting Davy at the courthouse, and that it might
have been healthy and normal if we did, but I couldn't, and I was
grateful that she sensed how I felt, and let it go.

After that, the morning passed quietly, apart from a typically unpleasant encounter with Dermot Lyons. I met him just before noon, as I was coming out of the tea-room.

'You sorted out my dear cousin Harry? He rang. We went out for a few nerve-settlers.'

'He seemed happy with the result,' I said. 'Did he say anything?'

'Well, he didn't complain. But it's no time for resting on laurels.'

'*Never*,' I said.

He had the grace to look amused. At times, I think it's all a game to him.

'And you were up at College too, I heard. Did you get talking to old Will Atkins at all?'

'A little. He seems nice.'

'He's mellowed. He was an awful man when he was young. Good tennis player, never affected by the gallons he'd put away the night before.'

'You knew him when he was in Cork, then?'

'He wasn't here long, but he made an impact. He was teaching us, but he was only a couple of years older, and worse than any of the students for going to parties and what-have-you. Not any more. I met him for a drink in Kinsale last week. He was doing part of the Wild Atlantic Way while he was over, and he was on the dry. Soda water. Something to do with his health, would you believe it? What is it they say? You won't live longer, it just feels that way, what?'

He paused. 'Will didn't, ah, happen to mention me, did he?'

'No, Dermot, he didn't.'

'Probably for the best. The stories would probably make your hair curl. I met him out in Melbourne during the World Cup in '03. We had a ball, marred only by the result, though Drico gave the Aussies a run for their money – I have to hand it to him, even though he's from Leinster.'

He was talking about rugby. Soccer didn't exist for Dermot because he'd gone to a famous rugby school, Presentation Brothers College, or 'Pres, of course', as Tina and I called it because that was Dermot's stock answer if anyone asked. I stopped listening until I realised he'd asked me a question: 'He's gone back, has he? Will?'

'Yeah, I believe he was taking the Aircoach to Dublin at an ungodly hour this morning.'

'Right, well, *sayonara*, Will, and so on, but you were out all of yesterday, and that kind of gadding hither and yon doesn't pay the bills. So, nose to the grindstone now, Finn, eh?'

I climbed the stairs to my attic room, revising my positive impression of Atkins with every step. If he was that close to Dermot Lyons, he couldn't be up to much.

Atkins and the conference and the various other guests didn't cross my mind again until the following Saturday when Agnes phoned me on my mobile to tell me about the murder.

SATURDAY

22

AGNES'S CALL CAME WHILE I WAS VISITING MY
parents. They live over the other side of town in the hundred-
and-fifty-year-old single-fronted two-storey terraced house I'd
grown up in, the house where I grew into the person I am now.
I was someone else before my parents took me in as a foster
child. Later, after my birth mother went away with the river,
they adopted me. I was their real daughter then. My surname
was the same as theirs. Legally. That might even have been
where I got the idea of studying law. Because the law was a
good thing. It gave me more love than I knew what to do with.
It gave me warmth. Certainty. No more the endless waiting for
the boom-boom of the door knocker, the stress of worrying
if *she* would show up for our court-approved access time on
Saturday afternoon and take me somewhere I didn't want to
go. Though that's not the full truth. A part of me wanted to
go with her. And that same part of me still believes that she
wanted to see me. But most of the time she wanted alcohol
more. Needed it so much that she was never able to stop.

Anyway, I was visiting my parents, which I didn't often
do on a Saturday. I dropped in during the week and usually
I was there for Sunday lunch, but this particular Saturday I'd
been pressed into service by my mother on the phone the day

before. In the course of our conversation, she'd told me she needed me to come to the house but that she didn't want me to visit until the next day, and that I'd understand why, that she had her reasons.

'You see what I mean?' she said, when I arrived. 'This time of year he'd normally be in the garden, night, noon and morning. Now, in the middle of the afternoon, he's watching golf.'

'I *like* golf,' my father said.

He was sitting in his armchair by the cast-iron fireplace in the front room. The fire was lit and he was wearing a cardigan as well as a jumper. The television was on with the volume turned down.

'Since when?' I asked. 'And Mam's right. You're not yourself.'

'Isn't a man allowed to have a sit-down?'

I exchanged a look with my mother, standing with her back to the window. She was a walker and kept the house spotless, and he walked too, and gardened, and they lived on Gardiner's Hill, so steep that anyone would say that was a workout in itself, and were up with the dawn every day. They were both in their seventies. As a rule, sitting wasn't something either of them did much of before the *Six One* television news, which they watched religiously.

'You need to go for tests,' my mother said.

'I don't,' my father said.

'Just the GP,' I said. 'That'll do.'

'The thin end of the wedge,' he said.

'See it as a way to get Mam off your back.'

No reply.

'Dad,' I said. 'Cop yourself on and go to the doctor.'

After a long silence, and without looking at me, he said, 'I'll think about it.'

❖

In the kitchen, I put on the kettle and my mother opened the back door. She gestured for me to follow her outside.

'Do you think he has the place bugged?' I asked.

She laughed. 'I didn't think of that, but he'd be well able.'

An electrician, he'd worked in the ESB before he retired, shimmying up poles in all weathers.

'How long has he been like this?'

'I've noticed him over the last few weeks, but I'm not sure. It could be longer. He's exhausted all the time and, like you saw, watching telly during the day, which normally he wouldn't dream of.'

'What's wrong with him, Mam?'

'I don't know. But he's sore as well, aches and pains, and cranky. And he's …'

She didn't have to say anything else because I'd felt it too. He was afraid.

We talked some more about the next stage in the plan to get Dad medically investigated. Even though he'd more or less agreed, stealth was required. We decided that I'd be the one to phone the GP for the appointment on Monday, and that I'd book time off from the office to drive him. Having me take a half-day piled extra pressure on him to go. But there was another reason.

'You don't ask for much,' my mother said. 'That's why he can never say no to you.'

We sat for a while longer drinking tea. When the phone rang in my handbag, Mam told me to take the call. I did, and told Agnes I'd be back to her in two minutes. I hugged my mother more tightly than I'd felt the need to in a while. As I was leaving,

I put my head round the front-room door. Dad was asleep, his mouth open. He looked wrecked. I squashed down the swell of dread in the pit of my stomach and called Agnes from the street outside the house. Afterwards, when the shock of what she'd said had subsided a little, I rang my mother to say that something had come up and that I couldn't make it to lunch the next day. I debated telling her about the death and decided against. My parents didn't know I'd been to UCC the previous Wednesday. When the story hit the news, they wouldn't connect me to it. There was no reason to add to their current woes by informing them that I was murder-adjacent yet again.

I took the vertical route to the city centre, down Gardiner's Hill through St Luke's Cross, further on down Summerhill, past the Coliseum Corner and over the river to the bus station. Having thought about what Agnes had said all the way in, I wanted to make notes as soon as I could on what I remembered of the conference and the dinner in particular. I also wanted to come up with a plan for the following morning.

Town was busy with cheery Saturday afternooners clogging footpaths, dawdling. I needed to go somewhere I could work in peace, preferably somewhere I'd meet nobody I knew.

There was only one viable option. I ducked into the anonymous buzz of Webworkhouse.com, an internet café, bureau de change and Western Union money transfer outlet on Winthrop Street, a place where it was always night no matter the time of day.

Grabbing a large coffee and a terminal, I logged into my gmail account and started typing.

23

THE AFTERNOON SLIPPED AWAY AND BY A QUARTER
past four I had done as much as I could. But the moment I
stopped typing he was back in my head: my father; beside the
fire in the middle of the day; wearing more clothes indoors than
he normally wore outdoors; watching a sport on television that
he'd always considered an utter waste of anyone's time.

I looked away from the screen and around the internet café.
The lighting was dimmer than it had been. The number of
patrons had thinned. In the corner, by the Western Union desk,
two men stood abreast at the top of the queue but not talking
to each other. When a spot opened up, the taller one went to
the window and conducted his transaction, glancing back at the
other every so often, then beckoning to him. The smaller man
moved forward and bent over the desk, as if checking something,
then stepped back. After a time, the taller man finished at the
window and turned around. On seeing him full face, even in
the half-light, I recognised him as Ian, the Thin-Lizzy-T-shirt-
wearing conference techie. I let him walk past and thought
about following but spent too long thinking. By the time I'd
gathered up my bag and coat, sent what I'd typed to my work
email and deleted it permanently from my gmail for security

reasons, logged out and paid, Ian and the man with him, whom I didn't know at all, weren't on Winthrop or Oliver Plunkett Street. They'd disappeared.

In other words, I couldn't see where they'd gone. I was being over-dramatic. But a man had been murdered, and McAnespie was as much of a suspect as anyone else in the East Wing that night. What he got up to on a Saturday might be significant, or it might not. Nevertheless, having lost them, I drifted westwards and, at the corner of Princes Street, turned right.

In the market, some of the canopies had come down, mops and buckets were being put away and cloths laid over display units as stalls closed for the weekend. A few units were still open. One was the Farmgate shop and, by a miracle, a single portion of fish pie was left in the fridge. I paid and made my way further into the market. By the fountain, a man stood holding a child in his arms; the little boy was pointing at the decorative leaves and painted birds (herons, like the clever ones who gathered every morning by the market gates, foraging for fish); the man, his father, was saying the words aloud – 'birdie', 'cabbage'.

Because I hadn't got used to seeing him with short hair and without his beard, it took me a moment to realise that it was Davy and his baby son Tom. As soon as I did, I stopped, intending to turn and leave the way I'd come in, but it was too late. He'd seen me, and he was coming in my direction.

He beamed. 'Twice in one week. How are you getting on? This is Tom, by the way.'

'Fine,' I said. 'He's gorgeous. I'm in a rush. Need to get some fruit and veg.'

'We'll walk with you, if that's okay? Maybe we could go for a cup of coffee. I'd like it if we could be friends, Finn, or even civil.'

Instead of telling him to fuck off, like I should've, I ended up telling him about my dad being unwell. Because they liked each other. And because Davy was always a good listener.

And all the time we stood there, the child in his arms cooed and smiled. It took every gram of willpower I had in me not to reach out and take his chubby little hand in mine. But I stayed strong and, as soon as I could, left the two of them there. Walking away, I pretended not to hear Davy saying that he'd phone me 'sometime'. It meant nothing. Less than nothing. We both knew that, in the highly unlikely event he ever did, I wouldn't take the call.

I made it to Superfruit, always the last place to close, in time to get a red cabbage, a bag of tomatoes, six plums, a few oranges and a bunch of carrots. After, as I laboured up Barrack Street, my mood sank deeper with every step. At home, I threw the shopping bag onto the kitchen counter and the fish pie into the freezer. Then I flicked on the telly and phoned for a pizza.

SUNDAY

24

THE PRESIDENT LIVED ON WESTERN ROAD, A FEW
minutes' walk from College, in an angular glass-walled penthouse
apartment with spectacular up-close views of St Fin Barre's on
one side and the limpid green of the river on the other. I arrived
as the bells for the eleven o'clock service were pealing. The
president flapped her left hand in the direction of the cathedral.
'The call to prayer,' she said. 'And we need all the help we can
get, I'm sad to say.'

She was wearing freshly pressed khaki chinos and a crisp white
shirt. She didn't look like she'd ever needed anyone's help. She
looked grimly competent, like a general in wartime. The vague
thought that had skirted around the edges of my mind since
I'd met her the previous Wednesday came into sharper focus.
What was she doing here? In this city? In this job? Though most
Corkonians would disagree, the inescapable fact is that Cork is
not the centre of the universe. With her elite background, there
had to have been other places she might have gone. I followed
her along an interior corridor painted midnight blue and hung
with a series of large multi-coloured abstract canvases.

In the living room, along with Agnes, PhD student Sophie
Dignam and Professors Casey and de Barra were seated at a

round glass table on uncomfortable-looking designer chairs. In front of her, Sophie had a fresh hard-backed A4 pad with a few lines of nearly microscopic handwritten notes on the front page. She was pale and seemed younger than before, in a loose aquamarine sweatshirt, her light brown hair in a low ponytail. Beside her, Casey looked like he'd received a diagnosis of a terminal illness. Next to him, Agnes looked equally shell-shocked. Lia de Barra, wearing a floaty floral midi dress with white Converse sneakers and a fitted white cardigan, was the only one who appeared unaffected by the tragedy. I wondered about that. And I wondered how long they'd all been there, and what they'd been talking about before I arrived.

But as I tried to read Sophie's notes upside down from across the table, she closed the cover and placed her pen firmly on top.

25

'LET'S BEGIN,' THE PRESIDENT SAID, 'BY REMEMBERING, in silence, the late Professor William Atkins.'

'Let's not,' Lia de Barra said. 'We all know what's happened. Like, it's sad *obviously*.'

Martin Casey said, 'Isn't that the trouble? That we bloody well *don't* know what's happened? The only bloody thing *I* know is that the last time I saw him he was hale and hearty and now the poor bastard's lying dead—'

'Stop it!' Agnes said. 'For once, just stop and listen to yourselves!'

'Perhaps we should move on,' I said, 'to why we're here this morning.'

'No,' Casey said. 'First of all, I want to register my, well, my unease. You're new, President, but even so, there are tried and tested ways of doing things around here. What I mean to say is, I'm concerned that this important meeting is taking place in the absence of any representative from the university's Office of Corporate and Legal Affairs.'

'Thank you, Martin. It's an excellent point. And you may rest assured that OCLA are aware of this meeting and that I'll be keeping them fully informed of what happens here today.'

'And they've approved this course of action, have they? Because I—'

'Corporate and Legal Affairs have *advised*, of course,' the president said. She steepled her fingers. 'But the buck stops with me. Calling this meeting is, and was, *my* decision.'

Which didn't quite answer Casey's question. He lapsed into miserable silence.

Lia de Barra said, 'President, I find myself in unusual agreement with my colleague's concerns. And I have a *further* concern. I *do* understand why you'd want to meet with me, and with Professor Casey and, to a lesser extent, with Dr Heaney, though I suppose she *did* organise the conference, so she probably *has* to be here. But why, in the name of *God*, are we burdened with the presence of a PhD student? No offence, obviously, Sophie. But the clue's in the name, President. She's a PhD *student*, not an *employee* of the university.'

Sophie went bright pink and bowed her head.

The president said, 'Try to think of this meeting as a talking circle. A move away from the staid old hierarchies.' She looked around at the group. 'Something terrible has happened. Something that has *never* happened before. If ever there was a time for doing things a *little* differently, surely it's now.'

Lia muttered, 'So far it's more like a listening circle than a talking one.'

Agnes looked pained, but Casey appeared slightly cheered by Lia's retort.

The president carried on, 'The university is faced with two initial primary concerns. The first, PR – in other words, communication with students, the media and the public at large – is well under way and is being spear-headed by the head of our in-house publicity department. We're dealing with a murder, which is an awful, not to say dreadful, one-off, for want of a better word. Though I've been assured that, in many ways, it's not so very different from any other crisis such as staff or student misbehaviour, academic plagiarism, disputes, suicide and so on.'

She made university life sound like one miserable event after another.

She continued, 'The advice I've received is that we simply need to acknowledge, sympathise, downplay and deflect in the usual way. And under no circumstance does any of us, in particular, or any other member of staff, in general, talk to the press or make any comments *whatsoever* on social media.' She made a point of looking around the table at everyone individually.

'The second issue, however,' she went on, 'is the murder investigation itself. *Terra incognita*, as it were. Which is where you come in, Finn. You've done this before. Last year. With that death at your firm. We want you to do the same kind of thing for the university.'

Agnes had told me as much on the phone. But before I agreed, I wanted to know more. 'You're staying in-house for PR, and the College has its own lawyers so why not stay in-house for legal too?'

'They're corporate. They deal with contracts,' the president said. 'Nothing like this.'

'It also has a law school,' I said. 'I'm not a criminal-law expert whereas the law school has several accomplished lecturers and tutors in criminal law.'

'*Nemo iudex in causa sua*,' Agnes said.

'You can't be a judge in your own case,' I said. 'Therefore, you're saying, the lawyers in the law school are disqualified from advising?'

'Exactly,' Agnes said. 'Apart from which, we're academics, not practitioners. I can't speak for anyone else, but I'd be utterly useless.'

She was right, of course. 'Nevertheless, they wouldn't be judging anyone. They'd be ...' I paused. 'Actually, I'm not sure I understand what exactly you want from me.'

The president spoke again. 'We want you to be the interface between us and the Garda Síochána.' She pronounced it Gawda Shickawna, which was a reasonable effort for an Englishwoman new in town. She either had a good ear, or someone had given her a few pointers.

With a trace of a smile, Agnes said, 'The guards have designated one of the investigating officers as their primary liaison. We want you to be ours. We think you're the ideal candidate. The garda liaison is someone we both know, by the way.'

And the scales fell from my eyes. Newly promoted Detective Sergeant Sadie O'Riordan had been my best friend since we'd been classmates at UCC. The same class Agnes had been in. The same class to which Professor Martin Casey had taught property law. I didn't know for sure whose idea it had been to have me act, but I reckoned it was Agnes's. Which was interesting. And clever. Because Sadie was ideal too, someone who knew the law school from the inside. Someone who, in the guise of rapport-building and supportive coffee-drinking, would actually be watching out for those accidental admissions and incidental giveaways that might steer the investigation in the right direction. Appointing me as buffer kept everything on a much tighter leash.

'Interfacing wasn't what I did for the firm,' I said. 'As anyone who heard my paper at the conference would understand, and I know that you weren't there, President, what I did was more in the nature of an investigation.'

I kept one eye on Agnes as I was talking. I thought I saw her give a tiny nod.

'That's the second part of your role,' the president said. 'Investigating within College.'

I raised my eyebrows.

She went on, 'You're the ideal person. You were there that night but you were first to leave so ...'

'So presumably I'm not a suspect.'

'However, the rest of us *are* in that utterly ridiculous position,' Lia de Barra said.

'Putting it bluntly,' the president said, 'I believe that this was a horrific but random attack by some disturbed individual or psychopath. But, for the good of the institution, the identity of the murderer, whoever that may be, must be ascertained. Sooner rather than later.'

26

THE TOKEN OBJECTIONS I'D PUT UP WERE FOR MY
attendance note, so that I'd have back-up if it all went wrong. In
reality, I wanted the job. Though I barely knew him, I wanted
to find out what had happened to William Atkins who, by
right, should've breathed his last in a comfortable bed a couple
of decades from now on the other side of the world. And, I'm
ashamed to say, because William Atkins had died, and in horrible
circumstances, I wanted the excitement of a new investigation.
I craved anything that might help me escape from the sinkhole
I'd fallen into. Nevertheless, I had to impart a few home truths
before I went any further.

'None of you can say for sure at this point that no one at this
table did it.'

The president replied, 'We know you have to say that,
especially at this early stage. We also know that the police will
be of a similar view. You see, that's the nub of why we want
you involved. To keep a close eye on the garda investigation
while simultaneously carrying out a parallel investigation where
you're looking for evidence that exonerates us and assists with
discovering the guilty party.'

In my experience, that wasn't how investigations worked.

Once you peeled back the rug, all kinds of dirt and secrets tended to be revealed, often unrelated to the original problem.

'So you want me to prove that you're all innocent.'

It sounded ridiculous when I said it out loud but the people seated around the table, lawyers who should have known better, didn't appear to think so.

I went on, 'As you know, in our system, an accused doesn't have to prove anything. It's up to the prosecution to establish sufficient guilt beyond a reasonable doubt to enable the jury to convict. But mud sticks and, as of now, you're right, all of you *are* in the frame. The only reliable way to prove that any one of you is innocent is to find the murderer. I don't need to tell you that that's the guards' job and that they have tools at their disposal – forensics, DNA – that I don't and—'

'Stop,' Martin Casey said. 'This isn't a first-year lecture in criminal law.'

The president said, 'Are you taking the job?'

'I'm taking it,' I said. 'Subject to a few terms and conditions.'

'Which are?' Lia de Barra asked.

'Who is my client?'

The president replied, 'The university, of course. Your fees – your employer MLC's fees – will be payable from a fund to be used at my absolute discretion to advance the interests of the university.'

'The interests of the university?' I asked. 'Or your personal interests?'

'Both of which, in this case, coincide,' the president said.

'Arguably they do. But, if your decision to engage MLC comes under external scrutiny at, say, a parliamentary committee, is it truly justifiable? After all, it's public money …'

'It *is* public money, though originally the fund from which

I'll be drawing was donor money. The Toomey bequest, a wonderfully generous Irish-American gentleman. I'll provide a full account of my spending to the Finance Committee and to the auditors, but I have every confidence that they will agree there can be no better use of these monies than the protection of the office of president and some of the university's most senior staff from guilt by association with this, em, tragedy.'

I caught Sophie's eye. She was making a big effort to appear impassive, and failing. As a PhD student, she didn't come within the definition of 'senior staff', yet here she was, inside the tent. She didn't seem at all sure that it was a good place to be.

I said, 'President, I'll need to get you to sign MLC's standard client retainer agreement and the Section 150 costs notice.'

She replied, 'We can do that later, before you leave.'

'Okay. Tell me about the garda investigation. Have any of you been interviewed?'

The president said, 'I was contacted on Saturday morning, I'm not sure how long after the body was found, but pretty soon. I spoke to a uniformed policeman first and then to a detective, two of them actually.'

'What did they ask you?'

'The first concern was to do a preliminary identification of the body – he had his passport on him so that made it easier. But they did show me a rather grisly photograph … Anyway, the next issue was when he'd last been seen and—'

'Let's not go into that for the moment. Has anyone else been spoken to?'

Agnes said, 'I have, twice. Not an interview but they wanted some more background information and contact details from me as conference organiser. I think for everyone else it's just been once.'

The others confirmed they'd been spoken to once, and that no formal interviews had been carried out yet.

'By the sound of it, you've all spoken freely thus far,' I said. 'But—'

Lia de Barra interrupted: 'You can take it that we're aware of the right to silence. Even the president here has a PhD in law. From *fucking* Cambridge.'

'What I was *going* to say is that I can't advise you individually if I'm acting for you as a group. And that I can recommend other solicitors to you if that becomes necessary.'

'Fine,' Lia de Barra said. 'Whatever. I have nothing to hide.'

'I'm sure we're all happy to cooperate with the investigation,' the president said, 'and obviously we're aware of our rights in theory. But, as Agnes said, we're academics, not practitioners. We *do* need your assistance.' She cleared her throat. 'So what's next, Finn?'

'I'll start by interviewing each of you individually and in private.'

'There's a room you can use,' Lia de Barra said quickly. 'In the law school. An office belonging to someone who's on sabbatical.'

'Who's that?' Casey asked.

'Eamon Fitzsimons,' Agnes said. 'Remember him? You've worked with him for the last six years? He's at Notre Dame for the semester?'

'Oh, yeah. Lucky bugger. If I'm allowed to use that expression, these days.'

'You're not,' Lia de Barra said. 'Not that that's ever stopped you.'

'Children, children,' the president said. 'Please continue, Finn.'

'The offer of a room is helpful, Lia, thanks,' I said. 'I'll conduct initial interviews as soon as possible. In your own offices, probably. And I have to warn you that, in all likelihood, I may need to visit you at home too.'

Because seeing where they worked and lived would tell me more than mere words ever could.

'You've been here. Presumably you won't need to return,' the president said.

'I'll interview you here,' I said, 'after the others have gone, if that's okay. Given that your office is inaccessible at present, as is the entire quad and the President's Garden.'

'How do you know?' Casey asked. 'Are there photos online? I didn't see any.'

'I went to College for a look on the way here. I didn't get far before I was stopped by a uniformed garda in a hi-vis. I assumed you were aware of the access restrictions.'

'We were,' the president said.

'We just didn't know *you* were,' Casey said. 'Resourceful, aren't you?'

'I'll take that as a compliment,' I said.

Casey grunted.

I said, 'I'll need full cooperation from each of you, and full disclosure of *all* the surrounding facts, no matter how seemingly irrelevant. I'll be asking you about the motive too, any reason you're aware of why someone might want to kill Professor Atkins.'

'Naturally,' Agnes said. 'Though I'm also of the view that we're most likely talking about something in the nature of an accident, manslaughter rather than premeditated murder.'

The president, Sophie Dignam, Lia de Barra and Martin Casey remained silent.

27

INTERVIEWING THE PRESIDENT STRAIGHT AFTER THE meeting wasn't one of my better ideas. She'd returned to the living room after seeing the others out. I was still sitting at the glass table, my barrister's notebook and pen at the ready. She made no move to rejoin me. Instead she walked to the balcony and opened the door, letting in a stiff breeze. With her foot, she rolled a cannonball-sized stone sphere into place as a doorstop. She turned to me, her head on one side, her face crinkled with apology. 'I didn't want to say it in front of the rest of them. I wanted to show willing. Let's get the retainer forms signed, obviously. But as for an interview, I know you'll understand when I tell you we'll have to do it another time. I don't have the space in my schedule for this right now. For *any* of this. I have a million things to do day to day, even without this, um, event.'

'I've heard you call it an event. And a one-off. You seem to have a problem with the word "murder".'

'Doesn't everyone?'

'With the fact of it, sure. Less so with the word.'

The president's expression hardened. 'I *do* need to get on,' she said.

'Tell me what happened after I left the dinner.'

'I'll send you an email. Tonight. You'll have it first thing in the morning.'

I shook my head. 'I left the dining room at about ten,' I said. 'What happened next?'

'For goodness' *sake*, that's the whole point. *Nothing* out of the ordinary happened. I have *nothing* to tell you. That's why … I mean, people just sat. Talked.'

'Was there any resumption of the big argument from earlier on?'

She sighed. 'There was no more drama. Proceedings wound up around eleven.'

'Was everyone apart from me still there at that point?'

'All the guests were, other than you. The chef may have left by then or he may have been finishing up in the kitchen – I didn't see him – but the waiting staff were still there and presumably a security guard or two, though not physically in the East Wing at eleven p.m., at least not that I saw.'

'And the conference technician, Ian McAnespie?'

'I didn't see him. I assume he was long gone.'

'So what happened at eleven?'

'Agnes said a few thank-yous. So did I. We got up from the table. Stood around for a while in the hallway. People said their goodbyes, which seemed to take for ever, the way these things do.'

'Is there CCTV footage? The guards will be asking for it and I'd like—'

'I'll arrange for you to view it, such as it is. There's security footage for most of the exterior, but not inside the East Wing. It's a workplace, not a nightclub. Though, in retrospect, it was a bad idea to remove it. But it's easy to be wise in hindsight.'

'*You* removed it?'

'It was one of the first things I did. I have a thing about excessive surveillance. The gradual erosion of human freedom to just *be*. My first degree was in philosophy, you know.'

I did. It was another of the things she'd gone on about in the press puff pieces around the time of her appointment. I made a mental note to ask her the question that none of the journalists had asked, or got an answer to, 'Why the move to Cork?', but I had more pressing concerns to deal with first. 'When did you last see Professor Atkins?'

'I was beside him as people came up to pay homage.'

She turned away and gazed beyond the balcony into the river below.

'You knew him well. He was a friend?'

She faced me again. 'Hadn't seen him in real life in years. But I was young when we met. He made an impression.'

'You're the second person who's said that to me,' I said. 'A man I work with, Dermot Lyons, said much the same thing.'

She spoke softly: 'I think you'll find it's a common response. A lot of people are going to miss him.'

'Do you know anything about his family?'

'Not much. I know he was married a long time ago and divorced. No children. Never remarried. But he was rarely lonely, I imagine. Women found him attractive.'

'Did he have someone in his life at the moment?'

'He didn't mention anyone but that doesn't mean he didn't. There was little opportunity for one-on-one personal exchanges. It wasn't that sort of evening.'

'Did he say anything that would indicate concern for his personal safety?'

'Not a thing.'

'Have you any idea why someone might want to kill him?'

'None whatsoever. He was a highly respected legal scholar with an international reputation.'

'Had he any enemies in the academic world?'

She shook her head. 'It's entirely possible, but I don't know of any. As far as I do know, he was popular. Well-liked.'

'When was the last time you saw him?'

'When we parted. About eleven thirty, or perhaps a little later. At the garden side of the East Wing. All the others had gone out via the small door onto the quad by then, I believe.'

'The garden door was open at that time?'

'Someone had shut it, one of the security staff, I suppose, but I opened it from the inside. We stood outside for a moment. It was chilly, very chilly, by then. He ... Yes, well, this is the thing. He went back inside. To use the lavatory. And I ... I'm afraid I went home. I offered to wait. I even suggested walking him back to his hotel but he assured me there was no need.'

'Where was he staying?'

'Hayfield Manor. The rest of the conference visitors were at the River Lee.'

I leaped on that piece of information. 'Is that unusual? For one of the speakers to be given five-star treatment while everyone else gets four? The River Lee *is* lovely but Hayfield is a lot more expensive. Did he *ask* for that? Or was it the sponsor? Do you *know*?'

'Those kinds of details are below my paygrade,' the president said.

Which put me right back in my box.

I said, 'You went home. He went to the loo. Who locked up?'

'A member of the security staff undoubtedly and don't ask because I haven't the foggiest which one. I lock my own office. Other than that, there are a lot of doors in UCC, in case you hadn't noticed. We pay people to lock and unlock them. It's their job, not mine.'

I could tell that she wanted me to disappear but I kept going.

'Agnes told me that the body was found in the East Wing. Exactly where?'

'At the bottom of the gallery stairs. By a nosy schoolgirl.'

She paused. 'That poor child,' she said. '*She*'s the innocent victim in all this.'

I thought it an interesting thing to say and waited for her to say more.

She backpedalled. 'Of course Will was innocent too. He didn't deserve …' Then, leaving no room for doubt, she said, 'We've done enough for today.'

'I agree,' I said, even though there were more questions I wanted to ask. Taking her through the retainer forms, I pointed to the place where I wanted her to sign and gave her a duplicate to keep. But I wondered how we'd got from 'We need all the help we can get' to this uncomfortable silence, and where the hinge point in the conversation had been.

I put on my coat and picked up my bag and notebook. The president was still standing by the door to the balcony. I heard her sigh again as I left the room and I thought it was with relief.

28

I'D ARRANGED TO MEET AGNES AT THE LAW
school. She'd texted to say that she'd got through the garda
cordon. But she had a College identity card and, as a serving
staff member, a good excuse to go somewhere that didn't lie in
the direct path of the area under investigation. I had nothing
official connecting me to the university apart from an out-of-
date student card in a shoebox at the bottom of a wardrobe in my
parents' house. I could've asked the president for a pass, but that
would've taken too long. And I could've phoned Sadie about
access, but I didn't feel like explaining my role to her just yet,
especially as I was still trying to figure out what it was.

A security barrier had been set up at the bottom of Donovan's
Road and the main gate had uniformed guards blocking access.
Also, earlier in the day, I'd tried and failed to enter from the
College Road side. There was no hope of getting in by any of
the obvious ways without the right ID. I kept walking west and
turned onto Gaol Walk where a garda car was splayed across the
road, just past the bridge over the south channel of the river and
in front of the old county gaol entrance, effectively restricting
access to several areas of the college at once.

And it struck me forcefully for the first time that unnatural death was nothing new on this campus. Over the centuries, the gaol had seen many executions, and I'd heard somewhere that the cadavers of the executed had previously been used by the medical faculty for dissection, but I didn't know if that was true. What was incontestably true was that two men had died on hunger strike here in 1920; and that in 1921 six IRA men were shot by firing squad on what was now an integral part of the university estate; and that their memorial, a stone's throw from the main restaurant, was passed by thousands of oblivious students every day; and that, as late as 1940, a man was shot and killed here while trying to help prisoners escape.

It wasn't until the 1950s that the gaol finally closed and was absorbed fully into the grounds of the university. It was demolished eventually, apart from the impressive stone gateway and some of the exterior wall, to make way for the massive modernist Kane Building, known as the Science Block back when I was a student.

'Where are you going?' the garda asked. She was leaning against the bonnet of the car. I mustn't have looked like much of a threat.

'Up to Highfield Avenue,' I said.

'Go on so,' she said. 'Fast.'

I rounded the corner and headed up the narrow hill, sticking to the road rather than the path at the other side, skirting the high former prison wall. Above, at the junction of Highfield and College Road, a garda stood facing away from me, blocking the traffic coming down. I was out of view of the cops at both ends of the lane. I had to hope they weren't in radio contact.

When I reached the rear service entrance of the Kane Building, the gate was open and unmonitored, as I'd hoped. I ducked inside and made my way up the stairs from the basement to ground level. I stood on the plinth in front of the glass doors and took stock. Though there was a garda and a barrier blocking access to the quad, and two more guards stationed on the College Road entrance, no one seemed to be much bothered about people going in and out of the Kane. I've been told that the building is even accessible to staff on Christmas Day, and rumour has it that there's a communal mattress on one of the upper floors, which gives me hives just thinking about it. The gardaí must've decided to let the scientists do whatever they do.

As soon as the guard on duty by the former College Bar turned away, I crossed quickly and moved unseen, down the path and past the Civil Engineering Building, to the law school.

29

'I THOUGHT YOU WEREN'T COMING,' AGNES SAID.

She was loitering on the grass in front of the building by an upright yew tree, the kind you find in graveyards. She said, 'I'd give anything for a cigarette.'

'Sorry, I don't smoke.'

'Neither do I. Allegedly. I've given up and I don't want to start again but …'

'Is anyone else here?'

'Sophie had a party to go to, would you believe? Casey went home. I did happen to notice that Lia de Barra is in her office, though.'

'You didn't walk up together from the president's flat, then?'

She laughed. 'That would be a no.'

'Which of them is harder to cope with?'

'Depends on the day. Casey mostly. He's a dinosaur. But he's straightforwardly boorish and sometimes that's easier to handle than de Barra's fiendish mind games. Do you remember her from when we were doing our degree?'

'Not much. Other than thinking she was a lot more sophisticated than we were.'

'That wouldn't have been hard. We were all fairly basic back in those days.'

'Let's go in,' I said. 'Before the persons in blue decide we shouldn't be here.'

The entrance hall was plain with dark wood panelling, unremarkable apart from the elaborate scales-of-justice-tiled mosaic beneath our feet. The main lecture theatre and some tutorial rooms were on the ground floor. Before the campus tour the previous Wednesday, I hadn't been inside that building since I couldn't remember when, but I'd spent three years there as a student, as had Agnes, walking back and forth over the scales of justice ten times a day during term time. Now the place felt both familiar and strange to me and I thought about how little I'd done in the years since graduation to honour the ideals I'd had back then. My career had run into the sand. In truth, my life had too. And I didn't even want to think about my father and how that might go. But this investigation, this was something to hold onto. An opportunity to reset. Maybe.

I followed Agnes up the stairs. We stood at the front window on the second floor for a look out at the garda operation. A couple of vans. Five or six people standing around, some in uniform, some not. No one I recognised. A protective membrane had been laid over the grass on the quad.

'They thought of that covering a bit late,' Agnes said. 'I heard it's carnage underneath. Footprints and tyre tracks apparently. Hopefully they'll make a better job of the investigation.'

From the landing where we were standing, an enclosed

glass walkway led to a new extension built onto the rear of the main structure. The extension hadn't been there when we were students. Agnes gestured in the direction of a large door made of honey-coloured hardwood visible beyond the far end of the walkway. It was ajar.

'That's Lia's office,' Agnes whispered, though Professor de Barra was too far away to hear.

'Fancy-looking,' I said. It was convenient that Lia was there – I could call to see her after I'd finished with Agnes. I didn't have an appointment but it would do no harm to drop in on the off-chance. Besides, I wanted a look at her office.

'Yeah. But it's south-facing and baking hot whatever the weather and they can't open any of the windows. There's a wooden louvred thing on the exterior that's supposed to regulate the light and temperature but doesn't, which nobody realised because they were all too busy fighting each other for the biggest room and the best view.'

'You didn't enter the fray?'

'They're welcome to it. Give me a good old-fashioned window every time.'

Agnes's office was neat and well-organised, with a peaceful east-facing vista of trees and sky visible from both of its tall, narrow windows. The bookshelves were well-stocked and orderly. The desk was enviably tidy. A side table held a clear plastic gallon container half filled with water, a Barry's tea caddy, a kettle, a Nespresso machine and a bowl of multi-coloured pods.

Catching my glance, Agnes said, 'I like to be well set-up. I do a lot of my work from home, but if I'm in the building, I spend as much of my time as I can in here. Less chance of getting sucked into the latest argy-bargy. Do you want a coffee?'

'No, thanks. Your room is lovely. And so clean!'

'I'm a compulsive declutterer. Helps my stress levels no end.'

I clicked the door shut behind me. 'Was stress the reason you asked me to speak at the conference? I was surprised to get the invitation. I've been wondering if it was your, ah, employment issues.'

She looked at me blankly.

'With Martin Casey and Lia de Barra?'

Agnes reddened, blinked a couple of times, and said, 'I'm perfectly capable of handling the two of them. I'm a tenured senior lecturer ...' She pressed her lips into a line.

'Now isn't the time, I get that. But you *can* tell me, and perhaps we ...'

'Finn, my employment situation wasn't the reason. Honestly.'

'What *was* the reason, then?'

'Will. The late Professor Atkins. *He* was the reason. *Him*. The murder victim. He wanted you there.'

30

'I THINK I'LL TAKE THAT CUP OF COFFEE AFTER ALL,' I said, because I couldn't think of anything else to say. My thoughts jumbled, I sat on the chair in front of Agnes's desk. From behind me, I heard the mechanical whine of the Nespresso machine and watched as Agnes placed a cork coaster and small beige ceramic mug in front of me.

'Is black all right?'

I nodded. Took a sip. It was barely lukewarm.

'Is it hot enough? Maybe it wasn't switched on long enough.'

'It's grand. Now, *please*, Agnes, tell me everything.'

31

'I WAS PLANNING THE CONFERENCE,' AGNES SAID. 'I had a wish list. Professor Atkins was on it. He's eminent in the field. You know that. I didn't expect him to come but I knew vaguely about his connection to the School of Law from his time teaching here. I thought, Nothing ventured, nothing gained, you know? I was surprised and *absolutely* delighted when he accepted. Now I'd do anything not to have asked him, needless to say. What's happened, it's horrific.'

'Tell me about the invitation and the acceptance. How it went.'

'Let me check.'

Agnes sat at her desk and opened a window on her computer.

'I have a separate folder for each speaker,' she said.

Her pace was too leisurely for my liking. I wanted to tell her that I didn't give a shit about her filing system, that I wanted to see the emails and find out why the late Professor Atkins had wanted me at the conference, and after that I wanted to scream at her and ask her why the fuck she was only telling me all this now. But I didn't. I waited.

'Ah,' she said at last. 'Here he is. Invitation. June. Questions. Emails back and forth. Acceptance comes in ... yes, July. After that, some travel queries. Flight info. Blah blah. February. Early draft of his paper, which was, of course, brilliant, as you'd expect. Final draft early March. Something about the hotel. I can send these on to you? Print them now, even?'

'Printing would be good. Or I can look at your screen?'

'Printing's no bother.'

But she was out of paper and she had to get some from a cupboard, which took what felt like four hours. Eventually the printer coughed into life and spat out pages at a glacial pace. Standing beside it, I scanned them one after another. I sat down again.

'There's no mention of me in the emails,' I said.

'That's because you're not in them. He asked me about you by phone.'

'When?'

'Just last week. He'd come for a short holiday before the conference. He was doing the Wild Atlantic Way.'

'That's what Dermot Lyons said.'

'Who's he?'

'I work with him. He was pals with the deceased back in the day when he lived in Cork. Did Professor Atkins say anything about him, was that how he'd …?'

'He didn't mention Dermot Lyons. Or anyone else. He only seemed to be interested in you. And, well, I could be wrong but …' She went quiet for a while before continuing. 'I had the impression that it was less *you* he was interested in than your work, the investigations you'd done. But I don't know for sure.'

I took that in. 'What did he say? What *exactly* did he say?'

'I didn't make notes,' Agnes said, 'but he phoned me on his mobile …'

'Do you have his number?'

'Yes, of course. Is it relevant?'

'I don't know. Send it to me anyway.'

She picked up her phone and started fiddling with it.

'Not *now*,' I said.

She gave me a look and put the phone back gently on the desk.

'Tell me what he said. Please.'

She spoke slowly: 'He started by talking about the investigations and then asked me if I'd heard about them. Of course I said I had. Then he asked me if I knew you and obviously ...'

'Go on.'

'He asked me if I could arrange for the two of you to meet. I said I'd do my best. Then he asked if I could invite you to the conference. I had no problem with that until I realised he meant I should invite you to *speak* at the conference and, specifically, he wanted you to speak about the investigations. I don't know if he was a true crime fan or what it was but he was like a dog with a bone, I swear to God. I felt boxed into a corner. He was my guest, he'd travelled from the other side of the world and he's sort of a star. I wanted him to be happy. Rather, I couldn't afford for him to be *un*happy. But it didn't suit me. My programme was full. I had to shoehorn you into the opening session. And you, you know yourself, you didn't quite fit.'

'It felt all wrong. I couldn't figure it out.'

'Anyway, that's the explanation for the invitation,' Agnes said. 'All I know.'

'Why didn't you tell me? Last week? The day of the conference? On the phone yesterday at least?'

'There didn't seem to be any point in discussing it yesterday. I thought the news of the murder was enough. Anyway, the main reason for my phone call to you was that Nell, President Deady, had asked for your assistance and wanted you to come to her flat.'

I thought about that. There was no escaping the fact that my engagement by the president on behalf of the university, and the method of it, was unorthodox. And that this additional information made it more so. But I had a signed retainer agreement confirming UCC as my client and I wasn't going to look that kind of a gift horse in the mouth. 'Why didn't you say it before?'

'He asked me not to.'

'That's *it*? He asked you not to tell me and you complied?'

'Yes. The day of the conference, I *could* have told you then, *should* have, but I was so busy it was the last thing on my mind. Running an event like that is akin to herding cats.'

I paged through the emails again. 'And there's nothing at all in writing?'

'Unfortunately not,' Agnes said. 'You'll just have to take my word for it.'

'If you'd told me on the morning of the conference, when we met in the bathroom, even, I'd have made it my business to talk to him, and find out what he wanted of me.'

'I assumed he was going to say something to you during the day. Though you didn't hang around for lunch and that might have been when he intended to talk to you. He'd asked to be put sitting beside you. At lunch *and* seating. Then there was that argument between Béatrice Mbemba and Martin Casey, which changed the seating plan unexpectedly. But did he not say anything to you at all, at any point?'

I slumped back in the chair, overcome suddenly by an unaccountable sense of powerlessness and something like regret. Or loss. After a time I said, 'We were introduced by ... I can't remember who. I think it was at the start of the tour. No, it definitely *was* then. Apart from that, he spoke to me only ... twice. And both times, yes, he *did* mention my investigation work. At the time I thought he was being polite, making conversation. But maybe ...'

Agnes said, 'Maybe he wasn't.'

32

I'D COME TO THE LAW SCHOOL WITH ONE IDEA of why I'd been asked to speak at the conference. What Agnes had told me just now painted an utterly different picture, and I felt like I'd been sucker-punched. My instinct was to retreat somewhere on my own to think it through and come up with a strategy for moving forward. It's what I usually do. It was what I wanted to do then.

But I had a job to do too. I had to interview Agnes about what had occurred at her end of the table during the dinner, and what had gone on afterwards, what she'd observed. All I'd found out thus far, from President Deady, was that 'nothing' had happened. I felt sure that Agnes would have more to add. Because of that I tried to park what she'd said about Professor William Atkins's interest in my investigations and continue with the interview.

'At the president's apartment earlier, you mentioned manslaughter.'

'When you mentioned motive, that's right. Will's death must have been accidental. Whoever did it panicked and tried to hide the body. That's what I think.'

'Do you have any idea who that might have been?'

'None. Last time I saw him, in the East Wing corridor around the time we were all leaving, he was very much alive. And before you ask, I don't know of anyone who might have had a motive to murder him deliberately, least of all me. His reputation preceded him, but I'd never met him before. The idea that I would invite him all the way to Cork and then murder him?' She shook her head. 'The same goes for anyone else in the East Wing that night. A deliberate killing makes no sense.'

We spent another twenty minutes or so going around in circles, which was my fault because I was asking long-winded, unfocused questions and not listening properly to the answers. In the end I apologised for my woolliness and told Agnes I'd have to see her another time. She said that that was fine. I managed to remember to ask her for a printout of the dinner attendees' contact details. She said she'd email me a PDF too. I knew I could track them via the conference programme but Agnes's list included personal mobile numbers, which would make my life easier.

As I was putting on my coat Agnes said, 'I suppose you're going to talk to Lia.'

In reality, I'd entirely forgotten about Professor Lia de Barra, whose door we'd seen ajar earlier on, but I said, 'Yes, I'm going to touch base with her briefly, if I can … Any tips on how to handle her?'

It took a while for Agnes to respond and when she spoke again her tone was sour. 'Flattery always helps. Also, even if you think she's wrong, don't let her know. She interprets anything less than total subservience as a betrayal.'

After that introduction, I half hoped that Lia might have left the building and gone home. She hadn't. Crossing the glass walkway to the new extension, I heard her voice long before I reached her office. I couldn't hear what she was saying but she didn't sound like she was in a good mood.

33

'GIVE ME A SEC,' LIA DE BARRA SAID LOUDLY, WHEN I knocked, and then, more quietly, 'I have to go.'

I took that as an excuse to poke my head around the door. 'Could I have a word?'

As I stepped into the room, I saw Lia shove something black that looked like an old-style Nokia phone into her handbag. There was another phone, a smallish iPhone from a few generations back, on the far side of the desk. A lot of people have two phones, but Lia seemed to be hiding one of hers. Which I found interesting.

'I *said* I needed a moment. That's what I meant when I said, "Give me a sec."'

'I'm so sorry. I'll wait outside. Do you want to call that person back?'

Her face wore a mildly annoyed and slightly bored expression. She didn't appear at all worried that I might have overheard her side of the conversation. But if she genuinely wasn't bothered, why did she feel the need to hide the phone?

'You're here now. Might as well take a seat. I didn't know there was anyone else in the building but obviously you are.'

'And Agnes,' I said, as I sat down in the chair at the front of the desk. It was rock hard and seemed to have been selected for the purpose of inhibiting students seeking special treatment and colleagues foolish enough to drop in for a casual chat.

'Ah, yes, the ever-diligent Dr Heaney. And what is it you want from me? I have children and they have school tomorrow and I have to go to the big Dunnes to do a shop because otherwise they'll *starve* and you wouldn't want that on your conscience, would you?'

I realised she was making a joke. 'Definitely not!' I said. 'I won't keep you long. I know you have a lot of demands on your time. Your job can't be easy at the best of times but with all this going on …'

Lia had been standing behind the desk. Now she sat, pulled her lavishly padded high-backed chair into place. She moved the mouse to wake up the screen and went about shutting down her computer before I could see what she'd been working on. While I waited for her to finish, I took in my surroundings. Just as Agnes had described it, the rear wall behind Lia's desk was glass and south-facing. I recalled too what Agnes had said about her mind games. The wooden louvre shades were fully open. I was willing to bet that she scheduled her most awkward office meetings for sunny days between noon and 2 p.m. to maximise her advantage. But by now the evening sky was filled with clouds. The glare was minimal.

The interior walls of the office were lined with shelving, much of it unused. There was a seating area in front of the shelves with a single elegant but comfortable-looking armchair upholstered in a mustard yellow print with green leaves and large white flowers that resembled daisies. Beside it, a low, square, blond hardwood table held a reading lamp, several chunky law books, some loose pages, and scattered notebooks of differing sizes. There were no photographs or pictures anywhere. In a corner, various boxes were stacked in two untidy piles.

'I like the armchair,' I said.

'It's a good spot for marking exam scripts. I brought it in from home because I'm often here quite late. I can't get anything done back at the house, unfortunately.' She added, 'I haven't moved in here properly yet. I should pay an undergraduate to unpack everything for me. But there's so much pointless admin in academia these days that I haven't time to think, which is ironic given that, teaching aside, thinking is supposed to be my primary role.'

She stopped talking then and fixed her attention on me. I should have been able to ask her the forensic questions I needed answered. But my confidence had leached away over the course of my afternoon at the law school, and instead of a muscular serve, I went for a gentle lob. 'Tell me what you remember about the end of the conference dinner.'

'*Just* the end?' Her tone was needle sharp.

'What I mean is, what happened after I left?'

'Well, if you're *sure* that's all …'

I sensed I'd either made a big mistake or, more likely, that she wanted me to think I'd made one. It was a girls' school playground tactic, and it would have been effective if I hadn't been the foster kid, the butt of every joke in Gardiner's Hill primary. If I hadn't learned to hold my own when I had to. I straightened myself and went back hard. 'Do rest assured, Lia, this won't be our only meeting. And you probably recall that you've promised President Deady your *full* cooperation with my investigation. So with that in mind, for now, I want to focus on what happened, from your point of view, leading up to and at the conclusion of the evening's activities, in particular in the period of time after I'd left the premises. After you've answered that, my next question will be whether or not you remember anything at all at any stage during the day or the evening or, for that matter, before or since then that you now, following the tragic death of William Atkins, consider to be significant in any way. And, Lia, the sooner you answer, the sooner we'll both be out of here.'

Professor Lia de Barra held her head very still for a long moment. Then she gave a little nod. After that she started talking and it was a while before she stopped.

34

'I WAS SITTING BETWEEN AGNES AND KIRSTY MacMillan. Padraic O'Flaherty, the ginger hobbit from Galway, was beside Kirsty, needless to say. He was sitting across from you. I'm sure you noticed that they have an unhealthily close relationship. I recall exchanging a few words with the two of them during the evening, though nothing of any importance and nothing at all after you left, as far as I recall. I was opposite Sophie Dignam, Agnes's PhD student, and she is still *only* a student, however much she might like to think otherwise. Dr Cormac Ryan from UCL was beside her, to her right. I spent most of my time talking across the table to him. He's an ex-student of mine, one of the finest graduates this school has produced, apart from yourself.'

I made the obligatory chuckling noise, though I'd rarely been less amused. The woman was a gorgon. I had no doubt she'd checked my grades and seen that they weren't in Ryan's league or anywhere close. It probably accounted for her prior snarkiness about my inadequate line of questioning. But she appeared to have decided that my skills lay in other areas and that I was worthy of her attention, if not her intellectual respect.

She went on, 'I taught Cormac tort, as I'm sure you're

aware. He's doing so well in London. I thought at one time he might … but that's not relevant to what you want to know. As regards Atkins, Professor Atkins, I didn't speak to him one-on-one all night. He was monopolised by Agnes, the president and that rude French woman most of the time.'

'Béatrice Mbemba? I didn't notice him talking to her.'

'Oh, but he did,' Lia said. 'He was sitting directly opposite her and he even swapped places with the president at one point and sat beside her and they had quite the little chat. Ten, twenty minutes at least. I didn't hear what they were saying. Cormac might have, I suppose.'

'When was that? The place swap?'

'It was probably soon after you left but I can't be a hundred per cent sure.'

'Agnes didn't mention it, I think. Maybe she forgot.'

I thought back over my conversation with Agnes. After the big reveal about the real reason for my invitation to the conference, I'd been a bit all over the place for a while. Still, though I couldn't be certain if Agnes had told me, I was nearly sure that she hadn't. I took a note to check back with her.

'If I know Agnes, she's forgotten to mention quite a few things.'

'What do you mean by that?'

'You know that saying "If you want to know me, come and live with me"? They should add "or come and work with me" to that, in my opinion. But I know she's a friend, and former classmate, of yours so … Besides, as you know, that wasn't the only musical-chairs type activity.' Lia paused. 'But, no, I can see from your face that no one's told you.'

She opened her mouth, shut it again. Finally she grimaced –

or smiled, it was hard to tell – then continued: 'Look, you didn't hear it from me. It's just that, after he'd spent time with Béatrice Mbemba, the victim moved into your seat. I didn't have a great view and I didn't hear what was said but it can't have escaped your notice that your seat was directly beside, well, Professor Martin Casey, dean of this school. And you asked if I'd noticed anything significant. It was this – that Professor Atkins spent the remainder of the evening sitting beside Casey. At least half an hour. Possibly longer. I'd call that significant, Finn, wouldn't you?'

35

LIA DE BARRA WAS RIGHT. IF WHAT SHE'D SAID WAS
true, it *was* potentially significant that William Atkins had made
an effort to spend a good portion of his last hours on earth
sitting beside Professor Martin Casey. But it might have been
equally important that Lia had been the one to tell me, while at
the same time making abundantly clear that she hadn't spoken to
the murder victim at all. And perhaps the ten or twenty minutes
Atkins had spent with Béatrice Mbemba would prove to be even
more crucial. It was too soon to make a definitive judgement on
any of it.

Which was what I said to Lia. 'Time will tell how significant
it is.'

'That's not the reaction I expected,' she replied. 'I expected
some gratitude.'

Too late I recalled what Agnes had said about Lia's tendency
to interpret anything other than total subservience as a betrayal.
I tried to claw my way back into her good graces. 'Don't get me
wrong. My time with you has been more helpful than anything
else I've done today. If you don't mind my saying, your memory
and powers of observation are, em, quite extraordinary. But
it's early days with the investigation. I'll, uh, I'll be able to give

you a better steer on things when I meet you again at your, um, house, at some, ah, point ...'

I didn't know if my tardy flattery had worked but I thought I detected a trace of a smile. Nevertheless, I pushed my luck a little further. 'When we were down at the president's apartment you said something about an office I could use? Belonging to someone on sabbatical?'

'That's right. I did.'

'Do you know where I could find a key?'

'I have one. If you're quick, I'll show you the room on the way out. Don't delay, though. It's late and I'm not coming back to rescue you if you get locked in.'

She smiled sweetly. But her friendliness might have been an act. And I hadn't finished with her quite yet. 'When did you last speak to Professor Atkins?'

She bristled. 'I thought we were done here? And, anyway, I told you already, didn't I, that I didn't speak to him all night? Other than about the food, momentarily, across the table.'

'So you didn't say goodbye to him?'

'Of course I said goodbye.'

'Tell me about it.'

'It was in the corridor of the East Wing, everyone milling about. I said something like "Lovely to meet you again" or whatever, the usual. The dinner was a duty as far as I was concerned. I was invited by the president and I had to go, obviously, and it was great to have the opportunity to chat to Cormac, but I couldn't wait to get home. I left as fast as I possibly could. After you, I was the first to go.'

'You said "again". You'd met the deceased before?'

'Yes. Briefly. At a conference at the University of Liverpool.'

'Can you tell me about that prior meeting?'

'It was two years ago, I think. I was introduced to him. We were in company together. Same hotel, I can't remember the name of it ... Cormac might. He was there too.'

'What did you talk about?'

'Generalities. Nothing memorable. Flights, probably. The weather.'

'Do you remember anything else?'

'No. And before you ask, I have no idea who might have wanted to kill him. I'm inclined to agree with Agnes, which doesn't happen too often, that it was an accident. Or, like the president said, a random attack by a disturbed individual.'

'And, returning to the night of the murder, can anyone else verify what you've said, that you were first out of the East Wing?'

For the first time, she faltered. 'I – I'm not sure ...'

'Which way did you go?'

'The back door of the Aula.'

'I've been told that many of the others left via the door onto the quad.'

'It was shut when I was leaving. I didn't open it. Like I say, I was first out.'

'So you were alone?'

'Well, ye-es, I suppose I was.'

'What time was that, Lia, can you recall?'

'I can't. After eleven. About a quarter past, a little earlier or later?'

'And how did you get home?'

'By car.'

'Yours?'

'I walk or cycle normally but I like bringing the car to College events. And in case you're wondering, I'd had one tiny Pimm's at the reception and a thimbleful of white wine with my starter. I was in precisely *zero* danger of being over the limit.' She thought for a moment. 'I parked in that spot by the Aula. You can check the CCTV, can't you? You'll see me leaving if you do. I exited via the Gaol Cross gate.'

'Where was Cormac Ryan at that stage?'

'With the others, I assume, the conference guests staying in the River Lee Hotel. Look, to be completely honest, that's the main reason I scuttled off early. I didn't want to get stuck with giving lifts to any of them, especially Casey, who was *abominably* drunk by then.'

It had the ring of truth about it but I would need to check the CCTV.

'Did you notice anything or anyone as you were leaving?'

'The library was still open. There were quite a few students going down Main Avenue but I didn't really pay any heed. Though, now that I think of it, there *was* someone connected to the dinner. You know that viewing area where you can look down at the river?'

I nodded.

'Someone was standing there, having a smoke. A man. I think he was the chef. The catering van was nearby, a big white thing, I don't know what the make or model was but it has "Nibblz" on the side – that's "nibbles" spelled with a classy *z* so it's hard to miss. But, yes, he was there. I didn't talk to him but *you* should. He might have seen something. Or, with a bit of luck, maybe he was responsible for the murder. A College outsider. Probably an immigrant. Yes, if it turned out like that, it'd be a great relief to all concerned, I'm sure.'

36

CONSCIOUS OF WHAT LIA DE BARRA HAD SAID
about the danger of being locked in, I spent little more than a few
minutes in the office I'd been provided with as a base. It belonged
to Eamon Fitzsimons, a lecturer in Roman law, currently on
sabbatical approximately four thousand miles away at Notre
Dame University Law School in Indiana. I didn't know if anyone
had asked his permission before giving me licence to occupy his
space but I doubted he would have cared. Situated to the rear
of the ground floor, the room had the feel and dimensions of a
stationery cupboard. A large evergreen bush directly outside the
window blocked most of the light. Those in power at the law
school didn't appear to afford much status to Roman law, and
I was beginning to wonder if that was how they felt about my
investigation too. Giving me an office looked like cooperation,
but it would have been hard to find a place more remote from
the action.

I wasn't bothered. I'd accepted the offer of a room for the
excuse it gave me to be on site in the Horgan Building without
repeated explanations for my presence to the law school staff
and An Garda Síochána.

And there was no one but me there now. I might never again

get as good a chance for an uninterrupted poke around. I locked the door behind me and went exploring.

With a notebook and pencil, I climbed the stairs to the top of the building. There were three storeys made up of smaller teaching rooms and offices. I worked my way down, noting the nameplates and the rough location of each staff member as I went. I didn't intend to talk to each and every one of them but, by cross-referencing the names I was taking now with the law school website and my own interview notes, I planned to ensure I missed nobody with knowledge potentially relevant to my investigation. Because it was a Sunday evening, almost all of the internal doors on the upper storeys, apart from the bathrooms, were inaccessible to me. The only unlocked room – probably because it gave access to a massive industrial-sized printer and photocopier – was a communal office on the first floor used by support staff. I wrote and underlined a note reminding me to have a chat with the law-school secretaries. If anyone would know what was really going on here, they would. Plus, they had all the timetables, which would make it easier for me to track everyone down.

By the time I got to the ground floor, I had a reasonable grasp of the current layout, including the new extension. I checked that the main entrance to the building was still open – it was – and told myself that I should go straight home. It was almost dark outside and I had a busy Monday ahead.

But I didn't leave. I doubled back across the scales-of-justice mosaic, turned left and walked along the corridor. At the end, I pushed open the heavy door – the movement caused the main lights to flicker on automatically – and stepped into my past.

37

THE LECTURE THEATRE, WITH ITS STEEPLY RAKED
benches and narrow writing ledges, looked the same as it had
when I'd sat there day after day listening to tall tales – of snails
in ginger-beer bottles and carbolic smoke balls, of leaking cargo
ships and careless sailors – that had gone on to become important
precedent-setting cases.

Martin Casey had taught me property law there. He'd seemed
so different back then: energetic, fiercely intelligent, a full
professor at thirty-nine, with two important books under his
belt. I wondered what had happened to change him. Or what
hadn't.

I moved further into the room. It smelled of old wood and
dust and, when full, I knew it would smell of damp coats and
smoke and chewing gum and, sometimes, alcohol. I knew too
that, from the dizzy heights of the back row, there was a fine
view of the sky and the treetops because I'd spent a good chunk
of my time there gazing out the small square window panes at
clouds scudding by and birds on the wing. I remembered Sadie,
my best friend then and now, nudging me, or giving me a
kick, if I daydreamed too much; Sadie who had gone into paid
employment with An Garda Síochána after College instead of

opting for the extended poverty and torturous study that the Law Society FE-1 exams required; Sadie, who was most likely out on the quad even now with the rest of the detective team from Coughlan's Quay station; Sadie, who had been appointed liaison officer with the law school and who would be my point of contact with the murder investigation.

I was going to have to talk to her about all of this soon. Knowing her, I was expecting a blowback when she found out about my involvement. I figured it was best to get it over with.

Night was falling as I made my way down the narrow, winding footpath, lit intermittently by dim footlights, that led to the side of the library. A quiet rain was falling too. It had been sunny the last time I'd walked there during the campus tour, and William Atkins had been there then. Now, more than a day and a half had passed since his dead body had been discovered. I assumed that it had been removed from the East Wing and that it was stretched flat on a slab in the morgue awaiting post-mortem examination. But, even if the corpse was gone, the crime scene below me remained active. The extra lamps that had been set up to supplement the existing lighting and the strips of blue-and-white tape fencing off the entire area made the quad look like a film set, but the horror felt real.

All of which is by way of explaining that, when I heard a man's voice behind me calling my name out of the dark, I jumped sky high.

When I managed to turn around the voice said, 'You're not

allowed to be here, Finn. I'm on duty. I'm supposed to keep everyone away.'

The voice belonged to the novice security guard on whose watch Professor Atkins had been murdered. Which didn't exactly fill me with confidence.

And, straight away, two things occurred to me. The first – how he knew my name when I had no recollection of introducing myself to him – I dismissed as unimportant. He might have overheard other people addressing me while we were in the East Wing watching the argument between Béatrice Mbemba and Professor Martin Casey.

The second was more serious. Because, unless I was very much mistaken, the man standing in front of me, the man who had just told me he was guarding the scene, must also be a suspect. Even if he had had nothing to do with the murder, having him anywhere near the operation might lead to evidence being compromised. I had to let Sadie know.

Right after I'd asked him a few questions.

38

'YOU GAVE ME A FRIGHT,' I SAID. 'I THOUGHT FOR a second that it was a ghost calling my name. And, I'm so embarrassed, I don't remember yours.'

'It's Rory, Rory Donnelly.'

I put out my hand and he shook it. He was in his mid-twenties, very skinny and slightly stooped, taller than me by a few inches, with thin fair hair falling in a long side sweep across his forehead that he touched repeatedly and pressed into place. He seemed nervous.

'You've been busy today and yesterday, I reckon.'

'You can say that again. I was supposed to have the weekend off but we were all called in to help. It's a massive job keeping everyone out. Library's shut. Ructions about that so close to exams. Students up in arms. Organised chaos.'

'Have you spoken to any of the guards yet? Any of the detectives?'

'A few of the uniformed ones. Just "How's it going?" and that kind of thing.'

'So they don't know you're an important witness yet, then?'

'I'm still new,' he said. 'I didn't want to mess up.'

'I see what you mean,' I said. 'Maybe I can help you fix that.'

I beckoned him to follow me beneath the overhang of the library, a multi-storey 1980s building made of horizontal bands of pebbledash-effect concrete and recessed tinted glass, regarded with considerable affection by generations of students nevertheless. We sat on a wooden bench in one of the ground-floor window alcoves. It was dark inside, but for a few emergency lights that served only to deepen the gloom.

'It's dry here, at least,' I said. 'Even if it's not very bright. Or private.'

'It's not much like your office, I suppose,' he said. 'You're a solicitor, aren't you? I might need a solicitor sometime, you never know.'

I had been about to give him my business card but thought better of it. Instead, I took the barrister's notebook and pen out of my bag and wrote his name in block capitals at the top of a fresh page. 'Let me explain my role, Rory. I've been appointed by the president to be the link between College and An Garda Síochána, and the first thing I need to do is take a few details from you, starting with your mobile number and where you live.'

He called out his number and said that he lived on Prosperity Square, just off Barrack Street. I stopped writing and looked up in surprise. Later, I would realise I'd failed to note the house number.

He added, 'You live around there too, don't you? I've seen you a few times. I recognised you when I saw you in the East Wing on Wednesday night.'

I felt a scratch of unease at the back of my neck. 'You must be new to the area.'

'I'm from Waterford originally. After I got the job, I took

a room in a house share about two months ago. Not a student house. But I don't plan on being here too long. I'm applying for the guards.'

'Great experience for you today so. And about that, Rory, I'm a bit surprised to find College security on duty. I thought no one was allowed near the scene.'

'We're not supposed to be. We're supposed to be just minding the periphery and staying on duty outside the gates to assist An Garda Síochána, but when I saw you I had to do something. You were heading straight for the quad.'

'Which gate are you actually on?'

'Up there.' He gestured vaguely in the direction of College Road. Earlier in the day, I'd noticed that all the gates were shut, apart from the main College Road entrance, and that was staffed by gardaí in high-vis vests. It seemed that College security was assisting them now, though I wasn't sure how Donnelly could have seen me from way up there. Perhaps he'd been patrolling along the exterior railings. It was something I could check later if it became an issue. I had to move on. 'Talk to me about Wednesday night. When did you start work?'

'I was on the evening shift. Started at seven, finished at three the next morning. A private security firm comes on duty then. On call and monitoring the exterior with a vehicle.'

'So you weren't long on duty when I met you.'

'I signed in, and straight away I was deployed to do a general sweep because this time of year there's a lot of activity at night and you never know what might happen. The campus is well covered by CCTV but we like to have a visible presence. I was just heading back to make my report when a student told me there was trouble on the lawn.'

'You're talking about the argument in the President's Garden.'

'That's right.'

'And you stayed around the East Wing for a while during dinner. Can you tell me what you saw?'

'I saw you going to the toilet and you told me it was quiet and I headed off then but I suppose you know that. And I saw the Black woman on the quad talking on the phone.'

'Dr Mbemba. Did you see her talking to anyone else?' I was thinking about the woman I'd seen her talking to earlier in the day.

'No. I'm sure she was alone.'

'Who else did you see in the corridor?'

'The two waitresses. Plus the fella who was supposed to be doing the film.'

'Ian, the technician. When did you see him?'

'I'm not sure. Early on, I'd say.'

'What about the chef?'

'Didn't see him. Only people I saw were from the dinner, a few who went to the toilet while I was there. You, some others, and that old guy from the law school who was shouting and roaring on the lawn earlier.'

'Professor Casey. Who else?'

'I don't know any names. I might know their pictures if I saw them. The dead man was one of the people who came out to the hall. He made a phone call. He was talking but I couldn't hear what he was saying. I– I didn't talk to him myself. I don't know if he even saw me. After a minute or two he went back in. Didn't go to the toilet. After a while you came into the corridor. You *did* go to the toilet. And you spoke to me and you told me to leave – remember? So that's what I did. I checked back again later and it was still quiet so I didn't bother any more after that, just kept going with my other work until about eleven.'

'What happened after eleven?'

'I helped with the lock-ups. There's a lot of doors and gates so it takes a good while but we're normally all done before twelve. But that night we were leaving the quad area a bit later than usual because we didn't know what time the party was going to break up. And, of course, a couple of gates are left open until the library closes at half past two. Well, officially it shuts at two, but it's not locked till half past. And the remaining gates are locked then as well. The only one left open all night is the revolving pedestrian one on Western Road and that only opens outwards so no one can get in that way.'

'What did you do next?'

He swallowed. 'I was due a coffee break. I'd missed it earlier, but I, ah, said to the supervisor that I didn't mind taking a stroll over to the East Wing to see what was happening.'

39

THE RAIN WAS HEAVIER NOW, AND LOUDER, THE drops bouncing off the ground. We were sheltered from the wet – and from being seen by the gardaí on the quad – by the library and the trees, but the lighting was so subdued that I could barely make out my scrawled notes on the pages in front of me. Taking a statement on the fly like this had been a bad idea, but I had to keep going. I asked, 'What's the supervisor's name?'

'Kasper Nowak. He's my line manager too.'

'Can you give me Kasper's phone number, please?'

'Em, okay, I suppose.' He called it out and I wrote it down.

I went on, 'But it was *your* idea to go over to the East Wing?'

'It wasn't anything special. Covering the East Wing is a normal part of the job, only we hadn't done it yet that night because of the dinner. I was happy to go over because of being there earlier. Curious, I suppose. But we both hoped I'd be able to get *some* of the locking out of the way at least.'

I said, 'Tell me what you saw, Rory. And who.'

'I'm not sure where to start.'

'Walk me through it step by step from the time you decided to check the East Wing.'

'I was up by the Electrical Engineering Building, so I wasn't all that far away. I just went down by the security hut and past the monument and I turned right to go towards the quad. There were a few people walking against me – I think they were all students on their way home from the library. I don't think any of them were at the party in the president's dining room, but I'm not sure. I came along just below the steps here and walked down by the front of the East Wing.'

'You were back by the East Wing around what time?' I asked.

'Coming up on midnight, a bit before, give or take.'

'And what did you see?'

'There were people around.'

'People from the president's dinner?'

'The weather was dry. A lot of the guests were still hanging around. Talking.'

'What was the mood like? Any arguing?'

'I don't think so. They were in a couple of different groups. Maybe the ones that had been fighting earlier were keeping away from each other.'

'Can you remember who was talking to whom?'

'I told you I don't know the names.'

'That's fine, just do your best. Hang on, I've got an idea.'

On my phone, I googled the conference webpage and located a PDF of the programme. I started with a picture of the deceased, Professor William Atkins, and held it up. 'Was he one of the people you saw?'

'No. He's the one guy I'm a hundred per cent sure of.'

'You're doing great, Rory. What about Professor Casey?'

'The guy from the fight on the lawn? He was there. I saw him.'

'How sure are you?'

'I'm fairly sure.'

'Before I take you through any of the other photos, can you recall if you saw him talking to anyone?'

'He was talking to a tall older woman with grey hair and a big colouredy scarf, and she had her arm around a red-haired man a bit smaller than her. They were kind of an odd couple. It's why I noticed them. And because the three of them were laughing their heads off.'

One by one, I located programme photos of Professor Kirsty MacMillan and Dr Padraic O'Flaherty and held them up.

'Yeah, that's the two I saw with him,' he said.

'Can you remember anyone else? Even a rough description, or whether they were male or female? Or how many people were there?'

'There were a few more. I don't want to say a number because I don't want to get it wrong but there's CCTV of it, I'm sure. You need to talk to my line manager Kasper about it. The only thing I can say for definite is that Dr Mbemba wasn't there then. I'd have remembered her. The president wasn't there either. Or the dead guy. I said that already, didn't I?'

'That's good, Rory. And what about the doors? Were they open or closed?'

'The West Wing had been locked since soon after eleven and the two doors under the arch leading to the North Wing were done at the same time. As the party was over, I walked around the outside and locked the back door to the Aula. The kitchen door was still wide open but that's just a pull-out job when the caterers are finished so I didn't have to worry about that.'

'You're saying you remember the kitchen door being open after midnight?'

'Yeah, and the lights were still on.'

'Did you see any of the staff?'

'No, they were still there, though. The lights in the dining room and the East Wing corridor were still on too. The staff were there after midnight for sure.'

'What did you do next?'

'I checked the back doors to the East Wing and they were all locked, apart from the kitchen, like I said. I checked that the main door from the East Wing to the President's Garden was locked, but that's another pull-out job so it was no bother, and then I walked up along the front again, past the group. A few had gone, I think, but Professor Casey was still talking to the same two and there was another woman with them as well the second time I saw them.'

'What did she look like?'

'She had a long puffy coat. That's all I remember – I didn't take any notice.'

I showed him Agnes's picture.

'It could've been her,' he said.

'Had she been there earlier on talking to someone else, or had she just arrived?'

'I don't know,' Rory said.

'That's okay. What did you do next?'

'I went in the main door to the Aula from the quad and locked it from the inside and then I went in and locked the inside door to the Aula from the inside as well. I made sure of that. And then I walked down to the back of the Aula and I was going to, em, lock that door too and come back through the small pointy door onto the quad and lock it behind me. That was my intention because they all looked like they were finished inside apart from the staff so ...'

He stopped. 'This is the part I'm a bit worried about.'

'There's nothing to worry about,' I said. 'All you have to do is say what you remember and tell the truth.'

He said nothing for a while, stared at the ground. He was wringing his hands. When he looked up again, he said the last thing I expected.

40

'I'M NOT SAYING ANOTHER WORD WITHOUT MY union rep.'

He went to stand up and I put my hand on his arm. I thought for a moment. Whatever this was about, it was mainly about fear. His. He was afraid of something or someone, or of the consequences of something he'd done or not done. Pushing too hard might cause him to clam up completely.

'That's fine, Rory,' I said, 'though the chances of getting someone like that at this hour on a Sunday are nil, obviously.'

'Right.'

'You said you're a *bit* worried, but it's a lot more than a bit, I can tell.'

He made no response.

'Look, what I want to say to you is, there's no need to be. This isn't a workplace investigation in the normal sense. Or a disciplinary.'

'Yeah,' he said. 'But if you found out something it might end up being one.'

'I honestly don't think so. Anything you say to me now wouldn't comply with due process and couldn't be used against you. We're just having a chat. A serious chat admittedly. About serious things. A man died violently on the UCC campus, which happens to be your workplace. The whole college is under a cloud until the crime is solved. So anything you say to me that helps to catch the murderer, how could that do you anything but good around here?'

I couldn't see his face well enough to see if my words were having an effect. I kept talking. 'The other thing I was thinking about was your application to the guards. If what you told me helped – and you've helped loads already, Rory – it'd be a great thing to talk about at your interview.'

'Hah,' Rory said. 'This won't help me get into the guards, believe me. But I don't know, maybe delaying more might make things even worse.'

'Up to you,' I said. 'We can put this off till tomorrow, if you like.'

He was staring at the ground again.

'Is there something in particular you're concerned about?'

'It's the locks,' he said.

I waited for him to continue.

'I think someone tampered with the locks. And I'm afraid that because I didn't say it at the time they'll think it was me who did it.'

'You're saying it now,' I said. 'That's the most important thing.'

I still didn't know what he was talking about but I gave him a chance to tell me himself before I pressed him with more questions.

'The door at the back of the Aula that leads to the East Wing. My key wouldn't work. The lock was broken and I think now that someone did it deliberately. I looked at it and I fiddled with it but it needed to be replaced. I meant to say it to Kasper that night but I forgot. And another thing, the door to the gallery. I didn't check it because it's nearly always locked except for those special private tours. But it couldn't have been locked that night. It must've been interfered with and left open too. Otherwise how would that girl have found the body?'

He put his head into his hands. 'You see now why I'm in trouble. *Two broken locks.* And I did *nothing.* Didn't even know about the second one. But if I had, if I'd checked the door to the gallery, like I was supposed to, I'd have known something was wrong. I might've been able to stop the murder before it happened. Or catch the murderer in the act. Save that man's life. I fucked up big-time. I know it. You know it. Soon, everyone will know it. The gardaí. My supervisor. And I'm still on probation. I can get another job if I'm fired, I know I can, but a dismissal from a security job always looks bad. And that's not even it. It's what might have been. If I'd only checked the door to the gallery.'

'You might have been killed as well if you had,' I said. 'We might be dealing with two corpses instead of one.'

He looked straight at me for the first time in a while. 'Didn't think of it like that.'

After a beat, I asked him, 'Did you see anyone inside the East Wing at that point?'

He shook his head. 'Like I told you, the caterers were there. I heard them, but didn't see them.' He hesitated. 'I didn't check the toilets either. I thought there was no need. That's all.'

I talked to Donnelly for a few minutes more. He confirmed that he didn't know Professor Atkins and that he hadn't spoken to him at any time during his visit to the university. I took him through pictures of dinner attendees he hadn't mentioned to see if he remembered them. He didn't. I told him that was fine and I gave him my card after all and told him to call me if he remembered anything else. He said he would. I walked with him towards the main College Road entrance, leaving him at the gate, by the security hut. I told him he should carry on with his work as normal and wait for me to contact him again. I also told him that if he was tasked with patrolling the periphery, that was where he should stay, and that no matter what he saw, he shouldn't venture onto campus again without clearing it with the gardaí. He agreed.

What I didn't say was that, as far as I was concerned, his evidence did considerable damage to any suggestion that the dead man was killed spontaneously in an unplanned or random attack. One broken lock might be wear and tear. But two? The unlawful killing of William Atkins was looking more and more like premeditated murder.

41

IT WAS TWO MINUTES AFTER NINE AND THE RAIN
had stopped. Before I'd met Rory Donnelly, I'd intended to
make contact with Sadie on campus but my interview with him
had taken a long time so I decided to call her later. I thought
back on what Donnelly had said. It was useful, though I'd need
to check it independently. And it undoubtedly made him even
more of a suspect in the murder. He was on site at the relevant
time in the East Wing and, according to himself, he was alone.
Whatever about motive, he had the means and the opportunity.
I wondered if he realised. He'd seemed more concerned about
his job, but that might have been an act.

I headed along College Road, up Wycherley Terrace and
through the arch onto Bandon Road. The Centra shop had shut
for the night and the street was Sunday-night quiet. As I walked, I
texted Agnes for Ciara Boyle's mobile number and email address
because, in addition to being our tour guide and a waitress at the
president's dinner, Ciara was also a law student. As a lecturer in
the law school, Agnes would presumably have access to students'
personal information, their *confidential* personal information,
strictly speaking. But Agnes had promised the president full
cooperation with my inquiry. I hoped that that meant she'd

push aside any data-protection concerns. If not, I knew that I could connect with Ciara and the rest of the party staff via the caterers, though a direct phone number would be faster. Nevertheless, I quickly googled Nibblz and saved their address and contact details to my phone, noting that their website said that Nibblz was the 'executive events' division of Complete Solutions Catering, known as CSC, the company with the main College catering contract. I'd been under the impression that the dinner had been something special, but it seemed not. I realised that, with so many different departments in the university, such occasions might not be all that unusual.

When my phone buzzed, at first I assumed it was Agnes, but it was the president's name on the screen. I was annoyed. I wasn't even a day into the investigation. If she was looking for an update already, it didn't bode well. Still, I had to take the call. It might be a break in the case.

It wasn't. She said, 'I hear you're asking for student contact details.'

Agnes must have asked for her clearance to give out Ciara Boyle's number. 'Yes,' I said.

'For your information, staff don't have routine access to student information, other than their College email. All student information is stored centrally ... but I've authorised the release. Emergency situation. Um ...'

'Thanks,' I said. There had been no need for her to ring me, other than to remind me of where the power lay. She *was* looking for an update but I made her ask for it.

'Is there any news?'

'Three initial interviews done, in addition to yours.'

She didn't respond straight away. 'Who?'

'Agnes, Lia, and one of the security guards.'

'Did you find out anything useful?'

'Hard to say yet. And don't forget I need to see you again. Do you want to—'

'Contact my assistant,' she said. 'I'll send you her number.'

She ended the call. Seconds later, a ping told me that the contact card for the president's assistant had arrived on my phone. Even though I had no intention of using it to arrange an appointment, I saved it. When I wanted to talk to the president, she was the one I'd be talking to. If she had direct access to me, I intended to have direct access to her.

Because from what I'd learned so far Rory Donnelly wasn't the only one who'd admitted to being alone at the pertinent time in the East Wing with the means and opportunity to murder William Atkins. The president had too, and it looked to me like she might have been the last person to see him alive.

Apart from the murderer, obviously.

42

MY HOUSE WAS A FIFTEEN-MINUTE WALK FROM College, which was handy. It was also just up the hill from Prosperity Square where Rory Donnelly had said he was living. Though he hadn't produced proof of address, I had no reason to doubt him.

But it bothered me that he'd said he'd seen me around the area, because I'd never noticed him. The same as any woman living in a city, I liked to keep an eye on the neighbourhood. If I'd missed Donnelly, what else had I missed? I'd let my sharpness blunt in the long months since the break-up with Davy. As I turned off Barrack Street onto the narrow dark lane, barely wider than a wheelie bin, I told myself, not for the first time, that the rot had to stop.

At the end of the lane, a grey door was set into a high stone wall. Behind it was a small garden with stone paving and gravel, a few pots, shrubs, a herb bed, and the house I'd built some years before on a tight almost landlocked site when the banks were dishing out money for all projects involving property without looking too closely at anyone's bank balance. The crash had come, but I'd been able to keep up the repayments and I still had my house.

My architect had told me that the tiny footprint meant that in order to achieve a decent floor area, I needed three storeys. I remembered Rapunzel, my favourite fairy story when I was a child. I told her I wanted a round tower, with the living space at the top, an en-suite master bedroom in the middle, and an office, a shower and laundry room, and a small spare room on the ground floor.

It had turned out better than I could have hoped. The top floor had a flat roof, and the walls were glass, encircled by a perforated-steel balcony. Double doors opened to the evening sun, and there was a kitchen island, a dining table and benches made to fit the space by Sadie's husband, who had a successful craft furniture-making business. Plus there was a slouchy sofa, and books, and music, and views from everywhere in the room. Which was all great.

It was also the place where Davy and I had first kissed, and where we'd spent so much of our time as a couple. There were memories everywhere I looked. Which was less great.

I clicked on the kettle and grabbed a plastic tub from the fridge, opened it and gave it a sniff: the previous Friday's leftover bolognese sauce. Despite everything that had happened in the meantime, it was still only Sunday. The leftovers were fine. I spooned half of them into a saucepan and threw what was left of a packet of spaghetti into another with boiling salted water. While I was grating the Parmesan, I thought about calling my mother to check on how my dad was. But I'd phoned her that morning and she'd said he was the same. And I knew they'd both be watching the nine o'clock news now. I called Sadie instead.

'That's a coincidence,' she said, when she answered. 'We need to talk. Do you have any food, by the way?'

I said, 'Well, as it happens …'

There was no more pasta but I put the rest of the bolognese into the meat saucepan. I badly needed to do a big shop but the way things were going it would be a while before I had the time. I roughly chopped some red cabbage, a little onion and a couple of carrots and made them into a coleslaw with Dijon mustard, natural yoghurt and mayonnaise. In another bowl, I made a sliced tomato salad with vinaigrette dressing.

Sadie arrived and I buzzed her in. We sat at the table and ate without saying much. When she'd finished, she leaned back in her chair. She said, 'When were you going to tell me you're a murder suspect?'

'You're joking!'

'Yeah, obviously. I think I'd know by now if you were the kind to go around strangling people. But you were at that dinner, so you *are* a witness. You're going to have to make a statement. At the station. You can tell me what you remember now anyway.'

'I will, of course,' I said, 'but, full disclosure, and you're probably not going to like this, I've been appointed—'

'As *liaison* between College and us? Yeah, I knew that too. And that you were on campus illegally for several hours today without making contact with me.'

'I did nothing illegal so don't give me that. But how do you know all this?'

'The president informed my superintendent, who was *not* impressed, let me tell you. And Fogarty saw you canoodling in the love nook at the library with that security guard. I told him to leave you there but to keep an eye on you. After ye parted, he picked up Donnelly for a little chat. Seems he might be a useful witness. At the very least.'

Olly Fogarty was Sadie's main work partner. I knew what his chats were like. 'If you know so much, why didn't you call me?'

'To *liaise*?'

'Yeah,' I said, and laughed.

Sadie didn't. 'I've had enough to deal with. It was my decision to close the library. Student representatives seeking meetings with the superintendent. Hundreds of emails to the ministers for justice and education. Those *fucking* students. If they'd worked harder during the year, it wouldn't be such a big deal to have the library shut for a day or two. Which, operationally, was one hundred per cent the right thing to do, by the way. But because the super's getting heat from above, I'm getting it in the neck from him. Not my biggest fan in the first place, either.' She sighed. 'Talk to me.'

I saw no conflict between full disclosure of my personal recollections and my representative role for the university. As a solicitor, I was an officer of the court. And, whatever my professional role, I had an obligation to cooperate with the garda investigation.

'Agnes invited me to give a paper. I didn't want to go, obviously, but …'

'Yeah, she's invited me a few times as well. To talk to the students. Can't very well say no, can you?'

'Not really, but the reason for the invitation was interesting. She told me—'

'I heard about it already. Agnes said that you spoke about the Mandy Breslin case. Which I know all about, of course. You can give all those details later in your full statement. I'm more interested for now in when things got interesting. I believe there was a row in the President's Garden?'

I summarised what had happened there, and when I moved on to talking about the dinner, I showed her a page in my barrister's notebook on which I'd drawn a plan of the table.

'That's handy,' she said. 'Can I have a copy?'

I took a photograph and sent it to her on WhatsApp.

She looked at it. 'What about the waiters?'

I amended the plan to include the three catering staff, the conference techie Ian McAnespie and Rory Donnelly, the security guard. 'I never met Davide Rossi, the chef, by the way.'

'What about the guy from Limerick, Senan Dunford, that you mentioned a few times? I don't see his name here.'

'He was gone before dinner.'

'Was he around for the fight on the lawn?'

'No, but he's still worth talking to. Bright guy. Might've seen something earlier in the day.' I made a mental note to get in touch with him as soon as possible.

Sadie said, 'I've had some preliminary conversations with a number of the locally based guests. Now it's your turn, Finn. Tell me all.'

43

I SAID, 'I WAS STUCK BESIDE NATHANIEL "CALL ME Nate" Simpson. He's a complete sickener. His idea of conversation consisted of him giving a monologue on his entire CV.'

'Anything of interest?'

'Kind of. He was talking about how his company started their sponsorship of the law school. He said they'd employed a few UCC law graduates in their HQ at the Financial Services Centre in Dublin and then they opened a branch in Cork at the Airport Business Park and now employ even more UCC law grads. He said he saw "synergies in ethos and outlook" with the school.

'Whatever the fuck that means,' Sadie said.

'According to him, UCC law was a perfect fit, considering the company name. Lexbonay. From *lex bona* meaning, and this is the interesting bit, because Martin Casey chimed in and more or less shouted, "Good law," at that point. It was the *way* he said it. Through clenched teeth. He seemed really *angry*. Even though, earlier that morning, he'd been licking Simpson's arse and thanking him effusively. But *something*, whatever it was, changed during the course of the day. I thought at first that Casey was drunk, and then I wasn't sure. He seemed sober again all of a sudden, though he was definitely plastered by the end of the evening.'

'How did Simpson react?'

'He thanked him. He said that "Good law" was precisely what Lexbonay meant because it's an ethical investment company, though he prefers the term *sustainable fund*. He said he's banned the term "hedge" unless it refers to the biodiverse plantings on the office building roof.'

'Oh Jesus Christ,' Sadie said.

'I thought Casey was going to explode when Simpson said that. The only mercy was that the starter arrived and Padraic O'Flaherty managed to distract Casey by asking if he was hungry and talking about how hungry he was himself.'

'What's he like, O'Flaherty?'

'Nice. Funny. He spent a lot of time massaging Casey's ego about a recent article he'd written for the *Journal of Comparative Law*, which helped keep him under control. And when he wasn't talking to Casey, he was talking to Kirsty MacMillan. She used to be his PhD supervisor and they're still close.'

'You were stuck with Simpson all night so?'

'No. He transferred his greasy attention to the person on his other side, Sophie Dignam. She seemed to enjoy his company more than I had. Or maybe she had a higher pain threshold.'

'What was going on with the rest of the table?'

'Stilted talk, back and forth. At the start it was like a conversational relay race, people taking turns to keep things ticking over. Let me think. There was a discussion about bone broth and old-fashioned recipes coming back into fashion precipitated by the starter.'

'Which was?'

'Prawn cocktail. Tasty but a lonely few prawns. I might have been better off going for the minestrone.'

'Main course?'

'A choice of wild garlic risotto or lamb tagine and pomegranate couscous. I went for the lamb. It was delicious, in fairness.'

'Dessert?'

'Rhubarb crumble. Too sweet and jammy for my taste.'

'But you ate it anyway.'

'I did. Then we had a selection of County Cork cheeses.'

'That was a nice touch,' Sadie said.

'I thought so too.'

'What was the atmosphere like?'

'Tense. Watchful. *Deeply* unpleasant. It felt as if hostilities could break out in an instant again. But they didn't. Things loosened up a bit later, but I didn't hear too much of what was being said in the other groups. The table sort of divided into islands, and down in the far corner, I was confined to the most distant and least hospitable constituent of the archipelago.'

'What about Atkins during all this?'

'He was chatting mainly to the people near him, as far as I could see, but I couldn't hear what was being said, unfortunately.'

'Did anything else happen? Did you find out what the fight on the lawn was about?'

'No, though I did try. There was no point in asking Casey but Béatrice Mbemba got up to go out at one stage and I went after her. We'd had a nice chat earlier and she'd been about to tell me something about Nate Simpson when we were interrupted so I wanted to follow up on that with her. And, of course, I was planning to ask her about the big row too.'

'What did she say?'

'Nothing. On the way out of the dining room, I asked Magda, the catering manager, where the East Wing loos were. When I got into the corridor, I looked for Béatrice and spotted her through the window. She'd stepped onto the quad and she was talking on her phone but I couldn't hear if she was speaking English or French. She caught me watching, covered her mouth with her hand and turned away. Not fast, but with determination. As if to say, "Piss off, this is none of your business."'

'Did you go straight back to the dining room after that?'

'No, I went to the loo. To run down the clock, pass a bit of time. On my way, I noticed the door to the men's closing but I didn't see who'd gone in there. Could have been the chef. I went to the women's, and immediately checked my phone, obviously.'

'Obviously.'

I smiled. 'Actually, Senan Dunford had sent me a photo of a Freshways chicken and stuffing sandwich from the Circle K petrol station in Blackpool, which was amusing but sad too. I'm pretty sure I got his seat at the dinner, even though he had a tutorial to give the following morning. But still. Then on the way back, I talked to Rory Donnelly, the security guard – he was still on duty by the door. I told him he could go away, that things had calmed down.'

'And did he?'

'Yeah. Nothing stopping him coming back, obviously. I wouldn't have seen it if he did.'

'What happened next?'

'More of the same, really. Chit-chat. There was a lull at one stage when Simpson – the only non-lawyer in the room but as far as he's concerned he knows more than all the rest of us put together – said he was surprised that, as it was a conference about truth, none of the speakers had talked about truth in *criminal* cases. And then he asked that question laypeople *always* ask,

"Would you defend someone if you knew they were guilty?"
Nearly set off Casey again. He went all red, *purple* actually. He
definitely has a short fuse. Exacerbated by a lorry load of alcohol,
obviously.'

'Who answered Simpson's question? Or did anyone bother?'

'Atkins did. The deceased. He made light of it. Said something
like "Lawyers would have no clients if they only defended
innocent people." And then he said that everyone is entitled to a
defence, and that it's the bedrock of our legal system, et cetera,
et cetera. The usual. He handled it well and managed to steer the
conversation onto something else.'

'Were you talking to Atkins during the dinner at all?'

'Just near the end. At about ten p.m., I signalled to Agnes that
I had to go. I got up and walked to the far end of the table. Stood
there behind Cormac Ryan. Thanked the president and Agnes
for the invitation. And he, Atkins, said he was sorry we hadn't
had an opportunity to talk. Actually he said, "I'm sorrier than I
can say, but it wasn't to be." I gave him a business card and said
to call me if he was hanging around for a few days. But he said
he was heading off later on the Aircoach and flying home the
following morning with Emirates from Dublin.'

'Did he specify what time he was catching the Aircoach?'

'He said "stupid o'clock".'

Sadie said, 'The poor man. He was booked on the two a.m.
bus but never made it.' She paused. 'So you've left the dinner. Is
that the end of it from your point of view?'

'Nearly. I bumped into Ian McAnespie, the conference
technician, in the hallway. He said he was collecting
equipment.'

Sadie stopped writing and drew a circle around McAnespie's

name. 'I keep thinking about the motive,' she said. '*Why* would someone kill Atkins?'

I shrugged. 'The popular theory in the law school is that it was an accident, a manslaughter situation.'

Sadie nodded. 'Or some randomer wandered in from outside ...'

We were talking for a long time. Theorising. Coming up with different scenarios.

Afterwards, I regretted that I hadn't made a point of mentioning what Agnes had said to me: that Atkins had specifically asked for me to be invited to speak at the conference. I assumed that she had told Sadie. But she hadn't.

I didn't make it clear either that, when I'd met McAnespie, it was because I'd returned to the East Wing to retrieve my coat. I regretted that as well.

And it wasn't that I forgot to say either of these things. At the time, I knew I'd be making a full statement later. I'd be able to fill in any minor gaps then.

I had no idea how severe the consequences of my omissions would be.

MONDAY

44

IT WAS AFTER MIDNIGHT WHEN SADIE LEFT. I'D gone to bed and fallen asleep immediately, which was unusual for me. I was still exhausted when I woke at six forty with the feeling that I'd forgotten something. I groaned and stretched, and then I remembered my father. I swallowed a sob and leaped out of bed into a sixty-second cold shower.

Afterwards, I dressed quickly in generic lawyer gear – black opaques, black knee-length long-sleeved dress – and slathered on age-defying serum, an expensive ongoing act of faith because the wrinkles seemed to be gaining the upper hand, and tinted SPF50 moisturiser. Upstairs, I grabbed my phone and bag and headed down Barrack Street and across the Nano Nagle footbridge. At Gusto, on Washington Street, I paused long enough to purchase a flat white. I took a sip, snapped on the lid, and made for my office on MacSwiney Street. I had a lot to do and there was no time to waste.

Walking, I ran through the list of people I needed to contact. Talking to Sadie the previous night about the guests at the dinner had made me realise afresh how many people I had left to interview and that up to now, subconsciously, I'd been concentrating on the ones who'd appeared to have been last to leave the East Wing: the caterers, the president, the security guard Rory Donnelly, and Ian McAnespie, the conference technician, whom I'd seen there late when I'd called back to collect my coat.

But there were several others I hadn't properly considered. I'd be able to fill in some of the gaps when I got the CCTV from the quad – I'd already sent a text message to security supervisor Kasper Nowak to contact me about that – but the absence of CCTV from within the East Wing was a huge disadvantage. Sadie had agreed.

Last night she'd said, 'The president's decision to remove the CCTV is puzzling. And taken together with her decision to remove the permanent security presence ...'

'What's that? I didn't know about that.'

'There used to be a permanent security guard in the East Wing. She said she didn't need it. The security officer's room has now been repurposed as a private hot desk for important campus visitors. I imagine it's very rarely used but I suppose it sounds good.'

'Nobody could have expected this to happen,' I said. 'But ...'

'They were two dopey decisions that she made, the end result of which is that, in the absence of a confession, we're unlikely ever to be able to say exactly what time the victim died. But there are some things we *do* know, which I'm telling you confidentially and strictly *not* for wider dissemination.'

I nodded. We'd worked together like this before. She knew I could keep schtum, College liaison role or not. And in the previous two cases we'd collaborated on, I'd identified the murderer before she had, a fact of which I only occasionally reminded her.

Sadie continued, 'The weekend discovery of the body has delayed things but we're hoping to have the full results of the post-mortem by Tuesday morning. Toxicology and other forensic tests will take weeks. The cause of death is almost certainly asphyxiation by strangulation. There are visible ligature marks on the neck, and pinpoint haemorrhaging on the skin and in the eyes. He may have been hit over the head with a cosh of some sort to disorient him first, or that injury might have occurred post mortem.'

'What kind of ligature? Was it left with the body?'

'Unfortunately not, but from what we can gather something thin was used.' She paused. 'Removed from the body after death.'

'Oh,' I said.

'We think he may not have been killed in the stairwell where he was found. We reckon the murder might have happened somewhere else, possibly the loos, and that he was moved to the bottom of the staircase one to three hours after death.'

'What makes ye think that?'

'The president told us that the victim went back into the East Wing to go to the loo and she didn't see him after that. But also, and more importantly, there appear to be inconsistencies in the bruising, the lividity, though it's too soon to say for sure. We'll have to wait until we get the post-mortem results ... But if it does turn out to have been the loo, we're working on the theory that it was an assignation gone wrong.'

I made no response.

She said, 'A secret meeting for sexual purposes?'

'I know what an assignation is,' I said.

'But you're not buying it?'

'Anything's possible obviously. But what about the locks?

You saw the broken locks on the door from the Aula Max and the door to the stairs?'

She nodded. 'We'd found them long before Donnelly told us about them.'

I said, 'I was taking the broken locks as evidence of premeditation.'

'Unless they were broken afterwards. To allow the perpetrator to escape?'

'And go where? From the unsurveilled East Wing to the Aula Maxima, which I know *does* have CCTV coverage because I've seen the cameras myself?'

Sadie said, 'Yeah, that's the problem with that theory. Though the main part of the Aula and the doors on the outside are covered by CCTV, the part under the gallery isn't. Whoever broke that lock, if it was broken deliberately, we won't be able to get video of it.'

We'd talked on, back and forth, for another hour and agreed that as soon as the East Wing was declassified as a crime scene, which she expected would be Monday evening, she and I would do a walk-through before the staff were allowed back in. It was another thing on my to-do list for the day. I didn't know where I was going to find the time for everything.

I arrived at the office and took the stairs to my attic room in twos. By 8 a.m. I'd sent out a slew of text messages and emails to the conference guests I hadn't yet spoken to, explaining my role and asking them to contact me.

At 8.10 a.m., I received my first call back.

45

IT WAS SOPHIE, SUPREMELY EFFICIENT CONFERENCE organiser and PhD student. I found it hard to think of her as a suspect. Maybe it was the Miss Marple outfit she'd been wearing the day of the conference, or that I knew her from when she'd been a summer intern at the firm.

I suggested meeting at her office but she told me she didn't have one, that she worked from a desk in the library mainly, which made sense. She said she could make it into town to MLC for any time that suited me that morning. I checked the availability of a client meeting room and slotted her in for 10 a.m. I ended the call without going into any of the questions I wanted to ask her. I preferred face-to-face meetings, though it would be nearly impossible to see all the witnesses in person for this case, even those on the island of Ireland. I thought about that for a moment. I hadn't yet discussed expenses with the College president. Maybe I could get her to agree that it was necessary for me to travel to interview witnesses.

On the other hand, depending on how things went with Dad's medical check-up, maybe I'd want to stay close to home. I was counting down the minutes to 8.30 a.m. when the GP's surgery opened. I still had fifteen minutes to go.

And I needed to talk to Gabriel. I had to let him know that the firm had a new client, the president of UCC, and that I'd taken on another investigation, more of the kind of work that wasn't within the strict confines of my original job description. I hadn't cleared it with him in advance and, I had to acknowledge to myself, that omission had been deliberate. It was partly to do with lack of time, and more to do with knowing that, sometimes, it was better to present Gabriel with a fait accompli. His middle name wasn't 'Caution' but it should have been.

Besides, once he got over complaining, I knew he'd be delighted. Getting the firm's foot in the door of the university was a coup. They had their own in-house legal team but often needed outside expertise. MLC hadn't yet had a share of what was presumably quite a lucrative pie. This case was a start.

Though it was early, and a Monday, I didn't need to check if Gabriel was in. I nipped downstairs to his office. The door was open.

Dermot Lyons and Gabriel were standing in front of Gabriel's desk. Lyons was at work an hour earlier than normal and his face was red, his eyes puffy. I guessed that he was hung-over. Though, if I hadn't known him as well as I did, I'd have thought he'd been crying.

To my surprise, it became very clear very fast that that was exactly what he'd been doing, and that Gabriel was comforting him, his right hand patting Lyons's left shoulder.

'I'm so sorry,' I said. 'I didn't realise. I'll go. Um, I hope …'

I turned and went to leave the room but Gabriel called me. 'Hang on, Finola, come back and shut the door. This concerns you, in a way. Or, at the very least, you might be able to help.'

We were sitting on the wing-backed armchairs in front of the window, Dermot Lyons and I. Gabriel was perched anxiously on the corner of his desk. Lyons was still crying intermittently.

'It's such a shock. I was away for the weekend and I only just heard this morning. Will Atkins was a hero of mine, you know, a big hero. Yours too, wasn't he, Gabriel?'

'Yes, yes,' Gabriel said. 'Though you were much closer to him, of course.'

'You know what he was like, Finn. You met him.'

'He seemed like a lovely man,' I said.

'Have you heard any details about the murder? About the garda investigation?' Lyons's voice was stronger suddenly, and his eyes had regained some of their laser focus.

I gave them a little more information than had been in the media – that the body had been found in the stairwell and that it looked like Professor Atkins had been strangled – but not everything that Sadie had said. I also told them about the meeting at the president's apartment the day before, and that I'd been engaged to investigate.

'What hourly rate did you agree?' Lyons asked.

I told him.

'It's not good enough,' he said. 'But it could be worse.'

I caught the glint in Gabriel's eye and the slight upward tilt of his lips. 'Normal service has resumed, I'm glad to see. And, Finola, I don't need to tell you that you shouldn't have taken on a client or a case of this magnitude without running it by me. But, in these *very* unusual circumstances, I'll allow that it may work out for the best. You'll give Dermot and me regular updates on progress?'

'Of course I will,' I said.

I left Gabriel's office and returned to my attic room. My mobile was on my desk where I'd left it. I had six missed calls. Two were from my mother. I was already half an hour late phoning Dad's doctor. The day was off to a blistering start. And it was still only 9 a.m.

46

I GOT THROUGH TO THE GP'S SURGERY ON THE
fourth attempt and took the earliest available appointment. I
booked the time out of office in the firm's case-management
system diary and, simultaneously, called my mother back and told
her the details. After that, I phoned my father. I was expecting an
argument from him. It didn't happen. He agreed to go. His voice
sounded different – weaker and older – and I realised that it had
probably been like that for a while but that I hadn't wanted to
hear. I told Tina about him when she came up with the post.

'Don't catastrophise,' she said. 'He's bound to have some kind
of health issue one day. He's no spring chicken. But it mightn't
be as serious as it looks now.'

'Or it might be,' I said.

'Don't write him off. Worry when, or if, you have to.'

I took in what she'd said. 'You're right but …'

'No buts. And, hey, who's this client you have in your diary
for ten o'clock, Sophie Dignam? Is she the same Sophie who was
a summer intern here a few years ago?'

'Looks different now, but that's her.'

I gave Tina a rundown on our new case and raced through a
list of the tasks arising from the morning's post and emails that

I wanted her to follow up on. I would be relying on her to keep things moving with my regular workload while I concentrated my attention on the UCC case, though she'd also be working on that with me, as needed. We had a complicated few weeks ahead of us.

Checking my phone, I established that none of the missed calls I'd received while I was with Gabriel and Dermot Lyons had come from Professor Martin Casey. He hadn't replied by email either. He was Cork-based, and his should have been one of the easier witness interviews to arrange. I had to get it out of the way. I asked Tina to chase him for me.

'With pleasure. But are you sure? He sounds like a dose.' She laughed.

Before I could reply, a message from Reception popped onto my screen, letting me know that Sophie had arrived for our meeting.

On the way downstairs, I reflected on what I'd been thinking earlier, about how difficult I found it to regard Sophie as a suspect. I reminded myself that she was. But she was also both an insider and an outsider in the law school, involved in tutoring and in organising the conference but, crucially, not an employee. She was, potentially, a source of high-grade background information.

She was also, by a mile, the most overtly cooperative witness I'd met yet. She was seated at the round table when I opened the door but she stood, as I walked in, and smiled. Dressed in a fitted dove-grey soft wool dress, she was channelling 1950s librarian chic, her hair in a chignon, her glasses big and black.

'I like the dress,' I said.

'Charity shop. I don't buy new any more unless I have to. The planet ...'

'Of course.' I felt tired all of a sudden. I didn't know why. I sat at the table, Sophie a beat after me.

She started talking. 'I've prepared a statement of my recollections of all my contacts with the late Professor Atkins and a timeline of the day. It's here in this folder.' She pointed to a cardboard envelope. 'You were missing at lunchtime on the day of the conference. I thought it would be useful for you to know what happened then so I've done a comprehensive note on it. The folder also includes a full list of all attendees. Everyone, not just the people at the dinner. And I've got my laptop here. I can email everything to you as well, if you like.'

Without saying a word, I slid the folder towards me and opened it. I took out the dossier and leafed through it slowly. It was incredibly detailed and I had no doubt that it was accurate in every respect. We could have spent the next two or three hours going through each of the documents, and it occurred to me that that was exactly what Sophie expected and, perhaps, what she wanted. In preparing them, in effect, she was setting the agenda for the meeting.

Which made me wonder what she was trying to hide.

47

I WASN'T TIRED ANY MORE, BUT I WASN'T SURE what to say next, except that it had to be something she wasn't anticipating. I shuffled the papers together and replaced them in the cardboard envelope. I made a point of closing it fully.

'This is going to be really useful, Sophie,' I said. 'I'll read it later and follow up with questions when we meet next. I, ah, didn't notice your home address in what you gave me, just your College email and mobile-phone number, both of which I have already. Is your address in here?' I tapped the folder.

Sophie flushed. 'I didn't think.'

I tore a page from my barrister's notebook and passed it to her with a pen. 'Write it out there for me, if you wouldn't mind, please.'

I waited in silence as she wrote. When she was finished, I said, 'You were sitting beside Nathaniel Simpson from Lexbonay Investments, the conference sponsor, at the dinner. You seemed to be getting on well with him. Do you remember what you were talking about?'

'My goodness,' Sophie said. 'Let me think. The food. A little about the conference. My work. The papers. But mainly about his company, I suppose, his vision, that type of thing.'

'All night?'

'What?'

'That's what you talked about all night? I was there. Nathaniel Simpson was sitting beside me. Your conversation seemed considerably more light-hearted to me. That was my observation at the time. You seemed to be laughing a lot.'

'Nate's very entertaining. Amusing. I found him to be so.' She was biting her lip.

'Clearly,' I said. I knew I was being mean to her, but she was definitely hiding something. I was sure of it now. I thought for a moment about where to go next.

I asked, 'Did you stay sitting beside Mr Simpson, *Nate*, or did either of you change seats at any point during the evening?'

'We stayed where we were.'

'And did anyone else change places?'

She took in a long breath. 'Yes. It's all in my statement.'

'Can you find it please? The particular section?' I handed her the cardboard envelope.

Her hands were shaking slightly but she located the spot and pointed it out to me.

I read it aloud, '"W. Atkins swapped places with president. W. Atkins then spoke to B. Mbemba. Duration 10 minutes approximately. W. Atkins then moved to F. Fitzpatrick vacant seat. Duration 30 minutes approximately."' I looked up. 'But there's nothing here about who he spoke to while he was sitting in my place.' I paused. 'Who did he talk to, Sophie?'

She swallowed. 'We-ell, let's see. For a lot of that time, obviously, he talked to Professor Casey and also to Padraic O'Flaherty.'

'The two of them together? Or to each of them separately.'

'I'm not sure. *Really* I'm not. Mainly Professor Casey, I think. Padraic was talking mostly to Professor Kirsty MacMillan, I suppose.'

'Duration of Professor Atkins's chat with Casey?'

She took too long to reply. 'Probably fifteen minutes.'

'And for the other fifteen minutes he was in my seat, who did the victim talk to?'

'He, em, he turned around to his other side and talked to Nate.'

'And you talked to Cormac Ryan beside you and Lia de Barra opposite then, did you? Though you hadn't talked much to Lia during the evening before that, I noticed.'

'Lia doesn't talk to me except about work things. She and I used to get on but she asked me to fill in for her last year doing something and I couldn't, and I wasn't being paid anyway, not that I would've minded, but I was away, I just couldn't do it. But since then …'

Something occurred to me. 'What's the antagonism between Lia de Barra and Martin Casey about?'

'I did hear that they were close for years and fell out after Lia got promoted to full professor. I'm not sure why but I suspect he didn't like having her as an equal.'

I thought of something else. 'And what about the row on the lawn between Casey and Dr Mbemba? What was that about?'

'That's not the kind of information I'm permitted access to,' Sophie said quickly.

It was an interesting answer. I filed it away with the intention of coming back to it.

'Where were we? Oh, yes. Atkins and Nate were chatting and you were left with no one to talk to.'

'No.' She paused. 'Nate pulled back his chair to include me in the conversation.'

'So the murder victim spent fifteen minutes talking to Nate and you.'

'Yes.'

I waited a beat before asking, 'And what was the conversation about?'

She sighed. 'You're probably not going to believe me but it was about the company again. Professor Atkins hadn't been around when we, Nate and I, were talking earlier so it was new to him, and he was interested. In everything to do with the company.'

'Like what?'

'For example, Nate told him how Lexbonay has employed lots of UCC law grads.'

'Was that something you and Nate had discussed too? Employment opportunities?'

'Well, I suppose we had. A little.'

'Is Lexbonay somewhere you'd consider working?'

'An academic job used to be my plan, but it's getting harder all the time, you know? Restrictions on hiring, and even if you do get a post there are promotion freezes. It's dire. But I don't see myself in practice as a solicitor or barrister either. The internship here was a wonderful opportunity but it made up my mind for me. I'd like something with a more identifiable career track. I *had* thought of Lexbonay.'

'Okay,' I said. I picked up the dossier again. 'I'm wondering why you omitted your conversation, yours and Nate's, with the dead man from this *forest* of paper?'

'It was late when I was typing it. I wasn't trying to conceal it, really I wasn't. I mean, why would I? There were other people at the table. You would've found out.'

'Eventually,' I said. 'And when did you type it all up?'

'Last night.'

'Agnes told me you'd gone to a party.'

'That's what I told her. I was supposed to go. I couldn't face it in the end. I just wanted to do something to help ...'

She stared down at the table. I couldn't see her face but she sounded sincere. I felt even meaner than I had earlier, but I still had a few questions left.

'What happened at the end of the night?'

'Everyone said goodbye. In the East Wing corridor. That was the last time I saw Professor Atkins before he died. Standing beside the president there. Then people went out on the quad and a few stood around for a while chatting, I think.'

'What about you, Sophie? Did you stay and chat?'

She shook her head slowly. Then she burst into tears.

It wasn't yet 11 a.m. and this was the second crying person I'd had to deal with, the third if I counted myself in bed that morning.

'I'll be back in a minute,' I said.

I went outside to Reception and returned with a box of tissues. Handing them to Sophie, I said, 'Things are never as bad as you think,' which was a lie, but a well-meant one.

'Sometimes they're worse,' she said, which was very much my own view.

I sat down again.

Speaking quietly, I said, 'Are you saying you had something to do with the murder?'

She blew her nose. 'No. Not that.'

'Then what is it?'

She sniffed loudly, but she appeared to have regained her composure. 'I understand the need for truth in a situation like this, but I don't want anyone to know.'

'Sophie,' I said, 'a man was murdered.'

'What I'd be telling you has *nothing* to do with the murder.' She waved her hands about. 'This isn't a garda investigation. I don't mind saying what happened – well, I do, but I don't want everyone in College to know. I'll only talk if you promise me that what I say is confidential.'

I made no response. I was thinking.

She went on, 'I was *there* that day in the president's flat.'

'Yesterday,' I said.

'Jesus, is it only yesterday?'

I nodded.

'Finn, the president didn't ask you to report on every single thing you find out. You have two roles. The first is to keep the guards at bay and to find out as much as you can about what's going on from your friend Sadie and feed it back to the president. Second, she wants you to investigate the murder, like you did on that case for your firm last year. And she's only interested in results. She's already badly wounded by one of her guests having been murdered. She doesn't want to be tainted even more by being the person who invited the murderer to dinner. But she's not a fool. She knows it's possible. If she's involved in finding the murderer, it'll help repair some the damage.'

'I don't disagree with what you say,' I said. 'I can offer you conditional confidentiality.'

'What does that mean?'

'It means that, if what you say isn't relevant to the investigation, there may be no need to reveal it to anyone, including the president. So I won't tell anyone for now, *provided* you go on the record with the cops. I'll put you in direct touch with someone on the murder team after this.'

She sighed. 'Okay.'

I waited for her to continue.

'I can't tell you what happened on the quad. I didn't see how the evening ended. I wasn't there. I left straight after dinner.' She sucked in a breath. 'I spent the night with Nate Simpson.'

48

'I WAS A LITTLE DRUNK, NOT PISSED, THOUGH. I knew what I was doing. It seemed like a good idea at the time. Obviously it wasn't. Apart from anything else, Nate's married. Happily, he said. After we'd ... Anyway, I won't be applying for a job at Lexbonay now, as you can imagine. I'd die of shame. Especially if anyone at College found out.'

'Where did all this happen?' I asked.

'We'd been flirting all night, you were right about that. I was laughing and we weren't just talking about the company, though he does talk about it a *lot*. Then at some point he produced two room-access cards – I mean to his hotel room. He was staying at Hayfield Manor.'

'Professor Atkins was booked in there too, wasn't he?'

'Yeah. Nate paid for the hotel rooms and travel expenses. The company did, I mean. Lexbonay. That was what the sponsorship was.'

'So was he the one who decided Atkins would be upgraded to Hayfield? Because the rest of the guests were in the River Lee.'

'I don't think Nate had anything to do with the reservations, he just paid a lump sum to the law school. I made the reservations on Agnes's instructions but I had nothing to do with the money side of things. You'd need to ask her about all that. She was the one paying.'

'I will,' I said. 'Who booked Nate's room? Was it you?'

'His assistant maybe? Or him? It wasn't part of the conference arrangements.'

'And did Nate know that was where Atkins was staying?'

'We didn't discuss it. The first I knew about Nate staying at Hayfield was when he produced the two room cards and asked if I'd like one. It was during the cheese course. He held them under the table so that no one else could see them.'

'And you said yes?'

'I did. And then all during the time that Professor Atkins was talking to us, I was thinking about what would be happening afterwards. I wasn't taking a full part in the conversation. I was sort of excited, sort of very, actually ...'

'What happened after dinner? Everyone was in the corridor. What did you do?'

'We'd arranged that I'd go up alone first, and he'd follow. I headed out the back door of the East Wing onto the President's Garden and then out the side gate onto Donovan's Road – you know the pedestrian one a bit down from the Honan Chapel, past the service entrance? The hotel's only a few minutes' walk away. When I got there, I went straight up to the room.'

'What number?'

She told me and I wrote it down. 'And then what?'

'There was champagne chilling in a bucket. He'd called and ordered it earlier.'

I wanted to ask if she thought he'd put in the order with the hotel before or after the cheese course but I restrained myself.

She went on, 'He said I should open it and have a drink and

run a bath and that he'd follow along when the coast was clear. He hung on for a while – he was out on the quad talking to some of the other guests, he told me when he arrived at the room later.'

'When was that?'

'Not too sure. But not *very* long, I think. I wasn't checking the time but there was plenty of champagne left and I was still in the bath and he, you can probably imagine …'

'Right,' I said.

'It was a lot of fun, though I truly wish it hadn't happened now. But I didn't know someone was going to die. And, anyway, none of this has anything whatsoever to do with the murder. There must be CCTV of me leaving College and arriving at Hayfield and not leaving until the following morning. And Nate the same.'

'Have you had any contact with him since?'

'He phoned me after the media reports about the discovery of the body. After the name was announced on Sunday morning. He asked me not to say. About us. He was terrified his wife would find out. I guessed we'd have to tell sometime. But I did my best to delay it.'

'You told me yesterday that you'd spoken to the guards once. Who was that?'

'Detective Garda Olly Fogarty.'

'And you told him nothing of what you told me. Nothing about you and Nate.'

'No, I just told him the time I left the East Wing and the exit I went out by, and I said I had a bath and went to bed soon after. I, em, gave him *sort* of the impression that I went home, and not to Hayfield. I didn't exactly lie, but they'll know from the cameras that I was gone from College before Atkins died so I figured that a little ambiguity didn't matter.'

I tried to be diplomatic. 'If the CCTV backs up what you've told me, hopefully the guards will be able to rule you out fairly quickly,' I said.

But I wasn't at all sure. She'd lied by omission at the first opportunity. And even if ultimately she did end up being eliminated from suspicion, I had a feeling things mightn't go as easily for Nate Simpson. Sophie would be dragged deeply into the garda investigation whether she liked it or not.

49

'WHAT NEXT?' SOPHIE ASKED.

I didn't want to come straight out and tell her that she was inevitably going to become a suspect. And that her efforts to keep secret the one-night stand with Simpson, if that was all it was, were doomed to fail. I did my best to be helpful. I wanted her to understand that she needed to be careful.

I said, 'I have a couple of suggestions for you. The first is that, after you leave here, you go to the City Library on the Grand Parade and prepare a full typed version of your statement on your laptop and call me when it's done. By then, I'll have found a solicitor who can attend the garda station with you when—'

'Solicitor? But I haven't done anything wrong.'

'Sure,' I said. 'This is as much for me as for you, Sophie. I can't be your solicitor – no one at this firm can. We have a conflict of interest. But you *do* need to take independent legal advice. It's a murder case. We need to do everything by the book. Having a draft of your statement ready will make it easier for your solicitor to get up to speed on things.'

'Okay,' Sophie said. 'I suppose you're right.'

'The next thing I want to do is talk to Nate. Do you know where he is?'

'He lives and works in Dublin most of the time, but he's based in the Cork office this week. It's—'

'In the Airport Business Park. Yes, he told me.'

I took my mobile out of my pocket. I'd had it on silent during the meeting. Nate Simpson had been one of the people I'd texted earlier that morning about making an interview appointment. I checked my messages. He was one of those who still hadn't reverted. I typed out another message and showed it to Sophie before I pressed send. She approved it.

Hi Nate, Finn here again. Wondering if you could get back to me to arrange an appointment to chat? Heard you're in Cork this week but if you'd prefer to wait until you're back in Dublin, I can visit you at home no problem. By the way, I've been talking to Sophie.

Less than a minute later, Sophie's phone rang. I answered. 'Thanks for calling back.'

He agreed to meet me at the Cork offices of Lexbonay Investments at 2 p.m.

50

ON MY WAY BACK UPSTAIRS, I DROPPED INTO THE room Tina shared with some of the other secretaries. I gave her the handwritten notes I'd taken at my meeting with Sophie and asked her to type them up. 'You'll never guess,' I said. 'It turns out—'

'No, don't tell me! You'll spoil the reveal.'

I laughed. 'Okay, okay. Any other news?'

'Only that Prof Casey was unable to resist my charms. You're seeing him at noon.'

'Where?'

'His place on the North Mall.'

'Nice,' I said.

I told her about the meeting with Nate Simpson at Lexbonay Cork. 'Depending on how things go, I probably won't be back here,' I said. 'Most likely, I'll have to go straight to College after the Airport Business Park, but I'll let you know.'

On my return to my office, I had time to make a few calls. With the first, to Kasper Nowak, I arranged to attend the security camera room in the North Wing during the afternoon to view the CCTV. I told him I wasn't sure what time I'd get there but estimated it could be 4 p.m. He said that was fine and that I should sign in at the security hut by the College Road entrance and give my name and destination there. I asked him if it was possible to download extracts of the video footage onto a memory stick. He told me I'd have to bring my own as he didn't have any. I said I would.

My second call was to Sadie. I held off on telling her what I'd learned from Sophie. I wanted to give her a chance to get her statement down and to obtain independent legal advice. I felt sure that she had nothing to do with the murder, but she was going to end up seriously compromised unless her statement to the guards was dealt with in the right way.

'I'm calling about the walk-through of the crime scene you promised me,' I said.

She sounded stressed. 'Yeah. The scene is more complicated than expected, as per fucking usual, but you could chance phoning again around five. If the scene's going to be released today, and if everyone's being allowed back on campus tomorrow, we should know by then. You can liaise that info back to the president, if you like.'

'Will do. I can actually be at College at five. Will I call by the East Wing? I'm—'

'No.'

I laughed. 'Okay. I'll phone first.'

'Make sure you do.' She ended the call.

I paged through my almost full barrister's notebook and ran my index finger down the expanding to-do list stapled inside the front cover. It told me what I knew already: that I was making slow progress with the investigation and that I had a huge amount of catching up to do. I waited for the sinking feeling, so familiar from the last few months, to come, but it didn't. Because being busy felt good. I smiled to myself.

Then I made myself remember what this was all about. The murder of Professor William Atkins. A man I didn't know but who, for some reason, was interested in my investigation work, and who had ended up dead. I realised I'd been giving too much attention to a perpetrator having the means and opportunity to commit murder. I needed to start looking more at motive. If I was to do that, I needed to find out more about William Atkins, and why he might have needed investigative help. Had he been afraid of someone? And if so, who? I grabbed a fresh barrister's notebook and headed down to MacSwiney Street.

51

IT WAS IMPOSSIBLE FOR ME TO CROSS THE CITY'S central island without meeting someone I knew, and meeting only one or two would have been almost as much of a miracle as meeting nobody. Navigating those streets involved repeated scanning of the middle distance, modulating the appropriate level of greeting: a wave and a smile, a double eyebrow and chin raise (smile optional), a passing hello or a pause for a chat. Sometimes it seemed like I knew everyone, but I didn't. Cork was a lot bigger than it felt. There were whole swathes of the city I encountered only rarely, and some areas and newly built estates I hardly knew at all.

Walking around town and through the parks also meant simultaneously hearing multiple languages and accents: Polish and various Eastern European, French, German, Italian, Spanish, Portuguese, Arabic, Yoruba, Urdu, Cantonese and other tongues. English too, but less than you'd expect, because much of the native population lived and shopped in the suburbs. They came into the centre for entertainment or work, and left again. Maybe Cork had always been like that, inward- and outward-looking at the same time. A port, with strong connections to Europe and the wider world: people had been passing through the city for centuries. Some sailed up the river and established settlements. Some came and worked for Apple computers or one of the big pharmas around the harbour. Some went home again after a time. Many stayed. If they stayed long enough, they acquired Cork accents and started giving out about Dublin.

As I walked, I rang the president and told her that the declassifying of the crime scene might take place this evening and that I'd confirm with her as soon as I knew.

'We've been hoping for that,' she said. 'I've been in touch informally with the various heads of schools but if we could make it official tonight we could get the announcement out on all our channels. The sooner you can get back to me the better, though realistically a full reopening is unlikely before Wednesday.'

'I'll be back to you as soon as I hear more.'

'Any other progress?' I heard her tapping on a keyboard in the background.

'Some. Though I haven't yet started on the non-Cork-based witnesses. I envisage completing most of the non-Cork interviews by phone, or FaceTime, but in the event that it becomes desirable to travel to pursue a line of investigation, I wondered if—'

'As long as the expenses are properly receipted and justified, and if they're not exorbitant, I'll approve them. Provided you tell me where you're going beforehand.'

I didn't respond immediately. I didn't like the idea of giving her advance notice of my movements. 'Travel may or may not be necessary,' I said. 'I'll get back to you on it.'

'One more thing,' she said. 'We've been contacted by the Australian Embassy. They're sending a representative down here for some reason or another, probably to do with the dead man's family, I don't know. I've given them your number, so you can expect a call. Of course I'll meet them in due course, and we'll extend the ambassador and the relatives every courtesy, but perhaps you could find out what exactly they want first.'

It struck me that she'd called William Atkins, for whom she'd arranged an elaborate dinner party, 'the dead man', and that she appeared to have little empathy with the bereaved. It seemed oddly callous, but she'd hung up before I was able to ask her anything else.

52

THE NORTH GATE BRIDGE HASN'T HAD A GATE for hundreds of years, and the days are long gone when those approaching from the dangerous unconquered lands outside the city walls were met with a display of severed heads mounted on spikes. The current bridge dates from 1961. It is flat and functional, with four lanes of traffic and an oblong concrete island. And yet, to my mind, it retains some of its former drama. It's still the main access route to the northside, to Shandon Steeple and all that, and the views from it are spectacular. Also, it's the most straightforward way to get to the North Mall from the city centre.

I was a few minutes early for my appointment with Professor Casey. I took the opportunity to check off one of the items on my to-do list ('ask president about expenses') and add another two ('Australian Embassy to call' and 'family/friends/work colleagues Melbourne – contact? interview?'). I replaced my notebook in my bag. There is no wall between the Mall and the river, only trees and pretty railings and painted benches and a timeless feel. The line of south-facing period houses made it easy to imagine it was horses' hoofs and carriage wheels I heard going past rather than the chug of a car or the buzz of an electric bike. Some of the dwellings had been restored to mint condition using best conservation practice. Others looked like they hadn't been touched in centuries. A few had been converted into flats.

I crossed the road and walked along the footpath to find the house number that Casey had provided to Tina. As instructed, I rang his mobile phone and he came to the front door to let me in. He was wearing a baggy navy zip-up fleece with sagging pockets and what looked like a blob of porridge – grey and crusty – a few inches below the left shoulder.

He led me down a wide flagstoned hall, past an elegant staircase, towards the back of the building and into a flat: north-facing, recently decorated, spacious, with high ceilings, but impersonal, a distinct executive-let flavour to it. There were no pictures and almost no books but for a low stack of texts and folders on one corner of the dining table, next to an open laptop, and a massive hardback that looked like a library copy of a recent John Connolly thriller. It appeared that Casey hadn't lived there long. And, on his salary and with his position, according to Cork's well-established social rules, he shouldn't have been living there at all. I hid my considerable disappointment at not getting the chance for a look around one of the grand houses, and being confined instead to a ground-floor apartment, and accepted the offer of a cup of tea. I sat on a spongy magnolia-coloured sofa and waited. Through the sash window, I could see the high walls of the rear garden, and the red sandstone cliff face, tangled with ivy, but not the sky.

'That assistant of yours is persistent,' he said. 'She seemed to be under the impression that I was trying to *dodge* talking to you. Not at all. I *did* intend to call you back. But I didn't see any need to rush. Your investigation is a misstep by the president, in my opinion. I've voiced my objections, you know that, but I'm quite happy to talk to you. You should know that I've already spoken to the guards. Twice now. And in some depth. In as much as anyone can be, I'm totally out of the picture as regards being a suspect. I mean, you saw me. I was sitting beside you at dinner. When I left the East Wing, Will Atkins was still alive. After that, I was chatting to several, for want of a better word, alibi witnesses for half an hour or possibly even more out on the quad. I couldn't have killed him. Simple as.'

'I've heard that when I left, Professor Atkins came and sat beside you.'

'He did, but he didn't spend long talking to me. Ask Padraic O'Flaherty. I assume you'll be taking a UCC all-expenses-paid trip to Galway to talk to him?'

'Was Padraic the one talking to Atkins, then?'

'Hardly. Atkins talked mainly to the sponsor, Nathaniel Simpson.'

'I have the impression you don't like Nate very much,' I said.

'I don't know what gave you that idea. I, along with everyone else at the School of Law, am very grateful to Lexbonay Investments for its sponsorship, not just this year but over the past number of years. It's safe to say that we wouldn't have been able to attract such distinguished visitors as Will Atkins without their very welcome cash injection. That it all turned out so unfortunately couldn't have been predicted, of course.'

It was a repeat of the sentiments and many of the words from his interminable conference opening address. But however dull that had been, at the time the gratitude had felt genuine. Now it rang false. Like I'd said to Sadie, something had altered in his attitude to Lexbonay during the conference. Over the course of that day, he'd gone from fawning over Nate Simpson to animosity. During the dinner, I'd put down the mood change to his alcohol consumption, but perhaps there was more to it.

And it wasn't the only incidence of his aggression that I'd observed.

'What was your argument with Béatrice Mbemba about?'

'I wouldn't call it an argument.'

'Would fight be a better word?'

'Dr Mbemba and I had a minor professional disagreement, which, I can assure you, had nothing whatsoever to do with the murder. Subject closed.'

'You were shouting at her.'

'I think you'll find that it was the other way around.'

'Both voices were raised, Martin. I was there, remember? College security almost had to intervene. What was it about?'

'What it was about has nothing to do with what you're being paid for.'

I asked him a couple of times more but got nowhere. Eventually, I said, 'Fine, I get it. You're not going to tell me.' I paused. 'So who do you think killed William Atkins?'

'Maybe you should ask the last person to see him alive.'

I knew who he meant but I wanted his version. 'Who's that?'

'I departed the East Wing, after giving Will a goodbye hug. Everyone hugged him as they were leaving, except you, now that I think of it. Anyway, when I was leaving, there were only two people left, Professor Atkins and the president. She must have seen where he went and with whom. If not, the only other explanation, however unwelcome, must be considered.'

It was something I'd thought of myself, though I didn't want to talk to Casey about it. But I found it interesting that he wanted to point the finger in the direction of the president.

'What do you think of the president?'

'I hardly know her, thankfully. I try to keep out of College politics and governing-body bullshit.'

'Was she a surprise appointment?'

He smirked. 'It would be more correct to say that she was a surprise *applicant*. A downright shock to some people, I imagine. But once she was in the mix, with her background and expertise, it was inevitable that she'd get the job. And, until now, she's been quite sure-footed. Prior to this, she hasn't fucked up once, much to the chagrin of certain people. Those same people are at this very moment rejoicing in her current ill-fortune, I'm sure.'

'Who? Which people?'

'It's not for me to say. And again, what exactly has this to do with the murder?'

I pressed on. 'Were there internal candidates who resented her getting the job?'

'My *dear* Finn, it's a university. Resentment is an integral part of the job.'

'Was there anyone in particular who resented President Deady's appointment?'

'Oh, where's the harm, really? And someone is bound to tell you eventually.'

I waited.

He smirked again. 'I'm given to understand that the person who was most miffed, entirely wrongly in my opinion, was Lia de Barra.'

53

HE WENT ON, 'LIA HAS A DELUSIONAL VIEW OF HER own competence, and a highly inflated sense of entitlement. Not content with promotion to professor, and colonising the largest office space in the new extension to the Horgan Building, she set her sights on the East Wing, despite having zero administrative experience. I don't even know why she wanted it. Her skills, and I am willing to admit that they are considerable – let it not be forgotten that I championed her promotion – lie in her academic work. Plus she's a very talented teacher. Maybe it was the jump in salary she had her eye on. But she was never going to get the post. And once Deady applied, she was finished. Anyone else would've withdrawn at that point. Not Lia. She stayed in the race till the bitter end. And was very pissed off indeed when night followed day and she failed to be appointed.'

'You said that you championed her promotion?'

'Oh, here we go. Yes, I did. And *no*, whatever you may have heard, Lia and I never had an affair. Our relationship, what I'd *thought* was our friendship, both professional and personal, ended as soon as she got her promotion. She used me, then dropped me like a hot potato. But there was no affair. I loved my wife, you see. Note the use of the past tense.'

'Are you separated or …?'

A separation or divorce would explain the apartment.

'We've undergone the ultimate separation, I'm afraid. She died last year. After a long struggle with MS.'

'I'm sorry,' I said.

He looked around the room. 'It's easier being in this place than back home in our house. No reminders of Fiona here. Or her illness. The safety bars. The wheelchair ramp. We even installed a lift. I'm getting all of it taken out now. The builders are in there at the minute. After that, I'm getting painters to do over the whole place in Brilliant White. A fresh start for me. And the house. Or I might sell it. I don't know yet. After fifteen years of life being about just one thing, it's hard to move on. Fiona's decline was slow at first but precipitous towards the end, all-consuming. I took my eye *right* off the ball as regards my career. Had to. That article I wrote for the *Journal of Comparative Law* that I was discussing with Padraic O'Flaherty on the night of the dinner, that was my first academic publication in many years. Now I have plans for a book. I'm filling my time as best I can …' He trailed off. After a silence, he spoke again: 'I don't know why I'm telling you all of this. None of it has anything to do with the murder. Lia, bad and all as she is, wouldn't ever … And as for the president? No, take it from me, whoever the murderer is, it's not one of the guests at that dinner, you may be sure of that.'

'Do you have any idea why anyone would want to murder Professor Atkins?'

'None whatsoever.'

❖

Later, as I sorted through my notes on the interview with Casey, I re-examined what I'd learned. Of most import to me initially, apart from his lack of cooperation, was that his memory of the evening's events appeared to be remarkably sharp for a man who'd seemed to be drunk from early on. I'd also learned about his life, both private and working, and about his opinions of Lia de Barra and the president. At the end of our conversation I thought I knew something of why he'd changed so much from the energetic lecturer I remembered as a student to the bitter man he'd become in later years.

But I still knew nothing about the reason for Casey's row with Dr Mbemba, or why he appeared to have fallen out with Nate Simpson of Lexbonay.

All of a sudden Casey's own words came back to me: 'I don't know why I'm telling you all of this.' I didn't know either. He'd over-shared on some topics, and clammed up on others. I couldn't help wondering if he'd been trying to distract me from delving too deeply into his disputes with Simpson and Mbemba.

And if the two disagreements might be connected.

54

HEADING UP NORTH MAIN STREET ON THE WAY TO
collect my car, I got a call from Cormac Ryan.

'Sorry for the delay,' he said. 'I know you've been looking for
me but it's been so busy since I got back to London. How can I
help?'

'I've been tasked by the president to—'

'Yes, yes, I know. Lia told me to expect your call.'

'Did she say anything else?'

'Sorry, am I missing something? I thought you wanted to
know what time I returned to the River Lee Hotel and if I'd
seen anything suspicious?'

'I do,' I said. 'But I find it interesting that Lia phoned to—'

'You think she called to warn me or something? It wasn't like
that.'

'What was it like?'

He spoke slowly and patiently, enunciating each word, as if
he was speaking to an elderly aunt who'd forgotten to change
the batteries in her hearing aid. 'We are friends, Finn. We talk
to each other occasionally. In one of those conversations – and
it might surprise you to know that we've had several since the
murder because, believe it or not, when someone gets killed like

that, it's a topic people tend to discuss – she told me you'd been to see her and what you wanted to know.'

'Right,' I said.

'I can email you a typed version? I've already sent it to An Garda Síochána.'

'That would be great, but first I wanted to ask you about any previous meeting you had with Professor Atkins.'

'I've met him twice. Once at the University of Liverpool and another time in London. Briefly, on both occasions. In Liverpool, I met him both at the university and at the hotel later. The Beatles Hotel. Very nice. And rather fun. Have you ever stayed there?'

'No,' I said. 'I'm sure it'd be a memorable experience.' *Though not, apparently, for Lia de Barra who'd told me she couldn't remember the name of the hotel.* 'And the other time?'

'Here at UCL, my own university. I went along to hear him deliver his paper, spoke to him for a few minutes after he'd finished. But I didn't see him socially. I wasn't closely involved in the event. I don't know any more about that visit. I could possibly find out if you want?'

'Thanks. Have you any idea why anyone would have wanted to kill the deceased?'

'None at all. As I'm sure you've been told by many, people liked him. Also, even if you didn't like him that much, he lived in bloody Australia. He wasn't going to be bothering you on a day-to-day basis. I don't understand why he was killed. It's mystifying, really.'

'Can you tell me your memories of the dinner and anything odd that happened?'

'Apart from the equally mystifying argument on the lawn

between Dr Mbemba and Professor Casey, all was exceedingly quiet. As I recall, you were first to leave. Then, when the party broke up, a group gathered in the hallway to say goodbye to Will.' He paused. 'My goodbye was rather perfunctory, I'm afraid. *That* I regret. But no one could have guessed what would happen afterwards. It's a tragedy.'

I waited for him to continue.

'I believe that, after you and next Lia – she was driving home, of course, as she's told you already – I was the first of the group to exit the East Wing after dinner. No doubt the CCTV will confirm the exact sequence. I didn't dally. I walked quickly along the front of the North Wing, through the arch, rounded the corner and headed down Main Avenue. I noticed the catering van, but I didn't see anyone standing beside it. Lia said that she did, but *I* didn't. We both assume it must have been the chef she saw and that perhaps he'd finished his cigarette and gone back in by the time I was leaving.'

'Or maybe you just didn't notice him?'

'Yes, I'll allow that as a possibility. I *was* in a rush.'

'You had an early plane to catch the following morning, I believe.'

'Yes, that's right,' he said. 'That's the reason.' He went on, 'Upon my return to the River Lee Hotel, I spoke to the receptionist whose name, according to her badge, was Colleen. I remember because I always find that amusing. As you know, presumably, it comes from '*cailín*', the Irish for 'girl', yet you never find boys called 'Gorsoon' from '*garsún*', the Irish for … But I'm being flippant, I *do* apologise.'

'Why did you talk to her, to Colleen?'

'To double-check on my taxi and my alarm call for the

morning. Obviously I was also going to set the alarm on my phone, but I was being careful.'

'Fair enough. I never get any sleep if I have to catch an early train or flight the following morning. I usually drop off just before the alarm goes.'

'Exactly what happened to me that night,' he said. 'I got almost no sleep at all.'

As he spoke, he sounded cheerful. But it was hardly a surprise. If what he said checked out, he was in the clear.

55

BUILT ON A HILL TO THE SOUTH OF THE CITY AND
prone to coastal fog, the airport is one of my favourite places in
Cork. I turned off the access road to the terminal with a pang of
regret. No holiday for me. Instead, the map app on my phone
led me to the adjacent business park, to the offices of Lexbonay
Investments, an anonymous grey concrete square with four
storeys and, on the ground floor, an empty sloping glass and
steel porch that spanned the width of the building. It looked like
an extension intended to add character. It didn't.

I arrived at 1.59 p.m. I was met by a very young female
assistant loitering by the front door. She wore high-waisted
stone-washed jeans and a tucked in white cotton T-shirt.

'He's expecting you,' she said. She had braces on her teeth.

'Have you been working here long?'

'I'm still in school. Work experience. Finished now. Boss gave
me a half-day.'

She didn't look happy about any of it. In the lift, she pressed
the button for the top floor and stepped backwards out. As the
doors closed, she was typing something on her phone. Nate
Simpson was waiting for me when the doors reopened. He
looked different. The oily smile had disappeared, replaced with
what looked like cold rage. I wouldn't have cared.

Except we were on an open roof.

56

A LANDSCAPED ROOF, ADMITTEDLY, WITH WIND-
burned trees in pots, pea gravel, prairie planting and picnic benches,
surrounded by a grimy glass wall. The sheltered space near the lift
and the cigarette disposal bin looked the most used. Off to my
left, green fields and trees slid all the way to the coast at Kinsale.
Overhead, a propeller plane, making its descent, juddered past,
too close for comfort, though Simpson looked casual about it. He
was casually dressed too, in jeans and a Barbour jacket.

'Let's get this over with,' he said. 'I think it's going to rain.'

He made no move towards the picnic benches. It crossed
my mind that none of the regular staff members knew I was
in the building, and that, by meeting on the roof, he'd made
sure I wouldn't see inside the Lexbonay offices. Either he was
desperate to ensure that his wife got no whiff of the Sophie story,
or something else was in play. I looked at the sky. He wasn't
wrong about the rain. I figured I'd be seeing the CCTV from the
quad later on and that that would tell a lot. As it happens, I was
wrong, but I didn't know that then. I decided that, rather than
getting bogged down on timings and when-was-the-last-time-
you-saw questions, I should leapfrog straight to the topics I was
most interested in.

'Was last Wednesday the first time you met Sophie?'

'It was a one-night stand, okay?'

'I asked if it was your first time meeting her.'

'I fail to see how it's any concern of yours but, yes, it was. We'd only spoken on the phone before then. I suppose there had been a frisson, even on the phone, but I hadn't expected anything like that to happen, a *carpe diem* scenario, I suppose you might call it. We got on well and she was, ah, rather eager to deepen our acquaintance.'

'She said you were the one who suggested adjourning to your room at Hayfield.'

'I love my wife. Casual sex was the last thing on my mind. But if it's offered on a plate like that, there's not a man in the universe who would refuse. Although I *was* punished for my transgressions. I slept like a top, but I had a *dreadful* hangover the next morning and I hadn't even drunk all that much. And she was still there, of course, hadn't had the good grace to melt away in the night. That said, she *has* provided me with a dinky little alibi so I suppose I should be grateful.'

His story differed slightly from Sophie's but I opted not to press him on it for now.

'Had you met Professor Atkins before?'

'I'd never even heard of him. The content of the conference was of minimal interest to me. Our sponsorship was about building links with the law school and, mainly, the students themselves. We need intelligent, well-educated employees. It's as simple and, in this competitive market, as difficult as that.'

'Why did you pay extra for Atkins to stay at Hayfield rather than at the River Lee?'

'I had *nothing* to do with booking hotel rooms, either my own or anyone else's. I hadn't a clue where the fellow was staying. And, by the way, he didn't make it back there that night, or hadn't you heard?'

'Professor Atkins came and sat beside you after I left the dinner.'

'So what? He was a friendly guy.'

'What did you and he talk about?'

'This and that. Tourist things he'd done on his visit to Ireland. And my company. He wanted to hear about Lexbonay.'

'Tell me about the dispute between you and Professor Casey on the day of the conference.'

'What dispute?'

'You were all buddy-buddy at the start of the day. By dinnertime, everything had changed. I was sitting beside Casey. His animosity towards you was almost palpable.'

'That would be the alcohol, I'm afraid. Casey can put it away by the bucketful but he can't handle it, unfortunately.'

'That's all there was to it? Casey drank too much and—'

'Sophie *did* mention that his wife had died recently. All very unfortunate. I think he was just lashing out at the world in general and I happened to get in the way.'

'So your future sponsorship of the law school is unaffected?'

'*Well*, I don't know about that. The murder isn't the best connection for us, as you can imagine. But if it's all cleared up satisfactorily and doesn't impinge, then who knows?'

'What's your theory on the murder?'

'Random attack by drug-crazed student, of whom there are plenty, I'd imagine. Atkins in the wrong place at the wrong time. Tragic. But it could have been any one of us.'

'What was the row between you and Casey about?'

'I repeat, there *was* no row. No dispute. Casey was plastered. End of.'

'How do you know Béatrice Mbemba? I got the impression you two had history.'

'Unfortunately not.'

'Answer the question. How do you know her?'

'I do assure you that, before last week, I'd never met the woman.'

'She seemed to dislike you.'

'I can't help it if she liked me or not but, for what it's worth, I agree with you. My legendary charm didn't work with her. Or with you, as I recall, though I tried a lot harder with her, for obvious reasons. She's a very beautiful woman.'

'You're saying that you came on to her and she didn't like it? That's it?'

He shrugged. 'It happens. Rarely. But it does.'

'I don't believe you.'

'Which part?'

'Any of it.'

Simpson made no reply. He held out his left hand, palm up. It had started to rain, a few fat drops at first, then a downpour. He took out his phone and pressed the screen.

I kept talking, shouting over the rain and the engine of an ascending Aer Lingus Airbus A320. 'There *was* a dispute between you and Casey. There was *another* dispute between you and Mbemba. I think the two disputes are connected.'

Behind me, the lift doors opened and two large security guards stepped out. One on either side of me, they hustled me inside. Before the doors closed again, I saw Simpson standing by the edge of the roof, facing away from me, his hands gripping the glass wall. He was getting soaked.

As we descended, I smiled to myself. I should have been terrified. Disappointed, at least. I was being manhandled out of the Lexbonay office, and I'd learned nothing of substance.

But it appeared that, somewhere towards the end of the interview, I'd struck a nerve.

All I had to do now was figure out what it meant.

57

KASPER NOWAK WAS A SUPERVISOR ON THE
security staff at UCC, but he had the demeanour of a senior
policeman on a television crime series. He wore a crisply
ironed white shirt – the regular security staff wore blue – navy
trousers, epaulettes bearing the College crest, shoes polished
to a high shine, slicked-back hair and wire-framed spectacles.
Without preamble, he showed me into the CCTV suite. He
dipped his head in the direction of the door, indicating to the
other security guard who had been on duty in the room to leave.
When he'd gone, Nowak gestured towards the bank of screens.
'The president said I should give you what you want.'

'I'm especially interested in the quad, after the party broke up,
and the exits to and from the East Wing, including the kitchen.'

'The campus has many, many cameras, but not everywhere. I
will show you.'

I'm used to watching CCTV for my regular work. It crops up
in all kinds of cases – personal injury, unfair dismissals, careless
driving and, of course, criminal prosecutions. But most of the
time I get the edited highlights, the five minutes containing
the offending incident. I quickly realised that this was nothing
like that. There were hours of footage and multiple locations,

on top of which I didn't know what I was looking for. It would take a whole team of watchers, and considerably more expertise than I had, to make sense of it. This was a job for the guards.

I checked with Kasper. 'I suppose you've already handed this over to the cops?'

'It was one of the first things they did. I was in here all day Sunday with them. They downloaded everything and the map of where all the cameras were.'

There was no need for me to waste any more time on this, but I couldn't let it go.

I asked, 'Any cameras not working?'

'Everything was perfect. Like it should be. When something breaks, we fix.'

'Immediately?' I was thinking of the locks.

'If it's a camera, we fix soonest. Other things can take a few days. Sometimes we don't know. If the fault isn't reported to us. Or if we have to order something that's not in stock.'

'What about locks?'

'That's for the Buildings and Estates Department. If we find, we tell them.'

'There were two locks broken in the East Wing.'

He shrugged. 'Maybe it's true. But for this information you must ask Buildings and Estates. And the CCTV? What do you want to do about it?'

The honest answer, that I was overwhelmed and hadn't a clue, I didn't give. 'I'm going to need you to copy a number of sections of it for me to take away, but let's start with a look at the main door to the President's Garden after eleven p.m.'

'None. No camera inside East Wing. And no permanent

security presence there either. Replaced with a stupid hot desk. Crazy. Thanks to the new president.'

I'd known that, but I wanted to find out what Nowak thought. 'Did she give any reason for the removal of the cameras?'

'She said it was privacy. Her privacy and everyone who visited her. She sent an email to the whole college that anyone could make an appointment to talk to her with total privacy. An open-door policy, that's what she said it was. Good idea, some people said. This university is full of gossip. Everybody talks. All the time, believe me. But now everyone can see that it's a very bad idea, actually. As soon as the police leave, we're putting the cameras back.'

'Did she ask for that?'

He nodded. 'She said it was to help with the garda investigation, but I don't think that's the real reason.'

'And tell me, Kasper, what do you think the real reason is?'

He lowered his voice. 'If anyone asks, I didn't say it, but I think she's afraid.'

58

CIRCLING AROUND BY THE OLD COLLEGE BAR, I
made my way to the front of the library where I'd arranged to
meet Sadie. She was waiting for me. I'd never seen her looking
so tired and drawn.

'We'll have to make this quick. There's *massive* pressure from
higher up to release the scene and return the campus to normal.
But I really want to hear what you have to say. Anything you've
learned so far.'

She was being unusually open to my input but didn't give
me a chance to reply. She took off down the steps to the quad
and I followed. Ahead of us, a team of College gardeners were
rolling up the protective membrane that had been covering the
grass. It hadn't been enough. The formerly pristine lawns were
unrecognisably scarred.

'Jesus Christ,' I said. 'The state of it.'

'It could've been worse,' Sadie said. 'When I saw what was
happening, after the forensic lads from the Bureau had been
over the area, I organised the tarpaulins. Well, I made one quick
phone call to the head gardener and he arranged everything else.'

'See? Graduate entry to An Garda Síochána pays dividends
after all.'

Sadie said, 'Come on, we'll go in by the Aula.'

'Is that how you think the murderer got in? Or out?'

Inside the door of the Aula Maxima, Sadie stopped, turned towards me. 'We don't know enough to say. Between ourselves, Finn, and I *mean* that, whatever the opposite of "Gardaí are following a definite line of enquiry" is, that's where we're at. This investigation is running on fumes.'

59

INSIDE THE EAST WING, I WAITED WHILE SADIE talked to a couple of garda colleagues, from Coughlan's Quay, I assumed, whom I didn't know. I guessed that now she'd finally accepted the promotion to sergeant she'd long resisted, she'd taken on every responsibility going. I tried listening to their conversation but they were too far away for me to hear what they were saying.

I glanced out the window onto the quad again. The tarpaulin had been removed entirely and the four squares of lawn were visible. While the gardeners moved back and forth across the gravel paths, crouching on their haunches every so often to survey the damage, a knot of guards and security staff had gathered at the south-western corner. I was surprised to see that one of them was Rory Donnelly, the guard on duty there on the night of the murder. I snapped a photo of him with my phone, to remind me to ask Sadie how his statement had gone. I wanted to ask her about Sophie's statement too – she'd texted to let me know that she and her solicitor had attended at Coughlan's Quay garda station but told me no more than that.

After her colleagues had left, Sadie beckoned me towards

the entrance to the gallery where, I knew, schoolgirl Annabelle Leahy had made her gruesome discovery. Sadie opened the door. 'He was squashed in here, at the foot of the stairs.'

The floor there was badly stained with a dark liquid that didn't look like blood. A residual foul odour and a few flies remained.

'The body had started to break down,' Sadie said. She handed me a folder with a set of photographs. 'You can look at these while you're here but you can't keep them.'

I took the photographs and examined them one by one. Atkins had been arranged in a seated position, his knees pulled up to his chest, his head lolling sideways on the steps. His eyes were open, staring and bulging in a way they hadn't been in life, and red with broken blood vessels. A purple and black bruise encircled the end of his neck, the mark left by the ligature that had squeezed the last breath out of him.

After a time, Sadie went on, 'If Annabelle hadn't found him when she did, by Sunday or the return to work Monday the smell would've been unbearable.'

'Yet nobody noticed anything before Saturday?'

'Apparently not,' Sadie said. 'The corridor, bathrooms and offices in the East Wing are cleaned every weekday. And the Aula, the Stone Corridor and the West Wing are normally open at weekends, and the East Wing is normally locked but you know about the broken locks to the East Wing and the gallery. The gallery is nearly always locked. The important thing too is that it's cleaned only once a week. On Mondays. People worked and walked by here all day Thursday and Friday blissfully unaware of what was behind the door. Nobody who worked in the East Wing would even think to open it – they would've assumed it was locked as usual. The disastrously efficient cleaning of all these areas hasn't made our task any easier, mind you.'

'If the gallery hasn't been cleaned, there's bound to be DNA,' I said. 'Maybe too much of it. Like I told you the other night, we all went up those stairs to view the stained-glass window. But it's going to be hard to distinguish the multiple DNA profiles.'

Sadie sighed. 'Laypeople are obsessed with DNA. The first things we look for are fingerprints.'

'And?'

'Apart from poor Annabelle's, there's not a single one.'

60

'THE SURFACES MUST HAVE BEEN WIPED DOWN,' I said. 'By the killer. Or an accomplice.'

'Give the girl a medal,' Sadie said. 'And presumably you can guess why?'

'The killer wanted to leave no trace.'

'Yes. But the big question – one of the many big questions – is *when*?'

I thought for a moment. 'I don't know when that could've happened.'

'You were here. Ground Zero. Start thinking. Timing is everything, Finn, and never more so than on this murder. Now come on. Part two is next.'

'We've had the same problem here,' Sadie said. 'It's been cleaned at a minimum twice since Wednesday evening. And almost certainly in the aftermath of the murder by the killer as well.'

We'd moved to the East Wing men's bathroom. If they were giving out prizes for places I'd never expected to be, this would be right up there.

'You think he was killed here and then moved?'

'He didn't die where he was found. I told you about the lividity pattern. The pathologist confirmed what we'd surmised. We know that he was flat on his back for some time after death. He had an injury to the back of his head. That happened first. He must have been dazed or knocked out. We thought initially that an implement was used, a cosh, but if you look at the photographs again, you'll notice a distinctive curved shape that became properly visible once the head was shaved during the post-mortem.' She pointed at the urinal. 'It matches this.'

'Might he have fallen?'

'Look at his face. There's a very minor injury that no one noticed at the scene but the pathologist picked up on it during the post-mortem. We think he was punched or hit on the chin. Whether that happened before or after he fell it's impossible to say, but it makes sense that he was assaulted, then fell backwards and hit his head. We think he lost consciousness. It was a serious injury. On its own, it might have been enough to cause death.'

'But the killer made sure, and finished him off by strangling him.'

'The tie was removed to facilitate the asphyxiation. That's why we think he must have lost consciousness in the fall.'

'That was the ligature. He was strangled with his own tie?'

'We think so. The dimensions fit. We know for sure that he was wearing a tie because of the numerous photos that were taken during the day, and the video of his presentation. And the tie is nowhere to be found so it must have been taken away and disposed of by the killer. The fact that an improvised ligature was used supports the theory that the killing was a spontaneous act, not premeditated – like I've said before, an assignation gone wrong, or using the tie could be intended to make it look that way.'

I let that sink in. 'Was the murderer a man or a woman?'

'The location points to a man. There might have been an argument. The first injury, to the chin, was light. Atkins may have been shocked and slipped or tripped, hit his head off the urinal, lost consciousness, probably. There are no signs he fought back or tried to defend himself. In fright or panic, the killer might then have decided to be hung for a sheep as a lamb. And with the victim incapacitated, the perpetrator could have been a man *or* a woman.'

'Right- or left-handed?'

She shook her head in the it's-not-like-the-telly way I was familiar with.

'I get it,' I said. 'No way to tell … The body was moved, though.'

'Yes. Pulled by the legs before rigor mortis had set in fully. Some strength would've been required and, again, that points to a man. Though not necessarily. A lot of women would've managed it. You or I could've done it, no bother. But either before or after the corpse was moved, and probably before *and* after, he – or she – wiped the face, neck and clothing well with what we think were bleach wipes that might have been in situ here in the supply cupboard.'

'Or the killer brought them if all this was premeditated. Was it?'

'Don't know,' Sadie said. 'It was certainly *post*-meditated. A lot of care went into the clean-up, aided by the College cleaning staff in the few days after the killing. A few residual hairs and fibres were found, but it's a bathroom, what would you expect?

I'm not ruling out the possibility of getting DNA, but there's nothing obvious to go on. And those kinds of tests are slow. The results take months.'

'Plus even if there's a tiny fragment of DNA, what does it mean? He was in close contact with at least a dozen other people. Hugged many of them too, I've been told.'

Sadie said, 'There's one more thing. He was terminally ill with an inoperable brain tumour. Showed up on the post-mortem.'

'Oh, my God. Did he know?'

'It seems he did, though apart from a couple of close friends back home, and his solicitor, he hadn't told people yet. His colleagues at Melbourne Uni didn't know a thing. He'd refused chemo apparently, but he'd accepted radium treatment. We haven't released that information so it's between us. Strictly.'

'Gotcha,' I said. A moment later, I added, 'The killer didn't know, presumably.'

'There's no way of knowing. And, of course, it's still murder or, depending on the circumstances, manslaughter even if it was a dying man who was killed.'

After a silence, I said, 'The killer had to have known there was no CCTV.'

'Very useful email sent by the president to everyone. Staff *and* students.'

'And while a visitor *might* have assumed that this place was surveilled …'

Sadie nodded. 'Any student or member of staff who'd read the president's email would've known for sure that it wasn't.'

61

IN THE PRESIDENT'S DINING ROOM, SADIE AND I
sat at the table and talked through the staff and guest list.
Quickly it became clear why she'd emphasised the 'when' aspect
of the investigation.

'We've conducted preliminary interviews with everyone who
was in the East Wing that night, and done an initial comparison
between what they've told us and the CCTV that we have.
Bottom line, the people in the East Wing might have been able
to kill him but, according to the cameras, they left campus.
No one we're aware of at present could've done the clean-up.
Unless they were lightning fast. Or, potentially, they might have
done some of the groundwork earlier or later. The body wasn't
found for three days. People were traipsing in and out of here on
Thursday and Friday. There's no way of knowing who did what
and when because there's no camera footage. It was a bloodless
death. Aided by the cleaning staff. Trace evidence is hard to find.'

'What about Ian McAnespie, the conference techie?'

'We talked to him. He told us the time he left. It checks out.
So far.'

'Could he have come back?'

'Yes, he *could*. But he didn't, as far as we've been able to see.

Unfortunately. And the same goes for everyone else. The trouble is that, with exams coming up, campus was heaving, library packed till midnight, busy right up until the time it closed. One person in a hoodie and rucksack looks much like another. Time and close analysis are needed to harvest info properly from the CCTV. It's a massive task.'

'I gathered that,' I said.

'McAnespie *does* interest me, though,' Sadie said. 'He's got a bit of history.'

'What kind?'

'The chemical kind. He got the Probation Act for possession of MDMA.'

'When?'

'Two years ago. We're not talking Pablo Escobar, but still. It's something.'

'What if he was using drugs in the loo, Atkins surprised him, a fight ensued?'

'Something like that, maybe, though would you be bothered killing someone for interrupting you? Who knows? Maybe you would. Mind you, McAnespie says he's off everything. Offered us a blood test and all. But he has no alibi for the second half of the night. That helps us. Except we have him on CCTV exiting campus way too soon for him to have done any of the clean-up, and probably too soon for the killing, even though we don't know when exactly that happened.'

'So you *do* think he might have left and come back?'

'Yes. The CCTV isn't complete. There are gaps, on campus and the surrounding streets, but how does he get back into the East Wing? And it's so risky for him to return.'

'Unless he has a key.'

'He says not. Anyway, why would a guy like him have a key to the East Wing?'

I said, 'He's involved in the Film Soc. He was covering the event. Maybe he'd done that kind of thing before and, somewhere along the way, was given a key, to the Aula maybe, and held on to it. And there's someone else too. The security guard. Donnelly. He was in the East Wing at the time of the murder. He told me he didn't check the toilets but what if he did? What if *he* was the one Atkins caught taking drugs? If Atkins reported it, Donnelly would lose his job. And apart from the job here at UCC, he told me he wants to apply to join An Garda Síochána. Plus he's *very* interested in the crime scene. Hanging around it all the time.'

'I'm not ruling him out but the video shows he exits the East Wing, locks up, and doesn't return. And he's on video again, here and there, all over campus, till he clocks off.'

'One of the other security staff, so? They had keys and knowledge of the CCTV.'

'Yeah. But when? And, let's get real here, Finn, *why*? Where's their *motive*?' She got up from her seat and walked to the head of the table. She said, 'There *is* another person. Who had access to the entire *bunch* of keys. Who knew *all* about the absence of CCTV. Who'd ordered its removal, in fact. Who had plenty of time and opportunity to clean the crime scene in the days after the murder. Who knew the victim from before. Who organised a dinner in his honour …'

62

I SAID, 'YOU'RE TALKING ABOUT THE PRESIDENT.'

'However unlikely it might seem, she had the means and the opportunity. And she knew the guy back in Melbourne. She's the only one I've seen with anything like the potential for a motive, even if we don't yet know what it is. And this weird liaison role she has you doing? What's that but a way of getting you to spill the beans on the investigation to her?'

'Which I won't do. If you tell me that something's in confidence, then—'

'Relax, Finn. I know you won't blab.'

After a time I said, 'A few of the guests knew Atkins – had a passing acquaintance with him at least – apart from the president. They're all on that academic conference and sabbatical circuit. Off the top of my head there's Professor Lia de Barra, who met him once, in Liverpool, and Cormac Ryan, who met him twice. Kirsty MacMillan seemed to know him too. There could be more.' I paused. 'Who do you really like for the murderer?'

'McAnespie. Something smells off about the guy. Something he's hiding. Can't put my finger on it.'

'What about the staff? The chef, Davide Rossi.'

'We have him on video in the front seat of the Nibblz van

with the manager Magda Kozlowska at twelve forty-five a.m. She dropped him into town where he went to Barbarossa on Oliver Plunkett Street and re-emerged at two forty a.m. He *could* have done it, especially if he got help from Magda, but the trouble with that theory is that law-student-slash-waitress Ciara Boyle was also there at that time. She left a little before the other two. All the same, a killing and clean-up would've been a hard trick to pull off.'

'But not impossible.'

'Not impossible, no. But the person for whom the entire operation was *most* possible, like it or not, was the person who controlled the scene of the crime, the president, Nell Deady. Plus *she* was the last person to see Atkins alive. Not that I'll be detaining her for questioning any time soon. There's zero actual evidence against her.' She took a deep breath. 'The murderer will probably turn out to be some randomer who wandered in from the garden.'

I said, 'A detail-driven, ultra-hygienic, forensically aware randomer.'

Sadie laughed. 'Well, it *is* a university, Finn. This place is probably crawling with people like that.'

63

SADIE HAD LEFT ME WITH A LOT TO THINK ABOUT. I parted from her on the quad by the main arch and made my way to Perrott Avenue, a pleasant leafy street off College Road where many of the attractive early-twentieth-century houses had been colonised by the university; and where, earlier, following my return to town after seeing Nate Simpson, I'd parked my elderly VW Golf in front of the History of Art Building. On the way, I texted the president to confirm that, as expected, the crime scene had been released. She called me straight back but I put the phone on silent and let it ring out. There was nothing else I could say to her.

I sat into the car and scanned my notifications. I had numerous missed calls and messages but, in what was probably a Fitzpatrick family record, nothing from either of my parents. I took a deep breath and called my father.

My mother answered after half a ring. 'He's asleep.'

'Oh,' I said.

She said nothing. In my mind's eye, I saw her keeping watch over him. I said, 'I'll be over to collect him around half past eight.'

'Will you be needing your breakfast?'

'No.'

'Right.'

'Grand.' I could hear my mother breathing at the other end of the line.

'See you in the morning so,' I said.

'Bye-bye, Finn.' She ended the call.

I sat in stillness for a moment, then rang Tina. 'I might need more than tomorrow morning with Dad, Teens. I'll let Gabriel know myself but will you fix any other stuff for me? I can't think what's happening.'

She told me she'd take care of everything and that I wasn't to worry. But she sounded worried now too. Probably she always had been. Positive thinking only gets you so far.

I rang Gabriel. I told him that my father's health seemed to have deteriorated and that I was concerned things mightn't end at the GP's surgery. I said that I'd need the full day if a hospital admission was involved. Gabriel said to take as much time as I needed.

After that, I didn't know what to do. I didn't want to go home. I didn't want to eat. I didn't want to reply to messages or deal with missed calls. I didn't care who wanted to talk to me or why.

I flicked the car radio from the arts chat show on Radio 1 to John Kelly on Lyric and got chaotic wordless jazz instead. I shut my eyes for a few minutes. Tried to breathe.

When I opened them again it hit me that I was looking directly at the red-brick gateway to Hayfield Manor, where the late Professor Atkins had been staying, Nate Simpson and Sophie too, on the night of the murder. I locked the car and walked up the short slope to the hotel.

64

NESTLED ON A SNUG SITE AMID TASTEFUL PLANTING
and neat, curving paths, the hotel was about two hundred years
younger than it wanted you to think it was. In the far corner
of the lobby, a pianist competently plink-plinked harmonious
arrangements of pop songs and Irish ballads. On the left, inside
the door, a receptionist sat behind a narrow rectangular period-
style table.

Talking to her wasn't a complete waste of time. I learned
that Hayfield Manor is a five-star hotel and that it takes the
privacy of its guests extremely seriously, even the dead ones. I
also learned that, if there was nothing else they could help me
with that evening, Jonathan the porter would be *very* happy to
show me back to my car. I said there was no need for that. The
receptionist insisted it was no trouble whatsoever.

Jonathan was short and wiry. He looked at least seventy
but probably wasn't. We walked towards the gate, past a
glasshouse.

'You're not the first person who's been asking questions,
you know. We've had reporters calling in. Even someone from
the Australian Embassy, so I heard. The guards were here for
hours too, of course. They took the dead man's things but his

room was useless to them apparently. There were another four guests in there since Wednesday and sure he'd checked himself out on Wednesday afternoon long before the murder and his bags were in the luggage store to make it easy for him to collect later. He was supposed to be travelling to Dublin on the two a.m. Aircoach. Sure, that's why no one spotted he was missing.'

That was all he said about Atkins, despite several more questions from me. I asked him about Nate Simpson and Sophie. He said nothing about them either but he clearly knew who Simpson was, and it occurred to me that he might be a regular visitor to Hayfield Manor during his trips to Lexbonay's Cork office. He hadn't given that impression when I'd met him. He'd been at pains to say he'd had nothing to do with the choice of hotel. But how realistic was that? And if Simpson did know the hotel well, it might be significant. Or not. Either way, it was enough to shake me out of my stasis.

Back at the car, I finally listened to my voicemails. Two were from Matthew Cameron, third secretary at the Australian Embassy in Dublin. He said he'd been given my phone number by the UCC president and that he was on his way to Cork; then that he'd arrived and he'd like to meet up in the morning. I called him and suggested that evening instead. He said he was staying at the Imperial Hotel on the South Mall and that he needed to eat. He asked if I could recommend somewhere. I suggested Orso, a good but casual option down the street from his hotel, and said I'd meet him there.

I started the engine and did a U-turn, facing the car for my house, though I wouldn't have time to call in. Driving, I sniffed under my arms. Not great, but I had deodorant in my handbag, besides which, I wasn't going to be hugging the guy. I squeezed the Golf into a tiny but precious space on Barrack Street – I could leave it there as long as I wanted, thanks to my residents' parking permit. Hurrying down the hill, along Sullivan's Quay and beneath the trees, I crossed the south channel of the river onto the island via the elegant arch of Parliament Bridge.

65

MATTHEW CAMERON WAS AT ORSO BEFORE ME,
sitting under the awning at an outside table, by the window and
directly underneath the heater. He was not the muscle-bound
footie-playing clichéd Australian type I'd imagined during our
brief phone call. Dark-haired, fine-boned, olive-skinned, and
wearing horn-rimmed spectacles, he looked like the kind of
Spanish or Italian man who might carry a man bag. 'Full inside,'
he said, after he'd introduced himself. 'But I'm okay if you are?'

I said I was happy to eat outside. He ordered a glass of house
red and the lamb shank and I quickly requested sparkling water
and picked two small plates at random instead of a main course.
Everything on the menu at Orso is good. I wanted to get down
to business. My role was to find out what the Australian Embassy
wanted and relay it back to the president. Simultaneously, I
wanted to find out more about William Atkins the man, to see
if something in his life might offer clues to the manner of his
death.

'The president asked me to pass on her condolences and those
of the entire UCC community. And to let you know that the
resources of the college are available to the ambassador and the
late professor's family in whatever way would be of most help.

Such a terrible thing at any time, but the distance makes it so much worse, I'm sure.'

'His Melbourne Uni colleagues are gutted. Friends too. As for family, he lived alone. Divorced, though he had an ex-wife he got on well with and what seems like a *lot* of ex-girlfriends. He had an older brother who's in a care facility outside Melbourne. Parkinson's, unfortunately. There's an older sister living in Tasmania, a few other relatives scattered around the place and some nephews and nieces. No kids of his own, though.'

'Sounds like none of them are going to be coming over here.'

'Not any time soon. And the body isn't going to be freed for a while, I reckon. I've been in touch with his solicitor. There's a will specifying cremation, which makes things easier.'

'So there isn't much for you to do?'

'No, but it's the optics of it. He was a high-profile man who died a high-profile and tragic death. Someone from the embassy had to make an appearance, but right now, it's just a formality. My main task is to talk to the gardaí, tell them to leave no stone unturned and that they can be assured of our cooperation et cetera and, most importantly, that they need to keep us in the loop so that the minister can issue a press release saying we're across it. I'm meeting the superintendent heading up the investigation in the morning. I've already been to the hotel, which was uneventful. No call girls. Or boys. No drugs. Nothing for the media to get their teeth into. It's a big story back home, as you can guess. There's a lot of speculation.'

'Like what?' I asked.

'Robbery gone wrong. Mistaken identity. No one knows. He wasn't a fellow who was ever going to end up murdered. Only he did.' He drained his glass. 'Well, that certainly went down a treat. Actually my second. Earlier, I spotted that the minibar in my room offered Penfolds Bin 389 Shiraz by the quarter-bottle and …'

'It was your patriotic duty, obviously.'

'That's what I thought. You don't imbibe?'

'No,' I said. 'I won't bore you with the reason.'

'Doesn't sound boring at all.'

'Believe me when I say it is.'

I hoped he'd leave it at that, and he was a professional diplomat, so he did.

'You don't mind if I get another?'

'Why would I?'

He went inside to the counter. Night had landed heavily on the city and the municipal lighting wasn't strong enough to hold off the dark. The rest of the tables along the street were sparsely occupied with smokers and other fatalists, and lit with flickering pools of candlelight. It was too cold and too damp to sit outside but it suited me.

It suited Matthew Cameron too. When he came back he said, 'This is nice. And I'm reliably informed that dinner's on the way.'

I smiled and asked him for the email address of William Atkins's solicitor. I said I thought the president might want it. I had in mind that College might send a wreath to the memorial service, whenever that was. Cameron sent me a contact card from his phone.

'Thanks. And it's probably not necessary but maybe you could give me names and contact details for the professor's colleagues in Melbourne. I can google them obviously. Or get them from the School of Law. But just in case.'

'No problem.' He scrolled through the contacts on his phone

and sent me another contact card. 'But the solicitor is who I've been dealing with mainly. Knew him well, I gather.'

At that moment, our food arrived and the conversation moved on to more general topics. How long he'd been stationed in Ireland. Dream embassy postings of the future. If I'd ever visited Australia. Barbecues. Bush fires. Climate change. Along the way, Cameron got one more glass of red wine and, at the end of the evening, he insisted on paying for both of us. He said he was on expenses, that Canberra would be more than delighted to stump up.

Then he said, 'There's just one thing I've been wondering about.'

'What's that?'

'It's been a pleasure dining with you, but am I the only one who finds it a little strange that you're the official representative of the university? A solicitor. Who doesn't even work for the institution?'

'I don't disagree. I can see it looks off. But all of this has been seismic for College. And the president's quite new to the role. The word is that she's doing a great job. Maybe one of the reasons she's so effective is that she's good at delegating?'

'It's not *just* the president, though, is it?'

'What do you mean?'

'The wife, for one. I'd have thought she'd have wanted to—'

'Whose wife?'

'The president's wife.'

'The president has a *wife*?'

'That woman who organised the conference, what's her name again?'

'Dr Agnes Heaney?'

'That's her, yeah. Agnes.'

66

STUNNED INTO TEMPORARY SILENCE, EVENTUALLY
I asked, 'How do you know that the president and Agnes are a
married couple?'

'Because they've both ... Sorry, did you not know *any* of
this?'

'No,' I said. 'And they've both done what?'

'I've said too much already, I don't think I should ...' He
stood up from the table.

'Sit down again,' I said. 'One more minute. Please.'

'I'll sit but I'm saying nothing else. It's not relevant. And my
job's too important to me to risk it on gossip.'

'That's perfectly okay.' A few beats later, I said, 'This is where
me being a solicitor comes in handy. If you tell me something
in strictest confidence, you can rely on me not to blather. In my
job, I know *so* many secrets. And I never tell any of them.'

He shook his head. 'I'm not biting.'

'Okay. Try this on for size. I'm sure you googled me?'

He nodded. 'You're an investigator as well as a lawyer.'

'Yes. And an Australian citizen has been murdered.'

'True.'

'You have a duty to cooperate with—'

'The police. *Not* with you, Finn. Sorry.'

'Agreed. You have no duty to cooperate with me. But I believe that for some reason, related to my investigation work, Professor Atkins wanted me at the conference,' I said. 'Actually, I have no idea any more if that's true. The person who told me he'd requested my attendance was Agnes. She was the one who said he'd been asking about my work. He did seem interested. Vaguely. But not enough to seek me out privately.'

Cameron made no reply.

'Come on, Matthew. I've been dragged into this, on what might be false pretences. At the very least, Agnes and the president have been economical with the truth.'

After a long silence, Matthew Cameron said, 'I'm relying on what you said about confidentiality. And I'm only telling you because you've made me realise that this may somehow be relevant to your investigation ... The reason I know the president is married to Agnes Heaney is that they've both applied for Australian working visas. Because, in the application form, a person has to name their spouse. And there's more. I mightn't have noticed except Melbourne's where I'm from, though I went to uni in Sydney, not there.'

'What are you saying?'

'That Professor Nell Deady, the current president of UCC, stated in her working-visa application form that she's applying to be vice-chancellor of the University of Melbourne. The vice is the top gig, by the way. The chancellor's only a figurehead.'

'And what about the president's wife? Agnes?'

'Her application didn't refer to a job. It wouldn't need to. But, come to think of it, the murder of William Atkins means that Melbourne Law School has a vacancy.'

'Oh, come on,' I said. 'Agnes was in my class. I know her. The idea of her and her wife murdering someone for a job, it's too much.'

'I'm sure you're right. Yeah.' He rubbed his chin. 'There's a famous quote about ambition, isn't there? I can't quite recall ...'

'It's from *Macbeth*,' I said. 'I studied it for the Leaving Cert: "I have no spur to prick the sides of my intent, but only vaulting ambition which o'erleaps itself ..."'

'Macbeth. That's the guy. He killed a few, didn't he? Him and the wife?'

67

HOME SOON AFTER ELEVEN, I MADE STRAIGHT FOR my ground-floor study and started typing a note of what I'd learned. I'd barely begun when I remembered something.

From my bag, I took the memory stick of CCTV footage from the quad that Kasper Nowak, the security supervisor, had given me a few hours before. I fast-forwarded to the piece that Sadie had shown me on her phone while we were in the President's Dining Room. It seemed even more questionable the second time around.

Agnes chatting in the quad, phone in her right hand.

Getting a message.

Re-entering the East Wing by the small side door.

The short way.

Returning to the quad six minutes later.

The long way.

Walking around the corner of the East Wing from the President's Garden.

Meaning that she must have exited by the back door.

The side with no camera.

The same door the president said she'd left the East Wing by.

The president who'd removed all CCTV from the East Wing.
The president who'd arranged the dinner.
The president who'd said she'd parted with Professor Atkins, her
supposedly honoured guest, when he went to the bathroom, leaving
him to return to his hotel alone.
The president who was also Agnes's secret wife.

However suspicious it seemed, there had to be an innocent explanation. Why else would the president have engaged me in the first place and instructed Nowak to give me the CCTV?

Unless what the president had *really* wanted was to have an extra pair of eyes on the investigation. Because she, and her wife Agnes, had something more to conceal than that they were married?

And why had they bothered hiding their marriage anyway? It made no sense. Nobody would have cared.

But I couldn't see Agnes as a murderer. Or the president. Or both of them. It was too much of a stretch. I needed time to think all of it through before I said or did anything. Also, I needed to get some rest before Dad's medical appointment. I went to bed. And failed to sleep.

At 2 a.m., I went upstairs to the living-room sofa, pulled a blanket over me. As the orange night haze of the city seeped through the glass, I started scrolling Australian press reports.

Matthew Cameron had been right. The death of William Atkins was a huge story down under. I read a few obituaries and interviews. One was with a man called Dan Grant, described as a 'prominent solicitor and old friend of the late Professor Atkins', who revealed that Atkins had been 'suffering from health problems in recent times'. I figured he knew about the brain tumour. And Matthew Cameron had given me Dan Grant's mobile-phone number.

It was the middle of the night in Cork. But in Melbourne it was lunchtime the next day. I sent a text message explaining who I was and asking if he was free to take a call. While I waited for a response, I flicked on *Pieces of the Sky* by Emmylou, the volume low. The second track, 'Too Far Gone', was playing when my phone screen started to flash. I pressed pause on the song and took the call.

68

'WE WERE CLASSMATES AT UNI,' DAN GRANT SAID. 'Friends all down the years since. I feel like I've lost my right arm. Not just me, my wife too. And my kids grew up with him as a fixture. An honorary uncle. To have him go like this, so far from home, it's … I can only hope he didn't suffer too much.'

I thought before replying. I couldn't reveal what Sadie had told me in confidence about the post-mortem results. 'I hope so too … You mentioned in an interview I read that he'd been having health problems.'

'That's right. It'll come out at the inquest, I suppose. It's ironic. He hadn't wanted people to know. He said, "If people know I'm crook, they'll wrap me in cotton wool and treat me like a fucking invalid." He said he'd end up dead long before the actual event. And he wasn't having that. But now everyone'll find out. Not that it matters in the scheme of things.'

'What was it exactly, the health issue he was dealing with?'

'Inoperable brain tumour. Could've killed him in six days or six months but the docs told him he probably had a year and maybe a little longer with chemo. He said no to chemo, and yes to radium. It was quite successful, though the improvement was only temporary. He knew that. He kept working and went ahead with the visit to Ireland. The only change he made was that he gave up alcohol. He said that in whatever time he had left he wanted to see the world clearly, not through beer goggles. But I think it was more to do with knowing where he stood, with being fully aware of when he was going downhill. To have nothing interfering with his knowledge of what was happening to him.'

'Was he a big drinker before this?'

'Not really. Or, yeah, sometimes. If the occasion demanded. Big games. Birthdays. But he didn't have a problem with alcohol. He was just a bon viveur.'

'One of the people I work with met him out in Melbourne during the Rugby World Cup in 2003. He said they had—'

'Is that Dermot? I met him then too. Great guy. I'm surprised he wasn't deported. Wild times we had.'

'So I believe.'

'You work with good old Dermot, eh? That must be fun.'

'Ah, yeah, it is,' I said. 'Em, when was the last time you spoke to Will?'

'I talked to him on the phone the night before he left for Ireland so that's a couple weeks ago. I got a few WhatsApps from him. We're in a group, just jokes and political memes – I believe that's what you young ones call them – and he phoned me the day he died, I think it could only have been a few hours beforehand, and left a voice message to say he wanted to come to see me professionally when he got home. He said he wanted to make another appointment to talk about his will.'

'*Another* appointment?'

'He'd already been in my office about it approximately three weeks before he left for Ireland. You're a solicitor so you know.

Wills are something people like to take care of before embarking on big trips. And he had his diagnosis too. Something that might have affected his legal competency later. So he got everything done and dusted before he left. But he might've wanted to tweak something, who knows?'

'Do you mind me asking, what's in the current will?'

'I don't mind you asking, but before probate issues I'm obviously not allowed to tell you. What I *can* say is, there's nothing controversial in it. It's a perfectly normal, sensible document. I'm the executor. I've barely started the process but I don't expect any trouble with it.'

'Do you know if he was worried about something or someone?'

'Apart from being terminally ill, you mean?'

'I'm sorry, that was a stupid thing to say. I mean was he afraid of someone, or did he feel there was a wrong he needed to set right?'

'Not that I know of. Everything was fine until he started getting headaches.'

'What was he like?'

'Political in a champagne-and-smoked-salmon-socialist kind of way. Successful. Would've done well whatever path he'd chosen to follow. Generous. Well-regarded by his colleagues. Bloody good golfer. *Serious* tennis player in his day.'

'He sounds almost too good to be true.'

'Well, everyone has their Achilles heel, I suppose.'

'And what was his?'

'The ladies. One after another. My wife stopped inviting them to dinner. We'd have just got used to them, and they'd be gone. He'd let them down gently. Usually, it was the girls who'd break it off because he'd never commit.'

'Girls? *Young* girls?'

'Sorry. I should've said women. He wasn't trying to cling to his youth by dating younger than his own age. Five maybe ten years of an age difference max.'

'He *was* married once, wasn't he?'

'It was over in six months but chugged along for about two years before she called it quits. She remarried. He was at the wedding. Godfather to one of her kids. They had none themselves. He had this ability to stay friends with all his exes. Remarkable. That's why I think his death must have been an accident. Will Atkins hadn't an enemy in the world.'

TUESDAY

69

'SHOULDN'T YOU BE BACK AT WORK?' MY FATHER asked.

I told him I had loads of holidays due to me, which was true. To make all of this seem unexpected, I told him I hadn't planned to end up there on my day off. We both knew that was a lie. He'd found the short walk to my car early that morning a struggle, and a few minutes after we'd left the house, my mother had texted me to say that his bag was packed and ready by the door if we needed it. Only forty minutes later, after a short but decisive consultation with the GP, we did.

Now it was past 3 p.m. and we'd finally concluded the seemingly endless hospital admission process at the Bon Secours on College Road, universally known as 'The Bons', the private hospital where my father had been directed for what the GP had called 'a few run-of-the-mill tests', a term sufficiently vague to leave room for benign interpretation, if you were so inclined. Dad had been allocated a spacious single room on the second floor in the newer part of the complex with a view of the car park. He was surprisingly jaunty about his situation. 'I'm getting value out of it at long last,' he said.

He was talking about the Medical Provident Fund, a benefit

scheme he'd paid into most of his life as an ESB employee and retiree. It allowed him to jump the queue, to avoid what might be days on a trolley as a public patient in Accident and Emergency at Cork University Hospital. It wasn't fair, but I could handle the guilt. I could handle anything except him looking so small and unlike himself, propped up on three pillows and a tilted mattress in the narrow plastic bed. He hadn't lost weight. It was more like he'd shrunk, his muscles sagging and limp from inactivity.

'I was lucky with the free upgrade to the private room. That'd be on a more luxurious plan than mine is normally.'

'They might put you out on a ward in a few days, though. They said they might have to if they need the bed back.'

'He won't be here that long,' my mother said.

She'd come in without us noticing and was standing by the door to the en-suite bathroom, a bulging Dunnes Stores carrier bag hugged to her chest. New pyjamas. Meaning that she expected him to be in hospital for considerably longer than she was prepared to say out loud.

'Did they feed you yet?' she asked.

I answered for him. 'He's to get tea and toast shortly. Then nothing till after he's finished the scope tomorrow, whenever that will be.'

'I'm not hungry anyway,' he said. 'Hanging around all day would kill anyone's appetite. And there's no air here.'

'Will I open the window?'

'You'll do no such thing,' Mam said. 'Do you want to give him pneumonia?'

Dad gave me a little smile. 'You should go, Finn. I'm in good hands, I'd say.'

My mother added, 'I'll drive myself home. I'll stay as late as they'll let me.'

She moved to the side of the bed and got busy rearranging the locker. I knew that the moment I left she'd sit next to him, hold his hand and allow herself to shed a few tears. For now, both of them were keeping it together for my sake, which was the ridiculous but compulsory kind of behaviour all families resorted to at times like this, I supposed.

I left, because they wanted me to, and rambled out, blurry-eyed, through the old part of the hospital, the wide polished-linoleum hallways, the holy statues around every corner.

Emerging onto College Road, my recent discoveries swam back into focus. It was too late to bother going into work at MLC, and going home to stare sightlessly at the telly for the night wasn't an option I was prepared to contemplate. Instead, I dumped my car on Highfield West, in front of a house with a full-grown rowan tree in the garden. Now that I'd had time to think about it, I knew exactly where I needed to go. And who I needed to see.

70

MY RETURN TO THE CAMPUS WAS A POINTLESS exercise. I failed to locate the president, and Agnes, failed utterly in my intended task of finding out about their marriage and their Australian visa applications, and what any of that had to do with the murder of William Atkins. It wasn't something I wanted to talk to them about by phone. I needed to speak to them about it in person. Judge their reactions. Though I still couldn't see Agnes as a realistic murder suspect.

But I recalled that she'd told me Atkins had been 'on her wish list'. That on Sunday in her office, she'd left me with the definite impression that his acceptance of the invitation had come as a surprise to her.

I thought about it afresh now and came to the conclusion that the *acceptance* might well have been a surprise but, in light of what I'd learned from Matthew Cameron, the *invitation* looked more like deliberate scheming on her part.

And if she'd done that, and booked him a room at a separate hotel to the rest of the conference guests, what else might she and the president have done in the East Wing on that Wednesday night? The murder, the moving of the body, and the clean-up, whether that had happened in the aftermath of the dinner or early the next morning: seeing it as a two-person job made a lot more sense.

Except for all the bits about my former classmate Agnes and her wife, the current president of UCC, being potential murderers. That made no sense at all.

As well as the East Wing, I stopped by my temporary room on the ground floor of the Horgan Building. Someone had taped my name to the door but no messages had been left in my allocated pigeonhole in the communal administrative office. The entire law school had a hint of the *Mary Celeste* about it. People had been there, but no one was there now. I badly needed to talk in particular to the law-school administrator, but that interview would have to wait.

On the way back to the car, I rang Sadie. It took her a while to answer, and when she did, her voice sounded tinny and artificial.

'Hi, Finn, how's it going?'

'Have you got me on speaker?'

'Um, yeah, just typing something here. What's the story?'

Somewhere near the back of my mind I registered that I didn't hear her clacking at top speed on her ancient garda-issue keyboard, or any of the usual Coughlan's Quay station soundscape, and that she must have been away from her usual desk, or at home.

I said, 'Just calling to see if there are any updates.'

A pause before she replied, 'Anything in particular you're interested in?'

'No, I— Hang on a minute, Sadie, I'll have to ring you back.'

I ended the call and broke into a run.

71

I WAS ALMOST SURE IT WAS CIARA BOYLE, THE tour guide and East Wing dinner waitress, whom I could see heading east on Magazine Road, the street perpendicular to Highfield West. I raced up the hill and hung left, passing Sicilian Delights, a popular café that used to be a butcher's. Lots of places that used to be other things had turned into coffee shops, but this one served a full menu and drew queues. There was no queue now, and it looked like they were shutting up for the day. The galvanised security gate, unmoored from its tether, swung back and forth in the stiff breeze, its padlock clanking against the steel frame.

The woman – almost definitely Ciara – was ahead, walking surprisingly fast, and the thought occurred to me that she was trying to avoid me, even though she'd replied to my text message, and I was the one who hadn't followed up, with her and so many of the other witnesses I had yet to interview. I caught her at the pharmacy. It *was* Ciara.

Winded, I said, 'Can I talk to you for a minute?'

By the look she gave me, I knew she hadn't seen me, hadn't been trying to get away. She was just physically fitter than the sofa slug I'd become. 'Sure, but give me a sec?'

She went into the chemist and I waited outside, catching my breath and constructing elaborate reparative exercise regimens that, if recent months were any indicator, I wouldn't stick at long. Sadie's name flashed up on my screen but I rejected the call and put the phone on silent. I sent her a text saying I was tied up and would get back to her as soon as I could.

Ciara came out, carrying a small paper bag, sealed with a sticky prescription label.

She tapped it. 'Sleeping tablets. Five of them, all the College doc would give so that I won't get addicted. As if. Hopefully they'll help. I haven't had a wink since I heard about the murder. It's so awful what happened. And he was so nice. Funny too.'

'That's what I want to talk to you about, if it's okay. You know that—'

'I've been expecting to hear from you. Come on. I live down here.' She walked ahead again and took the second left, by the side of Horgan's Buildings, six rows of terraced brick-built cottages. Scattered among them were some of the most beautiful and unusual gardens in Cork, even though the houses had no ground of their own.

Ciara lived further down the slope, in Mount St Joseph's View, an enclave of later twentieth-century houses with red-tiled mansard roofs running alongside a grassy park with a few trees. On the far side of the park I noticed a grubby wall with a green metal gate and a sign: 'NO DELIVERIES BEFORE 8 A.M.'

'That's the rear entrance to Hayfield Manor, isn't it?'

Ciara said, 'Yeah, it is.'

'Did you ever think of applying for a job there? Only a minute from home.'

'I have enough going on. But Ian worked there. In the kitchen, I think. Don't know if he still does. Apart from the conference, I haven't seen much of him around College.'

'Ian McAnespie, the guy who did tech support at the conference?'

One of the people who hadn't replied to my messages.

'Yep. He's a law student too. Did you know that?'

I did. 'Is he a friend of yours?'

'He's a, well, he's a messer. He's not someone I'd want to …' She unlocked the front door. 'Best College house ever,' she said.

As I followed her inside and to the back of the house, my head started to spin from lack of sleep. I should've gone home, gathered myself after the day, but it was too late now. I sat at the small round pine table in the snug, scrupulously clean kitchen.

'Tea, coffee, water?'

'Water, please.' I took out my pen and notebook. 'Do you know where Ian McAnespie lives?'

'He used to live in a house share in one of those three-storeys on Connaught Avenue – I was at a party there once. Someone said he moved out. That he was occupying a vacant property as a protest against the lack of fairly priced student accommodation. Some people are living in cars. Or couch-surfing. It's a good thing to do, I guess. Occupying. Highlights the issue.'

'Where is this house he's occupying?'

'I don't know.'

'Doesn't sound like much of a protest if he's doing it on the quiet.'

'I don't think it's "on the quiet". I just don't know where it is.'

'Do you know anyone who would?'

She shook her head. I went through the questions I'd asked the other witnesses. I asked her about the end of the evening.

'The last thing I did was a final run over the dining room. I was finished by twelve forty a.m. And that's when I left, by the Donovan's Road gate below the chapel, and came home.'

'I'm surprised it was all done so fast,' I said.

'Most of the clearing up was finished by the time the guests left the dining room. Apart from glasses, and we don't wash those on site. They're just emptied and put in the van. Nibblz supplies nearly everything for these kinds of events – plates, glasses, napkins, cutlery and so on. Some of it's washed in the East Wing and reboxed, and some of it is scraped and stacked in plastic crates and taken away.'

'So there's a lot of in and out to the van?'

'Yeah. And before you ask, I didn't see anything out of the ordinary.'

'When was the last time you spoke to the deceased?'

'In the dining room, towards the end of the night. He gave me twenty euros as a tip. More than I got from the president.'

'How much did she give?'

'Zero, of course. I don't mind, like. No one tips at those events. He probably gave it to me because of doing the tour for him earlier. He was lovely. A good laugh.'

'When was the last time you saw him?'

'He was in a group in the corridor with some of the other guests. All of them apart from you, I think. Magda sent me into the dining room to gather the remaining glasses onto a tray and to collect the napkins, roll up the tablecloth and check the other surfaces. I did that and brought the glasses and the linen to the kitchen. And when I came back, they were all gone.'

'Apart from the guests, do you remember seeing anyone else that night?'

'Only the security guard and Ian McAnespie. Both were there quite late.'

'What time, roughly?'

'Sorry, can't remember. The security guard was there later than Ian, I think.'

'Can you think of anything else that happened, whether it's relevant or irrelevant to the investigation? Anything that struck you as unusual or unexpected?'

'There was nothing … although …'

What she said next made me change my plans for the evening.

Afterwards, I left the city, driving east in heavy rain to Midleton to meet Magda Kozlowska, the catering supervisor. I spent the remainder of the night trying and failing to track down Ian McAnespie and Davide Rossi, the chef, the one person present in the East Wing that night whom I'd never met, never spoken to, though after what Magda and Ciara had told me, I knew it was vital that I did.

I visited the address in Tivoli that Magda had given me for Davide Rossi – no one was at home. I tried calling him on his phone – it was out of service – and I found no social-media profile for him.

Ian McAnespie's phone rang out repeatedly and he didn't reply to my text messages. I found a Facebook profile for him, but he hadn't posted in over two years.

In between, I kept in touch with my parents at the hospital, and visited my mother on my way home from Midleton (via Rossi's place in Tivoli) when she returned to Gardiner's Hill around 10 p.m.

Back at my own house, I sat in my study, ran through my notes and typed them up, falling into bed after 1 a.m.

All of which is the long way of saying that I was too busy to phone Sadie back, despite three more missed calls from her – she didn't leave a voicemail – and a *Please call me* text message followed by a *Please call me NOW*. It was too late to get back to her by the time I noticed the text messages but I wasn't worried. I'd make contact with her first thing the next day. I knew she'd understand.

And, nine times out of ten, she would have.

WEDNESDAY

72

I RECKON IF YOU CARED TO DO A SURVEY, AND somebody probably has, you'd find that police forces all over the world overwhelmingly favour arresting people early in the morning. It's not that cops like getting up with the dawn, or before it, any more than the general population does. It's everything else. The chances of finding the person of interest tucked up in bed? High. The chances of running into organised opposition from said person, his or her family members and/or associates? Low. And there's the head start the morning provides, the time, oceans of it, to crank out paperwork, implement search warrants, get interview rooms set up, scoff breakfast rolls. Meanwhile the arrestee is blinking awake, dazed and shivering, at the edge of a concrete bed in a grimy cell wearing whatever pre-worn T-shirt and hoodie they've managed to grab off the bedroom floor before being pressed firmly into the back of a garda car. So whatever the other advantages, I think that's the main reason. Early morning has to be when the shock factor is at its highest.

At least, that was how it seemed to me.

When the doorbell went at 6.15 a.m., it felt like I'd just dropped off, though I realised later that I'd been asleep for a few hours. I jolted awake at the first ring, thinking automatically that it was bad news. I reached for my phone.

A text from my mother sent at 6.05: *Talked to the nurse. Dad had a good night. Still asleep. Going down for scope before 8.*

I replied, *Great, will call you later*, and got back a thumbs-up emoji.

By now, the ringing on the doorbell was constant. Looking out the window gave no clue as to why as I couldn't see the lane outside from it. I ran upstairs to the top floor and pressed the intercom: 'Who's this?'

A male voice, one I didn't recognise, speaking words that made no sense.

'Garda Síochána. Open the door. We have a warrant to search these premises.'

I rang Sadie. Straight to voicemail. I was too stunned to leave a message.

The doorbell started again and, from below, I heard loud knocking – hammering – on the gate. I had visions, from a thousand television shows, of a battering ram breaking it down and armed-response gardaí streaming through the front yard and up the stairs shouting, 'Clear.'

I pressed the intercom again. 'Give me a sec.'

I pulled on a T-shirt, sweatshirt, leggings. Had a pee, washed my hands, splashed cold water on my face, picked up my toothbrush, put it down again, didn't brush my teeth. And those minutes, those commonplace actions, are etched on my brain like stone carvings.

Because things were never the same for me afterwards.

73

I'D BEEN IN THE CELLS AT COUGHLAN'S QUAY garda station before. More than once. This was my first time being the client. The *potential* client. Because I hadn't yet sought legal representation. Hadn't even made a call to inform anyone where I was. Not the office. Not my mother. For now, I was saving my lifelines, like a too-clever contestant on *Who Wants to be a Millionaire?*.

I'd been cautioned. Fingerprinted. Photographed. Introduced to the member in charge, the sergeant tasked with my welfare. I'd been given the *Information for Persons in Custody* leaflet. I'd been told the reason for my detention in accordance with Section 4 of the Criminal Justice Act 1984 as amended. I'd handed over my keys, shoelaces, Fitbit, phone, earrings. Throughout all of it, I'd said nothing, watching silently as the custody sergeant noted my lack of response in the custody record.

And, throughout all of it, Sadie was nowhere to be seen. I knew she was in the station somewhere, and that she was aware of what was going on. But I didn't ask to talk to her.

Because she'd allowed this to happen. Might even have been the cause of it.

At 8.45 a.m., by the clock in the hall, I was moved to Interview Room Six. Left to sit there with a plastic bottle of water for company, I thought about the digital fingerprinting process I'd gone through. Often that wouldn't happen until later in the detention. Either they were taking this ludicrous arrest seriously, or they wanted to scare me. However bad things were, I hoped it was the latter. I reckoned it was. They hadn't bothered with a DNA sample. Maybe they didn't want to waste a testing kit on whatever this farce was about. Also, I *was* scared. Terrified. Their tactics were working.

The interview room was tiny and overheated. The kind of place uniformed gardaí might check car-insurance documents. A desk shoved into one corner. A camera in another, like a bulging eyeball, above the door. Nowhere to sit apart from a hard ledge underneath the window. I sat, fists clenched, body tense. Unmoving but for the churning in my stomach.

After a while, I felt like I was seizing up. Stood. Walked a few steps, put my hand to my lower back to rub it. A reflex action.

A sign of weakness too. I stopped. Took off my sweatshirt, formed it into a cushion. Sat again. Waited. Thought about my dad in hospital. Being scoped. Frightened. And my mam. Home alone. Whatever it took, I had to get out of there. Fast.

Time passed. Not as much as it seemed. When they entered the room, carrying a chair each, one of the gardaí said aloud, for the benefit of the video, that it was 9.17 a.m. I'd been in the interview room for only thirty minutes. But by now, the people at my office would have missed me, and I should have been letting them know where I was. I didn't want to. I wanted to hear what these two had to say first. I wanted to see the whites of their eyes.

Besides, any action I took would only delay matters. When it suits whatever purpose they're trying to achieve, things can move geologically slowly in garda stations. A phone call? At least half an hour of messing around. A request for a solicitor? An hour or two might go by before he or she arrived.

I knew both of the guards. Detective Garda Olly Fogarty had taken a statement from me in relation to a previous case. In my living room. Sadie's main work partner. She'd been promoted to DS since, but they were still tight. The other detective, Ruth Joyce, I'd met when she was in uniform, after my old car had been torched on Fort Street. Come to think of it, she'd been to my house too. The choice of personnel couldn't have been an accident. Two people who'd helped me, been kind to me, in the past. Good cop, good cop, intended to get me chatting?

Fuck that. I had the right to remain silent and I intended to use it.

74

FOGARTY OPENED. 'FINN, AH, JUST TO, AH, administer the oul' caution to you there again. You are not obliged to say anything but anything you do say will be taken down and may be given in evidence. And, ah, Detective Garda Joyce will be taking the memo. I believe ye know each other. And, ah, I've to get you to sign the form for the video as well. I'll read it here for you now first.'

Fair-haired, he was a few stone overweight, a big soft country boy in his early thirties, a lot more intelligent than he liked to pretend. Ruth Joyce was tall. Clever and diligent, as I recalled from when we'd met before. She had rosy cheeks and dark hair and was in her late twenties. She straightened the A4 pad on the desk in front of her, avoided my eyes. The three of us were squashed into the room, and the atmosphere was intense. Which, I assumed, was the point of the cramped accommodation. It was all rather obvious. And very effective.

Fogarty handed me the form and I signed it, though I needn't have. I caught him exchanging a look with Joyce. It might have been hope I saw in his face, but I wasn't sure.

He said, 'I need you to confirm your name, address and date of birth.'

I did as he asked.

He puffed out a breath. 'Right ... Sure you know why you're here?'

'No comment,' I said.

'Ah, Finn, don't be like that, for God's sake.'

I made no response.

'You're not helping yourself, Finn.'

I said nothing.

'Fair enough. If that's how you want to play it. As you know, Finn, you've been detained in connection with the murder of William Atkins.'

I made no reply.

After a time he continued: 'Could you tell us what happened last Wednesday?'

'No comment.'

'You gave a speech up at UCC. A good one, I believe.'

'No comment.'

'How did you get invited? Wouldn't be your kind of thing normally, would it?'

'No comment.'

And so it went on, Fogarty taking me through the day of the conference and the dinner that evening. I could've answered his questions. I knew I was innocent of any charge the Director of Public Prosecutions might choose to press, that there was no evidence to incriminate me. There couldn't have been.

But answering would have slowed things down. And, like I say to my clients, once you start talking, it's hard to stop. Better to say nothing at all. Listen to what Fogarty was saying.

Try to figure out what the hell I was doing there.

75

OLLY FOGARTY HAD STARTED TO SWEAT WHEN A
knock came to the door – three sharp raps. He and Ruth Joyce
got to their feet instantly.

He said, 'Interview suspended at ten twenty-three a.m.'

Both of them left the room.

Some minutes later, they returned, Fogarty had taken off his
jacket. He was carrying a paper cup and a thin buff-coloured
folder.

'Can we get you anything, Finn, a coffee or anything?'

'No comment,' I said.

He bristled. 'Your funeral,' he said.

Ruth Joyce gave her head a barely perceptible shake. Olly
Fogarty shut his eyes.

'Why were you at UCC that day, Finn?'

'No comment.'

'Because the late Professor Atkins insisted on you being there.
Isn't that it?'

'No comment.'

'A fact that you omitted to tell your pal Sadie, the DS. Why
didn't you tell her?'

'No comment.'

'Why were you trying to hide that from her, Finn?'

I thought Agnes had told her already! 'No comment.'

'Okay,' he said. 'Tell us about the end of the night. You left and came back. Why?'

'No comment.'

'We have it on CCTV. You left the East Wing. Crossed College Road. Came back. Went in a different door than the one you left by. Why did you do that? Who did you meet?'

The truthful answer – that I returned to the East Wing to fetch my coat, and, while there, met Ian the conference techie – was on the tip of my tongue, but I resisted the urge to speak. They should have seen on the CCTV that I was wearing a coat when I came onto the quad again, that I wasn't wearing it earlier. Presumably they *had* seen it. This couldn't be about a coat.

'No comment,' I said.

'You were interviewed by your pal Sadie, the DS. You told her the time you left but you never mentioned going back.'

I thought about it. I was sure I'd told Sadie about meeting McAnespie in the corridor. But maybe I hadn't said anything about returning. Maybe I hadn't been clear enough. Maybe I'd forgotten. Or maybe Sadie had. But now wasn't the time to get drawn into an argument about it.

'No comment.'

'Who did you meet when you went back, Finn?'

'No comment.'

'Was it Professor Atkins?'

'No comment.'

'Had you arranged to meet him?'

'No comment.'

'He *was* the one who asked for you to speak at the conference, wasn't he?'

'No comment.'

'Were the two of ye close?'

Weird question. 'No comment,' I said.

'Did ye have a fight, Finn?'

This wasn't going how I'd expected. Suddenly, I was boiling hot. I took a swig from the water bottle.

'You've gone a bit quiet, Finn. No "no comment" that time.'

I realised I hadn't replied to his previous question. 'No comment,' I said.

'Did I hit the nail on the head there, Finn? Is that it? Ye had a row so, is that what happened?'

'No comment.'

'We know you didn't do it yourself.'

This was getting more and more bizarre. 'No comment.'

'Who did you get to do it for you? Who did you get to kill Atkins?'

Holy shit, was this really happening?

'No comment.'

'Was it McAnespie, Finn? Was it him?'

'No comment.'

'Was it McAnespie's idea?'

Jesus Christ, was Fogarty for fucking real?

'No comment.'

'Finn, this is your opportunity to tell us your side of the story. Take it.'

'No comment.'

'You had to realise we'd find out, Finn. There's no secrets these days.'

He slid the folder in my direction. Tapped it with his right index finger.

'No comment.'

No clue where he's going with any of this.

My mouth bone dry, my stomach on the floor.

He opened the folder. Extracted a photocopied sheet. Handed it to me.

He said, 'Care to comment on that?'

76

I TOOK THE DOCUMENT, HELD IT IN FRONT OF ME.
The kind of thing I'd seen before. Loads of times. It should have
been easy to understand. But it wasn't. Because the information
it contained was nonsense. I read it and reread it and that's what
it was. Rubbish. Bullshit. Complete and utter.

And Fogarty was saying something, but I couldn't take it in.

Blood pumping in my ears.

Short breaths through my mouth.

Ruth Joyce talking. 'Finn, are you okay?'

Me hearing myself say, 'I'm fine.'

Then Sadie, her voice, saying, 'Interview suspended at ten
fifty-seven a.m.'

I was still holding onto the photocopied page but it was
crumpled into a ball now and I was afraid to open it again.

77

BACK IN THE CELL. LYING DOWN. BREATHING MORE
easily. Sadie standing beside me. 'I knew this was a bad idea,' she
said. 'I wanted to talk to you about it first but—'

'I didn't call you back.'

She nodded. 'Preliminary DNA results came in yesterday.
And, as Fogarty told you, there was a comparison done with
other people on the system. We didn't expect to find anything,
we weren't really looking for … '

A long silence.

Sadie said, 'You should've told me. It would've made all the
difference.'

I made no response.

'Finn, cut the "no comment" crap. I won't, *can't*, use anything
you say in here.'

'Okay, okay,' I said. 'I'll tell you. The truth is, I didn't know.'

'Ah, for Jesus' sake …'

'Really I didn't,' I said.

As if I'd said nothing, Sadie went on, 'If you'd told me, we
could've handled it differently but, when you didn't take my
calls, reply to my texts, and when you weren't at work, or at
home, well, you have to admit that it looked bad. I didn't agree

with the approach taken, the arrest this morning, it was too heavy-handed for my liking, but it was out of my hands. I've been under so much pressure because of the way I handled the scene, shutting down so much of the College grounds, that my objections didn't hold much weight with the superintendent. When this cropped up, he said you were to get no preferential treatment. But if you'd told me, I—'

I sat up. 'I didn't *know*. Can you not see?'

Sadie's expression turned icy. She walked to the door of the cell, turned around to face me again. 'I can't help you if you keep lying to me. On top of lying by omission.'

'I'm not lying. I'm *not* a fucking liar. When have I ever lied to you?'

'You've withheld the truth,' Sadie said. 'How many months did it take for you to tell me about your relationship with a cocaine addict?'

'Davy *again*? Jesus, Sadie. This is *different*. I *swear*. I. Did. Not. Know.'

Sadie made no reply.

'The search warrant,' I said. 'Ye've spent the morning combing my home from top to bottom and found nothing, right? No evidence of contact between me and him whatsoever? Because there's nothing to find. Sweet fuck-all.'

She leaned against the wall. Sighed. 'Allegedly, according to Agnes, Atkins was the one who asked for you to be invited to the conference.'

'I told you that. Or did I?'

'You didn't.'

'Unintentionally. We were both tired. I—'

'Come off the stage, Finn. Anyway, Atkins didn't tell Agnes

why he wanted you to speak at the conference. I sat beside you for three years in College. I think we can take it that it wasn't for your academic prowess.'

'Agreed,' I said.

'So let's assume that, whatever about you knowing or not, Atkins *did* know.'

I shrugged. 'Seems like a reasonable assumption.'

'And, despite that, you're asking me to believe that you were in his company all day at the conference, and that he said nothing to you?'

'I am. It was strange. It was like … He seemed as if he was always just about to talk to me, but never got around to it. We were supposed to be sitting next to each other at dinner but something happened and we weren't. And I missed lunch – I had to go back to work unexpectedly. Maybe he intended to say it then, but the moment passed and he decided not to? Agnes thought he was more interested in my investigatory work than—'

'He flies all the way around the world to see you and loses his nerve at the last minute? Finn, no one's going to believe that shite. *I* don't believe it.'

Something itched at the back of my mind, but I couldn't reach it.

'I know it's unbelievable,' I said. 'But it's the truth. I didn't know. Honestly.'

'And what about you leaving the East Wing on the night of the dinner, telling everyone you're going home, and coming back ten minutes later, what was that about?'

'It was more like five minutes,' I said. 'I forgot my coat. I didn't think to mention the coat but I did say I met McAnespie.'

'Though not *when*. And I saw the additional item of clothing on the CCTV. But there are people here who think the error was deliberate and that you *conveniently* not telling me about *allegedly* forgetting the coat was deliberate too. Stupid, but deliberate.'

'It wasn't.'

'Which?'

'Both,' I said. 'I forgot my coat *and* I forgot to tell you about it.'

She shook her head. After a silence she said, 'I don't know.'

'Please, Sadie, you have to believe me.'

'I don't, actually.' She paused, thought for a moment, then said, 'Say it.'

'I said it already. I didn't know.'

'No. The full thing. Say the full thing you *supposedly* didn't know.'

She waited for me to speak. Left me with no choice.

'I didn't know,' I said. 'I didn't know that Atkins was my birth father.'

78

SADIE'S FACE WAS BLANK, LIKE A LOCKED DOOR.

'You should eat something,' she said. 'I'll get one of the lads to arrange it.'

After she'd gone, leaving me none the wiser as to whether she believed me or not, I sat on the bed, back to the wall, knees bent. I pulled up the hood of my sweatshirt, tried to block out the world. The new, unknown, horrible world, revealed by chance because my DNA was still on the system after my part in the recent Mandy Breslin murder investigation. I hadn't been under suspicion then.

I was now. In an apparently motiveless killing, I was the one with the closest connection to the victim. The best motive. Hatred? Revenge? Money? Take your pick. It's why they always look at family first. Didn't believe I didn't know about him. Didn't want to. Because there's no such thing as coincidence. And, to be fair, this *was* no coincidence. Atkins *had* asked for me to be invited to the conference. Had *insisted* on it. Why? Whoever killed him had deprived me of the opportunity of getting an answer to that and any other question I might think of asking him. Ever.

What a mess.

Acid churning in my stomach, I thought again about asking for a solicitor. But, if I did that, it would mean telling someone else and, for as long as I could, I wanted to keep the awful knowledge here, inside the thick walls of the cell. With both fists, I tugged at my hair.

What a fucking mess.

I kept telling myself that, apart from the DNA test, there was no evidence against me. And that wasn't evidence of anything except that Atkins had had sex on at least one occasion with the woman who'd given birth to me. That he'd known her, though I couldn't imagine how. The woman I recalled wasn't the kind to hang around with professors.

Although, of course, he hadn't always been a professor. All those years ago he'd been a visiting scholar, a young man on an adventure, many thousands of miles from home. Young men went to pubs. As did she. I was almost certainly the result of a one-night stand.

But there had to have been more to it than that. Though she hadn't put his name on my birth certificate, somehow they'd kept in contact.

Or she'd got back in touch with him later. For him to have found me now, she had to have told him about me, and the names of my foster parents. Maybe his reaction to the news had disappointed her. Maybe he'd ignored her letter. It might have been the last straw for her. She'd gone away with the river afterwards. Taken her secret with her to her death.

But *he*'d known. And he'd never come looking for me. Hadn't cared.

I'd found out overnight that he'd made a call to his solicitor on the night of his death. Left a message saying he wanted to talk as soon as he got back. It had meant little at the time. It raised a lot of questions now. Had Atkins intended to change his will? To leave me something? Or was he trying to block my interests, to protect his assets, make sure I couldn't make a claim against his estate?

Either way, he needn't have bothered. I wanted nothing from the man. He'd been a stranger to me until a few hours ago. He was still a stranger as far as I was concerned.

But he hadn't deserved to die.

And the person who'd killed him deserved to be punished.

79

THE DOOR CLANKED OPEN TO REVEAL DETECTIVE Garda Ruth Joyce holding two sandwiches, one cardboard packet in each hand, and a small plastic bottle of water.

'Ham or cheese?' she said.

'I'm vegan,' I said.

'Oh, I …'

'Ham. I'll take ham. That was a joke. Gallows humour, you know?'

She placed the sandwich and water on the end of the concrete bed.

'Tea or coffee?'

'Tea. Black. And a purple Snack. Please.'

'Purple Snack? It's against regulations but I'll see what I can do.'

'It's only a Snack, for God's sake.'

'And it was only a joke. Gallows humour, you know?'

'Touché,' I said.

When she came back with the tea and Snack, I asked, 'Any word on when I'm getting out?'

I wasn't prepared to contemplate the only alternative to getting out.

Which was getting charged.

Ruth Joyce looked over her shoulder, though no one else was there, then said, 'I think it's going to be soon but don't quote me on it. Might change.'

I'd been thinking about calling Tina, letting her know where I was, and asking her to phone my mother. I hadn't made contact with the office since a quick *Late. Not sure what time I'll be in* message sent to Tina and Gabriel just before 6.30 a.m. Now, I stalled. Decided to take a chance on what Ruth Joyce had said.

The bet paid off. The next time the door opened, it was Olly Fogarty. 'You're getting out for now,' he said. 'Bit of paperwork first, though.'

Walking down the steps of the station and along by the river, I phoned my mother. She said, 'I didn't know where you were. I've been ringing and ringing.'

'Something wrong with my phone but it's okay now. I'll be right there.'

I texted Tina and Gabriel, sent the same text to both of them, *Sorry about today. I'll be in tomorrow.* I hoped that was true.

A little further along, I stopped walking. Stopped dead. My hands on the river wall, I held tight to the carved curve of the stone, smooth and rough at the same time. I'd been released because, other than my DNA link to the deceased, whether deliberately concealed or unknown by me until now, they had no evidence against me.

I thought about what Sadie had said, about how I'd withheld information from her in the past. She was right. I *had* withheld

— suppressed — information. I'd done it with her. And with others. With myself too. Tried to delete anything too awkward or uncomfortable to confront. Tried to keep control. Tried to stay safe.

But I didn't feel safe any more.

Before moving on, I checked my phone. Three voicemails from the president asking for an update on the investigation. One text message from Agnes asking for the same. I deleted them. This story wasn't about the president, or the university, or the law school any more.

Walking, I thought again about Atkins. Couldn't avoid him. I remembered a cliché I spout all the time with clients: 'Knowledge is power.' Despite that, I hadn't taken my own advice. The opposite was the place I'd chosen to live my life. Because *not* knowing the truth about my own past had *seemed* safer.

But not knowing the truth was the reason I'd ended up detained in Coughlan's Quay. Now I knew for certain that the truth was my only way through this morass.

Starting with who killed William Atkins.

80

I HOPPED IN A CAB AND WENT STRAIGHT TO THE
Bons. My mother gave me a funny look – excessively casual
clothes for a workday, lack of make-up, dishevelled appearance –
but that was as far as the investigation went. On another occasion,
I wouldn't have got away with it, but she was otherwise engaged
for now. Looking deathly white and completely exhausted, my
dad was sitting up in bed, doing his best to eat a bowl of jelly
and ice-cream.

'Have one more bite,' my mother said. She looked worn out
too.

'I don't think I can.' He gave the nearly full bowl a light
push in the direction of the newspapers, the *Echo* and *Irish
Examiner*, folded neatly on the over-bed tray. Both looked
unread, which told its own story. Normally, my parents were
avid newshounds.

'How was it?' I asked.

'I've been prodded with so many needles I don't know why
I'm not leaking. How are you anyway? Good day?'

He wasn't a complainer. I deduced that the tests had been
awful. I took a while to reply. 'Busy,' I said eventually.

But he was already asleep.

My mother said, 'His heart rate was too low for them to do the scope. He went down but ...'

'Oh, no,' I said.

She went on, 'The nurse said they're bringing in another specialist to look at the blood results. Is that a good or a bad sign, do you think?'

'We can hope that it's good,' I said. 'There's no harm in hoping.'

She got up off the chair and I pulled her into my arms. She buried her head in my shoulder and sobbed. Frozen, I kept my eyes on my father, my real one, willing him to live.

THURSDAY

81

I AWOKE WITH A START AND A SENSE OF DREAD. A door closing. Footsteps receding. Someone was in the house. It took a few moments to remember that I'd come home with my mother the previous night and slept in my childhood room. My parents had repainted it a few years before. The teenage tat and posters were long gone but it felt the same because the books remained, the wall of shelves built by Dad from stair-tread timber. I checked the time. Not yet 7 a.m.

Downstairs, while Mam ironed more pyjamas, I sipped black tea and checked my phone. Echolive and Cork Beo, two local websites, referenced the detention of an unnamed female in connection with the death of Professor Atkins, and her subsequent release without charge. At least there was no mention of a file being sent to the DPP. I wondered how long it would take for the rumour mill to carry the news to MLC that I was the woman in question. I'd have to come clean to Gabriel about it at some point, but not yet.

'I must go to the office,' I said. 'Home first to change.'

'I can drive you,' Mam said.

'No need. I could do with the walk. What time are you going to see him?'

'The night nurse said to wait till ten at least. There might be news by then.'

'You should get some rest.'

'I will,' she said.

'Meaning you won't.'

'Go to work. Is your phone fixed?'

'What? Oh, yeah. Fine now. New battery.'

I hugged Mam and headed down the hill. The way things were at present, there was no question of telling her or Dad what I'd found out the previous day about William Atkins. If I could avoid ever telling them, I would. I didn't even want to think about how I'd do it. For now, I filed it – him – away.

Concentrated on putting one foot in front of the other.

Normally, Tina knew most of what was going on in my life, either because I told her or by some other means, and I didn't rule out osmosis, but this time I left her completely in the dark. As far as she and everyone else at the firm were concerned, I'd spent the previous day at or close to the Bon Secours Hospital. My father's health was the only thing anybody had asked me about. Both Tina and Gabriel had come to my room separately during the morning.

'No news is sometimes good news,' Tina had said.

Gabriel had come out with something similar. 'It's only on television that medics know immediately what's wrong. In real life, accurate diagnosis takes time.'

After each of them had left, I went back to reading my emails, forwarding them to Tina with instructions for follow-up tasks.

Reading emails isn't real legal work, but it has to be done, and it kept me from staring out the window the entire time, and stopped me checking my phone every two minutes.

A waspish email from the president wondering why I hadn't been returning her calls. I sent a reply saying I'd been occupied with a family matter and that I'd revert as soon as I possibly could. Less than a minute later, she rang my phone again. I ended the call without answering. I didn't want her occupying the line.

But there was no news from my mother at the hospital. And, while Dad's health was in such flux, despite my best intentions, I was incapable of progressing the investigation.

When Katja buzzed me from Reception to say that Harry Bennigan, my recently settled divorce client, had dropped in downstairs unexpectedly and was asking for a quick word, I seized the opportunity for distraction, like a famished builder biting into a rasher sandwich.

In the small meeting room, Harry was standing by the round table in a green-hued tweed jacket and mustard-yellow corduroy trousers, the latter a brave sartorial choice for a man of his girth.

He said, 'I won't keep you but I'm looking for a copy of the divorce order, the one from the court office. I didn't get it yet.'

I had already explained to him at the courthouse the previous week after the settlement meeting that he wasn't divorced yet, and that I'd have to apply for a court date.

'But I'll know after next Tuesday,' I said. 'My Notice of Motion is listed before the county registrar then and she'll give us the date at that stage. It won't be too long, don't worry.'

'I'll be there,' he said. 'Just tell me the time and—'

'You don't have to come. I'll call you right after and let you know the ruling day.'

I'd told him that already too but often people don't remember the procedural details. He looked bothered. 'Harry, do you mind if I ask what's the rush? Is there something wrong?'

'Nothing, except I've seen a house in Kinsale that I like and I want to make sure that it's mine and mine only. I'd prefer to have the bit of paper in my hand before I start bidding. Now that things are sorted, I want to get out of that apartment. I've spent too long in there, staring at the four walls. Don't get me wrong, it was a good investment, but it's time to move on from Blackrock, and Rochelle is a desirable location. I'll get a frankly ridiculous rent for it, so it's a win-win, really.'

'You can start bidding on Kinsale,' I said. 'If you take it steadily, you should have the divorce order long before a single thing happens legally with the purchase.'

'Oh, what a *beautiful* day,' Harry said. 'I'd give you a big hug, Finn, only I'd probably get cancelled.'

'Weren't you cancelled years ago?'

'Heh-heh. Too true.' He paused. 'I found out from my youngest who your woman was, by the way.'

'What woman?'

'The one with my ex at the courthouse. The one walking down the steps with her.'

'Oh, I remember.' I did. And that she'd looked familiar, though I couldn't say why.

'Investment adviser. Samantha Fennell. Works for some company out at the airport.'

'Oh, God, you don't mean Lexbonay, do you?'

'I do indeed,' Harry said. 'You *do* know her, then?'

I took a breath. 'No. But I've met the company CEO. A guy called Nathaniel Simpson. From Cork originally. Quite posh. Possibly even posher than you, Harry.'

'Not a city boy or I'd know him. Landed gentry from the county maybe.'

'I reckon so,' I said. 'Went to school in Dublin. St Columba's.'

'We all have our crosses to bear, I suppose.'

Later, upstairs in my office, after I'd found a photograph of Samantha Fennell online, I had surprisingly little trouble recalling where and when I'd seen her before.

And with whom.

82

WHEREVER BÉATRICE MBEMBA WAS, SHE WASN'T in France. When I tried to call her, the ringtone I heard was the double beep used in Ireland and Britain rather than the long single tone of continental Europe. Her voicemail greeting was in French and English. I left a message and sent a text asking her to contact me with precisely zero confidence that she would. She hadn't responded to any of my previous attempts to connect with her.

A trawl of the Panthéon-Assas University website didn't help me pin down her current location. On Twitter, her profile was locked and I couldn't view her LinkedIn page fully because we had no connections in common. After too much time googling, I knew little more than I'd known already: that I'd seen her at UCC on the day of the conference talking to a woman whom I now knew to be Samantha Fennell, an employee of Lexbonay Investments. And that Mbemba had some kind of a problem with Nate Simpson, the Lexbonay CEO. Simpson had told me she'd rejected his advances. Even at the time he'd said it, I hadn't believed that explanation. I was even more certain now. But why had Simpson lied?

I thought about my meeting with him again, how he'd

made sure I hadn't met anyone else working for the company. I'd assumed that was because he hadn't wanted any of them to see him talking to me, but what if it was something else? That he hadn't wanted *me* to meet any of *them*, Samantha Fennell in particular.

I checked the Lexbonay website. Fennell wasn't named or pictured on it, and I could find no direct email address or phone number for her.

I went old-fashioned. Phoned the Lexbonay office. Put on a different accent. Gave a false name.

I said, 'I'm going through a divorce, and I need expert financial advice. I'm told that the person I need to speak to is Samantha Fennell. She's come highly recommended by a friend and—'

The receptionist cut me off. 'Samantha no longer works here, but I can put you through to someone else in that section, if you like.'

'I'll have to think about that.'

I ended the call and sat back in my chair. I was in possession of several important new pieces of information and I still had no idea what was going on. If only I'd paid more attention on the day of the conference. If only I'd listened properly to Mbemba's paper. If I had, I might have found out more about her and her connection to Simpson. All I remembered hearing was that she'd started off by talking about the duty of disclosure – something to do with insurance law? It didn't seem any more riveting now than it had at the time.

I drilled deeper into what I'd *seen*. Béatrice Mbemba and Nate Simpson on the quad at the start of the tour, Simpson whispering something to her, Mbemba pushing him away; and, later, during the drinks reception on the lawn, Simpson standing by the corner of the library, watching someone. Mbemba? Then, during the dinner, she'd gone out to the quad and made a phone call that, clearly, she hadn't wanted anyone to overhear. I tried calling her again. It rang out. This time, I didn't leave a voicemail.

I thought afresh about Professor Casey's argument with Mbemba in the President's Garden, and his refusal to tell me what it was about, other than that it wasn't relevant to the murder investigation. I'd have to talk to Casey again but I wanted to leave it until I knew more.

To have any hope of making progress, I needed to talk to someone else who'd been present on the day of the conference, ideally someone who'd take my calls. I considered Sophie first. Dismissed her for being too involved with Simpson.

Then I thought of someone better.

Senan Dunford was someone I'd intended to contact sooner but, because he hadn't been around for the dinner, I'd relegated him to low priority. I called his number now. He picked up on the first ring. 'Are you psychic?'

'Not last time I checked. This is Finn Fitzp—'

'I know who it is. Sorry, what I meant was, I'm in Cork. I was about to buzz you to cash in on the offer of lunch. That, em, sounds appalling, it's not ... I really *am* sorry and, obviously, I'll pay for my lunch, don't worry, I know you said you'd buy but, I'm making a total mess of this, what I'm trying, very badly, to say is would you like to meet? It—'

Laughing, I said, 'Yes, I'd like to meet and lunch is definitely on me sometime but I don't have time today. I have to, em, I have to do something at lunchtime.' *Visit my dad in the hospital. Talk to the doctor if I can.* 'But I'm free now. We could do coffee, if you like?'

We arranged to meet straight away at the Green Frog on Western Road, diagonally across from the main gate of the college and only a short walk from the Bons. As I made my way there, moving faster than I had in days, I noticed I was smiling and, for a brief interlude, I tried to pretend that the waking nightmare of the past week hadn't happened.

It wasn't so hard to do. None of it felt real anyway.

83

SENAN WAS WAITING OUTSIDE THE CAFÉ WHEN
I arrived, his hands in the pockets of his army-green parka. He
was dressed more casually than he had been on the day of the
conference. He seemed bulkier somehow. Stronger. Better-
looking than I'd remembered. And a little nervous.

'You look different,' I said. 'I'd hardly have known you.'

He smiled. 'That awful suit I had on at the conference, had to
get it for a wedding. Not the kind of thing I wear unless I have
to ... Didn't know where you wanted to sit.'

'Somewhere dry would be good. I felt drops. I think it's about
to start again.'

At the counter, he ordered a sausage roll and coffee, and I asked
for black coffee. He insisted on paying. I didn't bother to argue
the point, sensing that he was still embarrassed after the phone
call earlier. I chose a table down the back where it was quiet.

'Good to see you again,' I said. I was surprised how much I
meant it.

'Likewise,' he said. He smiled. 'You're, ah, probably
wondering why I'm here.'

I smiled too. 'It *had* crossed my mind.'

He spoke quickly. 'It's because I had to go to the garda station
in Coughlan's Quay to give a DNA sample. For elimination

purposes only. Obviously. They know I was gone back to
Limerick hours before the murder happened, but I was in his –
the victim's – company during the day, and we were up in the
gallery together, so that was why they said it was needed. In
fairness to them, they said I could do it at home, that a guard
could call to my house, but I was happy to come here. They said
it would be good if I did, that it would save time. And whatever
helps, you know. It was an awful thing to happen, like …'

He trailed off, looked down at his plate. After a moment, he
picked up his sausage roll, dipped it into a ramekin filled with
ketchup, and took a large bite. When he'd finished chewing, he
said, 'On the road crazy early. Starving.'

'Do you live in Limerick city?'

'Yeah,' he said. 'Do you know Limerick?' He took another
bite, a smaller one.

'Hardly at all,' I said. 'I've been to the prison a few times to
see clients.'

He seemed to choke and I realised he was laughing.

'I don't live *there*. Though at times it feels like it. I live at
home. It's grand like. I'm grateful for it. But I'm too old to have
my mother doing my laundry.'

'Are you far from the university?'

'Not far, no,' he said. 'We're near enough to Castletroy. Ah,
do you mind …?'

'Work away,' I said.

He ate. I was glad of the break in conversation. What he'd
said about the DNA test and his trip to Coughlan's Quay had
wrenched me back to reality. I didn't think the guards would
have said anything to him about my blood relationship with
Atkins, but they must have asked him about me, about what he'd
seen of me that day. Or maybe they hadn't. He didn't seem to be

looking at me strangely, though I couldn't tell for sure. I didn't really know the man.

But what I knew I liked, including the thing he'd said about wanting to help the investigation. As he ate, I told him about my role, how I'd been engaged by the president and given a temporary office in the Horgan Building. He didn't seem surprised by anything I was saying and it occurred to me that he'd almost certainly been talking to Agnes since the murder. I omitted to tell him I no longer trusted the president's motives for appointing me, and about her being married to Agnes; and nothing on earth would have persuaded me to tell him about my arrest. Instead, I stuck to firm ground: the questions I had about the day of the conference, in particular anything that had happened while I was missing during lunch and the afternoon. I kept it general to start with. The more I talked, the more he seemed to relax, though it might have been less to do with my talking and more the relief of getting food inside him.

'I left to go to the courthouse just before lunchtime. Tell me what went on. Who was talking to whom, where people were sitting, that kind of thing.'

He led me through the meander across campus and the arrival at the staff restaurant. 'It wasn't one big table, there were a few small ones set aside for the conference speakers. Initially, there was a vacant spot beside Will Atkins, and Agnes was rushing around the place looking for you because she'd put you beside him in the seating plan, but I told her you'd snuck off. I remember her being annoyed or, well, she *looked* annoyed, at least.'

'So who sat beside him instead?'

'She moved him to a bigger table, a combined table with—'

'Hang on, it was a table for *two* that I was supposed to have been at?'

'No, it was for three. It would have been you, Agnes and Will Atkins.'

'Okay. She never told me that was what she had planned.'

Even though she'd had every opportunity.

'Would it have made a difference?'

It might have. If I'd known, I might have said something to Atkins. Made other arrangements to talk to him. We could've skipped the tour. Talked instead, maybe.

'No,' I said. 'I had to go to work. Couldn't get out of it.'

'So, anyway, Will Atkins ended up sitting with the ever-uncharming Professor Casey, Sophie, Agnes, Simpson the sponsor and UCC Law's starry ex-student Cormac Ryan.'

A vinegary tang to his words. Understandable in his precarious position.

'Where were you?'

'I was at the other table with Kirsty MacMillan, Padraic O'Flaherty, Béatrice Mbemba and a few master's and PhD students.'

'And the president?'

'Not there. I didn't see her all day. Not till the Pimm's fiasco on the lawn.'

'Where was Lia de Barra sitting?'

'Didn't make an appearance at the conference until the tour of the Horgan Building, I think.'

I thought about that. She'd come late and, according to herself, was the first to leave the dinner. Minimal involvement with the events of the day. A deliberate choice on her part, presumably. Was that inconsistent behaviour for a gloryhound like Lia de Barra? Then I remembered. 'That's not right, actually. I saw her in the Aula during Atkins's speech. She was in the back row … Did you notice her talking to Atkins at any point?'

'I can't say that I did.'

'Me neither,' I said.

'Do you think it's significant?'

'I think it's a little strange, but she's kind of an odd fish, isn't she?'

'I suppose,' he said. He looked puzzled. 'You don't think …?'

'I don't know. Her reactions have seemed off to me. That might be her personality, or a response to the murder. I didn't really know her before this so I can't compare.' I went on, 'Did you hear about the argument on the lawn between Dr Mbemba and your nemesis Prof Casey? You were gone by the time that happened.'

He smothered a smile. 'Agnes told me.'

His response made me wonder what else she'd told him and if he knew about her marriage, though I was still no further along with trying to figure out the significance of that, or why she and the president had felt the need for secrecy. I didn't ask Senan about it because I'd promised Matthew Cameron I'd keep what he'd told me confidential. Besides which, knowing a secret is more valuable than disclosing it at the wrong time.

I said, 'Nobody's saying what the row was about. I know you'd left, but did you overhear anything earlier in the day that might give a hint as to the genesis of it?'

His face broke into a broad grin. 'Isn't it obvious?'

'Well, no, otherwise I wouldn't be asking.'

'It's what she said in her paper.'

'I wasn't actually listening. Something about disclosure. Insurance law, maybe?'

'It started off about the relationship between a moral obligation to be honest and a legal duty to disclose information.

She talked about that for a bit, then took a detour into academic independence. She's dead set against commercial sponsorship of any kind. She spoke about preserving the purity of legal thought, referencing the theme of the conference and the struggle to keep standards high despite the post-truth world, et cetera. All of which was mildly hilarious considering Casey had spent about twelve hours during his never-ending opening remarks extolling the virtues of Lexbonay and Nate Simpson who, according to Agnes, had splashed out a small fortune on the conference without even asking what the topic was.'

'A small fortune that included Mbemba's plane fare, presumably,' I said.

'Jeez, you really *weren't* listening to a single word, were you? There *was* no plane fare. She's not in Paris this semester, she's in Dublin, a visiting scholar at King's Inns. As was mentioned by Agnes in her introduction of her.'

Which explained the ringtone and the bilingual message on her voice mailbox. 'Did Mbemba talk specifically about Lexbonay?'

'No, she didn't mention them by name but it's hard not to think that they and companies like them were who she was indirectly talking about. I was amazed that no one took her up on what she'd said during the Q and A, but they didn't. Fair dos to Agnes. It was brave to invite her, considering how in thrall universities are to business, these days.'

'I should have been listening,' I said. 'I feel a bit stupid now.'

He laughed. Not unkindly. 'Never,' he said. Reaching across the table, he patted the back of my hand gently. 'There, there,' he said.

After he took his hand away again, I felt stone cold.

Which might have been why, when he asked me a while later if I'd like to go for dinner sometime, I found myself agreeing, even though the way my life had been going, dating anyone, let alone a soon-to-be jobless younger man, however attractive he'd turned out to be, had seemed impossible until about five minutes previously.

I parted from Senan at the side door of the café and headed west, resolving at first to make an as yet unascertained excuse the next time he made contact, then immediately changing my mind, going back and forth as I walked, eventually swinging more in the direction of yes. It was only dinner I'd said yes to. I might even enjoy myself. And it was a change. He wasn't Davy.

Walking on, I thought back on what Senan had said about the seating arrangements at the conference lunch. A table for three: Atkins, Agnes and me. Not a table for two.

Maybe he'd just wanted to see me up close, to get the measure of me. If he hadn't been killed, I might never have known who he was to me. Now, inescapably, and because of an act of brutality, I knew that I carried his DNA within me, but I could never find out more than that bare fact. I would never be able to ask him how he'd met my birth mother.

To my left, black cast-iron railings loomed high above my head, forming the lower external boundary of the main campus. Inside them lay the meadow where the annual spectacular wildflower display would bloom again when summer came. If it ever did.

84

I TOOK THE BACK WAY INTO THE BONS FROM
Western Road, intending it to be a shortcut, but had to circle
around by the service route to the main door, ignoring the no-
through-traffic signs, on finding that the entrance I'd hoped
to use required a security pass. What had been drizzle had
metamorphosed into a downpour. It streamed like tears on
my face and ran down the hill in rivulets as I went in the other
direction. I had no umbrella with me and feared for the phone
and laptop I was carrying in my shoulder bag, shielding it as best
I could with my raincoat.

By the time I reached my father's room, after leaving my
dripping coat on a hook in the corridor and drying myself off
with paper towels in the bathroom, I found my mother alone in
an armchair having a cup of tea and a slice of white toast from a
tray. She was facing in the direction of the television, which was
turned on with the volume low. She looked deep in thought but
smiled when she saw me. She seemed brighter.

'One of the girls gave me this,' she said. 'I'm sure they'd—'

'I'm grand,' I said. 'Where is he?'

'They're checking his heart again.'

'Is it to see if they can do the scope? If his heart-rate has gone back up?'

'They've decided they're not going to do the scope now at all.'

'Why not? Were you talking to the doctor?'

'No, but the nurse says he's improved. She says he's stable now.'

'What does that actually *mean*?'

'They're talking about releasing him tomorrow.'

'*What?* He's only been in for three days. Not even that.'

'Tomorrow's Friday. They say he's well enough to go home for the weekend.'

'They probably just want him gone. All hospitals clear patients on a Friday. But he's *not* well enough. What if something happens to him?'

'I think he *is* a tiny bit stronger, and even if he's not, at least he's not worse. He'll do better in his own bed. I know he will. And he wants to come home himself.'

'I'm sure that last bit is true. But is it wise, Mam? Ask yourself that.'

She pressed her lips into a line. 'Whether it's wise or not, it's happening.'

I looked around for his chart but it had gone with him, wherever he was. 'I'm going to ask for more information. There has to be *some*one in charge.'

'*I'm* in charge. He's *my* husband. They've prescribed a new tablet for him, and he's promised to take it and that's great progress. You know what he's like. He'll be back here for an outpatients' check-up next week. And that's that.'

Further resistance was futile. I'd been outflanked and outwitted. I plucked a pink iced caramel from an open packet on the bedside locker and popped it into my mouth. Flopping onto the bed, I opened Google on my phone and said, 'Tell me the name of the new pill.'

85

I LEFT MY PARENTS AT THE BONS, MY STOMACH A swirling pool of anxiety. Whatever infinitesimal improvement my mother had noticed in my dad, I'd seen none. When he'd arrived back to his room after the cardiac tests, he looked completely done in, but so happy at the prospect of being let out of jail the following day that I bit my tongue and smiled with him as best I could.

Struggling eastwards along College Road beneath a low gunmetal sky, I gave myself the advice I'd give anyone else: 'Trust that the doctors know what they're doing.' But the trouble with being a member of one of the other professions is that I know the truth from the inside. Nobody knows everything. However impressive someone's qualifications are, a lot of the time people are making it up as they go along.

On reaching the main vehicle entrance for the university, I remembered what Kasper Nowak had said: that the security staff were responsible for the cameras but Buildings and Estates took care of other maintenance issues. Had a report been made to Buildings and Estates about the broken locks in the East Wing? It was something the gardaí would surely have checked but I wasn't going to be getting any more back-channel information from Sadie on this investigation. She hadn't even sent me a text message since my release, and I'd been too afraid to contact her. And too angry. She'd allowed me to be arrested and, even worse, she hadn't believed me.

The irony of the situation in which I found myself struck me hard. I'd been engaged to investigate the murder of William Atkins. I'd thought I'd chosen to accept the job. Now it felt a lot more like the job had chosen me. And that I'd run out of options. That unless I could find the real killer, I'd always have a giant question mark hanging over my head.

I turned off College Road onto the campus. The Buildings and Estates office was just inside the gate. I took the footpath to the right and made my way to the door. Even if I learned nothing new there, at least it would be dry inside.

The sensible-looking woman in the office at the front of the building told me there was a running-repairs spreadsheet somewhere and that if I sent an email to the right person they'd definitely be able to give me the information I needed but, as that particular person wasn't back until Monday, in the circumstances I'd probably be as well off talking to the lads themselves – she was nearly sure she'd seen one of them passing not five minutes previously. She got up from her desk and pointed me towards the rear of the building.

'The inner sanctum is back there, second door on the left,' she said.

I followed her instructions and found a man tipping retirement age, a set of rain-soaked yellow oilskins, a fan heater turned up to the max, a recently boiled kettle, a small red Formica-topped table, a few kitchen chairs and a packet of chocolate Hobnobs. The man was sitting on one of the chairs. He looked up at me with interest. He asked, 'Who have we here?'

I told him.

Immediately, he got up from his chair and flicked on the kettle. 'Tea or tea?'

I laughed. 'Tea, please. Black, no sugar.'

'Sit down there now and I'll talk to you.'

I took off my coat and hung it on a hook, the oilskins reminding me of my father again, the late-night homecomings after life-threatening storm repairs, the joy of seeing him safe by the fire, my mother drying his hair with a towel. My eyes brimming, I pulled a chair beside the fan heater. I bent to warm my hands, regained my composure after a few quick breaths. The man handed me my tea.

'I'm Seamus, by the way,' he said. 'I heard about you being around the place asking questions. I was wondering if you'd come here. People forget about us, you know, but they shouldn't. This place would fall down without us.'

I asked him about the broken locks, if a report had come in.

'No,' he said. 'And I'm definite about it. There was no report.'

'So what does that mean?'

'It means that either there was a vandal going around independently breaking half the locks in the East Wing, which is possible, or it has some connection to the murder.'

'That's what I thought too. And it was just the door to the gallery and the one between the East Wing and the Aula?'

'Just those two. The locks that were broken were internal so nobody would have noticed them, not for a while anyway. We did get one report, though. On the Friday.'

'The day before the murder was discovered? What kind of report?'

'It was about the light in the East Wing supply cupboard. Used by the cleaning staff. The light in the cupboard wasn't working because the bulb had been removed, and the casing for it loosened too. It was a bit unusual. Normally if a bulb goes, it's left there until it's replaced. No one bothers to take it out. Which isn't to say that someone wouldn't, mind you. All the same, I told the guards but whether it's relevant or not, I don't know.'

I said, 'I don't know either.'

'Have a Hobnob,' Seamus said. 'They say your man Sherlock Holmes was a demon for them altogether.'

I sat with him for another while, drinking tea and munching biscuits, as the rain beat against the window and the world outside fell away.

86

I'D KEPT MISSING PROFESSOR KIRSTY MACMILLAN
every time I'd tried to talk to her, and vice versa. When her
name flashed up on my phone screen, I made sure I took the call
this time.

'Two seconds, please, Kirsty.' I ducked out of the driving
rain and into the lobby of the Horgan Building, striding swiftly
across the scales-of-justice mosaic. I wanted to be in the privacy
of my cubbyhole office before asking any questions of her. The
fact remained, I didn't know who I could trust in this place. 'It's
lashing down here. What's it like in sunny Belfast?'

She laughed. 'I don't think I've ever heard the words "sunny"
and "Belfast" in the same sentence before. Och, I suppose it's not
too bad today.'

'That's good.' I'd reached my room and, with a struggle
because the key was stiff, heaved the door open. I kicked it shut
behind me and snapped on the light, an ancient fluorescent tube
that sputtered alive and banished the murk. I sat on the desk, my
legs swinging.

Kirsty said, 'You're a hard woman to get a hold of.'

I might have said the same, but didn't. 'I'm sorry about that.

I've been wanting to ask about the aftermath of the dinner and the walk back to the hotel.'

Kirsty said, 'In the words of the bard, "And thereby hangs a tale."'

'What do you mean?'

'Put it this way, Finn, I was glad I'd worn comfortable shoes.'

'Always a good idea, I guess?'

'Especially when they give you an alibi.'

87

SHE WENT ON, 'AT THE TIME, WE THOUGHT WE
were doing our good deed for the night *and* the following day,
the entire month, in fact.'

'When you say "we"?'

'Padraic O'Flaherty and I. We walked Martin Casey home.
As you saw at dinner, he was very much the worse for wear, but
when the fresh air hit him, well, it was goodnight Vienna. He
was in bad shape. We lingered on the quad for a good amount
of time, hoping he'd sober up, but it wasn't happening. We
eventually got it out of him where he lived and accompanied
him there. We had thought about hailing a taxi but ultimately
decided it was safer to take him ourselves.'

'That was very good of ye. But you're not from Cork – did he
give you directions?'

'Hah! As if. No. Padraic mapped a route on his phone and
by the time we got to the North Mall, Casey had sobered up a
wee bit and was able to find his front door. We went into the
flat with him, put him sitting in an armchair with a blanket over
him. Didn't want to chance laying him down in case he vomited.
Between everything, it was after one thirty a.m. by the time we
got back to the hotel.'

Casey had told me none of this. Even if he remembered, he had presumably been too ashamed. 'So that rules out the three of you as regards the murder.'

'Aye. While we were on a late-night ramble around Cork, and complaining bitterly about it, I might add, Will Atkins was dying. It's awful, just awful.'

'You knew Professor Atkins from before?'

'Socially, yes. I'd met him many times at conferences in various locations. He was the ultimate extrovert. Would've done well in politics, I'd say.'

'No dark sides, then?'

It took her a while to reply. 'I hesitate to speak ill of the dead.'

I waited.

She went on, 'The womanising. There was *always* a new girlfriend and numerous brief dalliances. Never any suggestion of undue influence. If anything, the women were the ones doing the chasing. Glamorous, usually. His own age or close to it. He told me he preferred older women. He said, "Once the burden of reproduction is removed, it's just good clean fun."'

From nowhere, I felt a bubble of anger. 'Did he not like children, then?'

'He loved other people's. Never wanted his own. He was an old goat. A charming one, admittedly. And maybe I'm being a prude, and ageist, but I'm almost sixty and he was sixty something, and beyond a certain age, I think that kind of thing becomes grubby, no matter how willing the participants. Even rock stars settle down eventually. You do have to wonder what it was all about, a deep-seated insecurity, maybe, that urge always to be on lookout round the next corner for someone new.'

She didn't know about his illness, clearly. 'Did he have a current partner?'

'I *did* ask. He said no. I said I was sure it wouldn't be long. He laughed. We both did.'

'Do you have any idea why anyone would want to kill him?'

'No. It's incredible that *this* was how he died.'

I wanted to ask if she'd been one of his 'brief dalliances' but didn't know how.

She said, 'You've probably heard.'

I didn't respond.

She said, 'I can tell that you have.'

Winging it, I asked, 'Could you give me your side of the story?'

'We were both single. It was a holiday romance. I was never going to move to Australia permanently and Will was never going to move over here.'

'When did it happen?'

'Ten, twelve years ago. I was in Sydney for a semester, met Will – he was based in Melbourne, as you know, and he said to call him if I was visiting the city. Which I did. And one thing led to another. We spent a lot of time together but it came to a natural end. And whatever you may have heard, I *never* bore a grudge against him. The opposite, actually …'

Afterwards, I fired up my laptop and fast-forwarded through the CCTV files that Kasper Nowak had given me. Now that I knew what I was looking for, it was easier to see. As Rory Donnelly the security guard had said, Kirsty with her voluminous pashmina,

Padraic O'Flaherty and Martin Casey in a huddle together on the quad. But he'd been wrong in one of the details. It wasn't Kirsty and Padraic with their arms around each other, it was them with their arms around Casey. Holding him up, it looked like.

I reversed the tape to find the point at which the guests had exited the East Wing. Cormac Ryan first, walking off quickly; a little later Kirsty, followed unsteadily by Casey and, immediately afterwards, Padraic O'Flaherty. A break, then Nate Simpson and Agnes, and a few minutes after that Béatrice Mbemba, who moved away immediately and left the quad via the main arch. Agnes lingered, talking to Nate Simpson, who then went to talk to Kirsty MacMillan and Padraic O'Flaherty before leaving the quad and heading in a southerly direction towards the library and, presumably, the Hayfield Manor Hotel. Just before that, Agnes got a message on her phone, went back into the East Wing and reappeared some minutes later, coming around the library end of the East Wing, at which point she went to speak to Kirsty and Padraic.

Missing entirely from the quad were Lia de Barra, who'd said she was the first after me to leave, and that she'd gone out the back door of the Aula Maxima; Sophie, who'd told me she'd used the door to the President's Garden; the president, who said she'd done likewise; the three members of the catering staff; Ian McAnespie, whom I'd seen entering the East Wing as I was leaving; and, as I'd seen when I'd viewed the video before, William Atkins was absent too, as if he'd never been anywhere near the place.

I could hear Kirsty MacMillan's words ringing in my ears, 'It's awful, just awful,' and, for a time after I closed the video file and shut the laptop, I couldn't make the words stop.

And what she'd said about Atkins loving other people's children, and never wanting his own, it shouldn't have mattered to me. It wasn't new information. His solicitor had told me much the same thing over the phone from Melbourne. It hadn't bothered me then.

But that had been before I'd known. Before I'd found out the DNA results. Hearing it again, it *did* matter to me. Somehow, for some reason, it did.

When the next call came, I answered it gratefully, but I can't blame anyone except myself for what happened after that.

88

THOUGH I'LL BLAME THE RAIN A LITTLE, IF YOU'LL let me.

He'd said that he'd phone and he did. I shouldn't have answered but I did. When I told him where I was, and when he said that he'd finished work for the day and that he was free for the evening, and that he'd collect and drop me home, well, after the drenching I'd had earlier, it would have been foolhardy to refuse.

And when I got into the car, and when his hand brushed against mine, leaving a trail of electrical sparks, and when he leaned across to kiss me chastely on the cheek, leaving a burn mark, I didn't say no.

And when I suggested coffee, he didn't say yes or no, but parked the car tidily on Barrack Street and followed me to my bed without a word.

But I said something. I said, 'This doesn't have to mean anything.'

Even though I knew that it did.

FRIDAY

89

DAVY DIDN'T STAY THE NIGHT. AROUND TEN
o'clock I asked him to leave.

He said, 'Are you *sure* that's what you want?'

I glimpsed a flash of something in his eyes that I read as
triumph. Because, despite everything, I'd come crawling back.
For a second, I hated him again.

'Totally,' I said.

'Whatever you want,' he said, his words compliant, his tone
anything but.

He dressed agonisingly slowly and went quietly, his departing
feet like half-heard rumours. Left alone to cope with the long,
painful slide off the high moral ground, I changed the sheets.
Had a shower. Went back to bed. Did my best to ignore the
ghost on the other pillow.

And, the fresh linen cool against my skin, I slept well for the
first time in what felt like for ever. I'd thought that the shame
would keep me awake but it didn't. It might even have helped.
Gave me something fresh to ruminate on.

I woke early and forced myself to put both feet on the floor.
A deep sigh. Another. Standing before I made it to three. Pulling
up the blind to let in the dawn and, in half a dream, donning

black tights and one of my better black dresses, and make-up, including lipstick, despite the nearly overwhelming urge to stay in pyjamas, never leave the house again.

Dragging my mind back to the Atkins case. For any number of reasons, the stakes were a lot higher for me than they'd been at the start, but that was what it was still. A case. A job. I made myself focus on that.

Downstairs in my office, I got to work. It was 6.53 a.m. Too early to phone or text anyone. My first task was to corroborate what Kirsty MacMillan had told me the previous afternoon and get some extra information I'd forgotten to ask her. For that, I needed to talk to Padraic O'Flaherty. With my dad getting out of hospital later, and everything else I had on, a trip to Galway to see Padraic in person was impossible. I sent an email, asking him to contact me. To my surprise, he replied immediately by FaceTime. I took the call.

'You're an early bird.'

'Likewise. Was Kirsty talking to you since our chat yesterday?'

'She sent me a WhatsApp. Are you always at work by this time?'

'Up often, but not fully awake usually.'

'You still at home?'

I angled the phone in such a way as to hide as much of the mess as I could. Someday I really *was* going to hang those pictures and drop the multiple black plastic sacks of long-forgotten stuff to the charity shop. 'Yes, but my room at the firm isn't much better.'

He laughed. I asked him to take me through what had happened after the dinner. He backed up what Kirsty had said in every respect but I was more interested in what came next.

'Did you see anyone at the hotel when you returned at one thirty a.m.?'

'I went up to bed. We both did. Separately. Obviously.' He laughed again. 'We're the best of friends but nothing more.' Suddenly serious, he went on, 'She was my PhD supervisor. There was never anything between us. Nothing whatsoever. Not *every*one in academia is as ethical as Kirsty.'

He was either telling the truth or protesting innocence too strenuously.

'Would you like to expand on that comment?'

'Not particularly. I was speaking generally. It has nothing to do with the murder.'

Any other time, I'd have been straight in with a follow-up question, but I wanted to move on from the apparently eventful love lives of academics. I'd heard more than enough on that theme from Kirsty MacMillan the previous evening. I chose to accept what Padraic had said.

I asked, 'Can you tell me about the next morning?'

'There are few things in life I enjoy more than a hotel breakfast buffet so I went down around nine a.m. I noticed Béatrice Mbemba at the far side of the room. She had a table in the corner overlooking the river. She was obviously working. She had her laptop open and was typing. Hard at it. I didn't want to disturb her so I left her to it and settled down with my complimentary *Irish Times*, *Irish Examiner* and the full Irish. Two fried eggs. Pure bliss.'

'Did she see you, give you a wave?'

'I don't think so. She looked deep in thought. She was frowning. I suppose she'd had a rough day at the conference so ...'

'You mean the argument with Martin Casey?'

'Yes.'

'Did Prof Casey say anything about that on the walk home?'

'No, he just kept going on and on about his wife, how he couldn't bear being in the house any more, how he'd had to move into the flat and all. He's devastated. Drinking like a fish and not just that one night, I reckon. He kept asking why it had to happen. Though she'd been sick for years, I gather. Maybe he's grieving that lost time too. Kirsty knew him years ago. She said he's changed.'

'That's right,' I said. 'He taught me. He's not the same man I remember. Getting back to Dr Mbemba, did you talk to her at any point? At the hotel, I mean.'

'No, but I did see her later when I went to check out, in the seating area by the reception desk. She was talking to a woman I didn't know and they had some papers and two laptops open on the table in front of them. I wondered if they were working together on a book or an article, maybe. Béatrice is big on ethics, the area of ethics, academically speaking. That's what her work's about.'

'Could you describe the woman she was talking to?'

When he did, it sounded like she'd been meeting Samantha Fennell, the investment adviser who no longer worked for Lexbonay. I showed him her picture and he confirmed it. I ended the call and sent another text message to Mbemba. For once, I was confident that she'd reply, even though I didn't know what I'd say when she did. In the message, I'd said, *I know about*

Lexbonay. In truth, I didn't. But I had my suspicions. And they were getting stronger by the minute.

Later, after I'd noticed that Padraic O'Flaherty was now following me on Instagram and I'd followed him back, I wondered if I should have asked him about William Atkins, and if he'd known about the womanising, and about Atkins's affair with Kirsty.

But I couldn't face it. Instead of calling Padraic back, I dug around and found Senan Dunford's profile. I started following him and he reciprocated, sending me a private message a few minutes after saying that he was looking forward to meeting again soon.

I replied, *Me as well*, adding an *x* in a second message.

I let out a breath and told myself that the night with Davy had been a one-time regression. That it would be easily forgotten.

Soon it would be almost as if it had never happened.

90

I TYPED UP A SHORT NOTE MARKED 'OBSERVATIONS' in bullet points and was halfway through a longer list ('Next Steps' – on number five: 'Talk to Sophie again. Also Nate Simpson, if poss') when a text message from Ciara Boyle came through: *I found that address. Do you still need it?*

Going after Ian McAnespie meant shelving my investigations into Lexbonay for now, but it was still before 8 a.m., probably the middle of the night by his standards, and such a good opportunity might not come again. Also, it gave me another excuse not to reply to the president's latest text message. It arrived as I was leaving the house: *Please provide an update without further delay.*

I replied, *Sorry, just off to interview an important witness.*

She responded immediately, *What on earth is going on? You're clearly avoiding me and I don't understand why. Apart from being highly unprofessional, this was *not* the deal.*

I couldn't disagree. I was going to have to meet up with her. Broach what I knew about their marital status and, by right, tell her about my arrest. The trouble was, once I did that, I'd be officially off the case. I'd have to be. I could still carry on my investigation by myself but, without the president's imprimatur, and without Sadie's input, my progress would be minimal.

I just needed a little more time. I replied, *Sorry again, talk later, I promise.*

I meant it.

But I didn't know what was coming.

91

TWENTY MINUTES LATER, ACROSS THE ROAD FROM the Capwell bus depot on Summerhill South, I was standing outside a once-fine Victorian red-brick. Black paint flaked from the front door revealing generations of gloss in various colours underneath. I knocked on the door and got no response so I hammered on it, using the side of my clenched fist. There was still no response. I stepped back and looked up. A flicker of movement behind a filthy net curtain on the second floor. 'Open up, Ian. I just want to talk.'

Silence.

'Open the door, Ian, or I swear to you I'm calling the cops.'

As if. I'd had enough of them for a while.

A shout. 'What do you want?'

I waved my phone above my head. 'Last chance.'

'Do what you like. I've nothing to hide.'

'Why have you been ignoring my calls?'

Ironic, considering the text conversation I'd just had with the president.

'Because … Fuck sake. I'll come down.'

McAnespie directed me into what had been a formal dining room. A scratched mahogany table and a few mismatched chairs were all that remained. I waited for him to finish putting on a dirty vest over his low-slung grey trackie bottoms. He was barefoot and milk white, with unwashed hair and sparse stubble. As a third-year student, he must have been twenty-one or -two, but he looked about seventeen. In a few short years, if he got through the Law Society entrance examinations, he'd be working in a law firm, advising clients. A few years after that, he'd be climbing the ladder towards partnership. Or struck off the roll.

I took a seat at the head of the table. 'Sit,' I said, pointing at the chair beside mine. He sat. I asked, 'Do you pay rent for this place?'

'I can't afford rent. I'm sort of minding the house for someone. It's going to be sold once the title problem is fixed. A court application is needed. Listed for July.'

'Lease too short, maybe. They probably need to buy out the freehold.'

'That's it, yeah.'

'You're not "occupying" it so?'

'No.'

'Does the person you're minding it for know you're here?'

'Let's just say that I'm altruistically protecting his fleapit from burglars.'

'Who owns it?'

'My uncle. Why are you here?'

'To ask a few questions. First, I believe you work at Hayfield Manor.'

'The hotel? What has that to do …? Anyway, no. Not any

more. Haven't been inside the door in a year, maybe. Is that all you wanted to ask?'

'How did you end up getting the conference job?'

'There was another guy filming officially, from the university's audio-visual service. You probably saw him. The guy in the suit. But he left at five p.m. when the conference was over. My job was to do more spontaneous stuff. For social media. And to show the film about the university before dinner. Which didn't happen because of the fight on the lawn, obviously. Anyway, you wanted to know how I got the job. The answer is, Agnes asked me.'

'Did she ask or did you offer?'

He sighed. 'I offered. Begged might be more accurate. I have the equipment. Well, the Film Society does. I suggested uploading bite-size live video pieces to Instagram and Twitter. And I suggested showing a film before dinner too.'

'Were you the person in charge of the social media?'

'No, Sophie was. I sent my clips to her. She only used a few but they made an impact, in my humble opinion. More artistic than the usual corporate stuff.'

'Why did you want the job?'

'I needed the money. I have debts. An investment gone wrong.'

'What kind of investment?'

'None of your business but it wasn't drugs, I swear.'

'How much did you get paid for the day?'

'Two fifty.'

'Did that pay off your debts?'

'Nowhere near.'

'Not really worth it so?'

He shrugged. 'Every little helps.'

'What kind of investment was it? Because I *am* thinking drugs, Ian, and you're not a client of mine so I don't owe you any duty of—'

'It was a crypto thing. A sure bet that ended up being a pile of crap.'

'So you lost money on cryptocurrency. Had you borrowed to fund it?'

'No, actually. I used the money my parents gave me for living expenses. They do a big lodgement at the start of each semester. I got into the habit of using it for various little projects. Shares. Other things. Buying and selling. Then I got into crypto. All going great. Money for nothing, like. The problem is, I recommended the, ah, investment to someone and he lost too and blamed me. Told me he'd kill me. He was *very* fucking convincing, I can tell you.'

'He?'

'The chef. Davide Rossi.'

92

'HOW DID YOU GET TO KNOW HIM? WAS HE A student?'

'No, he's over here working. I met him around the place.'

'Around what place?'

'College. He was giving private lessons in Italian and then he got a few hours tutoring temporarily in the Italian Department when one of the regulars was on sick leave. He was doing the cheffing with Nibblz part-time too. He told me he was having to do more of that kind of work because of his own debts. He said he was in even more trouble than me.'

'What do you mean?'

'His story was that he told people back home in Italy. About the crypto. Not very nice people, he said. The whole thing was a shit show. I ended up as Davide's indentured servant or something. Working all the hours to make money. You were complaining that I wasn't replying to your messages. I didn't have *time*. That conference gig was only the tip of the iceberg. I have a weekend job going around the country stock-taking convenience stores. I get picked up in town at six a.m. on a Saturday and dropped back late in the afternoon. Same thing on a Sunday. And in between that, I've had final-year lectures, more than half of which I've missed so fuck knows how I'm going to pass my exams, and I've been doing fucking Deliveroo up the wazoo as well. Even the night of the conference, I had to do it.'

'Tell me about that.'

'When the video show was cancelled, Davide called me into the kitchen and told me I had time to do a few Deliveroos. And I don't have an electric bike either. It's all *me* doing the work, your friendly zero-hours contract exploitation-style gobshite. So I logged in. Made myself available. That was why I was so late picking up the tech equipment that night. I had to come back and give Davide my cash tips, then turn around and clear the camera, the video screen and the projector out of the Aula Max.'

'But you were in the East Wing corridor. As I was leaving, I saw you through the window. What were you doing there when you're telling me now that you were supposedly taking equipment out of the Aula?'

'I'd left the fucking equipment in the Aula Max earlier on. When you saw me in the East Wing corridor, I was going for a piss, all right? Is that allowed?'

'Em, yeah,' I said.

I took a breath, thought through what he'd told me, analysed it to see if it fitted what Ciara Boyle and Magda Kozlowska had said. Unlikely as it seemed, it did. Both of them had told me that McAnespie and Davide Rossi knew each other. Ciara had said Rossi had asked her to send in McAnespie to talk to him. Magda had said she'd seen McAnespie pass something small, hand to hand, to Rossi. She hadn't said anything to either of them at the time, but she'd told me she wouldn't be calling Davide Rossi for work again. After what Sadie had said about McAnespie's

MDMA history, like Magda, I'd assumed it was drugs. I still wasn't sure that it wasn't.

'This money that Davide owes in Italy, how does he pay it?'

'I don't know. Occasionally, he's made me do a Western Union transfer direct.'

'Where do you do that?'

'The internet café on Winthrop Street.'

'Does he give you an account number and you—'

'He wouldn't be so trusting! No, he comes with me. Watches me do it. The last time was the Saturday after the conference. Agnes had paid me for my Wednesday conference work, the money hit my account on the Friday, and I met him the next day to do the payment.'

'What does he look like?'

He described the man I'd seen him with, and put his identity beyond doubt when he showed me a photograph of him on Davide Rossi's Instagram profile: @perfectitaliancork. I'd searched for him online previously. With that profile name, it was no surprise that I hadn't found him.

Then McAnespie said, 'I've been doing all the talking and you've been saying nothing. Do you believe me?'

I took in a breath. 'Yeah, Ian, much to my surprise, I do.'

He got to his feet. 'Great. I have study to do. Did I happen to mention that I've final exams coming up?'

'And I've got a few more questions.'

'Five minutes is what you've got. Then I'm going back to bed. Which, by the way, is where I study. Because it's comfortable. Plus it's the only warm spot in this place. It's impossible to get a seat in the library this time of year unless you're up at six or something.'

'Take me through your time in the East Wing that Wednesday.'

'I've already done this with the guards.'

'I'm here and I'm going nowhere so do us both a favour. Talk. Now.'

'Jesus Christ, okay, don't get your knickers in a fucking twist, eh?' He went on, 'I was waiting for the drinks thing to finish. I'd set up the film in the President's Dining Room. You were there. We were looking out the door at World War 3 on the lawn. The film was cancelled. Every cloud and all that. But then Davide gets Ciara to call me into the kitchen and that's when he tells me to do the Deliveroos. So I'm missing for about three hours, give or take, freezing my balls off waiting for someone to order a Thai green curry or whatever. And then I get back a bit after ten, meet you, go for a slash, head to the kitchen, give the princely sum of twenty-seven euros to Davide. Giving him tips, I always made it uneven so that it looked more genuine. Otherwise he went apeshit. Anyway, he was pleased Wednesday. Gave me a plastic container with leftover dinner in it, a lamb thing. He heated it too. Not the worst sometimes, I s'pose. I sat at the back of the Aula Max in the dark and ate it. Then I did the clearout.'

'Where did you put the stuff?'

'There's a Film Soc overnight locker. That's where I went. Then I came home. Here. Once I left the East Wing, you can see for yourself, I'm all over the CCTV. I'm out of the picture long before the guy got done. That detective sergeant was dying to pin something on me, but she couldn't. Because I'm squeaky fucking clean. I had fuck-all to do with the murder. And, like I told her, I saw nothing and no one in the East Wing. Except you. No one who shouldn't have been there.' He paused. 'Just Davide Rossi. Ciara the waitress. And that manager woman.'

'Magda.'

'Yeah, her.' He paused again, looked pensive.

'Is there something else, Ian?'

'No,' he said.

'You don't seem sure.'

'I am. It's like I said, I saw nothing.'

'Did you *hear* something so? Something someone said.'

'I heard nothing. If I'd heard something, I'd have told you.'

'But something's bothering you. What is it?'

'I didn't tell the guards. It's kind of stupid, to be honest.'

'Tell *me*. I'll listen.'

'Promise not to laugh?'

'I promise.'

'Look, I *felt* something, okay? In the toilets. As if I wasn't alone. But there was no one there. I checked. The stalls were empty. And now I think it was a premonition I had. Because I heard that was where he died. That's the story around College anyway. That he was killed in the bog, dragged over to the gallery door and left behind there. So I think it was his spirit. Or another spirit maybe. An evil one.'

93

I KEPT MY PROMISE. I DIDN'T LAUGH AT MCANESPIE'S cheesy ghost story. Because I wanted to shake him. And not just for that.

I said, 'You do *know* that Davide's been committing a criminal offence?'

'Section 17 of the Public Order Act. Demanding money with menaces.'

'If you know so much about the law, why didn't you make a complaint?'

'I didn't want to. I was afraid. And at this stage, well, I'm too ashamed.'

'You have to do it now, Ian. It's not too late. What you've been going through, it's ridiculous. I mean, you didn't force him to make that investment, however foolish it was.'

'I didn't force him, no, I—'

'Where does he live?'

'He's gone home. It's April. His temporary tutoring contract is up and he's been told he's not getting any more gigs from Nibblz Catering. Or so he says. He'd have no problem getting other work like that, mind you, or in a call centre, with his Italian and he has perfect English too, but he doesn't want to. He says he's sick of the Irish weather. I thought he'd be too scared to return to Italy. Turns out he isn't.'

'Why's that?'

'None of it was true. That Mafia stuff he told me, it was a big fat lie. Seems like he never invested a *cent* in that crypto thing where I got burned to a cheese and onion Tayto. He just watched the prices for the laugh and when it crashed he used it against me. And he's not from the mean streets of Naples, like he said. He's from *Milan*. All these months, I've been funding his lifestyle. Or something more pharmaceutical – who the fuck knows? Either way, he played me. I'm such a fucking eejit. And now I'm going to fail my exams.'

However annoyed or frustrated I felt, kicking a man when he's down isn't in me. I dug deep. 'You're not,' I said.

'Not an eejit?'

'Oh, no, you *are* an eejit, but you're not going to fail your exams.'

'How can you know that?'

'I just do. I'm sure of it. If you knuckle down now, you'll get them. You'll learn from this and you'll move on.'

'I will, yeah,' he said, meaning he wouldn't.

I said, 'Apart from that Instagram profile, do you have any contact details for Davide Rossi?'

'Course I do,' he said, meaning he didn't.

'Come off it, Ian. How could you *not* have contact details for him? By the sound of it, you were in constant touch with him.'

'On an Irish burner mobile,' he said.

He called out the number. I rang it. No longer in service.

He went on, 'And his @perfectitaliancork Insta profile seems to be dormant now.'

'What about his account details in Italy that you transferred money to?'

'There's bound to be a record in the Western Union place but I didn't keep the receipts or anything. Davide did. I kept a record of the amounts I paid him in the calendar on my phone.'

I got up from the table and took a business card from my handbag. 'Call me if you hear from him, or if you think of anything else.'

I left before he had time to reply.

As I walked down the path, I was sure I'd been wasting my time. That the McAnespie visit had been a sideshow, that the beating heart of the murder investigation lay elsewhere.

Not the first time I've been wrong. Not the last either.

94

THE ONLY ADVANTAGE TO MY MORNING
diversion was that it meant I was already in town. Almost. In no
time, I was on South Terrace, site of the closed-down synagogue,
and crossing the footbridge, nicknamed the Passover by some,
onto Morrison's Island.

Turning over and over the information I'd gathered as I
walked, it seemed I was no nearer to finding the identity of the
murderer of William Atkins, and time was seriously running out
for me. In other cases, I'd have met up with Sadie, talked through
the evidence. Made progress. Now that avenue was closed. For
ever, perhaps. I still couldn't believe she'd allowed me to be taken
into custody. Some best friend. She'd told me that the arrest was
out of her hands, but was it? Even if I hadn't been returning her
calls, that was no excuse.

I reached MLC by 9 a.m. I planned to update Tina on the case
and get a few hours' work in before leaving for the Bons to take
Dad home. At all costs, I had to avoid running into Gabriel, or
Dermot, or any of the other partners who might ask me how the
investigation was going. If they asked, I'd have to tell them about
my arrest. If that happened, I'd be deemed to have a conflict of
interest, and I'd be off the case.

Except I knew I hadn't killed Atkins, and that finding his killer had become fundamental for me in a way I only half understood.

And so, if I managed to avoid meeting Gabriel, or Dermot, or any of the other partners, I'd be able to buy myself a little more time.

If I could have teleported to my attic room, I would have. Instead I slunk, making it as far as the first floor without incident.

But as I passed the boardroom door, it opened.

95

LIKE A BOND VILLAIN, GABRIEL STEPPED OUT AND said, 'Miss Fitzpatrick, we've all been wondering when you were going to make an appearance.' He handed me an envelope. 'We thought we were going to have to hand-deliver this. You've saved us the trouble. Take a seat and have a read.' He pointed to a chair by the wall inside the door. 'While you're doing that, I'll give you the edited highlights. Yes, you will be unsurprised to discover that you *are* suspended pending a disciplinary process that may result in your dismissal. And, yes, I'm saddened by your behaviour, both professionally and personally. And, yes, of *course* you'll have every opportunity to defend yourself and give your side of the story. But ...' he swallowed, went on '... for us to find out about your detention at Coughlan's Quay garda station from an outsider, it's a terrible breach of trust. You should have told us immediately. If you had, we might have been able to come to an arrangement of some sort. By not doing that, we're left with no option, not least because you're fully aware that it puts you in a clear conflict-of-interest situation as regards the case you're allegedly working on. Nevertheless, however unfairly *you* may have acted, fair procedures will be applied by us.'

It wasn't my first rodeo. I'd been suspended before. Back then, I'd felt aggrieved. Wronged. I'd talked a lot at the suspension meeting. Defended myself. This time, I didn't even try. Because they had a point. I *should* have told the firm about my detention by the gardaí. I should have explained to the partners what had happened and why.

I scanned the letter quickly. A situation of the utmost seriousness. Two weeks' suspension on full pay. Prohibition on engaging in any work whatsoever for clients of MLC during the period of suspension. Specific prohibition on all further activity regarding the Atkins investigation; UCC president informed of my unavailability, though not the reason. A three-person sub-committee appointed to investigate and report back to the rest of the partners. If necessary, the process would move to a formal disciplinary. Result not a foregone conclusion. And so on. I put the envelope in my handbag.

What they said on paper was more neutral than they appeared. The antique boardroom table was packed with every partner in the firm. Angry-looking all, most of them stayed silent. A few spoke. Said they weren't in any sense prejudging the issue, then proceeded to do precisely that, running the gamut from rage to disappointment with a dash of disgust thrown in. Understandable. Predictable. I could have written the script. In a way, I already had. What they were saying wasn't so very different from the criticisms I'd been levelling at myself.

It was only afterwards as I hit the street that I twigged the one voice I hadn't heard. He'd been there, in his usual seat halfway down the right-hand side. I'd seen him, he'd seen me, and he'd looked away, picked up a plastic biro, examined it like it was a rare jewel. He hadn't joined in the chorus of condemnation. Hadn't said a word. Unusual for him. Out of character, even.

But it wasn't only his silence that was odd. He looked shifty.

Which, at the very least, was interesting.

I slid my phone out of my bag and composed a text message: *We need to talk.*

The terms of my suspension forbade me to have contact with any employee of the firm during the course of the investigation. I couldn't even speak to Tina for fear of getting her into trouble. Anyway, she mightn't even want to know me. She might be upset that I hadn't told her about my arrest. I'd felt guilty about that. Now I was glad I'd said nothing. With a bit of luck, she might escape being cross-contaminated by my misfortune and stupidity.

Technically, though, Dermot Lyons wasn't an employee. He was one of the senior partners. A text to him was arguably within the rules, if anyone would be interested in applying them. From what I'd seen, they might not be. And what Lyons would do when he got my text was anyone's guess. I figured there was only one way to find out. I pressed send.

96

WHAT LYONS DIDN'T DO WAS REPLY. THE MESSAGE
was marked 'delivered' and, a few seconds later, 'read', but
nothing came back from him. It wasn't a good sign.

And it wasn't even 10 a.m. by the time I got home again. I had
a few hours before I needed to be at the hospital. I intended to
use every second of that time doing something vital, although
I didn't yet know what that was. Throwing my work clothes
onto a chair in the bedroom, I pulled on black jeans and a black
sweatshirt. Exhausted from the effort of that, and probably from
delayed shock, I went upstairs to the kitchen and made a large
pot of coffee.

Feeling utterly overwhelmed, I was halfway through my
second mug when the thing about the elephant came to me, the
way you eat him. One bite at a time.

The evening before and early that morning, I'd been
concentrating on Lexbonay, and I'd been making good progress,
though I still didn't know how it connected to the murder of
William Atkins, or if it did. Then, the text from Ciara Boyle
had come in and I'd gone on a wild-goose chase, haring after Ian
McAnespie and Davide Rossi, all to no avail.

I needed to wind the clock back and finish what I'd started.

Every avenue I'd tried to pierce the Lexbonay veil of secrecy had failed. Nate Simpson. Béatrice Mbemba. None of them would open up to me. Mbemba wouldn't even take my calls. Apart from Sophie who, whatever her temporary physical intimacy with Simpson, had no real connection with Lexbonay, there was only one person left. I needed to find Samantha Fennell, the mysterious ex-employee.

I pinged a text message to Harry Bennigan: *Any luck with tracking down that investment adviser your ex was using? Do you have any contact details for her?*

He replied, *I told you the name of the company, didn't I?*

I responded, *Yes, but she's gone from there. Does your ex have a mobile number for her?*

He messaged, *Despite all the money I gave her, I'm still persona non grata. Is it important?*

Was it? I had no way of knowing. I replied, *Vital.*

He responded, *Try her yourself. She might talk to you. She definitely won't talk to me.*

The next message was a business card with Harry's soon-to-be ex-wife's number on it. However tempting, it was useless to me. For now, at least, I was still a solicitor and direct contact with the client of another solicitor was not permitted. Ever. I deleted it straight away.

Nevertheless, it gave me an idea.

97

I'D BEEN UNDER STRESS. MY BRAIN HADN'T BEEN working properly. Otherwise, I'd have remembered to ask the former Mrs Bennigan's solicitor a lot sooner. Legal people share information all the time. Such as the contact details for expert witnesses. My hands shaking, and not only from excess caffeine, I scrolled through my phone and sent a text to Regina Dooley, my opposition: *Have you a mobile number for Samantha Fennell, the financial adviser you had in the Joanna Bennigan case?*

No further explanation was needed. If Regina had it, she'd send it to me. She'd assume I was planning to engage Fennell on behalf of a client. Which I was. Kind of. Though, by this point, the only client I had was me. And, as the old adage goes, 'A solicitor who acts for himself has a fool for a client.' So be it.

I got up from the table, poured the rest of the coffee down the sink. The waiting was killing me and my head was splitting. I took two paracetamol, paced for a while. Still nothing. I was downstairs in my en-suite bathroom having a wee when the reply from Regina came at last. Another business card with a mobile-phone number on it.

This one I saved.

98

SYCAMORE LAWN IN DOUGLAS WAS A MATURE
suburban estate of well-tended gardens and mid-range family-
sized vehicles. In summer, the evening air hummed with
lawnmowers. On this Friday morning in April, a soft rain soaked
the budding hydrangeas and dropped steadily onto the tarmac
driveways. Most of the residents were at school or at work,
many others down the hill at the big Tesco getting ahead of the
weekend rush.

But Samantha Fennell was at home. She answered before the
doorbell had finished buzzing. Mid-forties and slim with mid-
length highlighted hair, she wore shiny black leggings and a
cerise pink hoodie. She looked worried, spoke urgently. 'Come
in,' she said. 'I wouldn't put it past them to be watching.'

She took me into the front room of the house: flat-screen
television, wooden floor, flame-effect fireplace, grey mid-
century-style sofa and contrasting feature armchair, wafer-thin
laptop on a small round table beside the chair, a single accordion
file horizontal on a shelf, a yoga mat laid out in an open space
beside the radiator, a couple of brightly coloured blocks and
a folded wool blanket stacked beside it. All of her possessions

looked considered, from the Nissan Leaf parked outside to the abstract-pattern wool rug.

'Sit down,' she said. 'Do you want coffee or something?'

'I might go into orbit if I drink any more this morning,' I said, 'but thanks.'

She nodded distractedly. 'Know what you mean. Doesn't help the anxiety either.'

I took a seat on the sofa. She made for the chair, stood for a while, sat eventually. I had so little time left before I had to go to the hospital to collect Dad but something told me to let her do the talking. I stopped myself looking at my watch.

After a time, she said, 'I never thought I'd be a person who would do this kind of thing. That *I'd* be the one.' She went on, 'Lexbonay isn't the ethical investment company it says it is. It's rotten to the core. Every nasty business on the planet that you can think of washes through it. Coltan and wolframite from conflict zones in the Democratic Republic of Congo. Fracking. Strip-mining. Unethical testing by pharmaceuticals in third-world countries. Here in Ireland it's Direct Provision hotels. That's how I spotted it first. It's all so well hidden, chains of on- and offshore companies, but I was reading a report in a Sunday paper and I recognised one of the names.'

She continued, 'I'm an accountant originally but I branched into investment advice in a small way and built up a good client list. Nathaniel Simpson – Lexbonay – bought my business. Not huge money in the scheme of things, but this house is mortgage-free now. And I was kept on by Simpson to service my own roster of clients. I was on the sales side of the business, selling to what were, by Lexbonay's standards, small and medium-sized investors, and liaising with brokers. I wasn't involved in the high-finance side. But I'm a bit of a nerd. I read into what I'm supposed to be selling. A lot of people don't. They rely on the glossy fund reports, the summaries and digests, the coloured charts, the squiggly graphs. I look behind those, do more in-depth research. And, like I said, I was reading that piece in the *Sunday Business Post* about the vast profits that Direct Provision to asylum-seekers delivers for its investors and I saw it, one of the companies on our list. I said nothing at first, did some more research. The more I read, the worse it got. Direct Provision is horrible and demeaning, but it's one hundred per cent legal. The other stuff is in the greyest of grey areas, not exactly illegal but ...'

I said, 'The mis-selling *has* to be illegal, surely. Telling people they're getting one thing and actually selling them something different? A fake Rolex instead of a real one?'

'You'd think that, but the fine print, the terms and conditions of the contract, gives them an out. That's what Nathaniel Simpson said anyway. And I've read it. Arguably, he's right.'

'You spoke to him about it?'

'I built up a file and made an appointment to see him. Took the early-morning train to Dublin, went to Lexbonay HQ. His office is absolutely gorgeous, bespoke furniture, fabulous paintings, a stunning view of the Liffey. I got a warm welcome from him at first, lovely to see me, what could he do for me. But once I started talking ... Well, when you get on the wrong side of him, he's not half as polite as he seems at first. He's a piece of work. A sophisticated monster.'

I let that sink in, then asked, 'What did he say? Did he try to give an excuse?'

'He said there's nothing illegal in what they're doing and that side of the business funds the work they're doing on climate change, renewable energy expansion, micro-investing in disadvantaged communities, helping them to build resilience, and making money out of that too, shoring up his belief that Africa has the potential for strong economic growth. I said that a lot of people might call what he was doing "greenwashing" to hide the other stuff. That was when he reminded me, em, quite strongly, to say the least, that my contract of employment obliged me to keep secret everything I learned while working for him. And he reminded me about all the other people in the company. Their jobs. That if I didn't need the money, they did. He asked me if that was clear and I said, "Crystal," and he said that answer was from some film or other and started laughing and asked me if I'd like a drink and I said it was only eleven fifteen a.m. and he said, "I won't tell if you won't," so I accepted a gin and elderflower tonic and drank it and we parted on good terms, as far as he was concerned.'

'But not you.'

'I was very unhappy. He was right. I didn't need the money. I could've resigned. I thought about it. I could easily have managed for a while, rented out this place here, gone to Spain or Greece. Relaxed. I would've had to find another job eventually, a different kind because the restraint-of-trade clause in my contract prohibits me from working in a competing business for twelve months, but I have transferable skills. I'm an accountant. I would've done fine somewhere else. And maybe if I had a partner or kids, that's exactly what I would've done. But I don't. I was coming home here on my own every night and it got in on me what Lexbonay was doing. I decided to stay. Find out as much as I could, and if the moment was right, I'd think about doing something. Meanwhile I steered my clients away from the objectionable funds. I hadn't made up my mind definitively to talk until—'

'The conference at UCC.'

She nodded ruefully. 'In retrospect it was incredibly stupid of me to arrange to meet Dr Mbemba there. But she doesn't know Cork. And it was supposed to be a quick handover, spy-movie style. But we'd never met in person before. We let down our guard. Started chatting.'

'I saw you together,' I said.

'You weren't the only one.'

'Simpson?'

'I can't say for sure if he actually saw us, but he certainly found out that Béatrice had been talking to me and that was when the real trouble began.'

'Sorry, Samantha, I—'

'Sam.'

I smiled. 'Sam, can you roll the clock back and explain why? Why her?'

'Lexbonay fronts various dodgy mining concerns in DRC, the Congo, where Béatrice's family's roots are. She's written about this kind of thing a lot. I was aware of her work from my internet research, and then I saw that she was coming to Cork so I reached out to her before she came. Arranged to meet her. I gave her my file. By hand. I didn't think it was a good idea to leave a digital trail.'

'Had she known about Lexbonay before?'

'She had no real usable proof, but she knew. Her paper at the conference all but named and shamed them. If you read it, and insert what you now know about Lexbonay into the picture, it's damning.'

'Yet she accepted their hospitality, came to the conference, stayed in a hotel paid for by the company?'

'She accepted the invitation and the conference reserved her room but she paid her own bill the morning after. I met her at the River Lee. We're working together on a big exposé. But the legal proceedings that Lexbonay have begun against me complicate everything.'

'An injunction?'

'Not yet. But they're trying to gag me. I'll show you.'

She took down the accordion file from the shelf.

99

I LEAFED THROUGH THE SHEAF OF PAPERS SAM
handed to me. On top, on notepaper from Elliott Phillips, one of
Dublin's top law firms with offices worldwide, was a letter before
action threatening legal proceedings unless an undertaking to
cease and desist was received by them without delay. Below
that, another letter, dated the following day, enclosed a High
Court summons making a raft of non-specific claims of breach
of contract against Samantha Fennell, along with an interim
injunction application – a draft Notice of Motion, as yet
unstamped and unissued from the Central Office of the High
Court, and an unstamped but sworn grounding affidavit –
making detailed allegations of what she had allegedly done and
seeking interim relief. The documents also stated that damages
were not a remedy and sought full costs. This meant that, by the
time a case for compensation came to full trial, money would not
be able to fix the problem. Immediate temporary court orders
would be needed to stop her releasing company information.

Samantha Fennell was what we call 'a mark'. She'd already
told me that her house was mortgage-free. This case, if it went to
a full hearing in the High Court, would pauperise her if she lost.
But although proceedings had been issued, and the injunction

application was ready to go, they hadn't gone any further with the legal process. Not yet.

'Did Béatrice Mbemba get this correspondence too?'

'No.'

'Interesting. And they've made the High Court summons they've filed with the court office look like a common or garden employment dispute.' I thought for a while, then continued: 'Here's what I think. They don't want anything about this to leak out. And they don't *really* want to go ahead with the injunction because it would bring what you're saying about them into open court. It would make it public, reportable on by the press. But if they have to, they can. And they will. But for now, I think it's just a scare tactic.'

'It's working.'

'Have you replied to the letters? Entered an Appearance to the proceedings?'

'No.'

'Have you taken legal advice?'

'Other than from Béatrice, no.'

'She's not a legal practitioner, she's an academic. Plus she's not an Irish solicitor or barrister. The system in France is very different, and she's not independent, so you have to—'

'I know. But I needed time to think.'

I nodded. 'There's a lot to think about. Is there anything in particular?'

'Oh, just if I want to take the risk of losing everything. Maybe even my life.'

'Your *life*?'

'I'm being over-dramatic. Probably. But I can't help thinking about that Aussie professor. Atkins. I didn't know him, had never even heard of him, but Béatrice told me he was talking to Simpson for ages during the conference dinner. Maybe that's a coincidence. Maybe not. Either way, he's dead now.'

Her final words hung in the air like a full stop, black and final. I felt numb.

But, behind the numbness, I felt something else.

And, whatever it was, I didn't like it.

100

I PUSHED IT ASIDE AND RETURNED MY FOCUS TO Samantha Fennell, taking her through various possible responses to the proceedings, including no response at all and the consequences of that. I also gave her the names of some colleagues who might be willing to act on her behalf. I didn't tell her I'd been suspended, and that I couldn't represent her even if I wanted to. Mainly because she didn't ask. Which might have hurt my feelings, if I'd had time to think about it.

She said, 'I'm going to wait till Monday before making a decision.'

I said, 'That seems like a good idea. By the way, you might get another threatening letter by courier this afternoon around five or six p.m., when most legal offices will be closed for the weekend. If that happens, try not to worry about it. See it as more of the same tactic. Big-bad-wolf stuff. They'll want you to be stressed out of your mind for the next few nights with no access to legal assistance. They might then come to you on Monday with a more conciliatory approach. So if the letter arrives, send me a photo of it on WhatsApp and call me. We'll talk.'

'Will do.'

'There's one more thing. Béatrice Mbemba has been ignoring my messages and—'

'First, she's busy, *very* busy, working on how to get the information about Lexbonay out into the world. Second, she didn't want to be the one to tell you *my* story. She said it wasn't right. Now that you know it, she'll talk to you. I'll make sure of that.'

I said, 'Thanks.' I paused, then said, 'You're very brave, by the way.'

'I don't feel brave,' she said. 'I feel stupid. I feel afraid. I haven't left the house in days. I don't know what to do. But ...' she stood up from her chair '... you should go now. I'll call you if I get that letter.'

I heard her double-lock the front door behind me as I left.

101

DRIVING TOWARDS THE HOSPITAL, STALLED IN
heavy traffic much of the way but still on schedule, just about,
I thought through what I'd learned from Samantha Fennell and
how it related to the murder. *Was* there a connection between
Lexbonay and the Atkins murder? Sam Fennell seemed to think
there was and, at the very least, it was possible. Nevertheless,
however tempting it was to move the vile Simpson to the top of
my suspect list, he had an alibi. At the time of the killing, he and
Sophie were in a room at Hayfield Manor. Having sex. Allegedly.
While both of them might have been lying, the CCTV didn't.
They'd left campus. The evidence was incontrovertible.

But as I inched forward up the slip road from the N25,
I thought about that again. If Simpson had known about the
murder in advance, he couldn't have done a better job at ruling
himself out. It was almost as if he'd planned his night with Sophie
to ensure that he wouldn't be a suspect. He was certainly rich
enough to hire someone to kill Atkins. But why? Was Atkins a
threat to Lexbonay? Perhaps, but how?

Or was it personal animosity? That seemed less likely. Even
if he'd upset or annoyed Simpson, either at the dinner or in
some other way, Atkins was flying home the next day. Also, if

a hitman had been involved, surely the killing would have been more professional.

Or what about the two-person theory? What if both Simpson and Sophie had been involved? Wearing different clothes, they could have returned to the East Wing somehow, perhaps exiting the hotel via the rear gate, killed Atkins and done the clean-up with ease, then returned to Hayfield, both with alibis. And, unfortunately for that theory, no discernible motive.

The same could apply to Kirsty MacMillan and Padraic O'Flaherty. But on the CCTV, they seemed fully engaged with taking care of an extremely drunk Professor Casey, walking him home to the North Mall, apparently arriving back at the River Lee Hotel at 1.30 a.m. The timing didn't seem to fit, but Kirsty MacMillan might have had something of a potential motive: she'd had a historical affair with Atkins. Although she'd told me that the relationship had come to a natural end and that she felt no ill will towards him, was that true? And there was her close, though supposedly platonic, relationship with her devoted former PhD student Padraic O'Flaherty. Might *he* have been the one who bore a grudge against Atkins?

In my head, I ran back through the people at the dinner. The more information I had, the worse it got. I seemed to be no closer to finding the identity of the murderer of William Atkins. The man who'd travelled from the other side of the world to see me. And said nothing. And never would now. *Why* had he come to Ireland just to stay silent? It made no sense.

As I drove on, barely seeing the road, the need to know consumed me, my head splitting, my brain winding itself into spirals. Deprived of the opportunity of knowing him in life, I wanted to – had to – know the man in death. Who had killed him, and the reason for his murder.

And yet, for now, I also had to try to put the investigation on hold. I resolved to do just that. To concentrate on the man who'd been my real father, instead of the one who hadn't.

Still, barely fifteen minutes later, as I was driving into the Bon Secours Hospital car park, when a call came through to me from Béatrice Mbemba, I answered it automatically.

102

'I'VE BEEN RUDE TO YOU,' BÉATRICE SAID. 'FOR THAT I apologise. But I think you understand now why I haven't been responding to your messages.'

'Samantha Fennell told me about the work you've been doing.'

'The work is part of the reason, of course. It is also that we need to get the timing of the Lexbonay revelations just right. If I'd spoken to you sooner, I might have had to lie. And that goes against everything I stand for. I still can't say much but it will all be available to read soon, I hope and—'

'It's okay. Samantha gave me the gist.' I coughed. 'But may I ask you a few questions about the day of the murder?'

'Sure.'

'First, what did Simpson say to you? After you walked across the quad. Ciara, the guide, had been talking about the superstition associated with that.'

'He said, "Don't worry, I'm watching you." His hands were on me, his mouth touching my ear. It was disgusting. I pushed him away as hard as I could.'

'Disgusting is the right word for that man. Do you think he knew of your plans to expose his company?'

'When he heard my paper, although I never mentioned Lexbonay by name, he caught my meaning. At the coffee break that morning he said, "Interesting speech." He knew what I was saying, and he didn't feel threatened by me at that point. But he must have seen Samantha Fennell on campus. By evening, there was a change. His eyes never left me during the drinks on the lawn.'

'And talking of the drinks, what was the disagreement with Professor Casey about?'

'Agnes told Casey she'd invited me. He wasn't keen, but she insisted that it was too late to cancel. She told me he'd asked to read my paper in advance. So he knew its contents. That it argued against commercial sponsorship in academia. That was why he left the Aula Maxima before I started speaking.'

'Noisily, as I recall.'

'Very. And that evening, in the garden, he started talking to me about it. He said that it was ill-conceived. I told him that if he accepts sponsorship, the very least he should do is vet his sponsors more carefully. He demanded to know what I meant and I wouldn't say. Of course, he had been drinking also. Things got somewhat heated. As you saw.'

'It had an effect on Casey,' I said. 'It was clear during the dinner that he was having second thoughts about Simpson. There was an atmosphere. Sitting between them was—'

She laughed. 'I can only imagine.'

'I was told that you were talking to Professor Atkins. After I left?'

'During dinner, he was opposite me. We spoke but only a little. Later he swapped with the president, so he was sitting beside me for about ten or fifteen minutes.'

'What were you talking about?'

'About my work, my paper. He guessed what I'd been talking about. He asked me directly if I was referring to Lexbonay. I told him I couldn't confirm or deny it. So instead for fifteen minutes approximately we spoke *hypothetically* about the businesses that a *hypothetical* investment company might be involved in funding secretly. Then, he spoke to Simpson. Asked him about Lexbonay. Simpson gave the official line, as usual. The ethical-hedge-fund *merde*.'

'How do you know? Did you overhear the conversation?'

'Partly. Simpson wasn't speaking quietly. But also because Professor Atkins nodded to me from across the table when he got back to his original seat.'

'Do you think Simpson might have seen him do that?'

'I think perhaps he did. But what he understood by it, I can't say.'

I couldn't say either. A nod didn't seem enough to precipitate murder.

I went on, 'And, Béatrice, there's another thing I have to say. I've looked at the CCTV from the quad. You were one of the last guests to leave the East Wing.'

'I hadn't noticed that. I remember that I was talking to Professor Atkins.'

'Was it your first time meeting him?'

'It was. I really liked him. He was amusing, yes, but serious when necessary.'

'Who was left in the East Wing after you exited onto the quad?'

'Certainly the president was there. I don't remember anyone else. The staff?'

'And you went straight to the hotel?'

'I had an early start the next morning. My meeting with Sam. I needed sleep.'

'Do you remember anything else from your conversation with Atkins?'

'Yes. In the corridor he said he'd help me. That I should contact him. That he knew people.'

'Did he say who he meant?'

'No. It was just one sentence. I assumed he meant other academics or journalists.'

'Do you think anyone heard him say that?'

'It's possible. Probable. But as to who, I can't say.'

'Did he say anything else?'

'He did. Something interesting. A comment. He said he'd made many mistakes in his life and that some were too late to change but that helping me was something he could do. That was what I meant when I said he was serious. Beneath the laughter, there was sadness, I think. Regret. A lot of regret.'

Her words hit me like a kick.

After a silence, I ended the call.

But I didn't have time to think about any of what Béatrice Mbemba had told me. Manoeuvring my car as close to the door as I could, I went into the hospital to collect Dad and take him home to Gardiner's Hill.

103

I LEFT MY PARENTS BY THE FIRE AS THE *SIX ONE* news was beginning. When I say I left, what really happened was they told me to go.

'We're fine,' my mother said. 'Can't you see?'

The doctor had informed us that it would take a few weeks for the thyroxine to be fully effective but, though he was still very weak, I could see a slight improvement in Dad. He'd been diagnosed with hypothyroidism, a severe case, but treatable. He wasn't going to die, the doctor said. He would get better. I only half-believed it.

However long it took, half of me wanted to sit beside him and keep watch until he was well enough to go out and trim the hedge again. The other half was taken up with the case, talking to my parents, drinking tea with them, while simultaneously piecing together what I knew about the murder.

'You've taken *so* much time off,' Mam went on. 'You need to get back to normal. We all do. We missed him while he was on his holidays in the Bons but he's home now.'

'And there was no need for all the worrying in the end,' Dad said. 'I told ye.' He was talking himself up. He still looked and sounded awful.

My mother added, 'You'll lose your good job if you're not careful.'

She didn't know how close that was to the truth and that was what persuaded me to leave. I was carrying too many secrets. My humiliating non-reunion with Davy. My suspension from work. My arrest. And, most importantly, what the DNA results had revealed about the connection between me and Atkins. It was easier to go than to stay and lie by omission.

Turning the car, I headed down Gardiner's Hill, intending to go home, not feeling like it, contemplating the lone advantage to my suspension from MLC: that at least it had put a stop to the president's constant messages seeking updates.

Thinking about Sadie too, wondering how things were going for her, and if we'd ever talk again. I wasn't worried about being rearrested. The cops had got nothing from me the first time and, in the absence of evidence against me, that they were *never* going to find because it didn't exist, they weren't going to waste any more time on me.

As I got to the end of the slope, before it turns right onto St Luke's, I remembered that Lia de Barra lived around there, on Adelaide Place, a terrace of late-Georgians that mixed private homes and varying types of rental accommodation. I'd taken her address that first Sunday in her office. It had stuck in my mind because of its location, so near and yet so far from my parents' home.

Entering the enclave via a crumbling stone gateway, I parked at the outer edge and walked in along the front of the terrace. The houses were very large, comprising four storeys and an attic, and the view to the south over the city was extraordinary, even from ground level. But those homes were designed to reveal their full glory from the first floor and those above it. I had no expectations of seeing any of it. Knowing Lia, I doubted I'd make it past the threshold.

For once, I was lucky. The door was answered not by Lia but by her daughter, who looked about thirteen. She was wearing a green St Angela's uniform.

I spoke quickly. 'Hiya, I'm here to see your mother. I went to St Angela's too, by the way. Isn't the new building gorgeous? Makes going to school a pleasure, I'll bet.'

'Yeah, right,' the girl said. She looked me up and down with disdain, then shouted, 'Mu-*um*, a woman's here.'

When there was no reply, she said. 'She never answers. She *to*tally neglects her children *all* the time. You may as well just come in. She's in the drawing room. First floor front.'

I didn't need to be told twice.

104

'YOU MAKE QUITE THE HABIT OF THIS, DON'T YOU?
Showing up uninvited?'

Lia was standing by the sideboard when I entered, bathed in evening light. The room was beautiful: painted a chalky mid-blue, the high ceilings, decorative plasterwork and woodwork white, the original floorboards warmed with rugs, good furniture, a confident mix of contemporary and older pieces.

I edged further into the space, stole a glance out one of the sash windows, running almost floor to ceiling. The view was as breathtaking as I'd expected, the east side of the city and the river spread out before us. 'Em, I thought we'd sort of agreed that I would drop by at some point.'

She drawled a reply: 'We'll have to agree to differ on your interpretation of what I said, but even if you *are* right, six fifteen on a Friday evening, when I've just phoned for a takeaway for my family's Friday-night dinner and poured myself a well-deserved glass of red wine, isn't a time I would have chosen. That said, the fact that you're here now means I won't have to worry about you coming back again. So speak now or for ever hold your peace.'

'Worry? I didn't have you down as a worrier.'

It took her an extra moment to respond. 'What do you want?'

I smiled. 'To check over some things.'

She looked down into the glass of wine in her hand, didn't take a sip, placed it on the sideboard carefully, then eyeballed me. 'What things?'

She was still standing and she hadn't asked me to sit. I took the initiative.

'Let's both take a seat, Lia. This won't take long.'

105

IT WAS A BIG ROOM, SPANNING THE WIDTH OF
the house. As well as two sofas, there were three armchairs, an
ottoman, and a couple of pouffes. I opted for one of the sofas.
Lia moved towards the fireplace, threw on another log, turned
to face me.

'The food delivery is due around seven,' she said. 'They
accept cash only. I'll have to go down and pay. That will mark
the conclusion of our conversation. Because I will be eating
dinner with my children after that. And my husband, if he gets
home from Henchy's in time. Which he undoubtedly won't.
But when he does, probably between eight and eight thirty, he'll
eat the leftovers if there are any, raid the fridge if not, make a
God-awful mess either way, and promptly fall asleep on that sofa
there, the one you're sitting on. He won't be a bit happy if he
comes home and finds you in his spot. He'll go all Daddy Bear
on you, bless him.'

I'd planned on easing into what I wanted to know. Instead I
went for it. 'There's general agreement that the murder has been
embarrassing, damaging even, for the new president.'

'Is there now? Who told you that?'

'Staff members. People at UCC.'

'People at the law school, you mean?'

'Yes,' I said.

'Agreement in the law school about anything? That's rare. Also, as far as I'm concerned, untrue ... I don't agree that it was embarrassing or damaging. Unless the president turns out to be the murderer, no one's going to blame her. Shit just happens.'

'She was the person who removed the CCTV. If she hadn't, the murder might not have happened. Or it might not have happened *there*.'

'I'll give you that. But it wasn't an accident. The killing was intentional. *Mens rea*. Malice aforethought. All the constituent parts of the common-law definition. Someone was going to die that night. It was murder.'

It was subtly different from what she'd told me previously. 'You don't think there's any possibility of mistaken identity?'

'All I know for sure is that *I* didn't do it. But I don't *think* anything. You're asking me to guess the murderer. It's not Cluedo. I won't play that or any other game with you.'

'It's not a game. The president *did* ask me to ...'

By putting the request in the past tense, I hoped to gloss over any awkwardness if by some chance Lia had heard about my suspension.

She hadn't. 'A pointless exercise, in my view. Not one of her better ideas. Like the removal of the CCTV. But she corrected that particular error pretty fast and, overall, she's doing a great job. That's the main thing. Men are allowed to have the occasional fuck-up. As a rule, women aren't.'

'You sound like you're a supporter of the president?'

'Of *course* I am.'

'Oh ... I heard on the grapevine that you applied for her job.'

'I did and I didn't get it. Are you suggesting I should feel resentful?'

I waited a beat before replying. 'More that you might.'

She sighed. 'I'm going to let you in on a little secret and I don't care if you believe me or not. I applied for the top job out of duty. My duty as a feminist. There's a wall of past presidents' portraits in the Aula Max, all of them with penises, and it annoys me. I didn't even want the job. I just didn't want another man to get it. When Deady applied, she looked like a dead cert but I couldn't be sure, so I stayed in the race but, in all honesty, I was delighted to lose. To lose to someone with a vagina. The truth is, I like teaching. I like my room in the Horgan Building. I'm happily married, I have two very annoying and very demanding children, one of whom is almost certainly listening at the door. I didn't *want* to be president, but if push came to shove, I would have done it. Thankfully, I didn't have to. By the way, I would never have bothered having that conference dinner in the East Wing. It was another mistake, a legacy of the old boys' club academic theme-park Cambridge culture she came from. We should've gone to the pub, followed by a restaurant … You look surprised.'

'A little.' I didn't believe she'd have gone to all that trouble to apply for a job she didn't want at all. But she'd convinced me that she harboured no significant animosity against the president. Also, at the dinner, I hadn't noticed any tension between them. When Casey had raised the issue of a rivalry or conflict between them, it had come as a surprise to me.

I asked, 'Might sound like an odd question, but why do you have two phones?'

She laughed. 'Nothing sinister. I use the iPhone for work and people who can wait for me to respond. If ever. The dinosaur phone is for family. If that rings, I answer immediately.'

I thought for a moment, then asked, 'Professor Casey ... What's the real story of the bad relationship between you two?'

She sat down at last. 'You know his wife had a long-term illness?'

I nodded.

'He was amazing, took incredible care of her. But his work suffered. He feels thwarted. His career hasn't been quite as glittering as he imagines it might have been, though frankly his opinion of his own talents far outstrips the reality. Anyway, the point is, he hates seeing other people getting on, doing well. He's helpful to underlings but he has a problem with equals and with people he feels inferior to.'

'So when you got promoted, he ...?'

'I became the enemy.'

'Because you were both on the same level.'

'*And* because I wasn't grateful enough. I had the cheek to suggest that my promotion might have been partly to do with my own work as an academic and as a teacher, not *only* to do with the fact that he gave me a great reference and, allegedly, persuaded the rest of the interview panel to appoint me.'

'That's interesting.'

'Interesting if you don't have to deal with it maybe. It's tedious having to put up with him all the time, and to watch his machinations with other people.'

'What do you mean?'

'He had a hold over Agnes for a long time. It's probably why Agnes and I don't get on. Her PhD student Sophie, ditto.

Various others over the years too. Most of his attention these days is focused on Dunford, though.'

'Yes,' I said. 'Senan told me. Some historical conflict regarding his transfer from commerce into law when he was an undergraduate.'

'Oh, I don't know anything about that. And it's not what I'm talking about either. It's about Casey expecting him to be grateful. He helped Senan Dunford get that fellowship in Limerick. And *some* of us suspect, Cormac Ryan and I at least, that Casey's much-trumpeted article in the *Journal of Comparative Law*, the first since his wife became ill, blah, blah, *blah* – I heard him boring the arse off Padraic O'Flaherty about it at the conference dinner – well, *we* think Casey might've got more than a little uncredited help from Senan Dunford in the writing of it and— That's the doorbell so I'm afraid ...'

I had dozens of other questions I wanted to ask but my allotted time was up.

It was probably just as well. A bomb had gone off in my head. I needed time to pick up the pieces.

SATURDAY

106

IF SENAN DUNFORD HAD LIED ABOUT HIS relationship with Casey, what else had he lied about? And why?

I'd spent the whole night turning it over in my head. The obvious answer was that he was trying to hide something. Again and again, I asked myself, What?

Not wanting to admit it to myself.

That the reason it had been so hard to identify the murderer of William Atkins from the people in the East Wing that Wednesday night, the dinner guests and support staff, was because the murder might not have been committed by *any* of them.

Because Atkins might have been killed by someone who wasn't even there.

Only maybe he was.

107

WHEN I'D MADE THAT LEAP, OTHER PARTS OF THE deception started to become clearer, however slightly.

How Dunford had been the one to tell me about the conflict with Professor Casey, how even right at the very start of the conference, that hadn't made sense. I'd noticed Casey applauding Dunford's speech just as enthusiastically as everyone else.

It was possible that Dunford, resentful of Casey's power and influence over him, had intended to kill Casey and mistaken Atkins for him.

Or when Dunford's murder plans were upset after Casey got drunk, and had to be walked home by Padraic O'Flaherty and Kirsty MacMillan, had he killed Atkins instead?

The first scenario brought me back to the mistaken-identity theory; the second to the random-attack theory. I'd rejected both theories a long time ago. And for good reason.

Because I'd felt sure that the murder was planned.

With malice aforethought, as Lia de Barra had said.

Which meant that, if Dunford had killed Atkins, he'd *intended* to kill Atkins.

After a night without sleep, I couldn't even begin to understand why.

Around 5 a.m., I decided to concentrate on how.

108

SENAN DUNFORD HAD SENT ME A MESSAGE ON
the evening of the dinner, a photograph of a chicken sandwich.
I'd seen it when I was in the loo and hadn't deleted it. Now I
saved the photo to my iPhone and checked its location and time.
It confirmed that when he said he was in the Circle K petrol
station, opposite Blackpool shopping centre, on the Limerick
Road, that was where he was. Presumably he'd be visible on
CCTV if anyone cared to look. Also, he'd given his tutorial
at the University of Limerick the following morning. He was
the person who'd confirmed it to me, and as it was so easy to
disprove, I was operating under the assumption he hadn't lied
about that.

But what had he done in between? The pattern he'd created
made it look like he'd left UCC, stopped for a sandwich, driven
home, given his tutorial the next day. If I was right, he hadn't
gone home directly. He'd probably left the petrol station and
headed towards Limerick. Out of range of traffic cameras, he
would have had no trouble circling back to UCC by a different
route, using minor roads. He could have driven home to Limerick
later. Was that even possible in the time available to him?

I opened Google Maps. Hampered by the fact that I didn't
have a home address for Dunford, I made my calculations more

general. Limerick is sixty-two miles, or ninety-nine kilometres, roughly north of Cork. It takes an hour and a half to drive there if you're not stuck in traffic in Buttevant and Charleville for half an hour each. But in the middle of the night, there would have been no delay. He could have killed Atkins and reached UL in time for the tutorial with hours to spare.

And in UCC on the evening of the conference, with exams coming up, the College grounds were heaving. If he'd approached the campus on foot, dressed in a hoodie or a North Face jacket, he'd have blended in easily. Bided his time. Waited for his opportunity. But *where* had he waited?

I left my ground-floor office and went upstairs to the kitchen to make a cup of coffee. As I did so, the complete absence of motive began to niggle at me again. I forced myself to ignore it. For now, the motive didn't matter. I had to focus on the method. If I could get a grasp on the how of the murder, the why might emerge.

I walked to the window, leaned my forehead on the glass, took a few slow breaths, kept my eyes open. In the east, a softening of the darkness, the first stirrings of dawn. All around me, people would be having Saturday morning lie-ins, strolling downtown later on, going for a drink maybe. I felt no envy. I felt nothing but a cold certainty that what I was doing I had to do.

From somewhere, I recalled what Ian McAnespie had told me, the feeling he'd had that there was someone else in the East Wing men's bathroom.

And what Seamus from Buildings and Estates had said, about the bulb having been removed from the supplies cupboard, the loosening of the casing. Dunford could have done that at any time during the day of the conference, even early that morning, in anticipation of using the space as a hidey-hole that evening. Having the bulb gone meant that if someone *had* opened the door, they wouldn't have been able to see him, or what he might have stored there.

The problem was that I'd never seen the store cupboard or anywhere else Dunford might have used. On my previous visits to the East Wing, I hadn't been thinking along those lines. I had to return to the crime scene to check it over again with different eyes.

Except, now that the lock on the access door in Aula Maxima was fixed, the East Wing would be shut all weekend.

And I couldn't contact the president to arrange access. According to my suspension letter, MLC had informed her that I was 'unavailable' for any more work on the Atkins case.

But she had previously issued an edict that everyone in College was to provide me with full cooperation. With luck, she might not yet have reversed it.

109

'WE COULD MEET AT ALCHEMY,' RORY DONNELLY said. 'I need to have something to eat and—'

'No,' I said. 'We don't have time. After you've let me into the East Wing, you can go and get breakfast somewhere in College. It'll be my treat. As a small thank-you.'

Alchemy was the café at the corner of Barrack Street and Fort Street. I didn't want to meet him there because I didn't want him to think we were going to become friends. He lived too close to me for that to be a good idea, in a house on Prosperity Square, a pleasing quadrangle of late-nineteenth-century terraced cottages built by the Cork Improved Dwellings Company, only a two-minute walk from my house, some rental properties scattered among long-term owner-occupiers.

Donnelly's proximity was one of the reasons I'd thought of contacting him. The other reason was that, as a novice member of the security staff, he was far enough down the pecking order that he might not have been informed of my current 'unavailability'. I didn't know the house number, but on Prosperity Square, the neighbours would be able to tell me where he lived and whether he was at home or gone out. It was that kind of place. People looked out for each other. In summer, some of the women sat outside their doors knitting and chatting. They would have known exactly who I was too, wondered what I was up to at this hour on a Saturday. Having thought it through, I decided to try the phone.

He answered my text message asking if he was free to take a call with an enthusiastic quadruple thumbs-up. Picked up immediately when I rang. No, he wasn't at work but doing what I asked of him would be no bother at all, he said.

I arranged to meet him by the front of Choristers' House, tall and stone-built, on Dean Street, further along in the direction of the college. Across the narrow roadway rose the high wall of the cathedral graveyard and, beside that, the slope and steps leading down to Proby's Quay. Nearby too were the steps of Keyser's Hill, a steep track to the river used first by Vikings more than a thousand years before, the Scandinavian name still in use today. The past reaches out its hand to you in Cork. A cold hand it can be, sometimes.

Donnelly arrived a minute or two before the appointed time. I was pleased to note that he'd donned his work uniform even though he was on a day off. It would make his collection of the keys less noticeable.

As we walked, I said, 'I need you to be discreet, Rory. Can you do that?'

He nodded. 'It's like you said before, it'll all help with my application.'

'Your application?' After I'd said the words, I recalled what he meant.

He confirmed it. 'For An Garda Síochána.'

I took a long moment to suppress the shame that bubbled in my stomach. I was taking advantage of Donnelly, putting his job with UCC at risk, if it all went wrong. I was less concerned about messing with his hopes of joining the guards, though. From what I'd seen of him so far, that dream had to be a very long shot indeed.

'Probably best not to mention this part of the investigation without checking it with me first, Rory, eh?'

'Maybe you could help me filling out the application form?'

My guilt assuaged, I said, 'I'd be glad to. After this is all over, I reckon I'll have plenty of time on my hands.'

We arrived at College shortly after nine and entered the East Wing via the small, pointed Gothic door at the corner of the quad. My plan was to get Donnelly to open everywhere and then to ask him to step outside for a while to 'keep an eye on things'. In reality, I badly needed the silence that his absence would provide. The man never stopped talking. I couldn't hear myself think.

'Let's open up the access to the Aula first, Rory, and then you could ...'

My voice died in my throat. Donnelly unlocked the door to the Aula Maxima, looked at me quizzically, expecting me to continue. Then, spotting the direction of my gaze, he glanced down the corridor to the far end.

'Oh,' he said.

We were not alone.

110

'WHAT'S YOUR NAME?' THE PRESIDENT BARKED, addressing Donnelly.

He got out the two words somehow.

'Thank you. That'll be all for now. You can go.'

Donnelly looked at me uncertainly. I hadn't told him anything of my theory about Senan Dunford and I realised from his face that he had suspicions about the president. He was right to. My theory about Dunford was just that. And, as the last person to see Atkins alive, the president was still very much a suspect. Donnelly had spent the entire walk to College babbling incessantly, yet he hadn't mentioned that. He *had* been discreet. I felt a belated respect for him.

'It's okay,' I said.

He nodded at the president and said, in a loud voice, 'I'll wait *right* outside, so.'

After he'd gone, the president said, 'I've been talking to your managing partner Gabriel McGrath.' She pronounced it in the English manner, sounding the *th*.

I made no reply.

She continued, 'I'm told that you've been "redeployed". That you're "unavailable".'

She made quotation marks with her fingers. I said nothing.

'And before that, you were avoiding my calls and messages. Running your own show, it seems. Which is absolutely *not* what we agreed on. Reading between the lines, I imagine that your employers are quite as dissatisfied with your work on this case as I am. Which will be reflected in the fee to be paid. If any. So why are you here?'

I panicked. The more I thought about it, the less likely it seemed that the murderer was Senan Dunford, the more likely it was the woman standing in front of me, a woman with so many secrets and a past and a current connection to Atkins. I'd wasted so much time, made so many mistakes.

'I'm *waiting*,' the president said. '*What* are you doing here?'

From the corner of my eye, I glimpsed Donnelly. Outside the window. Looking in. If the worst came to the worst, I could signal to him and he'd come running.

'I know,' I said.

An unreadable expression crossed her face. 'Know what?'

'That you're married to Agnes. That you're both planning to move to Australia.'

The president dipped her head and looked to her right. Stared. Seemed oblivious to my presence. There was dead silence. Then she put her left hand into her jeans pocket.

111

SHE TOOK OUT A WEDDING RING, SLIPPED IT ONTO
the third finger of her left hand.

'That's a relief,' she said. 'I hate not wearing it.'

Before I could respond, Agnes stepped out of the president's
office. 'I'm so sorry, Finn,' she said. 'I *was* planning to tell you.
But we wanted to keep things on the down-low for a while,
until it was safe.'

'Safe? What do you mean?'

'I'm pregnant, well, we both are, but I'm the one carrying it.
That's why Nell moved here, took the UCC job. We met a couple
of years ago when I was on sabbatical at Cambridge. We just knew.
After that, things moved very fast. We wanted a family and …'

'Why the secrecy?' I asked.

'A lot of people *do* know, our families, close friends. We didn't
bother telling anyone else. We're private people. We didn't see
the need. Also, we thought it might be better for Nell's job.
Make it easier for her to settle in as the first woman president.
Who told you?'

'I'm not at liberty to say. The person who told me assumed
that I knew. But I didn't, obviously. And I didn't know about
the baby until just now.'

The president said, 'I think I can guess who it was. You had dinner with Matthew Cameron from the Australian Embassy. It was after that that you stopped answering my calls, but I didn't put it together until now. And Matthew Cameron didn't know about the baby.'

Agnes continued, 'Neither did we when we applied for the visa. We had an earlier pregnancy but I, we ... That was another reason we didn't want to ... Too much pressure. We wanted to wait. This one seems like a fighter, though. So the doctor says anyway.'

The president took her hand, gave it a squeeze.

Agnes said, 'We'd intended to stay in Cork but when the Melbourne job came up, it was too good an opportunity. And Nell was *asked* to apply. By the current chancellor. We decided that she would and that, if her application was successful, I'd take a career break from here and go with her. Inviting Atkins to the conference was all part of the strategy. He's influential – he *was*. That was why Nell had the dinner. Look, we had no motive to kill him, either of us. And it was my idea to get you in to help with the investigation. Whatever hope we had of keeping the Melbourne application on track, if the murder could be solved quickly, with as little damage as possible to Nell, we—'

'Why didn't you tell me about your relationship *after* the murder?'

The president said, 'Agnes wanted to. I disagreed. We compromised by agreeing that we'd tell you at the first appropriate opportunity. Which is now.'

'And what about the Melbourne plans?'

Agnes answered, 'We've both come to terms with the fact that Melbourne's not going to happen for us now. We're planning on staying in UCC. And, with the baby coming, we've realised too that we don't want to be so far from family.'

'Now will you tell us why you're here? And on a Saturday?' the president asked.

'You first,' I said.

She laughed. 'I'm in since before eight. That's why they pay me the big bucks. There's a lot of catching up to do. The murder's been taking up all my time. And Agnes isn't sleeping well at the moment. She decided to come along. Now you.'

'One more thing, Agnes. On the CCTV, I saw you. After you'd left, you returned to the East Wing. It looked like you'd got a message on your phone.'

'From Nell. She said she was at the far side of the East Wing and asked me where I was. I went back in and we spoke for no more than a few minutes, by the door to the garden. She was alone. She told me Will was in the loo. I returned to the quad by the outside, the long way. I didn't go back into the East Wing again.'

'What was so important? What did you talk about?'

'Nell said that Professor Atkins didn't want her to walk him back to Hayfield Manor. And that he didn't want to have a late drink. So that meant ...'

The president said, 'It meant that Agnes could come to my flat instead of going back to hers. If she wanted to.'

'I decided to stick with the original plan to go to my own house. I'd left stuff there that I needed for Thursday. It was nothing sinister. And I didn't see Will after I left the first time.'

I believed Agnes. My old classmate. I *wanted* to believe her. Because I wanted her and her wife to be free to bring their new baby into the world. I wanted them both to be innocent.

But it was still possible that I was entirely wrong about Dunford and that the president was responsible, that the late-night conversation between Agnes and her had gone entirely differently from how they'd related it just now.

And something else scraped at the edge of my mind, a question I needed to ask, but I couldn't reach it. Instead I thought again about what they'd said. Decided to take a chance.

Half a chance. I wouldn't tell them the full story.

112

'YOU'RE RIGHT,' I SAID. 'I'VE BEEN, EM, REDEPLOYED but I hate leaving a job half finished and that's why I'm here. I've had a few ideas overnight about where the murderer might have hidden.'

The president's face brightened. 'You think it might have been an intruder?'

I waited a beat before replying, 'In a way, I think I do.'

Both women looked unimpressed by my deliberate vagueness. The president seemed to be about to make a comment when Agnes shook her head. She asked, 'What do you need?' Her voice was sympathetic. She couldn't have failed to notice my exhaustion.

'I brought Rory Donnelly the security guard here this morning, on my own time, and his, I might add. I want him to open all the doors in the East Wing and then I'll need to go again to the CCTV camera room and—'

'You won't have to come inside my office?' the president asked, more sharply than I might have wished.

'I don't think so,' I said.

The president looked at Agnes, who shrugged. The president went on, 'In that case, I'm going to shut my door and let you and, er, Watson get on with it.'

I smiled, said, 'Thank you,' and beckoned to Rory Donnelly to come back in.

I kept my theory on the identity of the murderer from Donnelly. With a running commentary from him that I was able to tune out after a while, we spent most of the next hour checking every possible concealment location in the East Wing. There were hiding places other than the supply cupboard. Donnelly favoured the outside lavatory in the interior courtyard.

'The oldest flush toilet in Cork,' Rory Donnelly said. 'Still working. Though nobody uses it any more. No one would ever find you here. It would be an ideal place to hide.'

It might be. If hiding was your main aim. But nowhere in the East Wing was as convenient as the cleaning-supplies cupboard. Larger than the office I'd been allocated in the Horgan Building, one door, marked 'Staff Only', and boltable from the inside, opened off the men's bathroom. A second door, also marked 'Staff Only' but without a lock, led directly onto the corridor, adjacent to the main door to the President's Garden.

I remembered going to the loo during dinner, seeing Donnelly stationed outside there, letting him know that all was quiet. He'd left at that point. After he'd gone, it would have been easy for Dunford to slip unseen into the East Wing, conceal himself in the supply cupboard and, whenever the opportunity arose, murder Atkins.

Perhaps the plan had been to murder him earlier in the evening. But Atkins hadn't gone to the loo until the end of the night.

Or maybe Dunford had intended to do it later. To follow him back to his hotel, attack him on Perrott Avenue? Make it look like a mugging? If that were true, he might have been using the supply cupboard simply to keep an ear out for the break-up of the party.

But that felt too improvised. And far too risky. If someone had walked Atkins back to Hayfield Manor, the mugging attempt would have failed.

I thought about it again. There were two head injuries, one that might have been a punch, or a swipe with a cosh, and another with the distinctive shape of the urinal. Dunford might have surprised Atkins, hit him to disorient him, then smashed his head off the urinal.

There were only a few men in the building that evening. It was reasonable to expect that they wouldn't have gone to the loo together, if they could have avoided it. Dunford would have anticipated Atkins coming to the bathroom alone at some point. It was possible that the plan had been to make it look like Atkins had taken a tumble there during dinner, and hit his head with fatal consequences. Anyone coming upon him would have assumed illness or accident, at least initially. Attempts would have been made to revive him. An ambulance would have been called. It would have been chaos.

But Atkins wasn't drinking alcohol. And, when he finally did come to the bathroom, maybe he'd proved harder to kill than expected. The strangulation with the tie might have been a last resort, the hiding of the body an act of desperation.

If that was the case, it had been a good idea to conceal the corpse, in a toilet stall or the supply cupboard, and wait to move it until after the security check had been completed and all the exterior doors locked.

When the coast was clear, he must have dragged the body from the men's bathroom, keeping the lights off and staying low to avoid being seen through the windows leading onto the quad. Then, he broke the lock to the gallery door and arranged the corpse in a seated position at the bottom of the stairs and let himself out, most likely by the door to the President's Garden.

Strictly speaking, there was no need to move the body. He'd had access to a cupboard full of cleaning supplies, including bleach and wipes. He could have cleaned the body and the area around it, and left it in the bathroom. If he had, it would almost certainly have been found the next morning.

But by moving it, Dunford was helping his chances of evading detection even more. It might easily have been after the weekend when the body was found, when the gallery was next cleaned. The longer the delay, the more degraded any evidence would be. He hadn't counted on nosy schoolgirl Annabelle Leahy, of course. The body had been discovered a couple of days early, thanks to her.

Though it might have made little difference. The full set of DNA results might take weeks or even months to come, but the way Sadie had been talking, the guards were holding out little hope of finding much by way of forensic evidence.

I walked from the gallery entrance back up the corridor to the door to the President's Garden. 'This is how he got out,' I said. 'No CCTV. Has to be.'

Donnelly asked, 'Why break the lock to the Aula, though? To cause confusion?'

'Maybe. Or in case he was trapped, needed a second way out? Or a way in? An insurance policy to give him another escape route if he was spotted.' I thought about it. 'Alternatively, the Aula door could have been intended as an emergency access route *into* the East Wing if all the exterior doors were shut during the dinner. Even if they were, he could have banked on the Stone Corridor and the Aula Max being open until lock-up time.'

Not only that. I didn't tell Donnelly, but I now suspected that the breaking of the lock between the East Wing and the Aula was somehow related to the noise I'd heard first thing that Wednesday morning. That Dunford must have seen me arriving unexpectedly through the rear door, and hidden quickly. In doing so, maybe he'd dropped the tool he was using. Or something like that. He must have been terrified that I'd seen him. He'd made a beeline for me by the buffet table. But I hadn't seen a thing. My oblivious reaction must have reassured him. Yet he'd continued to keep an eye on me during the day, before the murder. And since. Met me for coffee. Asked me out. All in an attempt to deflect suspicion from himself.

Donnelly said, 'You reckon it was all planned.'

'Possibly not quite the exact way he ended up doing it, but it was planned.'

'Do you know who did it?'

It was the first time he'd asked me straight out. 'Not for sure, no.'

'Do you know why?'

'I still haven't a clue what the motive was.'

He looked in the direction of the president's office door, side-eyed me. 'You're certain it was a *man*, are you?'

He hadn't heard the conversation between the three of us earlier. I thought about my answer. Kept it simple. 'I think so,' I said.

He accepted it, but I didn't know if he agreed. 'Right, boss. What's next?'

'Another look at the CCTV.'

'Grand job.'

'If you want to head away and grab breakfast, Rory, you can.'

'No way, José,' he said. 'I'm in it to win it. Come on.'

I knocked at the president's office door.

'Come in,' she said.

Entering, I took in the scene: the president at her desk, Agnes in an armchair, her laptop elevated on several cushions.

'This is cosy,' I said.

Agnes gave a watery smile. She looked tired and pale. 'Are you finished?'

'Yes,' I said.

'If it helps, you were never here,' the president said. 'Not as far as your firm is concerned.'

'Thanks,' I said. 'It does. I'd prefer not to say any more for now. So far, it's just a theory I'm working on.'

'I assume you'll take your findings to the police,' the president said.

'If they amount to anything, yes.'

I backed out of the room and went to meet Donnelly on the quad.

113

IT WAS STILL BEFORE TEN. THE CAMPUS WAS QUIET,
eerily reminiscent of the Saturday when Annabelle Leahy had
found the body. The day was only getting going. Birds sang. The
weather was dry but overcast. How was Annabelle, I wondered.
Upset and traumatised, presumably. I hoped she was recovering
from the shock of it all.

It helped that Kasper Nowak was on duty in the North Wing
camera room. I explained that we'd come from the East Wing
where we'd been with the president.

'I thought you were finished with this job,' he said.

'Not yet. Talk to the president if you like. She's in her office.'

'It's okay,' he said.

It struck me that he knew precisely where I'd been because
the CCTV had been restored to the East Wing. Agnes and the
president's relationship would be all over the university by
lunchtime on Monday. I remembered Agnes rubbing her belly
in the way of all pregnant women. I groaned inwardly. They'd
think it was me who'd told. I'd contact Agnes later to let her
know to expect a deluge of well-wishers and gossip-gatherers.

I told Nowak and Donnelly that we were looking for a single
male figure, coming from the direction of the President's Garden,

and going straight out one of the gates alone, or mingling with a group of departing students. When we didn't find that, we started looking for someone heading back in the direction of the library.

It took a while, but I found him eventually, a hooded figure, carrying a small rucksack, standing near the railings by the Giant Redwoods, then falling in with a group leaving the library just before it closed at 2 a.m. I couldn't see his face, but I knew it was Dunford.

Once we had him, Nowak picked him up on three other cameras, head down, walking close behind a group of students down the steps onto Main Avenue and out the gate onto Western Road and off campus. We lost him after that.

I handed Kasper Nowak a memory stick. 'Can you download the relevant sections onto this please?'

'Who's it for? The president?'

'No,' I said. 'It's for the guards.'

'They have everything from me already,' he said. 'I told you this before.'

'I know,' I said. 'But do it anyway. Please.'

'Just saying,' he said. 'Calm down. I will do.' As he gave me the memory stick, he asked, 'Who is it?'

'I can't tell you yet,' I said. 'I'm not a hundred per cent sure myself.'

But I *was* sure that it was Senan Dunford.

On the other hand, Sadie took considerably more convincing.

114

I CHECKED FIRST WITH COUGHLAN'S QUAY. NOT on duty. Not replying to my *Please call me* texts.

Coming up to lunchtime on a Saturday? She could be anywhere but she was most likely to be at home. I drove across town to her house, a renovated bungalow near Rathcooney Cemetery in the countryside beyond Mayfield. Her husband Jack's furniture-making workshop was in a converted garage block in their beautiful overgrown garden. I texted her from outside to tell her I was there.

As I walked towards the front door, it opened. 'What's so urgent?' she asked. 'And, by the way, you shouldn't be contacting me. And you shouldn't be here. You're still a person of interest in, em, the Atkins investigation.'

She'd stumbled over his name but she hadn't called him my father. It made me think – hope – that she might have come to believe that I hadn't known about him.

'I know who did it,' I said.

She hid her surprise well. 'I thought you'd come here to grovel.'

The grovelling should have been the other way around as far as I was concerned. I didn't say that. Instead, I managed, 'I've been busy. And, in case you didn't hear me the first time, I know who did it. At least, I think I do.'

She replied faster than I'd expected. 'You'd better come in.'

'I need coffee and some kind of a sandwich before I fall down.'

'The grovelling didn't last long, I see. And cheese is all you're getting.'

You're the one who arrested me, I almost said. Almost. But then we'd have had to get into all of that again. The DNA test. What I'd known. What I hadn't.

'Cheese is fine by me,' I said. 'Toasted, preferably.'

We went into the kitchen: individual handcrafted furniture pieces, made by Jack, that Sadie had told me were pretty to look at but terrible dust gatherers, on top of which she had no proper countertop and had to do all her food preparation at one end of the refectory-style table on an array of beautifully carved hardwood chopping boards. She complained about it a lot. Loved it too. The only thing missing were the children she and Jack had always wanted, and still hoped to have, though it hadn't worked out for them so far.

As Sadie prepared lunch, I told her what I'd learned, beginning with the contradiction between what Dunford had said about his relationship with Casey and what Professor Lia de Barra had told me about them. I said it had started me wondering what else Dunford had lied about.

'I don't get it,' Sadie said. 'You find out a slightly different version of things from a person who hates Casey's guts and would say anything to do him down, including that he didn't write his own essay in that law journal or whatever. And even if it *is* true that Dunford wrote it and not Casey, what has it to do with the murder? Nothing, as far as I can see.'

'On the surface, you're right. But I think Dunford was worried I'd seen him that morning in the Aula Max interfering with the lock. I heard a loud noise as I was walking through it first thing. The place was empty and there was this sound, like a book falling off a shelf. Now I think he dropped something. Possibly the tool he was using.'

'And if he *was* going to break the lock, why wait until that morning? Why not do it sooner? A few weeks?'

'Presumably because it might be fixed?'

'Okay, that's a good point,' Sadie said. 'Go on.'

'So he came up to me in the coffee room. To suss me out. Must've realised pretty quickly that I hadn't seen him. But, just in case, he went ahead and painted himself as the outsider, telling me he was disliked by Casey, implying he was bullied by him, and saying that he'd be out of a job soon, getting the sympathy vote from me, and also befriending me, so I'd never suspect him. *And* he asked me out. After the murder. To dinner. I said yes, by the way.'

'*Now* we're talking,' Sadie said. 'Given your history in attracting criminals …'

I made no response.

'I'm talking about Davy Keenan. Your ex.'

'I know,' I said.

After a silence, she asked, 'He *is* still your *ex*?'

I shook my head. 'It was raining. He gave me a lift home. I slept with him. We didn't even talk. And he didn't stay the night. It was a one-time thing. Not to be repeated.'

She took in a deep breath and stood to clear away the plates. 'The less said the better, probably?'

I nodded. Then I told her about my dad, how sick he'd been,

how worried I'd been about him. We hugged each other and cried.

A while after that, as she loaded the dishwasher, Sadie said, 'I had a feeling about that guy.'

'Davy? *Again* with this?'

'*No!* Dunford. He was *too* helpful. Too sweet to be wholesome. No one normal would want to drive all the way to Cork to hang around a garda station if there's an alternative on offer. He could've made a statement and given a DNA test in a station in Limerick, or a local member would've called to his house by appointment.' She paused. 'But the part of Limerick he's from got me interested in him.' She named the area and went on. 'After I found *that* out, I liked him so much for the murder I even checked how long it would've taken for him to drive to Limerick and give his tutorial after killing Atkins and doing the clean-up on the night of the murder.'

'I did that too,' I said. 'The timing works.'

'So I talked to our lads up in Limerick, at Roxboro Road Station. Dunford's never come to their attention. Straight and narrow all the way. He's from a locality with a lot of social problems. But he's one of the success stories. Only child of a single mother. Father estranged. And this is where it gets interesting. Senan Dunford may not have criminal or gangland connections but his dad does.'

She said a name. A different surname from Dunford's. I recognised it from dozens of news stories over decades.

'Jesus.'

'Yeah. But Senan Dunford did well. Stayed out of trouble. And his mother is clean and always has been. She's worked hard her whole life. So it was a great theory. But, in the end, that's *all* it was. I ruled him out. Unless you found a surprise motive that I'm not aware of.'

'Maybe some killers don't need motives.'

'Rubbish. If that's all you've got, you're wasting my time. And your own.'

I said, 'Give me a chance. Let me tell you how I think he did it.'

MONDAY
AFTERNOON

115

'HOW'S IT GOING?' I ASKED.

Dunford had been arrested at his mother's home in Limerick at 6 a.m. and conveyed to Coughlan's Quay. Sadie had promised to phone me and let me know what was happening. It was after 2 p.m. and this was the first call I'd had from her.

'He's exercising his right to silence,' she said. 'Asking for plenty of breaks. Sitting cosily with his solicitor.' She sighed. 'The more I see of him, the more convinced I am that it's him, but we're making no progress.'

'Who's his solicitor?'

'Conleth Young.'

'He's good. And he acts for a lot of professional criminals.'

'Yup. And Dunford's in under Section 4. No special circumstances. No guns. No drugs. We have a max of twenty-four hours with the fucker at this stage.'

'Yeah,' I said. 'That's what I reckoned.'

We'd spent all of Saturday evening talking out the theory. And Sadie had worked through Sunday too, eventually persuading her superintendent that Dunford was worth arresting.

'There just isn't enough to go on,' she said. 'There's still no proof that Dunford came back to UCC that night. His alibi has holes, and it can be challenged by the prosecution, but the chances are it's not enough for a conviction. The DPP isn't going to recommend a murder charge based on little more than our gut feelings. The fact that there's zero motive is a major issue. Unless something changes, we're probably going to have to release him without charge.'

'Not yet, though,' I said. 'You have him until tomorrow morning, right?'

Silence at the other end of the line.

'Jesus, Sadie, tell me he's not gone already!'

'No, Finn, he's still here … but he'll probably be out by tonight.'

'Okay,' I said. 'Thanks for telling me. Keep him as long as you can.'

I ended the call, grabbed my bag and ran out the door.

116

I HAD IT IN MIND TO TALK AGAIN TO THE PRESIDENT
and to the four people from the law school – Agnes, Martin
Casey, Sophie and Lia de Barra – who'd been present at the
dinner. Legally, I wasn't allowed to tell them about Dunford's
arrest. Names aren't released before someone is charged. But
these things dribble out. I was fairly sure that the superintendent
would have informed the president and that she would inevitably
have taken Agnes into her confidence.

And if the president had told Agnes, now that the news was
out about their marriage, she would probably have had to tell
Casey and Lia de Barra too, to ensure that there could be no
accusation of favouritism. I dropped into Lia's office first.

Her opening words confirmed my suspicions. She said, 'I
assume you heard Dunford's been arrested.'

'Yes. I—'

She cut me off. 'Looks like he won't be applying for the job,
then.'

'What job?'

'There's a new permanent lecturing position coming up.
It's going to be advertised in the next month or two. It's not
quite Dunford's area, and obviously he'd still have to apply and

be approved by the interview panel, but Casey's been angling for him to get it. Recompense for the article in the *Journal of Comparative Law* and all the future books and articles Dunford was going to write for him, presumably. Casey's gone rather quiet, as you'd expect. His protégé appears to have let him down rather badly. All very unfortunate for our little Marty.'

'Is he in the building?'

'He came in but went home mid-morning when he heard the news of Dunford's arrest. Mentioned stress and taking early retirement, I believe.'

'Were you talking to him?'

'Heard it from Sheila, the school administrator,' Lia said. 'I would've expected you to have spoken to her already during the course of the investigation but, to my surprise, she told me you hadn't. She's been here forever and a day. There's nothing she doesn't know.'

'I need to talk to Agnes too. Is she here?'

'*Oh*, you mean the first lady. I've heard that that's what *some* people are calling her now. Or Mrs President.'

'*People* are calling her those names? Or is it just you, Lia?'

She laughed. Looking unperturbed, she said, 'Shut the door on your way out.'

I was pleased to find Agnes looking better than she had the last time I'd seen her, two days previously.

'I got some sleep the last couple of nights,' she said. 'I think I'm finally accepting what the doctor is telling me. That Junior's doing okay. That there's no medical reason he shouldn't be born happy and healthy.'

'He?'

'It's a boy. After what happened last time, we wanted to know as soon as we could.'

'I'm so happy for you. For both of you.' I paused. 'You heard what's happened?'

'I can't believe it,' she said. 'I *don't* believe it. Senan couldn't have done it. We're *writing a book* together. He's ... He can be intense sometimes. But he's not a murderer. It's not possible. Have you heard anything from Sadie as to why he's been arrested?'

I dodged the question. 'Not much. And I don't think we can do anything except leave it up to the guards at this stage. But, ah, there was one more thing. I meant to ask you on Saturday. It's this. How did Atkins end up in a different hotel to the other conference guests?'

'Because Martin Casey insisted. You'll have to ask him yourself. Pointless snobbery. Putting on a show for the posh visitor. It didn't make any sense to me at the time. Still doesn't.'

117

I NEEDED TO MAKE ANOTHER VISIT TO CASEY ON
the North Mall but first I had to talk to Sheila, the law-school
administrator. I'd tried to meet her several times before without
success. She hadn't been in the main office, the one with the big
photocopier, anytime I'd called in previously.

But she was there now, standing by her desk, a severe-looking
woman in her sixties. Guarded at the start. I explained who I
was. Said I was a graduate.

She thawed a little. 'I don't remember you. Trust me, that's a
good thing. Some students I remember all too well.'

I laughed. 'I wanted to ask you about—'

'Dr Dunford? In a little bit of bother, I hear. Funny thing,
he's one of the ones I *do* recall from their undergraduate days. He
transferred from comm. *Such* a palaver.' She wrinkled her nose.
'Didn't have the points for law day one. Got in the back door
after a lot of pushing.'

'Professor Casey was good to him, I believe?'

'He *warmed* to him, I suppose, shall we say? But it took time.
They're thick as thieves now, mind you, for some reason. Or
were, I should say. Today's events have—'

'Why do you think that is? That they became so close.'

'I couldn't possibly imagine. There was a touch of the you-scratch-my-back-and-I'll-scratch-yours about it, I suppose. Dunford had the youth, Martin Casey the power.'

We talked some more but I was conscious of time running out. I had to get to the North Mall, to Casey's flat. He had a solid alibi, but now I knew for sure that he was close to Dunford, that he'd been helping him to find employment. And I also knew that Casey had been the one to insist on Atkins staying at Hayfield Manor. Finding out why he'd done that might have nothing to do with the case but it was worth following up nevertheless, in case Dunford had been the one to suggest it. For as long as he was detained, I was determined to carry on digging for every possible scrap of information, no matter how obscure. After his release, everything would get more difficult.

'Thanks for your time, Sheila,' I said. 'I have to go now, though. There's a few more people I need to see.'

I was almost out the door when Sheila said, in what seemed like an afterthought, 'You know, it's funny, but the moment I heard about the murder, I thought of Martin. I thought it should have been him who did it. It wasn't, I know that. I heard he got drunk and had to be walked home.'

'That's right. Professor Casey has two alibi witnesses. But I'm curious. Why did you think it might have been him?'

After a long moment she said, 'It was his wife.'

'She was ill, I heard. Had MS.'

'She wasn't *always* ill, though. And she was very beautiful as a young woman. Beautiful and lively.'

'What do you mean by lively?'

'I'm fairly sure – more than fairly, actually, I know for definite that she had a fling with the late William Atkins when he was in

Cork back in the day. Thirty-eight, thirty-nine years ago now. When the Caseys were newlyweds. I was barely in the job. Very junior. But I had two eyes in my head. More sense than Martin too … It was a few more years before they had the kids. And Atkins wasn't the only one she played around with, I think. But she settled down, and after the children came along, they were so happy. She became ill years later, but they stayed happy till the day she died, despite her illness.'

'And you think that Casey knew about the affair with Atkins. And the others?'

'Oh, no,' she said. 'I don't think so. I don't think Martin ever found out. He couldn't have. He was so devoted, all those years while she was ill. He sacrificed so much for her.' She looked frightened. 'I shouldn't have told you. It was wrong of me. You won't say anything, will you? Promise me you won't?'

After a beat, I replied, 'I won't say a word to him, or to anyone in College.'

She looked sceptical. 'What does that mean?'

I said, 'It means that one man is dead, and another is in garda custody.'

'You're going to tell the guards what I said, aren't you?'

'It's what you expect me to do, isn't it, Sheila? It's the reason you told me.'

She didn't deny the truth of it, but turned her face away from me, said no more.

It occurred to me that she might have been in tears, but I had no time to comfort her. I had too much to do and too little time in which to do it.

❖

As I rushed downstairs, my head was spinning. If Casey had found out about his wife's affair with Atkins, even belatedly, what might he have done?

I remembered what Padraic O'Flaherty had told me, how Casey kept saying, 'Why did it have to happen?' At the time I'd thought Casey had meant 'Why did she have to die?'

And there was what he'd told me himself, how he couldn't bear to be in the house they'd shared, how he was clearing it out, planning to paint it white.

As if he wanted to erase every trace of his married life.

It had looked like grief, all of it. His tears. His heavy drinking.

But what if it wasn't grief? What if it was anger?

118

OUTSIDE THE DOOR, IN THE SHADE OF THE YEW
tree, I called Sadie. Her phone went straight to voicemail. I rang
Coughlan's Quay garda station, asked to talk to her.

'She's busy, I'm afraid. Do you want to leave a message?'

'Tell her to contact Finn. Tell her it's urgent.'

I ended the call and broke into a run, piecing it together on
my way.

In the public office, barely able to catch my breath, I asked the
member on the desk for Sadie again. Got no again. 'What about
Olly Fogarty?'

'Give me a sec.' The window shut in my face.

Two torturous minutes later came the response. 'Both of
them are busy. Can't be disturbed. They'll get your message
when they're free.'

'It'll be too late.' The window shut in my face again. Slammed
was more accurate.

The last time I was here, I'd been under arrest myself. The
lack of cooperation might have been understandable were the

situation not so serious. I rang the bell, hammered on the glass. The window was opened by a different garda.

'What?'

'Is Detective Garda Ruth Joyce here?'

'If I get her for you, will you fuck off afterwards?'

'Yeah,' I said.

'Take a seat.'

I didn't.

119

TEN MINUTES OF PACING LATER, RUTH JOYCE
appeared.

'You know me,' I said. 'I'm not a messer. The interview
with Senan Dunford needs to be suspended immediately. I have
vital information. I need to tell Sadie. Potential game-changer.
Honestly. Get her for me. Please. And don't tell me to take a
seat. There's no time for sitting.'

She said nothing, disappeared into the garda station.

I went out onto the steps. Tried to breathe. Hoped against
hope that Dunford hadn't already been released without charge.

Sadie came out to me sometime later. I don't know how many
minutes had passed. I'd stopped counting by then. She asked,
'What's the story?'

I said, 'Dunford wasn't the only one involved. It was a two-
man job after all.'

120

THEY FOUND CASEY AT HOME. I WATCHED FROM
the railing by the river as he emerged, escorted by Olly Fogarty.
Ruth Joyce followed, carrying two clear plastic bags containing
a laptop and phone, Casey's presumably. He was wearing a suit,
but the tie was crooked and his hair, normally smoothly combed,
was standing on end. He looked unwashed. And defiant.

He shouted, 'I'm suing you for wrongful arrest. And assault.
The very minute, the *second*, I'm released, I'll be going *straight* to
my solicitor.'

At the station, I was put into a side room with Sadie, watching
him on camera as Fogarty and Joyce conducted the interview.

'In case he says something you can help us with,' Sadie had
said.

They didn't need me. Casey cracked wide open when confronted
with his wife's affair. He broke down, said he'd been clearing out
his wife's things and found some old diaries of hers, discovered
the truth about her and Atkins. He'd thrown the documents on
the fire to no avail.

'The damage was done,' he said. 'I knew it off by heart. I could hear every word going around in my head. Our whole life together was a lie. Despite everything, all those years she'd been thinking about him. Recalling her trysts with that satyr. That animal. Even while we ... Even in our most intimate times of married love. *True* love for me. But not for her.'

He went on, 'The murder was all Senan Dunford's idea. After Agnes told me she'd invited Atkins to the conference, and that the *bastard* had accepted, I was horrified and, in a weak moment, I told Dunford about the affair. I was trying to find a way of cancelling Atkins's attendance, you see. I couldn't bear the idea of him being back in Cork where they'd both ... Couldn't stand to look at him.

'*Dunford* was the one who said that I should let him come. He said I should kill him. He told me he knew someone who could get me a gun. He's from Limerick. I don't know exactly what part, but I imagine it's easy to get a gun up there if you have the contacts.'

He took a long drink of water.

After a time, he continued, 'I dismissed the idea at first. Out of hand, obviously. But then he came back to me. With a plan. He said he'd do it *for* me and in return I'd get him a job at the law school. I told him that there would have to be a formal selection process, an interview, that my opinion would only count for so much. He didn't care. He said I'd got Lia de Barra a post at the school and that I could do the same for him. He kept on and on. Worked at me over months and months. Manipulated me till I became his creature. What happened, it was all *his* fault.

'I was in his control. I felt I had no choice except to agree. But then I gathered my courage. Told him not to do it. I was terrified of him. Even so, I did everything I could to *stop* him. But he was my master by then. I was powerless.

'Then, after the murder, Dunford came to visit me at the law school. He'd come down from Limerick to give a DNA test. Dropped into my office. *Warned* me we had to hold our nerve. And you'll find nothing on my phone or on the laptop, by the way. We never used technology. Senan was far too clever to leave a trail like that. He turned off his phone the minute he left Cork on the evening of the conference. Didn't turn it on till the following morning. If asked, he planned to say that the battery had died. He had it plugged in during his tutorial up in UL. Made sure the students saw it too, in case the guards enquired. He thought of everything.

'In the unlikely event that it all went wrong, and Senan was arrested, he said he'd never be charged. And even if he was, he'd escape conviction. He said there was a ninety-nine point nine per cent chance of acquittal. There was no blood. Any small fragment of Dunford's DNA or mine that might be found on Atkins could be easily explained away.

'But it would never get that far, Dunford was sure of it. And I was too. There was no evidence against Dunford. Nothing. Means and opportunity, at best. No motive. And juries like motives. The DPP would never agree to prosecute based on so little. I was certain of that.'

He took another drink of water, then continued: 'I was the *only* one with a motive. And no one knew what it was. Apart from which, I ensured I had a rock-solid alibi. If it hadn't been

Kirsty and Padraic, or someone else, escorting me home, I'd have taken a taxi. That was the plan. Though I drank more than I'd intended. It was the pressure, you see.

'I never wanted any of this, I swear. Senan Dunford made me do it. He's evil. Dunford *wanted* to kill. If it hadn't been Atkins, it would have been someone else. Of that, I'm sure.'

121

MEANWHILE, IN THE OTHER ROOM, AFTER HE'D been informed of Casey's arrest and what he was saying about him, Dunford was flailing, sweating, but still saying nothing of substance.

Though at least he'd stopped saying, 'No comment.'

Instead, he kept repeating, 'He's lying. He's a liar.'

And, after a while, 'I'm not well. I need to see a doctor.'

AFTERWARDS

122

CASEY AND DUNFORD WERE CHARGED WITH
murder. A while later, Casey was granted bail in the High Court
– he had applied at the first opportunity.

But Dunford was still in custody, hadn't yet applied. I
wondered if he was planning an insanity defence.

I went to the District Court in Anglesea Street courthouse
for one of the remand hearings. Casey was there. He looked full
of energy and less puffy than he'd been. Like he'd given up the
drink. More like the lecturer I remembered from my time at
the law school. He was all business, wearing a suit and carrying
a briefcase from which he extracted bundles of paper that he
passed to his unfortunate solicitor, even though it was only an
adjournment. He was one of *those* clients.

Dunford appeared on screen, by video link from Cork Prison,
slumped low, his shoulders hunched, eyes downcast, his solicitor
requesting his examination by the prison doctor.

Seeing Casey and Dunford like that was enough for me. I felt
sure that both would be convicted at trial. I was equally sure that
they'd keep the appeal courts busy for years afterwards.

But my thoughts and feelings were no longer relevant. Sadie
had told me I was unlikely to be called as a witness. She'd offered

to keep me informed about the trial and investigation 'in the normal way'. It sounded odd to me.

I'd asked, 'What does that mean "in the normal way"?'

She'd replied, 'The way I'd keep any family member informed. He was your—'

'No!' I said. 'He shouldn't have died like that. And I'm glad, relieved, that I was able to help find his murderers. But that's as far as it goes.'

So I'd chosen to be a bystander, to learn about the case from media reports, the same as any member of the public. I was processing how all of that felt when the letter came.

A handwritten envelope, marked personal, addressed to me at my office. I was still suspended so someone, probably Tina, possibly Gabriel, had forwarded it to me.

Inside, a folded sheet of white A4 copy paper.

Dear Finn,

I would very much like it if you would come to visit me, if you could find the time.

Regards,

Senan D.

'You don't have to go,' Sadie said. 'On the other hand, if by any chance Dunford confessed to you, it might help.' After a silence, she went on, 'It's totally your choice. I won't pressure you. Casey's confession will be enough. We can get both convictions over the line without this.'

Without thinking, I replied, 'Of course I'll do it.'

Sadie collected me from home. Drove me to the prison. It's on Rathmore Road, a bleak spot at the top of one of the steepest hills in Cork. In times past, it used to be connected to the nearby army barracks, part of a command and control complex stretching back hundreds of years.

But the old prison shut down a while ago. Dunford was in the new one across the road. As we pulled into the parking area, the rain was striking the windscreen like shotgun pellets. I got out of the car and put my hand on the roof to steady myself. The high walls of the two prisons, the old and the new, provided a degree of shelter from the gusts. It felt oddly calm, like we were in the eye of a hurricane.

And, walking up to the entrance, I wondered why in hell I'd agreed to come.

123

INSIDE THE MEETING ROOM, DUNFORD SAT AT A table. He had on a grey sweatshirt and sweatpants and, after only a few weeks inside, his skin had turned grey too.

I sat down opposite him. He looked clean but he smelled of prison. Boiled meat and onions and old sweat and dirty socks. I almost gagged and pulled away.

'You know that this isn't a legal meeting,' I said. 'I can't be your solicitor.'

He said, 'Of course.'

'And if you say anything to me about the murder, I'm going to have to report it to the guards immediately.'

'I'd expect nothing less.'

His tone was resigned, his eyelids heavy. His lips were dry and there were white flakes at the corners of his mouth. I remembered his solicitor's request for medical intervention.

I asked, 'Are you on medication?'

'Antidepressants. I'm not out of it, if that's what you're worried about. I know what I'm saying.'

'Why did you ask to see me?'

'Because I know you're the reason I'm here.'

124

MY FIRST THOUGHT WAS THAT HE'D SOMEHOW learned of my connection to the victim.

'What do you mean by that, that *I'm* the reason?'

'You're the person who put the cops onto me.'

I waited for him to continue. He looked straight at me. His eyes were bloodshot.

'I've thought about it these last few weeks.' He paused. 'I've made up my mind. I want to tell the truth.' He paused again. 'I did it. I killed William Atkins. But it was Casey's idea. If I keep on saying nothing, he gets to be the one to tell my story. People will get the wrong impression. And I can't have that.'

I let out a breath, sat back in the chair.

After a beat, I said, 'He says the opposite. That it was all your idea.'

'He's lying.'

'Convince me,' I said.

'I was born in Limerick. Tough area. My dad wasn't in the picture. My mother made sure of that. And she made me work hard in school ... I can see from your face that you know who he is. It saves me the trouble of telling you. My mother always told me I wasn't him. That I was my own person. But ...

'Mam worked as a cleaner in the university. Wanted me to go to UL. From when I was about five, she brought me there. We walked around the grass and … Anyway, when it came to going to college, UL was the last place I wanted to go. I wanted to get out of Dodge. That's why I applied to UCC. Did comm first, changed to law. You know all that.'

He sighed. 'I didn't think it through, the change to law. I loved it. But I didn't foresee what it would mean. When my father and his crew heard about what I was doing, they were all about me. Offering to pay for everything. A car. A flat. Saying it'd be great to have one of their own on the inside. I told them to fuck off. My father only laughed at me. Said I'd change my tune in time. But then I realised he was right. That if I ever went into practice anywhere, he'd follow me. If I was conveyancing, he'd be after me for money-laundering. If I got a job in the DPP's office, he'd be wanting inside information. I'd never escape. So that's why I decided to go down the academic route. Become a teacher. Write books and articles. He'd have zero interest in anything like that, I reckoned.'

He went on, 'It was going well. LLM. Tick. Funding for my PhD. Thesis. Viva. Tick. Tick. Tick.' He put his head in his hands. 'It was only afterwards that Casey came to me about the plagiarism. The *allegation* of plagiarism in my thesis.' He looked up again. 'When he showed me, I nearly died. It was unintentional. Completely. But it was there.'

He continued. 'I should've talked to someone else. The moment I discovered it. There are mechanisms for dealing with that kind of thing. I know that now. But I didn't then. I was a kid from the wrong side of the tracks. The son of a notorious criminal. And Casey was … well … I was no match for him, put it that way.

'So that's where it began. He didn't ask much of me at first. I wrote that article for him in the *Journal of Comparative Law* that he's always talking about. And I was going to help him with his book. But I was okay with all of it. I was *grateful* to him. I thought he'd saved me. And he had helped me get the post-doc fellowship in UL too. He knew about my mother working there. He knew all about my background. I'd have preferred somewhere else, but I didn't have another offer. And I was okay about going to UL by then. I thought I was free.'

'Casey said he didn't know where you were from, other than that you were from Limerick.'

'That's a lie. Another one. He knew exactly where I came from and who my father was. He knew everything ... Then, the Atkins thing.' He blew out a breath. 'Casey told me that I had to kill him. He wanted me to get a gun. To ask my father for one. He said if I didn't, he'd be forced to inform the authorities about my plagiarism. That I'd lose my fellowship and never get another academic job. He blackmailed me ...'

'But you didn't *use* a gun.'

'No. I decided to go my own way. Bad enough being in Casey's pocket. If I got a gun, I'd be finished. Even if I got away with the murder, my father would have me trapped.' He sat up straighter in the chair. 'I always reckoned you'd seen me. That if you did, you'd figure it out somehow.'

'Saw you when?'

'In the Aula that morning. I was down the back as you came in.'

'I didn't see you. I heard something. Didn't know what it was. But you pretended to hate Casey. Then I found out how close you two really were. That was when I started looking at you.'

'There was no pretending. By the day of the murder, I hated him all right. For what he was making me do.'

'Why did you break the lock?'

'I couldn't be sure that the doors would be left open, even though Casey was supposed to check, but I couldn't rely on him. I wanted to make sure I'd be able to get in and out of the East Wing if I needed to.' He stopped. 'The murder didn't happen the way it was supposed to. Atkins was supposed to take a piss a lot earlier. It was supposed to look like an accident. Like he'd hit his head. Someone was supposed to find him during the dinner, one of the other male guests going to the toilet, or one of the staff, and ... But I was stuck in that cleaning cupboard all night with the door open a crack and he never came in. When he eventually did, I was rattled and I fucked it up. The head injury wasn't enough to ... And I could hear the president outside the window talking to Agnes. I was afraid they'd come in and catch me in the act so I did it fast with his tie and pulled him into the cupboard and bolted the door. If they came in, I hoped they'd think he'd left already by the exit onto the quad. I waited and waited but no one came and eventually I was sure it was quiet so I got to work.'

He went on and on. The planning. The method. The clean-up. The escape. Words washing over me like a polluted wave.

In the end, he said, 'Do you believe me?'

'I do,' I said. 'Most of it, anyway.'

He shut his eyes and took a deep breath. He opened his eyes again, put his right hand to the centre of his chest, tapped it twice against the place where his heart should be.

'That means a lot,' he said.

I leaped from my chair, so fast that it clattered to the floor.

'Let me explain. When I said I *believe* you, what I meant was, I believe you're a murderer. I believe that that's *how* you executed it. But I don't feel *sorry* for you. I don't believe that you had no choice. What I *believe* is that Casey and you are two of a kind. That you *both* did it. You *both* planned it. And that you deserve everything you're going to get. *Both* of you.'

Dunford's expression hardened. He opened his mouth to speak.

'Enough,' I said.

Dunford's eyes looked like two black stones.

'See you in twelve years,' he said.

I left the room and didn't look back.

I said nothing to Sadie when I came out. Got in the car. Shook my head when she asked me how it had gone.

At the top of Military Hill, I asked her to pull in. Opening the door, I leaned out, bent my face as close to the ground as I could. Then, I vomited.

'You okay?' Sadie asked.

'Yeah,' I said.

'What happened with Dunford?'

I told her.

125

A FEW DAYS LATER, DERMOT LYONS FINALLY replied to my *We need to talk* text message. He phoned me. 'The bar of the Imperial Hotel. Four o'clock.'

Lyons was sitting in a booth, a glass of clear liquid in front of him that wasn't mineral water. 'We're not going to talk about your suspension so don't ask me about it. What I *will* say is, in light of recent events, a view might be forming that the partners might have been somewhat over-hasty in the circumstances. There has been some discussion of your usefulness. Representations have been made on your behalf. Some parties might consider it undesirable that you would seek employment elsewhere. I can put the matter no further than that at this time.

'End of discussion,' he said. 'That part of it anyway.' He sipped his drink. Then he said, 'You're adopted, aren't you? How much do you know about your birth mother?'

It wasn't a surprise, this line of conversation, I'd half expected it. And yet it was completely shocking. I felt like I'd been punched in the gut. I took a while to reply.

'Almost nothing,' I said. 'And what I remember, I've tried to forget.'

'And Will was your father. That was the reason for your arrest. The DNA match. A golfing pal in Divisional HQ passed on the information to me.' He sighed. 'As you've guessed by now, presumably, I knew your mother too. She wasn't always a drunk. What I mean is, she did drink, no one's denying that. A lot for these dull, puritanical times. A normal amount back then. But that changed. She went downhill.'

'I knew her on the downward slope.'

'Yes. But before, she was great. Everyone liked her. Men especially.'

I asked, 'How did you meet her?'

'There was a wine bar. Café Cervantes. A place people went after the pub. There were no late licences at that time. It was either nightclubs with music and dancing that required the serving of a substantial meal — chicken curry and rice reheated so often you'd be taking your life in your hands if you ate it. One time I got an awful dose of the … Anyway, the alternative was Café Cervantes. I never saw anyone drinking coffee, though. Wine only, quantity being more important than quality. It never closed, as far as I could see. Raided occasionally but most of the time the guards tolerated it. It was a sophisticated establishment. Bohemian atmosphere. But everyone was there for the drink. Warm Pedrotti as a rule. And that's where she worked.'

'My birth mother.'

'I can call her by her name if you'd prefer.'

'I don't,' I said.

'Anyway, she, your birth mother, worked there.'

'That's how you got to know her.'

'I met her in UCC at a UCC Law Society "Meet the Freshers" cheese and wine. She was in first year. It was my fourth. I hung around for an extra year after the BCL to do the LLB.'

'I didn't realise she went to College. I didn't know she did law.'

'She was bright. Could argue about anything. But she dropped out. Didn't come back in second year. Took time out, saying she'd return later. It might have been a money thing. Lack thereof. That only occurred to me years later. Did she never say that she was at UCC?'

'I was young when I was taken into care. I wouldn't have known what UCC was. Afterwards, when she turned up for access, she used to take me to the library on the Grand Parade, the kids' section, sometimes. I'd read the books. She'd sit there looking at me, or maybe at the clock on the wall, I don't know. I don't remember us talking, or any conversation, really. Maybe no child does. I just wanted to go home to my foster parents, my new mam and dad. To where it was always safe and clean and warm. I was frightened of her. Looking back, I think she was frightened of me too. Scared of hurting me. Or something else I can't put my finger on …'

Dermot Lyons shifted in his seat. He looked uncomfortable.

'Sorry,' I said. 'This isn't a conversation I ever expected to have with you.'

'Likewise.'

'You should cut to the chase. The Atkins bit. And don't call him my father.'

'All I can tell you is that he went there too. To Café Cervantes. Frequently, while he lived here in Cork. He met her, your … He couldn't not have. And one thing must have led to another. I don't recall anything about it, but it wouldn't have been unknown for your … for her, to, em, get off with, em, one of the lads. Where drink is involved, late at night, anything can happen. Consensual, by the way. Nothing hashtag Me Too about it or that sort of garbage.'

He looked embarrassed.

'Were you "one of the lads" too?'

'No,' he said.

I reckoned he was lying. 'So you don't know how or when but the DNA results prove that—'

'That Will and your birth mother did the nasty and you're the result.'

I flinched. 'A one-night stand? Or a relationship?'

'It couldn't have been much of a relationship or I'd have known about it. He shagged his way around Cork while he was here. I'm surprised there aren't more of his love-children about.'

'Did you know about him and Professor Casey's wife?'

'No. But Will was here for a year. That affair might have been two weeks out of the fifty-two. Meant nothing much to him, meant a lot to her. Even more to Casey when he found out.'

I felt my throat burning. 'But with her, with my birth mother, there must have been more to it than that. She kept in touch with him somehow.'

'What gave you that idea?'

'Well, he came here. To the conference. Asked for me to speak at it.'

Suddenly looking more serious, Lyons said, '*That*'s not what happened.'

What he said next turned everything I thought I'd known on its head.

126

'I WAS THE ONE WHO TOLD ATKINS ABOUT YOU, not her,' Lyons said. 'Only a few weeks ago, in fact. I told you already that I met him in Kinsale. We went to the Black Pig. Great food. Excellent wine list. Wasted on him because he wasn't drinking.' He went on, 'We were talking about old times and he brought up Café Cervantes.'

'Did he ask about my birth mother?'

'No, actually he didn't. It was me who mentioned her.'

'Okay,' I said. 'Did you have a reason for doing that?'

'Only because she was part of the furniture. For the few years Cervantes lasted, before the Revenue shut it down – an unpaid VAT bill the size of the *Titanic*, the place duly sank. She worked there all the time ... And, then, naturally, I told him about you.'

'Told him what, exactly?'

'I probably said something like, you'll never guess who we have working for us. And he said he hadn't a clue, and I said ...' He trailed off. Looked me straight in the eyes. Waited for the inevitable question.

I took my time in asking it. I had to because I felt like I'd been pushed off a cliff.

My voice low, I said, 'My name is Finn Fitzpatrick. How did *you* know about my connection to a woman whose surname was Whelan?'

127

'SHE TALKED TO ME ABOUT YOU AT THE TIME OF the care application. A few times. She was in a bad way by then. And I never acted for her officially. She had her own solicitor, someone in the Law Centre. But she talked to me as a friend. She thought of me that way. I used to see her around – I'd give her the odd pound here and there, a fiver every now and again. I knew she wasn't buying food with it, or clothes. It was all going down her gullet in one form or another. Vodka. Wine. Cans of cheap cider. Beer. Street drinking whatever she could lay her hands on.'

'So because of that contact with her, you knew who my foster parents were.'

'Not only who they *were*, I went to her funeral. To your birth mother's funeral. I *saw* you with them that day. Your foster parents. I made it my business to find out what had happened to you afterwards. All highly confidential information. Except in Cork, as you know, if you want to find out something, you can. I knew their names and where they lived approximately because she, your birth mother, had told me. It was nothing to ask a few questions and drive by and make sure all was hunky-dory. Once I did that, I knew you were safe. Respectable area. Decent people taking care of you.'

'You went to a lot of trouble.'

'Hardly any.'

The air was heavy with the next question. 'Did you think I was yours?'

'No. I never did. But for a few crazy minutes the day of the funeral I suppose I might have wished you were.'

'Did you think I was Atkins's child?'

'In all honesty, again, no. Your mother, she was free with her affections, shall we say, at a time when many girls of our acquaintance weren't. You could've been anyone's. Atkins knew that as well as I did. He was interested in seeing you. He genuinely was. A last connection with his misspent youth. But he didn't tell me he thought you might have been his. And he couldn't have known that you were. Not without a DNA test. Now that I know, I can see a bit of a resemblance. But it wasn't anything I'd spotted before.'

I didn't know if I believed him. 'He didn't contact you after he'd seen me?'

'No. And that Thursday, the day after the conference, I knew by how you were with me in the office that he'd said nothing.' He paused. 'Ah, the night at the Black Pig in Kinsale, I'd arrived before Will. I'd ordered a bottle of good white and a bottle of excellent red and, because he was off the sauce, I ended up drinking the two of them on my own. Anything else would have been a crime. It wasn't what you might call hardship, but it did lead my lips to loosen somewhat. I didn't think anything of it at the time. It was so unlikely, I suppose, the whole thing of him being your father. It never occurred to me. It probably never occurred to *him*. It's no surprise that he didn't say anything in the end.'

'I think he *did* know,' I said. 'Or felt it. When I was leaving the dinner he made a comment that he was "sorrier than I can say" that he hadn't had a chance to talk to me. And he said to another guest, Dr Mbemba, he'd made a lot of mistakes in his life that it was too late to fix. And he phoned his solicitor, his long-time friend, from the corridor in the East Wing. But he didn't get through. If he had we might know if he'd realised who I was. As it is …'

Lyons made no response except to wave at the barman and order another gin.

I asked, 'What about you? The quasi-friendship you had with her?'

'I associated her with my carefree days. I know you think I'm a stuffed shirt … You're not denying it, I see. But I wasn't always. And I liked her. She was a hollowed-out shell of what she'd been but she …' He grimaced. 'There's something else too. She phoned me. The day before she took her life. It wasn't that unusual. She'd be langers. Get hold of a phone card somehow and talk gibberish for as long as the credit lasted. Anyway, sometimes I'd take the call. More often I wouldn't. And that particular day, I didn't. I've always regretted it.'

I stared at him stony-faced.

'Say something,' he said.

'I have one more question. It's about me working for MLC.'

'Ask it.'

'Is it a coincidence? Me ending up in this job?'

'Would you like me to say that it was?'

'At this point in time, Dermot, the only thing I want is the truth.'

'You applied. Gabriel liked you. But he wasn't sure. Thought you were a bit of a risk. I might have helped him make the decision. I might have said that occasionally risks pay off or something like that. I don't really remember. You should ask him, though I wouldn't ask him anytime soon, if I were you. Your situation is still rather delicate.'

I said nothing.

Lyons went on, 'Employing you *did* pay off, in a way. Not financially, obviously but ...'

'Did Gabriel know her, did he know my birth mother?'

He laughed, a huge hooting sound, eventually said, 'Perish the thought. Gabriel was not and is not the kind to frequent late-night drinking dens.' He laughed again.

Throwing back the rest of his gin and tonic, he slid out of his seat. 'You'll be all right, will you?'

'I'll be fine.'

'You seem sure about that,' he said.

'I am,' I said.

Lyons nodded. He left without saying anything else.

128

THE MAIN REASON I WAS SURE WAS BECAUSE I
had my priorities right. I concentrated on what I had and
shelved what I'd never had. Since his release from hospital, my
dad had continued to respond well to the medication. Every
time I visited, I saw another improvement. And, apart from a
few residual niggles now and again, Sadie and I were back on
track.

As for my non-mother and my non-father, I knew I'd have to
think about them properly sometime. One day, I'd have to go
down to the river. Ask for answers there. But not yet.

The revelations about Lexbonay had started to come out. I'd
spoken again to Samantha Fennell and to Béatrice Mbemba.
They told me that what had begun as a trickle would turn into a
torrent. A *Prime Time Investigates* documentary was in the works
and Channel 4 News was compiling a report on the international
aspects of the story. Nate Simpson would get his comeuppance
and no one deserved it more.

Sophie Dignam was continuing with her PhD. Nobody had

found out about her mistake with Simpson. And, now that Casey was suspended from duty pending his trial, she'd been promised some teaching work in the law school next semester.

I was helping Rory Donnelly with his garda application. We'd met in Alchemy Café on Barrack Street and done some preliminary work on it. The submission deadline was months away yet but Donnelly was optimistic he'd succeed, however long it took.

Ian McAnespie got through his final exams. Even if he passed, he said, he'd decided to take some time out before studying for the Law Society FE-1s. But he'd stuck by his intention not to complain about Davide Rossi's enslavement of him and wouldn't be drawn further on the topic. I still reckoned he hadn't told me the full story. Probably he never would.

I had my job back, as Dermot Lyons had intimated. Tina had texted me in advance to let me know. She'd seen the letter being typed. The old band was back together again.

And I finally got a text message from Davy. Just the one. I replied, telling him what we both knew already. That our one-night stand had been a mistake. That we needed to move on with our lives without each other. He didn't reply.

On a sunny Saturday morning in late May, a few weeks after my return to work, I walked up to my parents' house: I'd been visiting daily since Dad had come out of hospital. I found him out front on his knees with a pair of secateurs, trimming the low box hedge that edged the garden.

'What are you doing? Where's Mam? You shouldn't be outside

yet. You're not well enough. Also, it's illegal to cut hedges from the end of March to the start of September.'

He ignored me, kept snipping. 'I'm going nowhere until I finish this.'

'Let me do it.'

He gave me a look. 'As luck would have it, I'm done now.'

With surprisingly little difficulty, he got to his feet, shrugging off my help.

'I really am better, Finn. Davy told me he could see a big change.'

'Who?'

'You know who. He's been up a few times. During the daytime. He's been helping me get back to full fitness. He said I could come to his gym, free of charge, if I wanted. He told me he has machines that'd be a great help. Not my thing, I said, but a nice offer all the same. Don't be cross with me.' He added, 'We all make mistakes.'

Dumbstruck, I followed him into the house. I didn't know how to feel about what he'd said. Pushing it into the furthest recesses of myself, I talked to him as normally as I could. It wasn't anger I felt towards him, or Davy. It was something I couldn't process yet.

Later, I walked back down the hill and along the river, lingering on Pope's Quay by the Shandon Bridge, gazing across at the steps on the far side as a heron stared back. I continued on, past the Friary Bar, and along the North Mall where I'd visited Martin Casey in his flat, via the tree-lined riverside path all the way to the

Mardyke and the main gates of the college. Heading up Donovan's Road, my feet took me into the grounds of the university chapel, the Honan, with its beautiful stone and wood carvings and Harry Clarke stained-glass windows; a peaceful place.

Not today. There had been a wedding. Pink and white flowers and ribbons had been tied around the ends of the pews and large pedestal arrangements stood at either side of the altar, a few forgotten mass booklets scattered here and there.

I left the chapel, went in the direction of my house, as far as my car parked on Barrack Street. Clicking it open, I drove to the sea at Fountainstown.

The beach was quiet. A few dog-walkers. A couple of families with small kids. I descended the rocky slope, the rounded pale grey stones sliding beneath my feet, and walked to the edge of the water. The tide was out and the sand was hard. I stood looking at the horizon, the arms of the little bay opening onto the wide ocean beyond.

And there, by the icy glinting shallows, I got my breath back at last.

Acknowledgements

A Lesson in Malice is my third crime novel but there would be no book without the guidance, support and kindness of my agent Luigi Bonomi, and Alison Bonomi, and all at LBA; and of my editor Ciara Doorley; and of Joanna Smyth, Elaine Egan, Ruth Shern, Stephen Riordan, Jim Binchy, and all at Hachette Ireland. Thanks also to the amazing Eileen Walsh; to copyeditor Hazel Orme; to proofreader Aonghus Meaney; to Lisa Brewster for the gorgeous cover design; and to Plunkett PR.

The decision to set a book in UCC, a place beloved of so many, brought with it extra pressure. Special thanks to John Mee of the UCC School of Law and to JP Quinn of the UCC Visitor Centre who read an earlier version of the manuscript and gave me very generous and incredibly detailed feedback. Any remaining errors are probably deliberate and are definitely my own. Many thanks also to Gemma Browne for answering (loads of) medical questions.

Thanks as ever to crime-writing guru Catherine Ryan Howard and to Claire Connolly, Eimear O'Herlihy, Fin Flynn, Jean Kearney, John Breen, Lynn Sheehan, Marguerite Phillips, Miriam O'Brien, Nick Daly, Paul O'Donovan, Rachel O'Toole, Siobhan Lankford and Tadhg Coakley who advised or assisted or corrected or encouraged or promoted or read or soothed or suggested at crucial moments; to Kieran O'Connor for my author photograph; and to Peter, Nicola, Laura and Alex Byrne.

Thanks to you dearest reader and double the thanks if you take the time to write an online review. Thanks to my friends and colleagues in Finbarr Murphy Solicitors; and thanks also to the legal community in Cork and beyond for your unstinting support.

Thanks to all media folk, especially Elmarie Mawe and Conor Tallon of *The Arts House* on Cork's 96FM, and to journalists, editors, reviewers and book bloggers; to book club members (especially Ballyphehane Library Book Club); to libraries and librarians everywhere especially Cork City and County Libraries (in particular the Youghal and Bandon branches), and DLR Lexicon, and Meath County; to event organisers and festivals, especially Murder One, Cork World Book Festival, Spike Island Literary Festival, West Cork Literary Festival, Kinsale Words by Water, Munster Literature Centre, UCC School of English, the CWA, Bookselling Ireland, Waterstones Cork, and to Danielle McLaughlin and Madeleine D'Arcy and the late-lamented Fiction at the Friary; and to all bookshops and booksellers with particular thanks to the people who arrange the window displays.

Thanks to the wonderful and inspiring company of authors who have been so kind and welcoming to me – you know who you are.

Thanks to my friends for putting up with me and supporting me so generously; thanks to everyone I thanked in my earlier books, because I wouldn't be here without you; and thanks to all those I forgot to thank previously, including Andrew Lane.

Finally, my eternal gratitude and love to my mother Breda Kirwan, to my late father Michael, to Marcia and Rob, to Neil and Nicola; and to my nephew Michael and nieces Molly and Elizabeth, of whom I am immensely proud and to whom this book is dedicated.